ALSO BY ROBYN HARDING

The Journal of Mortifying Moments

The
Secret Desires
of a
Soccer Mom

BALLANTINE BOOKS • NEW YORK

The Secret Desires of a

SOCCER MOM

A NOVEL

Robyn
Harding

The Secret Desires of a Soccer Mom is a work of fiction. Names, characters, places, and incidents are the products of the author's imagination or are used fictitiously. Any resemblance to actual events, locales, or persons, living or dead, is entirely coincidental.

Copyright © 2006 by Robyn Harding

Published in the United States by Ballantine Books, an imprint of The Random House Publishing Group, a division of Random House, Inc., New York.

BALLANTINE and colophon are registered trademarks of Random House, Inc.

Library of Congress Cataloging-in-Publication Data

Harding, Robyn.
The secret desires of a soccer mom / Robyn Harding.
p.   cm.
ISBN 0-345-47630-1—ISBN 0-345-47629-8 (pbk.)
1. Women detectives—Colorado—Fiction.   2. Suburban life—Fiction.
3. Neighborhood—Fiction.   4. Housewives—Fiction.
5. Colorado—Fiction.   I. Title.
PR9199.4.H366S43 2006
813'.6—dc22   2005053559

Printed in the United States of America on acid-free paper

www.ballantinebooks.com

2 4 6 8 9 7 5 3 1

First Edition

Book design by Susan Turner

For Susan Matthews

ACKNOWLEDGMENTS

Thank you: to my editor Linda Marrow for helping shape the concept of this novel (Without her suggestion, I don't think I would have tried the murder scenario and now, I'm so glad I did.); to my editor Charlotte Herscher for all her guidance and support, and to Arielle Zibrak, Signe Pike, and everyone at Ballantine who worked on this book; also, to my wonderful agent, Joe Veltre, for always being in my corner.

Thanks also to my dear friend Val Lawton for sharing her drawing class experiences; to the fabulous Darin Recchi (and his friends Jason Young and Cameron Newell) for all the insider info on Denver; to Sergeant Ross Milward of the R.C.M.P. (aka Uncle Ross) for his expertise on DNA evidence admissibility; to Brown Grandma for the (albeit rather short-lived) Thursday babysitting so I could write; and to Auntie Kerry, for taking over.

To my kids: Thank you both for being so funny and making Spencer Atwell so easy to write.

To my family: Thanks for everything. I love you.

The
Secret Desires
of a
Soccer Mom

We were loading coffee cups into the dishwasher when my friend Karen made a startling confession.

"I have something to tell you," she said.

"Okay." I continued tipping the dregs of cold coffee into the sink and plunking the empty cups into the top tray. It was a Wednesday, the day the five of us got together for coffee and conversation. This week, it had been my turn to host. When the others left to pick up various children from preschool, run errands, or go to the gym, Karen had volunteered to stay behind and help me clean up. Although . . . she wasn't really helping anymore. Now she was just standing there, leaning against the blue tiles of my kitchen island, with a strange look on her face.

"Don't judge me, okay?"

"Okay." This time, I stopped what I was doing and looked at my friend. Her cheeks were pink under her late-summer tan, and she seemed to be trying to maintain a somber expression while on the verge of hysterical giggles.

"Umm . . ." She cleared her throat. "I've been seeing someone."

I was silent for a few moments, choosing my words carefully. "Well, that's nothing to feel ashamed of. I've often thought I should get some therapy to deal with my parents' divorce. I know I was twenty-seven when they split up, but that doesn't mean that it didn't still hurt."

"I'm not seeing a shrink, Paige."

"Oh . . ." It took me a second. "Oh!"

"You promised not to judge me!"

"I won't. I'm not! It's just that . . ."

"What?"

"I'm just shocked, that's all. I thought that you and Doug were so happy."

"We were happy. But when I met . . . *this person,*" Karen said, blushing again and forcing away the delighted smile that was threatening to curl her lips, "I realized that my relationship with Doug just wasn't enough for me. I know it sounds terrible."

"Well . . . ," I said.

"If you're going to look down on me for this, then I won't say any more." Karen moved to retrieve her coat off the back of a kitchen chair.

"No, don't go," I soothed, realizing that I had offended her. "Let's have some more cake and talk." I cut two enormous slabs of Sara Lee apple-cinnamon coffee cake and led her to the breakfast nook. When we were seated at the pine kitchen table in the sunny alcove, I took a moment to study my friend. The sun streaming in through the bank of windows picked up the highlights in her chestnut hair and gave her complexion a golden glow. With her sparkling blue eyes and flush of delighted embarrassment, she looked almost impossibly girlish and pretty—far younger than her thirty-six years. Extramarital sex obviously agreed with her.

"Okay . . . ," I said gently. "Tell me how this happened." Of course, I was trying to be a supportive and nonjudgmental friend, but a small part of me was positively gleeful! This was the most exciting news I'd heard in years. Our Denver suburb was very quiet.

"Well . . . ," she began, daintily picking at the drizzled icing with her fork tines. "Like I said, Doug and I were happy. We have the big house, the nice cars, the time-share in Playa del Carmen. . . . I was content, complacent even. But sexually—"

I choked on my mouthful of cake. "I'm fine," I mumbled. "Go on."

"Sexually, I wasn't fulfilled. You know we've been trying to get pregnant for almost two years now, thanks to Doug's low-mobility sperm. That's really taken the fun out of it—the schedules, the ovulation predictor, the cold packs in Doug's shorts . . ."

I managed to refrain from choking again, but I was sure I'd never look at Karen's CFO husband the same way again.

"Sex should be spontaneous! Passionate! Sex should make you feel like you are the most beautiful, sensual creature on the planet, like you could conquer the world."

I was nodding along here, but it had been a very long time since sex had made me feel anything but . . . *good.* If it had ever made me feel like a world conqueror, I couldn't remember it.

"And that's how I feel when I make love with Javier. It's mind-blowing! I've never had this kind of sex with Doug."

"Javier?"

"He's Spaaaanish!" She said this like she was saying "He's covered in chocolate."

"Where did you meet him?"

"At my art class. I know it's wrong, Paige, but I swear, he's completely irresistible!" Cue the pink cheeks and girlish giggles.

"Spanish *and* an artist," I said. "That does sound pretty irresistible."

"He's not an artist. He's the model."

"Oh! Wow!"

"Yeah, I know," she practically squealed. "He's also a barista—to make ends meet. He doesn't care about status, and he doesn't want to get caught up in the rat race. It's a different culture, a different attitude."

"Well, I, personally, love coffee," I said gamely.

"He is just so beautiful, inside and out—and not in that plastic, Hollywood kind of way. His face has so much character. That's why he's so great to draw. And his body is unbelievable! And his eyes! Oh God, Paige, his eyes—they smolder."

"Smolder, eh?" I didn't know what else to say.

"Smolder," she said, flopping back in her chair with a positively postcoital sigh.

I cleared my throat. "He sounds amazing, but . . ."

"And it's not just his looks. He really gets me, you know? Like, he can see who I am—the real me—deep down inside. There's a bit of a language barrier, of course, but it's almost like we transcend words."

"Umm . . . okay. But what does this mean for you and Doug?"

She sat forward and stabbed a forkful of cake. "I don't know. When this all started, I thought it would be a fling. It was just passion, just lust in the beginning. But now . . . we have so much more." She stuffed the cake into her mouth.

"Do you still love Doug?"

"Of course I do," she mumbled through her apple-cinnamon confection, "but isn't it possible to love someone and yet not feel a real emotional connection to him?"

I thought about my own marriage for a second. Paul and I had celebrated our twelfth anniversary last month, but would I say we had a real emotional connection? We certainly did have one when we were first together, but over the last ten years, things had changed. His life revolved around his job in software sales, and mine had been focused on our two kids. But I still loved him. He was my husband, the father of my children . . . "I suppose it's possible," I said.

"And now I just want to be with Javier all the time! Honestly, Paige, I can't get enough of him—physically, emotionally, spiritually. I don't know how much longer I can keep up this façade with Doug."

"But, Karen," I said solemnly, "you and Doug have a life together. You and Javier just have great sex."

"Ha!" A humorless laugh erupted from within her. "Doug and I have *things* together, possessions. That's not a life, Paige: Javier taught me that. Seriously . . ."—she looked at me intently—"I'm beginning to think there was a reason I couldn't get pregnant. If I had a baby with Doug, I'd be tied to him forever."

"True," I murmured. My own fruitful marriage suddenly felt like a life sentence in Sing Sing.

Karen suddenly looked at her watch. "I've got to go." She jumped up. "I've got a bikini wax at noon." I followed her down the hall and into the front foyer, a large open space with an Italian tiled floor and high, coved ceiling. This "grand entryway," as the architect had called it, was a common feature in the area's newer homes. Undoubtedly, it was intended to give the impression of a Georgian manor or something, but the piles of kids' shoes, sporting equipment, and schoolbooks tended to detract from its grandeur. I waited patiently while Karen slipped into her chocolate leather blazer, zipping up her matching stiletto boots.

"Thanks for coffee," she said, taking my hands in hers. "And thanks for listening. Really, I was bursting to talk to someone, and you're the only person I felt safe telling my secret to."

I have to admit, I was somewhat surprised by this. Not that I couldn't keep a secret. I could. I felt fairly confident that I would take this information to my grave—even though it was the juiciest thing to happen in Aberdeen Mists for about eight years. But although Karen and I were very close, I wouldn't really have considered us confidantes. In fact, I would have thought she'd have had a more open and sharing kind of relationship with some of the other women in our clique. So why had she chosen me?

Karen was probably closest to Carly, who lived two houses away from me and six houses away from Karen. She was a more recent member of our social circle, having moved to the neighborhood just two years earlier. Carly had arrived a beaming newlywed, eager to start a family and immerse herself in suburban bliss. Shortly after relocating, her husband, Brian, left her for a middle-aged insurance adjuster with two young sons and an enormous pair of fake boobs.

Carly had been devastated. All she had ever wanted was to have a family. We had all rallied around our new neighbor in her time of crisis, and since then, she'd become an inextricable part of our social network. But I often wondered why she didn't move back to the city after Brian's cruel desertion. In Aberdeen Mists, she was literally surrounded by smiling familial units. It was like an alcoholic working in a bar or a Jenny Craig devotee living above a bakery! If it were me, I'd have moved to Washington Park or another trendy area full of restaurants and nightclubs and single men. I would have gone out dancing, done tequila shots, and made out with men much too young for me. But Carly stayed put, and thanks to time (and an ongoing prescription for Xanax), she began to heal.

Carly and Karen had a friendship unique to them: they were virtually the only women in the neighborhood who did not have children. This afforded them more free time to bond over drinks, to go out to movies, to go to the gym . . . Of course, Carly was busy with her home-based accounting practice, and Karen was busy having mind-blowing sex with a Spanish model/barista, but they still spent more time together than the rest of us.

I suppose it made sense that Karen had not confessed her affair to Carly. Given the adulterous demise of Carly's marriage, she might not have been as open-minded and understanding as I was. Carly was kindhearted and generous to a fault, but Karen's admission could have hit a little too close to home. Carly always assured us that she was healing, moving on, and putting Brian, and what might have been, behind her. But I often thought her smile seemed stretched a bit too tight, and her fawning over our children was a little forced.

Our friend Jane, on the other hand, would have been in no position to judge Karen's fling. Her marriage to Daniel, a fifty-eight-year-old oil company executive, was the product of just such an affair. Jane had been Daniel's secretary several years ago when they "accidentally" fell in love. She no longer worked for him, of course. Now she devoted her time to their two young daughters—and to her looks. Jane definitely qualified as a yummy-mummy. Thanks to regular salon visits, she had a lustrous mane of long, honey-colored hair; frequent facials (and, I suspected, a little Botox) had given her a glowing and youthful complexion; thrice-weekly Pilates classes had resulted in a body like Cameron Diaz; and a very talented plastic surgeon had provided her the perky breasts of an eighteen-year-old cheerleader. I had to admit, I really envied those boobs. They were just so . . . *perfect*. Mine were positively decimated by the breast-feeding. Not that I was particularly voluptuous before, but now they hung off my chest like two popped balloons.

As much as I coveted them, I knew I couldn't afford a boob job: It was evident that my ten-year-old daughter, Chloe, would be needing braces in a couple of years. I also harbored a deep-seated fear that if I ever did have my breasts done, I would have a reaction to the anesthetic and die on the operating table. On the slim chance that I did survive the procedure, one of the implants would be sure to burst, leaching toxic chemicals into my bloodstream, eventually killing me. While I would have truly loved a pair like Jane's, I could already hear my post-breast-implant eulogy:

> Paige was a loving wife and mother. Unfortunately, she was also an incredibly vain woman, whose quest for larger breasts has left her young children motherless, and her husband, a widower.

Perfect breasts aside, Jane was a very compassionate woman and a good listener. And she could have provided much wiser counsel on the whole affair situation than a novice like me. On the other hand, Jane's cheating streak appeared to be in the past. She and Daniel were extremely committed to each other—weirdly so. Due to the adulterous beginnings of their relationship, they had serious trust issues, which manifested themselves in multiple phone calls back and forth each day, numerous "date nights," extravagant gifts, and couple's holidays, all in an effort to prove they were still in love with each other and not screwing any of the staff. No, when I thought about it, it was probably better that Karen had confided in me.

The other member of our Wednesday coffee klatch was Trudy. There was no way that Karen would have divulged her secret to her! Trudy was quite possibly the sweetest, kindest person I knew. She was also the most virtuous . . . really, almost . . . *pious*. She was the type of woman who, after dropping a grocery bag full of canned goods on her bare foot, would say "Sugar"—but only if her toe was actually broken. Before she had children, she had been a nursery school teacher.

Trudy's marriage was something she kept private. Her husband, Ken, was director of marketing for a telecommunications company. With his nonstop travel and frequent eighteen-hour workdays, he made my husband, Paul, look like a slacker. But unlike me, her spouse's long hours and commitment to his job never seemed to bother Trudy. I'd asked her about it once, and she'd responded with a cheery "Well . . . sometimes it's hard, but I just thank my lucky stars that I've married a man who can provide for our family and allow me to stay home to be with the children. It's really a gift, you know."

"Yes, it is," I had responded weakly. Only moments before, I'd intercepted my son, Spencer, as he was writing the word *poo* on Jane's daughter's forehead with my lipstick.

So though we knew little about Trudy's marriage, it was likely as perfect as the rest of her perfect life. Probably a little bland, I would have to surmise, but solid. Trudy and Ken seemed like the "missionary-position-every-second-Friday" kind of couple. If Karen had confessed the sordid details of her extramarital sex romps to Trudy, she might have spontaneously combusted.

I guess it did make sense for Karen to open up to me. I smiled at my friend and gave her hands a squeeze. "Your secret is safe with me." Then I mimed locking my lips and throwing away the key. Corny, I know, but I couldn't help it. I spent a large majority of my time hanging out with a six-year-old boy.

CHAPTER 2

That afternoon, I drove to pick up my kids from school with Karen's confession replaying in my head. I knew that what she was doing was wrong, and I pitied poor, clueless Doug. But I couldn't deny the fact that my friend seemed so full of life, of joy, of . . . *joie de vivre!* And her skin looked fantastic.

It was the sex, I knew it was. Karen was experiencing the passion and intensity of a new relationship, while I was experiencing the same old thing I'd been experiencing for the past fourteen years. Not that there was anything wrong with the way Paul and I *experienced* together. We both knew the routine to follow to ensure the desired results. It was nice . . . *good,* even. But it wasn't exactly improving my complexion anymore.

I pulled the massive SUV into a parking spot bordering Rosedale Elementary's playing field and turned off the ignition. The digital clock on the dashboard indicated that I was seven minutes early. Since it was only Spencer's second week of school, I didn't want to risk turning up late. I could practically hear him telling his future therapist how he had abandonment issues because his mother wasn't there to pick him up one afternoon during first grade. It was a beautiful September afternoon, and the sun, filtered just enough by the yellowing oak leaves, warmed my face through the windshield. As I rested my head against the leather seat, my mind slipped back to Karen's admission.

It was a real dilemma. Despite her denials, Karen and Doug *did* have a life together. They'd been married for six years. They had a beautiful home. They were a part of the community. Doug was a good husband, offering her stability, security, and companionship— and that's not to mention the time-share and the BMW. It wouldn't be easy to walk away from all that. Okay, maybe he was a little dull in the sack, but was that really his fault? Any man could crack under all that baby-making pressure.

And if she were to choose Javier, what kind of life would they have? They'd end up renting a dingy one-bedroom apartment in East Colfax, scraping to get by on his barista wages and occasional modeling gigs. Karen would have to get a job. She'd left her event-planning career behind years ago; there was no way she could pick up where she'd left off now. She'd be forced to waitress at some late-night diner or a sleazy bar. They'd have to eat canned ravioli and ramen noodles for most meals. There would be no evenings out, no holidays, no meat that didn't come from a can . . . They would have nothing . . . nothing but each other and mind-blowing sex. I heaved a heavy sigh. It was a very tough choice.

Suddenly, the SUV lurched like it had been charged by a rhinoceros. I jumped in my seat, startled, until I heard the familiar giggling of my son and his friend Nigel, who had just propelled their slight bodies into the passenger door.

"Bye, poo hair!" Spencer called, opening the door to the backseat.

"Bye, snot eyes!" Nigel called back, as he was hurriedly corralled by his Filipina nanny.

"See you tomorrow, booger breath!"

"Okay, pee face!"

"Okay, . . . ummm . . . diarrhea brain!" Spencer screamed out the window.

"Spencer, that's enough," I said gently but firmly. I was glad he had a new school chum, but their entire friendship seemed to revolve around assigning rude adjectives to body parts. "Those words are not appropriate."

"What words?" he asked, climbing into his booster seat and buckling his seat belt.

"You know which words—*bodily functions,* okay?"

"Okay."

"So, how was your day?"

"Good. Can we go now?"

"As soon as your sister gets here." At that moment, I spied my elder child, standing in the school yard, ensconced in a gaggle of squealing and giggling girls. At ten years old, Chloe was at least four inches taller than her friends and looked gawky, coltish, even spindly. She also had enormous front teeth, which would be demanding braces in a year or two, and an unflattering center-part hairstyle, which worked with neither her fine hair nor her narrow face. Lately, when I looked at my daughter, the term *awkward stage* came to mind. "There she is," I said to Spencer. "She'll be here in a sec."

"I really need to go home," he responded, his blue eyes wide. "I'm starving and dying of thirst, and I have to go pee sooooo bad."

"How bad?"

"Bad."

"Can you wait until we get home, or do you want to go back in the school?"

"Umm . . . wait! . . . I think."

"Okay. She'll be here in a minute." But Chloe appeared to be in no hurry to join us, laughing, shrieking, and throwing pinecones at a group of nearby boys. To be fair, she didn't realize her brother was about to pee on the seat of our forty thousand–dollar SUV, but my patience was wearing thin. I tooted the horn briefly to catch her attention. Chloe's eyes darted nervously in our direction, but she angled her body away from us and continued her antics with her friends.

"I need to peeeeeeeeeeeeeeee," Spencer moaned.

"Let's go back in the school." I undid my seat belt.

"No. I want to pee at home in my home toilet."

"What's the difference? Just go to the bathroom here."

"It smells in there, and sometimes the toilets flood and there's wet paper towels stuck on the ceiling."

"Fine. Cross your legs and I'll get you home as fast as I can." I leaned on the horn once, following up with three staccato bursts. This time, Chloe didn't even turn around.

"I think the pee's coming!" Spencer shrieked.

"Hang on!" I cried. Hopping out of the car, I called to my daughter. "Chloe! Come on! We have to go!" It was obvious that she was pretending not to hear me. Despite being only ten, Chloe liked to give the impression that she had no family and lived alone in a small apartment, supporting herself as a cocktail waitress in the evenings.

From inside the car, I heard "Oh no! Oh no!"

"CHLOE ATWELL! NOW!" I bellowed. It had the desired effect. Not only did Chloe turn, but I now had the attention of approximately two hundred Rosedale students. Suddenly, I heard a car door open, followed by a sound like running water. I turned to see my son, standing on the sidewalk, relieving himself on the chain-link fence. The entire school yard erupted into laughter and horrified squeals. Chloe's face registered her mortification. She stalked silently to the car.

When we got home, I called Paul.

"Hey, babe. What's up?" I could hear his fingers tapping away at the keyboard as he spoke.

"Chloe wants to change schools."

"Why?"

"Her brother peed in front of the entire student population."

"What?" Paul chuckled and then called, "Hey, Mike! I'm gonna need the costings for the Wellington project ASAP. Conference call at 5:30! . . . Sorry, Paige."

"That's okay."

"So . . . yeah . . . ," he said distractedly. "The kids had a good day?" (Tap, tap, tap on keyboard.)

"Not particularly," I muttered. God, was he even listening to me?

"Good . . . good . . ." (Tap, tap, tap.)

Obviously, he wasn't. I heaved a sigh of exasperation. "I thought I'd get pizza tonight. It might cheer Chloe up. Is that good for you?"

"Mike! Call Monayim in San Diego! He should have half of those numbers ready to go." Paul turned his attention back to me. "Sorry, hon, but I've gotta run. We're having some problems with the Wellington pilot install. The server was dead out of the box, and the blah blah blah isn't interfacing with the blabbidy blah blah."

I'd never understood Paul's computer jargon. "Okay. So . . . pizza tonight? Or I could pick up chicken?"

"Don't count on me for dinner. I'm not sure if we can get the blah blah in time for the blabbidy blab blah . . ."

I hung up, feeling annoyed with my husband for his obvious distraction. Sometimes, it didn't feel fair. I'd forfeited a promising career in public relations to stay home and raise babies, while Paul continued to thrive out in the business world. It was my choice, I knew that. But at times, I really envied him his dynamic and exciting job—especially when I was stuck at home with a surly adolescent girl and her exhibitionist little brother.

I decided a glass of red wine and a little quiet time were in order. With Chloe pouting and blaring Avril Lavigne in her room and Spencer happily playing Bionicle on the family room floor, I moved to the front of the house. Opening the French doors, I entered the formal living room. Intended to host intimate gatherings or sophisticated cocktail parties, this room sat largely unused. A thin layer of dust coated the antique furniture, handed down from Paul's maternal grandmother. I always felt slightly uneasy in here, almost like an intruder. But on the other hand, it provided a wonderful escape from the rest of my frenzied household.

Taking a sip of Syrah, I wandered to the front window. Through the sheer curtain, I could see that it was getting dark. My neighbors' lights shone like beacons: a lone kitchen light signified that a wife was busily preparing dinner for her husband; a darkened house with only the porch light on meant that a couple would be arriving home from work, sooner or later; a home ablaze with electricity meant a houseful, all going about the chaotic business of being a family.

Pulling back the gauzy fabric, I peered into the street. At the end of the block, I could just see Karen and Doug's house. It was completely dark. Obviously, Doug was still at work, and Karen was probably off having multiple orgasms with Javier. Suddenly, I was overcome by an intense feeling of loneliness. Dropping the curtain, I moved to the center of the room, where I flicked on the floor lamp, then perched awkwardly on Grandmother Maple's chintz sofa. I took a deep breath and tried to quell the malaise that was overtaking me. It was strange: this feeling of emptiness seemed completely unprovoked. Paul worked late often; I was used to spending evenings alone with the children. What was so different about tonight?

After another sip of wine, I was back at the window. Karen's house was still dark, but as I stared, I thought I sensed movement inside. Maybe she and Javier were in there right now? Would she be so brazen? Could they be doing it, at this very moment, in a myriad of exciting positions, in Karen and Doug's own bedroom? Or the living room? Or kitchen? Maybe that added to the excitement—the fact that Doug could walk in at any moment. If I kept watching, I might see Doug's BMW pull up out front, and Javier would scurry out the back window half-naked. Or completely naked! I stared at the darkened house for another few minutes before realizing that my imagination had run away with me.

"Enough," I said, to the empty, austere room, shaking off my melancholy mood. I had absolutely no reason to feel down. I had a good life! I was happy! It was only natural to pine, just a little, for those early days of passion, romance, and multiple sex positions. After twelve years of marriage, it was perfectly normal to fantasize, occasionally, about raking your fingernails down some muscular stud's back or riding him like a young thoroughbred. But those days were over for me, replaced by comfort, security, a house in the suburbs, and an SUV. It wasn't like I was *jealous* of Karen's affair. God no! And I certainly wasn't *obsessed* with her love life. I mean, of course I was interested: I was her sole confessor, after all. But I hadn't turned into some voyeuristic sex maniac, peeking out the window at my friend's love nest. I was curious, that's all. Besides, I had many other things to occupy my mind. Like my children, who needed me to order pizza for them. I walked back to the kitchen to call Domino's.

CHAPTER 3

Every second Friday, Jane and I went power walking. Her trainer said that she'd get the best results if she varied her workout routine, so twice a month, she skipped her Pilates class, loaded herself down with ankle and wrist weights, and went for a walk with me. I wore no weights: keeping up with superfit, arm-pumping Jane was enough of a workout for me. She rang my doorbell at 9:45 A.M.

"Ready to go?" she asked, marching vigorously in place on my front porch.

"All set." We headed down the street, passing Carly's and then Karen's vacant-looking houses. I peered, as casually as possible, into Karen's front window. You never knew what you might catch a glimpse of in there.

"She's not home," Jane commented.

I blushed, as if she could have read my thoughts. "Uh, yeah . . . No, I didn't think so."

"She's been seeing this acupuncturist in the city. He's supposed to help her with her infertility."

"Oh."

"Yeah, she has appointments a few times a week, for hours at a time. Apparently, he's very good . . . very thorough."

"I'm sure he is."

"Still," Jane said, leaning forward slightly as we reached an incline—her trainer had told her this position would help tone her glutes—"it must be tough, not being able to conceive."

"Definitely," I agreed, copying her stance. A little toning wouldn't hurt my glutes either. "We're really lucky to have gotten pregnant so easily. It would be such a drag to have to have sex all the time." Jane shot me a bemused look. "I mean, it must take some of the fun out of it. It would be kind of like . . . work."

"True," she agreed. "It's much more fun to be spontaneous."

"Oh, yeah!" I said emphatically, hoping she wouldn't realize I was overcompensating. I knew that Paul's and my sex life wouldn't exactly qualify as spontaneous. We had sex once a week, on Saturday night. Occasionally, during the week, if we found ourselves in bed together before eleven, we'd get it on then, too, but this rarely happened. On the other hand, if Paul was going to be out of town for more than four days, we would usually squeeze in a quickie before his departure. That would have to qualify as spontaneous, wouldn't it? Sometimes, we were really quite daring. Once, we even did it in the master bathroom while the kids watched a movie!

"How is Spencer settling into first grade?" Jane changed the subject.

I was somewhat relieved. "Great, great! He really likes his teacher, and he's making friends."

"That's good. This is a whole new chapter for you, isn't it? Both your kids are at school all day. You're home free!"

"Right . . . ," I said rather hesitantly.

"So, what do you plan to do with all this time you suddenly have?"

"Well . . ." I cleared my throat and tried to match my arm-pumping rhythm to my friend's. "I haven't really thought about it yet. Spencer's just started."

"This is your time, Paige—time to think about yourself. You've given those kids your love and devotion, you've made huge sacrifices. And now they're out in the world, doing their own thing." She made it sound like they were in college, not elementary school. "What are your plans?"

"Umm . . . I guess I'll have to think about it."

"Good idea. You should make a list—you know, like your goals for the next five years. That's what Daniel does. He says that 87 percent of people who write down their life goals actually achieve them. He certainly has."

"True." I mentally envisioned Jane's husband's list of goals:

1. Make a squillion dollars.
2. Trade old wife in for younger model. Choose one who will ensure she always looks incredibly youthful and beautiful, no matter how old she gets.

Jane continued, "Of course, it's different for me, because I have Becca." Becca was Jane's "girl," a freakishly tall eighteen-year-old from New Zealand whom Jane employed to look after her two young daughters, clean her house, and generally run errands for her. Becca was never referred to as a nanny, a housekeeper, or a personal assistant; she was always referred to as Jane's "girl." While I thought it was kind of pathetic that a woman of leisure couldn't manage to look after her own children, clean her own house, or run her own errands, I desperately wanted my own giant Kiwi to do my every bidding.

"You're lucky."

"I don't know what I'd do without her." Suddenly, Jane placed two fingers on her neck. "Heart-rate check." I followed suit, though I had no idea what my heart rate was supposed to be. "Let's step it up a bit."

We walked in silence for a while, each focusing on getting our blood pumping. At least, Jane was focused on it; my own mind was racing. She was right: I'd reached a crossroads in my life. My children didn't need me anymore. Okay, they still needed me, but not as much as they had when they were younger. And every year, they would need me less and less. It was time to think about what I wanted. What would it take to make me feel fulfilled? Passionate? Alive? Unbidden, my thoughts drifted to Karen's love affair. I wasn't obsessed with it—really, I wasn't. But lately, Karen had become sort of synonymous with truly loving life. Before I could censor myself, I broke the silence. "This might sound weird, but . . . is your sex life with Daniel still satisfying?" There was no might about it. It did sound weird.

Luckily, I had chosen the right friend to open up to. If it had been Trudy, she would have pitched herself into traffic to keep from having to answer. But Jane reacted like I'd simply asked about her recipe for apple crumble. (Not that Jane would have had a recipe for apple crumble. Becca would've made it for her, of course.) "We have an incredible sex life, but we really work at it."

"Yeah?"

"You can't expect sex to stay amazing without putting in the effort." She looked at me then. "Are you and Paul having trouble in the bedroom?"

"No, I wouldn't say *trouble*." I could feel my cheeks getting hot. "Sometimes, I just miss the excitement of our early days, you know? Like when we were first together—the sex was so passionate and so uh . . . mind-blowing."

"You've desexualized him," Jane stated frankly.

"I've what?"

"*Desexualized.*" She enunciated clearly. "It's very common with married couples—especially when there are children. You now look at Paul as the family's provider, the father, the one who does the yard work . . ."

"I wish. It's like pulling teeth to get him to mow the lawn."

"And he looks at you as the caregiver, the cook, the housekeeper . . ."

"*And* the one who does most of the yard work," I muttered.

"It totally happened to Daniel and his first wife. That's a large part of the reason he fell in love with me."

Great. Now Paul was probably going to dump me for some hot young secretary. Jane read my dismayed expression. "You need to start looking at Paul as a sexual being again. You need to *resexualize* your relationship."

"Okay . . . how?"

"Go back to a time before the kids and all the responsibilities. Be more spontaneous, more adventurous, like when you were first together."

"Umm . . . ?"

"Wear edible panties! Go to his office and give him a blow job! Attack him when he comes home from work and make love to him in the grand entryway!"

"The kids would love that."

"You get the idea," Jane said. "Our marriage counselor says it's the secret to longevity in a marriage."

"You go to marriage counseling?"

"Preemptive measures," she answered breezily, holding her fingers to her pulse. "Daniel and I are committed to making this marriage work. He can't afford to go through another divorce."

When I got home, I showered and washed my hair, reflecting on my friend's advice. Jane was right. I probably had desexualized Paul, and he had likely desexualized me. I had been naïve to think that we would still be having wild, passionate sex without making any extra effort. A good marriage took hard work, and Paul and I had been resting on our laurels for too long.

I toweled off and then stood before the bathroom mirror, naked. The woman who stared back at me still looked pretty good for a thirty-eight-year-old mother of two. In fact, she could probably have passed for—I don't know—a thirty-six-year-old mother of one? Other than the two popped balloons hanging off my front, I didn't look half-bad. In fact, I was almost . . . kinda . . . hot and sexy. Paul was lucky to have me! And I was lucky to have him. Yes, he'd gained a few pounds over the years, and the hair on his head was receding nearly as fast as the hair on his back was advancing, but he still had broad shoulders, strong, manly hands, and those warm brown eyes that shone when he smiled. Two such attractive people should have no trouble kick-starting their love life! If Jane could have an incredible sex life with her fifty-eight-year-old husband, I certainly could with mine.

Still naked, I padded to the bedroom and rummaged through my lingerie drawer. Buried under a mountain of Jockey cotton briefs and A-cup bras were the garments I sought. I removed the black push-up bra, the G-string panties, and the garter belt with fishnet stockings, laboriously untangling them from one another. The outfit had been a gift from one of my college friends at my bridal shower twelve years ago. I had thought it was a joke; it probably was a joke. But for some reason, I had kept it, and desperate times called for desperate measures. I struggled into the complicated ensemble and assessed my reflection in the full-length mirror.

Not bad . . . not bad at all. Of course, it was a little depressing to note that my postbaby breasts no longer filled the B-cup bra, but other than that, I looked pretty damn good . . . definitely good enough to seduce my own husband. Soon, Karen Sutherland wouldn't be the only one in the neighborhood having incredible, passionate sex! I was determined. "Get ready, Paul Atwell," I said out loud. "I'm about to rock your world."

CHAPTER 4

Rocking Paul's world would have to wait. He was called to Cincinnati on the Friday-night red-eye. It was about a LAN or a WAN or a server—something had crashed. Paul called me with the news.

"The blabbidy blah's crashed," he said. "I'm going to have to fly to Cincinnati with the elite support team to see if we can remedy the situation. We're in danger of losing this account."

"Yeah, well you're in danger of losing your wife," I wanted to retort but didn't. I was really pissed off, though. How on earth were Paul and I going to develop a sex life to rival Karen and Javier's if he was never home? In his defense, I hadn't divulged my plan to surprise him in full porn-star regalia and ravage him like a nympho. Maybe then, he would have tried to get out of the trip. But lately, even on the evenings we did spend together, he seemed distracted, still absorbed with work. I wasn't feeling very positive about the current state of our relationship. Paul and I needed to talk. I still planned to put in the extra effort to improve our marriage, but it was going to take two of us.

Thankfully, I didn't have a lot of time to dwell on it. On Saturday morning, Trudy invited us all around to her house for homemade cinnamon buns. When Trudy said "homemade cinnamon buns," she did not mean premade Pillsbury dough-in-a-tube that you sliced, put on cookie sheet, and popped in the oven. She meant homemade dough that you had to knead and then let rise, and then knead and then let rise, and then knead and then let rise . . . Trudy was a throwback to another era.

Just before ten, I called up the stairs to the children. "Kids! Time to go play at Emily and Cameron's house! Don't forget your coats. It's chilly this morning!" Spencer bounded down the stairs joyfully, followed by his sister. "Okay, let's—" I stopped midsentence. "What are you wearing?" I addressed my daughter.

"What?"

"What do you mean 'what'?" I was incredulous. "What do you call that?"

"It's a *baby T*. Like duh? All the cool stars wear them."

"You're not wearing a T-shirt meant for an infant out in public. Go change."

"Why? What's the big—"

"JUST CHANGE!" I was in no mood for more of her insolence.

"God! What a nazi," she muttered, stomping back up the stairs.

Finally, with a petulant Chloe wearing age-appropriate clothing, we set off. Trudy lived a block and a half away. Spencer spent that entire distance trying to convince me to piggyback him because his legs were *soooo* tired. My son had a slight build and was a little small for his age, but I was not up to lugging an extra forty-eight pounds on my back. With much whining (Spencer) and pouting (Chloe), we finally reached Trudy's spacious nouveau-Victorian home.

"Hello!" My friend opened the door before we'd rung the bell. The smell of fresh bread wafted out from behind her.

"Hi!" I pecked her cheek. "It smells great in here."

Trudy leaned over and, adopting her former-preschool-teacher voice, greeted my children. "Hello, kids. Chloe, you look more grown-up every time I see you. And aren't you getting to be a big boy, Mr. Spencer Bo-Pencer!"

"Hi," the kids mumbled. "Yeah."

"Cameron! Emily! Chloe and Spencer are here!"

With much thudding and racket, Trudy's children lumbered up the stairs from their basement playroom.

"Hi, guys!" I said, with forced enthusiasm. Trudy was always so sweet to my kids that I would have hated for her to figure out that I wasn't all that fond of hers.

Emily addressed me. "Cameron thinks you're really a man be-cause your hair looks like Prince Charming's and you have no boobies."

Did I say I wasn't fond of them? I meant I hated them.

"Why don't you kids go down to the playroom?" Trudy inter-jected. "I'll have a special snack for you in a little while."

Trudy led the way through her pristine grand entryway, past the formal living room, burgeoning with family photos in silver frames and enormous silk flower arrangements, and into her French country-style kitchen.

Carly and Karen were seated at the oval kitchen table, steaming mugs of coffee before them. They greeted me in unison.

"How are you?" I hugged them each briefly, then took my seat at one end. It was the first time I had seen Karen since she'd admit-ted her affair. I felt a little awkward: Was I staring at her too long? Was I not looking at her enough? Was my discomfort evident to Trudy and Carly?

Trudy poured me a cup of coffee. "We'll just wait for Jane and the girls, and then we can have some warm cinnamon buns."

Carly laughed. "Like Jane would eat a cinnamon bun!" Carly was what you'd call *Rubenesque*—or else chubby, depending on how kind you were. She'd obviously found a lot of solace in food when her husband left. Who could blame her? I'd been known to spend a few lonely nights curled up with a pint of Häagen-Dazs my-self.

"Jane does watch her figure," Trudy acquiesced.

"I'll say," I added.

Karen changed the subject. "These flowers are gorgeous, Trudy." She leaned forward and inhaled the fragrance of the luxuriant bouquet of pink lilies, gerbera daisies, freesia, and miniature roses serving as the table's centerpiece.

"Aren't they lovely? Carly brought them," Trudy explained.

"You're always so thoughtful," Karen said.

Carly shrugged and waved away the compliment. "Well . . . it's just so sweet of Trudy to invite us all over here today. How often do we get homemade cinnamon buns?"

"So . . ." I cleared my throat nervously. "How has everyone been?" Part of me hoped that Karen would be unable to refrain from crying out "Fantastic! I'm having the best sex of my life with a hot Spanish barista!" I would have felt much more comfortable if her secret were out in the open.

But before Karen could speak, the doorbell rang. Trudy bustled to greet Jane and her entourage and escorted them into the kitchen. "Hello, everyone!" Jane breezed in, in a cloud of Bobbi Brown Baby. She was trailed by her two daughters, in matching pink twin sets and white jeans, and the statuesque Becca. She air-kissed each of us before taking a seat to my right. "You all know Becca, don't you?"

Since Jane went virtually nowhere without her, we all did. "Would you like some coffee, Becca?" Trudy asked.

"No thanks. I'll take the girls downstairs and play some games with the kids. You ladies enjoy yourselves."

God. I wanted to jump up, tackle her, and fireman-carry her home to live with me.

"So . . . ," Jane said, when a cup of black coffee was placed before her and enormous warm, gooey cinnamon buns sat before the rest of us. "What's new with everyone?"

"Not a lot," Karen lied.

"Emily has a piano recital next week, and Cameron's been making incredible progress at Young People's Theater. It's really helping him overcome his shyness," Trudy said.

"Good," Jane responded, as we all nodded our affirmation.

Carly cleared her throat. "I think . . . ," she began hesitantly. "I think I might have met someone."

"Great. That's wonderful. Fantastic," we chorused, supportive smiles pasted on our faces. Unfortunately, we had heard this line from Carly a million times. Very seldom did any of these "meetings" turn into a serious relationship; quite often, they didn't even culminate in a date. But somehow, Carly remained hopeful. It wasn't like she was unattractive: she had beautiful gray eyes and a glossy, dark bob. Yes, she was thirty-five years old and a little on the heavy side, but she was a great cook and the most giving person I knew. Really, Carly was an excellent catch. Unfortunately, most of the single men in her demographic seemed more interested in skinny, vapid Paris Hilton clones.

"Where did you meet this someone?" Trudy asked.

Carly blushed prettily. "At a client's office."

"I didn't know you were interested in one of your clients," Karen said.

"He's not a client. I met him in their lobby. He fills the vending machine. I wanted to buy a Diet Coke and he was refilling the machine, so he handed me a Diet Coke. I went to pay him for it, and he said, 'It's on me.' We just kind of had this moment, y'know? Like, a connection."

"Bought you a Diet Coke—very promising."

"Definitely a good sign."

"He sounds really nice."

"It probably seems silly, but it was just so . . . powerful," Carly said, her cheeks glowing with remembrance. "Our eyes met . . . time stood still . . . Really, it felt like we'd known each other forever."

"Oh no, not silly at all."

"I remember having 'moments' like that."

"How exciting."

"Anyway," Carly continued, "I have a meeting there next Wednesday, too, so . . . well . . . hopefully, he fills the Coke machine weekly."

God, it was so sad. I didn't know if I wanted to hug her or slap her.

Jane turned to me. "Did you tell them about your plan?"

"Uh . . . plan?" I could feel my heart begin to palpitate with panic and small beads of sweat break out on my upper lip. "I don't really have a . . . umm . . . plan."

"Paige is going to resexualize her marriage," Jane announced.

"Resexualize?" Karen asked.

Trudy laughed nervously. "What's that?"

"Just what it sounds like," Jane continued. "After so many years with one man, you need to take some extra measures to keep your sex life hot. You know, like role-playing, sex toys, doing it in daring places . . . Daniel and I discovered the concept shortly after our fourth anniversary. And since then . . . well . . . never a dull moment!"

"And you're going to try this . . . uh, concept, are you, Paige?" Trudy's voice was strained.

"Well . . . really, it's more about renewing our emotional connection," I said weakly. "I thought I might give it a try . . . when Paul gets back from his business trip."

"Oh! Where did he go?" Trudy asked. It was an obvious attempt to steer the conversation out of the bedroom, but Jane would not be put off that easily.

"You have to do it," she said, looking at me. "What are the other options? Boring sex for the rest of your life? An affair?"

Impulsively, my eyes darted to Karen, who was dissecting her cinnamon bun with rapt attention. Carly broke the nanosecond of uncomfortable silence. "Well, that's great, Paige. Good for you. Sex is a really important part of a relationship."

"Well . . . umm . . . I guess . . ." I shrugged.

Carly stood up. "I think I'll go see how Becca's making out with all your little monkeys," she said brightly. "It's just so nice to be able to spend some time with them."

When she had gone downstairs, Karen said sadly, "It's still hard for her."

"What?" I asked, through a delicious mouthful. Carly was always eager to help out with the children. I hadn't noticed anything odd in her departure.

Trudy elaborated. "The kind of pain and betrayal she suffered when Brian left . . . You do not get over that easily."

"You're kidding, right?" Jane asked. "She didn't leave because we were talking about sex, did she?"

"No, I think she just wanted to spend some time with the kids," I said, swallowing the remnants of cinnamon bun.

Trudy disagreed. "Sex is still somewhat of an uncomfortable topic for Carly."

"It's been two years!" Jane cried. "It's not like everyone else has stopped doing it just because she has!"

"A little compassion would be nice," Karen said pointedly. "Carly was devastated when Brian left."

"Okay, I'm sorry. But since she's not here . . . How's the baby-making going?"

Karen's composure was flawless. "We're cautiously optimistic. I've been seeing an acupuncturist, so . . . hopefully . . ."

Trudy commented. "A woman I know through Emily's music lessons has been undergoing IVF. The procedure's been meeting with more and more success these days."

"Maybe . . . ," Karen said. "I'm not sure I'm ready to take that step yet."

A lumbering noise on the basement stairs signaled that the children had decided it was snack time. Trudy jumped up, as if relieved. "Who wants a fresh homemade cinnamon bun?" All the children jumped up and down with anticipation, except my two. Chloe was too cool to jump. Spencer had a question.

"Umm . . . do they have raisins in them?"

"They do, sweetie," Trudy replied.

"I'm allergic to raisins."

"You're not allergic, Spencer," I said.

"I am!" he insisted. "If I eat one, I'll get bumps on me and my tongue will explode."

"That won't happen."

"Well, we don't want to take that chance, now, do we?" Trudy placated. "Would you prefer a homemade chocolate-chip cookie?"

"Yes, please!"

"Auntie Paige?" Cameron was standing beside me.

"Yes, dear?" I forced a smile of fondness. Trudy's children addressed us all as "auntie," which made me feel even more guilty for despising them. At least he hadn't called me "uncle."

"Spencer said that sometimes he touches his butt hole."

"Spencer!" I growled. He turned to me, his hand poised above the blue floral cookie tin Trudy was proffering. "What did I say about that kind of language?"

"What? It's not a body function. It's a body part. And sometimes I touch it, okay? Jeez."

"Ewwwwwwwwww!" the kids chorused. I think Jane may have joined in, just a little.

Trudy pulled the tin away. "Maybe you should go wash your hands, Spencer?"

"You are so disgusting!" Chloe shrieked.

"Go wash your hands, Spencer," I echoed, my face turning crimson.

"What's the big deal?" he huffed, as he headed to the washroom. "It's a part of my body."

"Ewwww! It's where poo and farts come out!!" Emily tittered.

"Emily!" Trudy whirled on her. "We DO NOT use that kind of language in this house!"

"But, Mom," she whined, "Cameron said 'butt hole.'"

"Cameron was just repeating what Spencer said," Trudy expounded. "You know better than to say that yucky word. Go get one of your toys to put in the naughty-word box."

Emily sniffled a little but obediently headed to the playroom. Trudy disappeared into the pantry, soon returning with a cardboard carton—obviously, the naughty-word box. Within a few moments, Emily rejoined us carrying a battered Barbie doll.

"In the box," Trudy said sternly. "Now, . . . what word will you use instead of that naughty one?"

"Pass wind."

"That's right. Now, off you go. Your cinnamon bun is on the table."

Spencer returned with his hands freshly washed. "Can I have a cookie now?"

"Sure, Mr. Spencer Bo-Pencer," Trudy said cheerily. "Help yourself."

I decided to follow the advice of Jane's successful, goal-reaching husband. It was time to make a list—a Life Makeover list. I could no longer deny the fact that my life was not exactly going as I had envisioned it. My son had apparently developed an obsession with bodily functions; my daughter seemed to have a case of early-onset teen hostility; and my husband, who had been away for four days, had called home only once, briefly, to say good night to the kids. And that was not to mention the fact that I suddenly had six glorious hours of freedom each day and no idea what to do with them.

With a mug of Serenity herbal tea (the uplifting blend), I took a pad of paper and a pen to the kitchen table. Taking a sip of the hot liquid, I inhaled the aroma of orange blossoms, essence of clematis, and something that smelled a little bit like mushrooms. Then I wrote:

LIFE MAKEOVER

I underlined it several times with heavy pen strokes.

Okay . . . first off, the kids.

1. Do research on Internet to learn if Spencer's fascination with bodily functions is a sign that he is a deeply disturbed weirdo or just going through a phase.

This was obviously a top priority. It was only a matter of time before this fixation had serious scholastic and social repercussions. Spencer was sure to call his teacher "barf hair" or something and get suspended if not expelled. And at some point, he was bound to become known to all his peers as "that weird kid who can't stop talking about diarrhea."

2. Find out why Chloe suddenly hates me.

I had absolutely no idea how to go about this, or whether it was even possible, but I was determined to at least try. Now, on to my marriage . . .

3. Resexualize relationship with Paul.
   • Wear sexy lingerie.
   • Initiate mind-blowing sex in room other than bedroom.
   • Multiple positions.
   • Increase number of blow jobs given. (Two per month reasonable?)

I took another sip of tea and tapped my pen on the paper thoughtfully. Surely there was more I could do to rejuvenate our sex life? It was a little disturbing that I couldn't think of anything else. Okay . . . time to focus on me. What did I want out of life? What would enrich my existence? What would make me feel more fulfilled as a person? I wrote down:

4. Bigger boobs.

No, I did not think bigger boobs would enrich my existence or fulfill me as a person, but still, I wanted them. I was not going to go the breast-implant route—too expensive and risky. But there were exercises I could do to build up my pectoral muscles, at least giving the *impression* of bigger boobs. And really . . . why stop there?

5. Begin rigorous exercise program.
   • Aerobic exercise: to feel great and have tons of energy.
   • Spot exercises: to tone and trim, ensuring I look very fit and gorgeous.

Both of these would undoubtedly help with my resexualizing efforts—but this was really about me.

6. Find stimulating and creative hobby.
   • Feed mind! Nourish soul!

7. Clean and organize household.

I scratched off the last one. Cleaning and organizing was a little mundane to be on a list entitled "Life Makeover." I felt better already. Daniel was right. Just putting these goals down on paper made them more tangible, more achievable. I was determined and energized. I would tackle item 1 immediately.

Paul had a tiny office tucked behind the family room, just before the entrance to the attached garage. Sitting in the swivel chair at his pressboard desk, I booted up the computer. I waited patiently as the machine initialized, feeling confident that, with a little insight, I'd be able to help my son overcome his problem. When I was finally on my search engine's home page, I paused. The empty white box sat waiting for me to enter my search topic. After considering for a few moments, I typed, **young boys fixated on pee + poo + snot + vomit.**

I clicked Go.

Ewww! I was immediately assaulted with a litany of pornographic websites that managed to turn my stomach within the span of their brief, ten-word descriptions.

I tried again.

Compulsive butt-hole touching in young boys

Oh God! This was even worse! I felt somewhat nauseous—not to mention paranoid that a kiddie-porn task force was going to kick my door in and arrest me at any moment. The office phone at my elbow rang loudly in the empty house. Oh shit! Oh shit! The cops must have been monitoring my computer!

"Hello?" My voice was thin and reedy.

"Hi. It's Karen."

"Oh, hi!" I was relieved. "How are you?"

"I'm good, thanks. Look . . . I have a couple of things I need to talk to you about. Is this a good time?"

My relief was short-lived. From her preface, I could deduce that either she was mad at me for some reason or she was about to divulge more details of her earth-shaking sex life. I wasn't really in the mood for either conversation. ". . . Sure."

"You didn't tell Jane about me and Javier, did you?"

"No!" I shrieked. "God, no! I told you I wouldn't say anything."

"Okay . . . It's just that . . . well . . ."

Her accusation annoyed me. I hadn't asked for the role of Karen's lone confessor, and I didn't appreciate her mistrust. "Why did you confide in me, then, if you think I can't keep a secret for more than a few days?"

"Sorry! I believe you! I believe you. It was just so weird at Trudy's house the other day."

"Weird how?" I was still simmering.

"All that sex talk. We don't usually talk about our sex lives around Trudy. It makes her uncomfortable. And poor Carly . . . She was really upset afterward."

"I wasn't too thrilled either. It was *my* sex life we were discussing."

"I know. I'm sorry. It just made me wonder if Jane knew something. She just kept going on and on about sex, sex, sex. She was relentless!"

"Well . . . You know Jane."

"You're right, I do. I'm probably just paranoid. Sorry I doubted you."

"That's okay."

"So . . . how *is* the resexualizing going?"

"Paul gets home tonight." I didn't offer any more details.

"Well . . . good luck with it. I'm sure you'll be, umm, great."

"Thanks." There was an awkward pause that I knew I was meant to fill. "How are things with . . ." God, what did I say? Your men? Your lovers? Or did I use their names—Doug and Javier? Finally, I chose ". . . you?"

"Good," she said weakly. "Well, not really. I'm so confused, Paige. I'm really torn."

"So, you're still seeing Javier?"

"Of course. I can't just walk away from what I feel for him. But then Doug . . . God, I feel so guilty. He's been really sweet lately and talking a lot about having a baby. It just makes it harder."

"Well . . . no one said adultery was easy."

"Apparently not." There was a slight pause before she spoke again. "I need a favor."

". . . Okay," I said hesitantly.

"I don't mean to draw you into this, but . . . I need you to cover for me tonight."

"Karen," I said firmly, "I'm not comfortable lying to Doug."

"You don't have to lie to him! You won't even have to talk to him. All I'm asking is that you don't call for me between eight and eleven tonight. That's not so much to ask, is it?"

"Well . . ." I still didn't feel good about it.

"And if you could just stay inside. You know, so he doesn't see you."

"So, you're telling him that you're out with me when you'll really be with Javier?"

"Yes, just this once."

"I don't like it, Karen."

"I know, but it's crucial I talk to Javier. There are some important . . . *issues* we need to discuss. I can't go on like this. It's not fair
to anyone. I need to have a serious conversation with him about
what the future holds. I'm not even going to have sex with him
tonight."

Sure, like she'd be able to resist his smoldering eyes.

I heaved a heavy sigh. "I guess it's okay—just this once."

"Thank you, Paige," she said, almost gleefully. She sounded aw-
fully excited for someone who was just going to *talk*.

"But if Doug calls here, I'm not covering for you. I'll just say I
don't know where you are, which, technically, will be true."

"That's fine. He won't call."

"I sure hope not."

"He won't."

I couldn't help but feel a little guilty about my small role in
Karen's subterfuge. It wasn't that Doug and I were close. Our relationship had always been pleasant but rather superficial. But I hated
lying. It made me feel like a bad person. Although . . . I wasn't actually *lying,* per se. I was just staying indoors and not calling Karen,
which, in fact, was what I had planned to do anyway. I decided to
stop beating myself up over it.

Instead of focusing (again) on my friend's dangerous liaison,
I would concentrate all my attention on my own plans for the
evening. Because tonight, at 9:00 P.M., my unsuspecting husband
would be landing at Denver International Airport. When he arrived
home, approximately forty-five minutes later, he would be greeted
at the door by his sexy, lingerie-clad wife, who was fully prepared to
ravage him like a horny teenager—quite possibly right there in the
grand entryway.

When the kids went to bed at eight, I began my preparations. I
had bought a do-it-yourself bikini-waxing kit and, for the first time,
gave myself a home bikini wax. The result was a rather lopsided,
chicken-skin look, but hopefully Paul would at least appreciate my

efforts. I then took a hot, lavender-scented bath, where I shaved off all other superfluous body hair. At 8:45, I toweled myself off, put my hair up in a loose, devil-may-care style, and applied my makeup. By 9:15, I was seated in the family room, a thick terry robe covering my garter belt, fishnet stockings, and rather too large push-up bra. Inexplicably, I felt nervous . . . or maybe just excited. This was a momentous occasion, after all: the first day of the rest of our marriage. To relax, I poured myself a glass of Syrah and flicked on a rerun of *CSI*.

I watched the entire program. And then I watched a VH1 *Behind the Music* episode on Mariah Carey. When the late news came on, I realized something was wrong. Paul was over an hour late. His flight must have been delayed. Or he'd had car trouble on the way home. Or his plane had been shot down by terrorists—although that would likely have made the news. But a car crash wouldn't! He could be lying, right now, in the twisted wreckage! My children could be orphans! It was a momentary panic. I still felt fairly confident that my husband was simply running late. But there was one thing I was absolutely positive about: I could not wear this lingerie for another second.

Upstairs, I gratefully peeled off the constrictive gear. An ensemble like this was obviously not meant to be worn for more than a few minutes before it was ripped from your body in a fit of passion. Extended wear could cause irreparable damage; I was lucky to have survived the experience with everything still intact. That's when I heard the sound of Paul's key in the front door. Damn! I tried to struggle back into the outfit, but it was too complicated. It wouldn't be very sexy if he came up here and found me awkwardly tangled in black elastic and lace. Throwing on the robe, I scurried downstairs to greet my husband.

"Hi!" I said, excited to see him.

"Hey, babe." We kissed. "Sorry I'm late. The plane was delayed."

I stepped back to look at him. His exhaustion was apparent. He wore a rumpled suit, a five-o'clock shadow, and bags under his bloodshot eyes. "You look like crap."

"I feel like crap."

"Poor baby. Did your thingamajig go well?"

"Well enough to salvage the account—I hope. But there are still some problems with the blah blah blabbidy blah . . ."

I made a sympathetic noise. "Come sit down. Would you like a massage? I could give you a massage."

"That would be awesome." He gave me an affectionate squeeze as we headed to the family room.

I poured my husband a glass of wine and wedged myself in behind him on the couch. Paul flicked on the news as I began to knead the tension from his shoulders.

"Ahhh . . . that feels great," he moaned.

"If you think that feels great, just you wait," I felt like saying, but decided not to ruin the surprise. "I missed you," I whispered sexily into his ear, as my hands continued to roam his shoulders and back. He really was still quite strong and muscular.

"I missed you, too. And the kids. How are they?"

"Fine." Now was not the time to alert my husband to our children's possible psychological problems.

"Good . . . good . . ."

I rubbed his shoulders for a few more minutes, sporadically kissing his neck and nibbling his ear. Though I was not an expert masseuse, his tension had definitely eased, and I felt he was primed for the big event to come. "I'll be right back," I whispered in his ear. "I have a little surprise for you."

It took about ten minutes to struggle back into the sexy lingerie, but finally I was ready. With a deep breath for courage, I headed down the stairs. "Surprise!" I called softly as I entered the living room. Paul snored loudly in response.

"Paulllll," I said gently. "I have a surprise for you. Wake up, honey."

Loud, unattractive snucking noise.

"Paul." My voice had returned to regular volume. "Hey, Paul." I shook his knee.

More horrible snoring sounds.

I felt frustrated. My plan seemed doomed to failure. I was also in incredible pain and desperately needed him to wake up and rip this lingerie off me. "Paul!" I said loudly, grabbing his shoulders and shaking him. "Paul! Wake up! Wake up!"

He sat forward with a jolt. "We'll provide a backup server while the elite team works on the problem!" His speech was slurred and his eyes still glazed with sleep.

For a long moment, I looked at my husband, the object of my seduction. In his disheveled and confused state, he really wasn't what you'd call sexually attractive. When I finally spoke, my voice had become distinctly maternal, despite my hooker getup. "It's okay, honey. You're home now. Come on up to bed."

CHAPTER 6

The next morning, Paul stayed and had breakfast with us. He usually left for the office at 6:30 A.M., but decided he wanted to spend some time with the children. He was fun and jovial, roughhousing with Spencer and teasing Chloe. If he remembered my resexualizing attempt of the night before, he wasn't letting on. He probably felt sorry for me—humiliating myself in that slutty outfit when he obviously wasn't in the mood. Or maybe he was so exhausted that he didn't even notice what I was wearing. Still, the sight of your wife in a garter belt and fishnet stockings should have some sort of stimulating effect, should it not?

I drove to Rosedale with a cartoon cloud of gloom hovering above my head. Carly was just backing out of her driveway as we passed, looking groomed and professional, ready to face the world. I waved, briefly, while mentally admonishing myself for my own slovenly appearance. We rounded the corner and headed down the hill toward the school, where I spotted Karen, out for a morning jog. She waved exuberantly, her cheeks pink with exertion and, probably, remembrance of her great "talk" with Javier last night. I was surprised by a sudden pang of envy. It should be me with the rosy cheeks and sly smile this morning. It wasn't fair. Karen had two men who wanted her. She had hot, passionate sex with Javier and perfunctory, baby-making sex with Doug. I had none of it! I couldn't get my husband to have any kind of sex with me—exciting *or* run-of-the-mill. God, when I tried to seduce him, he didn't even notice!

"Mom?" It was Spencer calling from the backseat.

I was thankful for the distraction from my silent fury. "Yes, angel?" I looked at my son in the rearview mirror, and the frost encasing my heart melted at the sight of him. His quizzical blue eyes . . . his freckled nose . . . He was growing up so fast. Already six years old and off at school. . . . My little man . . . My precious little man. I was the lucky one, not Karen.

Spencer continued. "What would happen if you had a fountain in your yard, and instead of water coming out, it had pee coming out?"

"There's no such thing as a pee fountain," I said irritably. This had a somewhat dampening effect on my lovey-dovey mood.

"What about a throw-up fountain?"

"No."

"Diarrhea?"

"Shut up, you gross pig!" Chloe screamed.

"Spencer that's enough! Chloe, don't tell your brother to shut up."

"But he's disgusting!" she hurled.

I pulled into our usual spot adjacent to the playing field. Slamming the vehicle into park, I swiveled to face my son in his booster seat. "I've had enough of that kind of language, young man. I hope you don't talk about things like that when you're at school."

"No." He blinked at me innocently.

"Because those things are not appropriate to talk about *ever,* but especially not in school."

He stared and blinked.

"Do you understand me?" I said firmly. "There will be no more talking about those things."

"Okay." (Long pause.) "What things?"

"You know what things!" I was aware that my voice was becoming shrill.

Blink. Stare. "Fountains?"

"Spencer!" I was definitely losing my patience. "Bodily functions, okay?"

"What are bodily functions?"

"You retard!" Chloe interjected.

"Chloe! Don't you say that." But I could only scold one child at a time. "Spencer, you know what bodily functions are," I said through gritted teeth.

"Ummm . . . armpits?"

"No, not armpits."

"Ummm . . . ?"

"Diarrhea! Throw-up! Pee! Snot!" I shrieked. "Those are bodily functions, okay?"

"Oh . . . ," he said, nodding his head with sudden comprehension. "Those things."

"Right. Now I hope I've heard the last about them." As I turned away from my son, I suddenly realized that all four car windows were partially open. A small crowd of primary school spectators and their parents had gathered on the sidewalk to observe my pee-and-poo tirade.

Spencer waved at them and smiled. He seemed quite pleased that an audience of his peers had witnessed his mom screaming all his favorite words. Chloe shot me a look of pure hatred.

"Oh hello! Good morning!" I waved. One or two of the mothers responded with a curt wave; most of them grabbed their children by the shoulders and marched them away from us.

"Thanks a lot, Mom," Chloe huffed, jumping out of the car and slamming the door.

"Bye, honey!" I called sweetly after her. "Have a nice day."

When I returned home, I was tempted to lie on the couch, watch soap operas, and eat the entire contents of the freezer (except the fish sticks). But I knew that wallowing in self-pity wasn't going to improve anything, and neither was gaining five pounds. From the corner of my eye, I glimpsed the edge of my Life Makeover list, peeking out from its hiding place in the back of my address book. I took a deep, fortifying breath. I would not let last night's failure deter me. I was still committed to improving my lot in life, and I knew just where to start.

Grabbing two family-sized cans of Campbell's soup from the pantry, I moved to the living room and lay on my back on the Berber carpet. With my arms outstretched, I began to lift the soup cans slowly, focusing on my pectoral muscles. I had read about it in a magazine—an article on toning your body using household items. There were all sorts of exercises that involved brooms and laundry baskets and hand towels, but this was the one that had stuck with me. I was realistic: I knew I wasn't going to recapture my teenage breasts with a few soup-can hoists, but it certainly couldn't hurt.

Just taking action toward reaching my goals made me feel much more positive. True, these soup cans were not very heavy, and it didn't feel like my pectoral muscles were actually doing any work, but the point was, I was moving forward. And really, it was silly of me to give up so easily on my resexualization mission. Paul was home now, relaxed and rested. And it was Friday night, the perfect night for romance. The phone rang.

"Hello?" I was actually a little winded when I jumped up to answer the phone: a good sign.

"Hey babe, it's me."

"Hi, honey," I cooed. "How are you?"

"Good . . . good . . ." (Tap tap tap of keyboard in background.) "Listen, hon, we've got some vendors in from San Jose. We're going to take them out for a beer after work. But don't worry, it'll be an early night."

"Great. An early night sounds great."

"Yeah, we've got a 7:00 A.M. tee-off time tomorrow, so I want to hit the hay by eleven."

I was so engulfed by anger and disappointment that I could not respond. There was a long silence.

"... Paige?"

"Yeah?" I managed weakly.

"I know I've been away a lot, but I'll make it up to you on Saturday, okay?"

"Okay."

I clung to that promise. Somehow, I did not succumb to the feelings of anger and neglect that simmered under the surface. Saturday would be the day—it was sex night, after all. It would mark the beginning of a new phase in our relationship! A hot and sexy phase! Despite my lack of progress, I was as committed as ever to turning this marriage around.

On Saturday morning, after I dropped Spencer at soccer and Chloe at her hip-hop dance class, I raced to the mall. A woman on a mission, I walked directly to Victoria's Secret and purchased the sexiest red bra and G-string panties I could find. There was no way he could not notice me in red! When I picked up the children, I drove toward home with a small smile of accomplishment. Within the hour, I had taken my children to their enriching, extracurricular activities and outfitted myself for a night of incredible passion with my husband. Really, I was pretty good at this whole wife and mother game. I seemed to have been able to achieve the perfect balance between kind and nurturing maternal figure and hot and sexy—

"Heyyyyy ... What's in this pink bag?" Spencer called from the backseat, interrupting my self-congratulations.

"DON'T TOUCH IT!!!" I shrieked. Keeping my eyes on the road, I flailed my arm in the backseat area, trying in vain to grab the lingerie bag, which had slid out from under the passenger seat and was now in Spencer's grasp.

"Why? What is it?" he continued, oblivious to my admonitions. I could hear the tissue rustling as he dug in the sack. "What is this thing?" He removed the sheer red G-string from the bag and proceeded to slingshot it into the front seat of the car.

"Spencer!" I hissed, as my new panties landed on the floor mat beside me. "Put the friggin' bag away!"

"But what is that thing? Is it a toy?"

"You are such an idiot!" Chloe screamed. "They're underpants for Mom! They're disgusting!"

"Thanks, Chloe."

"And what's this?" Spencer continued undeterred, pulling another garment from the bag.

"It's a bra!" Chloe said. "Like duh?"

"But why is it all squishy and lumpy? It sounds like there's water in it. Listen." He shook it for his sister. "See? It's full of water."

"It's a water bra," I said resignedly. "Now put it away."

"What's a water bra?" Chloe asked.

"A bra with water in it. Now, put it away please."

"But why?" she persisted.

The last thing Chloe needed to be made aware of was the fact that men were completely obsessed with big boobs. With the track she was on, this knowledge would see her saving up for breast implants at fifteen, which she would likely need if she took after me. "It's more comfortable," I lied.

"A water bra," Spencer mumbled, still playing with it. "That's weird, a bra with water in it. Could you put something else in it instead of water? Like pee?"

"Spencer, stop!!!" I shrieked. "Just stop! Put the friggin' bra back in the friggin' bag!"

"Jeez!" he muttered, but I could hear him replacing it. "You don't need to spaz."

Paul's car was in the drive when we arrived home. I tucked the pink bag into my purse as we entered. "Hey, guys!" he greeted us cheerfully. Spencer careened himself into his father, and even Chloe gave him an affectionate shove as she walked past. Paul moved toward me. "How are you?" He leaned in for a kiss.

"I'm good. How was golf?"

"I didn't play very well, but the vendors had a good time. And I ran into Doug Sutherland."

"Karen's Doug?" I felt my heart lurch for some reason.

"Yeah. I invited them around for a barbecue tonight. I thought I'd grill up a few steaks, have a few beers . . ."

"You invited Karen and Doug over here? Tonight?"

"Yeah, I thought it would be fun. They're a nice couple. We should get to know them a little better."

"Oh, I know Karen plenty well," I growled, stalking past him to the kitchen. "A little too well, in fact," I added, to myself.

Paul followed me. "What's the problem? I thought she was your friend."

"She is my friend."

"Then why don't you want to have them over?"

"It's fine," I said, banging around in the kitchen looking for nothing in particular. "Really, it's great." Yeah, it was just great. I had barely gotten used to being around Karen after her confession, and now I had to face Doug! Doug *and* Karen! It was going to be awkward and uncomfortable—*worse* than awkward and uncomfortable. And suppose Karen left him and moved into some tiny, faraway apartment with Javier? I could just hear Doug telling the neighbors "Paige knew about the affair all along. She even covered for Karen so she could cheat on me. And to think she had the nerve to invite me over to a barbecue at her house! What a horrible, deceitful woman."

"What's going on?" Paul interrupted my internal dialogue.

"Nothing."

"Tell me, Paige," he said sternly.

I wanted to tell him then; I really did. Sometimes I wonder whether things might have turned out differently if I had. But I couldn't break my promise to Karen. And besides, if Paul knew about Karen's affair, there'd be two of us acting awkward and strange around poor Doug tonight. I heaved a heavy sigh. "It's nothing. I'm just feeling a little tired for company, that's all. But you're right. It'll be fun."

"Okay . . . ," he said skeptically. "I'll go get some steaks."

"Great. And pick up some lettuce and croutons for a salad. And get beer . . . and some red wine. Get lots of red wine."

CHAPTER 7

Lots of red wine turned out to be a bad idea. But I thought it would help me relax! If I just had a drink while I made the salad, I'd be calmer. And a glass while I put on my makeup might make it easier to pretend that this was just a fun evening between friends who had no secrets. And then another, as I made the kids an early dinner of fish sticks and macaroni and set them up with a movie in the playroom, might make me forget that anything at all was amiss between Karen and Doug. When they rang the bell at seven, I was feeling quite cheerful and confident that I could handle the situation.

"Doug!" I swept him into a huge embrace that I might have held just a tad too long. "How are you? You look fantastic!" He did look pretty good. He was an attractive man of medium height, with a neat, graying goatee and stylish glasses. Something about Doug radiated intelligence. He was no artist's model, to be sure, but neither was he a hideous ogre who would drive his wife into the arms of the first good-looking barista to come along.

"You, too, Paige," he answered politely. "Great to see you, as always." He handed me a bottle of wine.

"Oh, you shouldn't have, but how thoughtful! Paul, Doug brought a bottle of wine. Isn't that nice? That's so nice, Doug."

"Well . . . thanks for having us over."

"Our pleasure! Really, Paul and I were just saying that we should do this more often." Paul took Doug's coat, and I turned to Karen. "Hi, stranger! Long time, no see." I laughed, as if it were actually funny.

"Hi," she said, smiling a little tightly. "Thanks for inviting us."

"Well, when Paul said he saw Doug at the golf course and suggested a barbecue, I just thought, what a great idea! We don't do nearly enough together as couples, do we?"

"No."

It was a warm autumn evening, so we all stood on the back deck and visited as Paul grilled the T-bones. I kept everyone's drink filled, including my own, and played the part of the charming and witty hostess. At least, I thought I was charming and witty. In retrospect, I can see that I was just drunk. But all in all, the evening went quite smoothly. Karen and Doug seemed very much a couple, teasing each other good-naturedly, exchanging fond glances, and touching affectionately. It would have been easy to forget that she was involved with someone else had I not developed a slightly unhealthy fixation with the subject.

Being with Karen and her husband only deepened my fascination—and confusion. Why did they seem so much closer than Paul and me? They seemed to revel in each other's company. They presented as a team, a unified front. Whereas Paul and I—well, he was in charge of steaks; I was on salads. Our connection didn't seem to go much beyond that. Did Karen's infidelity make her appreciate Doug more? Now that she was sexually fulfilled, was she more able to enjoy his companionship? Could Doug sense that his wife was happier, more passionate, and more alive? And did that all rub off on their relationship? God! Was the secret to a happy marriage a hunk on the side?

It was over a dessert of hot-fudge sundaes with fresh raspberries when things went a little off the rails. Conversation had previously been split along gender lines. Paul and Doug chatted about work, golf scores, and last night's football game. Karen and I covered the usual stuff: the new movie that she had seen and that I wanted to see, Carly's difficulty tracking down the vending-machine man, the workout regime I planned to start and the one Karen was already on. But as we sat around the dining room table, it seemed rude not to address Doug directly. I didn't want him to think that I was uncomfortable around him. As hostess, it was my duty to engage all my guests in conversation. Unfortunately, in my inebriated state, I might not have chosen the best topic for discussion.

"So, Doug . . ." I leaned toward him. "I hear Karen's seeing an infertility acupuncturist. I'm sure you'll have her knocked up in no time!"

Doug laughed, a little uncomfortably. Paul laughed, a lot uncomfortably.

"Seriously, though, once you have kids," I continued, my speech mildly slurred, "then you're really a family, you know? . . . Not that you aren't a family right now—you and Karen. You are! Very much so! But you know, kids . . . kids really kind of solidify a relationship. Not that they're always easy, let me tell you. Some days, I think, why couldn't I have been satisfied with just a dog or something? But kids are great, really."

At this point, I happened to glance at my friend across the table. Her eyes were filled with panic. Uh-oh. I realized I'd been steering our conversation in the wrong direction. If Karen was going to leave Doug soon, she probably didn't want me pumping up family life. "Although . . . you know, sometimes I think family is overrated. I mean, the whole concept of 'family.' " I did those annoying little air quotes. "Do people really need other people so much? Like, couldn't people be just as happy alone, without the burden of a spouse and children or trying to have children? If I were to find myself alone tomorrow, I'd be okay. Not, like, if everyone was dead or whatever, but just being on my own . . . it would be okay." I reached for my glass of wine, but Paul's hand stopped me.

"How about I make some coffee?" He was extending the offer to the whole table but looking directly at me.

"Actually, I think we'd better be going," Karen said.

"Yeah," Doug agreed. "That was a really early morning on the golf course. I'm exhausted."

When we'd said our good-byes, I trailed Paul to the kitchen. "So . . . ?" I said suggestively, closing one eye to keep him in focus. "What should we do now?"

"I'm going to clean up this mess. You should get to bed."

"I'll help," I insisted, grabbing a dirty plate. The cutlery sitting on top clattered noisily to the floor.

"You're going to wake the kids," Paul hissed.

"Sooooooooorry!" I sniped, sounding a lot like Chloe.

"Listen, hon," he said patiently, "I'll take care of the dishes. You get some sleep. You're going to have a sore head in the morning."

Sulkily, I headed up the stairs. I felt like a scolded child, sent to bed before she was ready. I certainly didn't feel tired: I felt full of energy! I wanted to do something wild and spontaneous, like take a cab into town and go dancing till dawn! At that moment, I remembered the pink bag tucked into my lingerie drawer. This was perfect! What better time to resexualize my marriage than right now, when I'd had a few drinks to enhance my sexiness and lower my inhibitions? I was going to do it! I was going to put on the new lingerie and jump my husband, right there in the kitchen. Right there in the messy kitchen! The messiness of it just made it that much more wild and spontaneous!

Thankfully, donning the crimson water bra and thong was much less complicated than my previous outfit. When I was dressed, I took in my reflection. The bra did a great job of boosting my minuscule breasts, and the thong . . . Well, who really looks that good in a thong anyway? But men go crazy for them, for some reason. Before I headed downstairs to ambush my husband, I slipped on an old pair of ridiculously high-heeled strappy sandals: the pièce de résistance.

"Hellooooooooo?" I cooed as I walked down the stairs, running my hand seductively along the railing. "Hellooooooo? Mr. Atwell? I'm sorry to interrupt your cleaning, but I desperately need—"

Suddenly, my ankle wobbled in its stiletto casing and, with a sharp, shooting pain, turned dramatically on its side. I grasped frantically for the railing, but to no avail. My body was pitched violently forward, and I fell flat on my face, sliding painfully, step-by-step, down the carpeted staircase. Paul burst around the corner and saw me lying in a crumpled heap on the hardwood floor.

"Jesus Christ! Are you okay?"

"Owwwwwwww!" I moaned.

"What's wrong? What hurts?"

Just my pride and, of course: "My ankle."

"Can you stand on it?" Paul took my elbow and tried, in vain, to get me to stand in my three-inch heels.

"Ouch!" I winced and burst into tears.

"It's not broken, is it?" Paul bent down to inspect my foot.

"It-it's not broken," I snuffled. "I just wanted . . . I just wanted to surprise you. I wanted to . . . re-, re-, resexualize . . ." Another wave of tears washed away my words.

Paul kissed my hair, then picked me up in his arms. "Off to bed with you, my little wino," he said, before laboriously carrying me up the stairs.

The next day was a write-off. As Paul had predicted, I had a throbbing headache, plus a swollen ankle and painful carpet burns on my knees and forearms. Mercifully, he let me sleep late, coming in to check on me at ten o'clock.

"How are you?" he asked from the doorway.

"Not good," I mumbled. It was true. I certainly wasn't feeling very healthy, but I was also incredibly sheepish. Lately, every time I tried to have sex with my husband, I humiliated myself. That was hard on my self-esteem, not to mention our marriage.

"I'm taking the kids swimming," Paul said. "You rest. Keep your ankle elevated. And you might want to put some vitamin E on your chin."

"My chin?" I sat up.

"Carpet burn."

I turned to look in my dresser mirror. Sure enough, my chin looked like a lump of raw hamburger. I flopped back onto my pillow.

"See ya later," Paul said, as he turned to go.

"See ya," I mumbled.

"Oh . . ." He turned back toward me. "Karen phoned. She wants you to call her as soon as you're up."

"Okay."

But I couldn't call her. I was embarrassed by my behavior the night before, and I was in no mood for a reprimand from my friend. She had a right to be angry with me; I'd acted like a complete jackass. While I might not have said anything about her affair outright, I had probably aroused Doug's suspicions. Hopefully, he would just think I was a drunken, babbling idiot. I might as well face it: Karen should never have entrusted her secret to me. I wasn't going to tell anyone, but I wasn't exactly handling the knowledge with a lot of grace. I acted differently around her now—at least when others were present. I couldn't spend even one evening with her and her husband without getting completely shit-faced. And probably worst of all, I couldn't get her affair out of my head. It was consuming me, turning me into a sex maniac—a sex maniac who couldn't get any action. I felt more dejected than ever.

By Monday, I was physically improved, but my mind-set was the same. I still hadn't spoken to Karen. I just couldn't face her. I honestly could not handle listening to her gush on about the intensity of her feelings for Javier, their passion, their connection, their word-transcending love. Nor could I stand to hear her moan about how conflicted she was between the two men who loved her and craved her and couldn't get enough of her. Maybe I wasn't being a supportive friend, but I had my own sanity to consider.

I spent most of the day moping. There was no other word for it: shuffling around the big, empty house in my fuzzy slippers and an old pair of track pants, my chin slathered in vitamin E cream. The Life Makeover list sat unread, my inspiration to turn my life around suddenly gone. I couldn't help but blame Karen. Hearing about her newfound passion and zest for life had highlighted the blandness of my own existence. I didn't want to cheat on Paul; I loved him. But is that what it would take to shake me out of these suburban-mom doldrums? I wanted something, *needed* something to change in my life. The phone rang.

"Hello?"

"This is Marilyn Chow calling from the principal's office at Rosedale Elementary."

This was not what I had in mind. "Yes . . . hello."

"Mr. Dennison asked me to call. He'd like to discuss some important issues with you, in person, and was wondering if you could come in for a few minutes this afternoon?"

The principal wanted to meet with me? In person? To discuss important issues? Oh God! But somehow, I remained composed. "Certainly. I could come in just before 3:00."

"Excellent. I'll put you in his appointment book."

I cleared my throat. "And what might this be regarding?" As if I didn't know. Spencer had obviously informed his teacher about how much he enjoyed touching his butt hole. Or possibly, that his fondest wish was to have a diarrhea fountain in his front yard. On the other hand, this could be about Chloe. Perhaps she had been sneaking minuscule T-shirts to school in her pants pocket and changing into them after I'd dropped her off. This meeting could be to discuss her parading around the classroom dressed like some chick in a Whitesnake video.

"Mr. Dennison didn't give me any specifics. We'll see you this afternoon."

Three hours later, I was sitting in one of the hard wooden chairs lining the wall in the school office's reception area. I felt just like I did in ninth grade when I got caught stealing Sandy Moresso's bra out of her gym locker and hanging it from the basketball hoop during the boys' gym class. It served her right for having such enormous boobs when some of us barely—

A door opened, and Mr. Dennison, a tall, fortyish man with an extremely obvious dye job, walked briskly toward me. "Paige Atwell. Nice to see you."

"And you," I said, shaking the hand he proffered in greeting.

"Let's step into my office so we can talk in private."

Obediently, I limped along behind him, my heart thudding loudly. When I was seated in the cramped, airless office, facing Mr. Dennison across his large oak desk, I took a deep breath. "I think I know what this is about," I said.

"You do?"

"Yes, and I agree that it's a problem, but I'm at my wit's end. I've tried, on numerous occasions, to talk to Spencer about his language. I've told him that there are parts of the body that are private and also that the things that come out of those private parts are a natural part of the body's functioning, and they are not funny or shocking but also private and not to be discussed, especially at school. But it's like an obsession with him."

Mr. Dennison looked puzzled and mildly amused. "Actually, I called you in today to talk about Chloe."

"Oh."

"But we can talk about Spencer's issue, too, if you like."

"No thanks."

"Well, Ms. Blackmore and I are concerned about Chloe."

I was not about to jump in with my theories this time. "Yes?"

"We suspect she may have some problems with her vision."

"Her vision?" Was it wrong to be relieved?

"Yes. Ms. Blackmore has noticed her squinting at the chalk-board, and she had to move Chloe's desk closer to the front. I don't know if you've noticed any strange facial movements or expressions at home?"

Other than constant sneers of disdain . . . "Not really."

"We've noticed some in class, which are most likely caused by the tension of eyestrain. We recommend she see an optometrist for a vision test. She'll probably need some glasses."

"Certainly, I'll make her an appointment right away," I replied cheerfully. It wasn't like I was *happy* that Chloe needed glasses, but the problem was so wonderfully cut-and-dried. Daughter has bad vision: see optometrist, get glasses.

"This can be a tricky subject to broach with girls Chloe's age.

They're just becoming aware of their looks, of fashion . . . That's why I wanted to meet with you in person—to make sure you felt equipped to bring this up with Chloe on your own."

What a thoughtful man! I was lucky to have such a caring principal at my children's school. Not many men would be as sensitive to the issues facing young girls today. I smiled at him. Really, other than the blackish red hair dye, he was not a bad-looking guy. If he let his natural hair color return and bought a better suit, Mr. Dennison would be almost attractive. And his hands . . . they looked quite strong and masculine, despite his desk job. Maybe he did carpentry on the weekends? I had always had a thing for manly hands. By looking at a man's hands, it was almost like I could feel them—

"So . . . do you feel comfortable talking to Chloe?"

"I think so," I said, smiling at him. "I may need to call on you for backup, though, if things get difficult. Would that be okay?" My tone was sweet, almost cloying. What was I doing? Was I flirting? Oh God! Sure, I felt bored and lonely, but dye-job Dennison? Come on!

"Of course. I'm here if you need me."

"I feel so much better knowing that." Ewww! It was like I couldn't stop!

When I had collected my children, I drove home on autopilot, lost in my own disturbing thoughts. I was perplexed by my earlier behavior. Never before had I considered Mr. Dennison even remotely attractive. Besides the bad hair and clothes, he was also married, the father of four, and my children's grade school principal. And there I was, so syrupy sweet: *I might need to call on you for backup.* God! I was sick.

Surely, this must be the kind of attitude that prefaces an affair. The lonely housewife starts to see extramarital-relationship potential in everyone. I would have to stay in my house lest I start something up with the pimply faced checkout boy at Safeway or the hairy old Greek man who owned the gas station at the entrance to Aberdeen Mists. What if I had to go to the dentist? Dr. Gillespie actually was quite good-looking! I'd have to find a new, female dentist immediately.

I pulled into our driveway and parked the SUV, standing patiently on the pavement as my children scrambled to grab their backpacks, discarded coats, and other school paraphernalia. Our mailman, Leon, was across the road, finishing his rounds. I returned his friendly wave. Gee, I had never noticed how muscular Leon's calves were. All that walking must really— I stopped myself short. "Hurry up, kids," I barked. "I don't want to stand out here all day."

I would phone Paul. Hearing my husband's voice would have a calming effect on my horny, adulterous imagination. This time, I would insist that we resexualize our marriage. There would be no more pushing it aside for work obligations or dinner guests. I was careening, out of control, into dangerous territory. I was terrified that I would destroy my marriage, my family, out of sheer loneliness and desperation. Something had to be done to stop me. Just as I reached for the phone, it rang.

"Hello?"

Jane's voice on the other end of the line was shaky. "Paige. Thank God you're home."

"What's wrong?"

"It–it's Karen." Jane seemed to be crying.

Oh no. Doug must have found out about the affair and kicked Karen out. Oh shit! I hoped I hadn't given it away last night. "What's wrong? Is she okay?" My voice was thin with panic.

"Oh God, Paige, no, no she's not."

"What happened?"

"Oh God! Oh God! I can't believe I have to tell you this."

"What? What!"

"Karen's dead."

CHAPTER 8

Karen couldn't be dead, she just couldn't. She was too young, too pretty, too full of life . . . And she lived in Aberdeen Mists, for Christ's sake. People did not just up and die in Aberdeen Mists! But Jane assured me that it was the awful truth. She had firsthand knowledge. Apparently, Daniel had decided to come home from work early to give Jane a little "afternoon delight." As he drove past Karen and Doug's house, he noticed an ambulance and two police cars out front. When he arrived home, he notified Jane, who raced to the scene.

"When I got there, she was already gone," she said, in a voice nasal from crying.

"Gone?" I was having trouble comprehending. "Gone where? Gone how?"

"Dead, Paige," she snapped. "She was already dead. The coroner said it was a head injury, probably caused by a fall. And Doug . . . Oh God, poor Doug . . ." She began to cry again.

"Doug was there?"

"H–he found her . . . lying in the attached garage. He's absolutely devastated. He'd been in Chicago on business, but Karen called him and said she needed to talk to him when he got home. Something in her tone made him decide to catch an earlier flight. He walked in, and he couldn't find her. Then he went into the garage and . . . and there she was!" Jane's voice dissolved into sobs.

I should have been crying, too. Why wasn't I? I loved Karen, would miss her terribly, but I felt numb, shocked, incapable of emotion. My thoughts were racing madly. Doug had found her, just lying there, dead in the attached garage? How could that be? Had Karen been heading to her car when she suddenly toppled over and cracked her skull? While this scenario was plausible in my own chaotic garage, I knew that Doug kept theirs organized and pristine. It just didn't sound right. It was too weird, too bizarre . . . especially with what I knew about Karen's secret love affair. "I have to go," I said blandly.

"Are you okay?" Jane asked, composing herself. "You don't sound like you're okay."

"No, I'm not. But I . . . I just . . ."

"You're in shock, hon. Let me come over."

"I'm okay, Jane. I just need some time to come to terms with this."

"You shouldn't be alone right now."

"I–I'll call Paul."

"Are you sure? Because I don't mind coming over. I know Paul's very busy."

Yes, Paul was very busy, but these were extreme circumstances. Of course he'd be there for me, wouldn't he? After all these months of physical and emotional unavailability, if Paul didn't grant me this request, I'd . . . I'd . . . Well, I didn't know what I'd do. But it would be something radical, insane even—like running outside and licking Leon's muscular calves. "He'll come home," I said. "He has to."

When I hung up from Jane, I took the cordless phone to the formal living room and closed the French doors behind me. The children were preoccupied with a Jimmy Neutron cartoon, but I didn't want them to see me in this state. I still hadn't broken down emotionally, but I wasn't myself. Perched on the antique sofa, I stared at the curtained front window. If I were to walk over there and draw back the drapes, I'd be able to see Karen's house. Was Doug still there? Was someone with him? Or was he at the hospital? Or the (ugh) morgue? But I couldn't do it. My legs would not carry me to the window to look. It was too devastating, too unfathomable. I dialed Paul's office.

"Paul Atwell," he answered, tap, tap, tapping on his computer.

"You have to come home," I said, my voice devoid of emotion.

"Why? What's wrong?"

"Karen's dead."

"What the fuck? Oh my God! What happened? Are you okay? Jesus Christ!" Paul tended toward expletives when he was upset.

"I need you to come home and be with the kids. I-I can't . . ."

"Yeah, okay, honey. Look . . . hang in there for an hour. I'll wrap up a few loose ends and head home."

" 'Kay," I said weakly.

"I don't want you to be alone. Can one of the girls come over? Jane? Or Carly?"

Oh my God, Carly! Carly was all alone. Did she know? Had she seen the police cars and ambulances? She worked from home, so she probably had. They must have come while I was off flirting with my children's principal, or I would have been alerted to the commotion myself. Poor Carly—she could be cowering in a corner, weeping hysterically, at this very moment. She and Karen were so close. She had no one . . . "Come home as soon as you can," I said, and hung up.

I would go to Carly: I had to. She only lived two doors down, and Chloe was responsible enough to look after her brother for a few minutes, but I didn't feel comfortable leaving them alone. Karen could have been knocked on the head by some crazed psychopath who was still roaming the neighborhood. Deep down, I knew this was not the case, but better safe than sorry. I called Mrs. Williams, an elderly lady at the end of the block who sometimes babysat for us. Chloe would be pissed off, of course. She felt she didn't need a babysitter anymore . . . or a mother, for that matter. But I'd rather my daughter be pissed off than attacked by some head-bashing maniac.

When I explained the gravity of the situation to Mrs. Williams, she promised to rush right over. I grabbed my coat from the front closet and then went to the family room to address my children. "I've got to go over to Carly's for a little while," I said, zipping up my jacket.

Jimmy Neutron held their attention. Eventually, Chloe murmured an acknowledgment.

"Mrs. Williams is going to stay with you."

Chloe's head snapped in my direction. "What! Why?"

"I've asked her to come over for a little while. End of discussion."

"That's so, like, totally stupid!" My daughter continued. "You can't leave me in charge for, like, ten minutes? You're only going to be fifty feet away!"

"Fifty *yards* away."

"Whatever. I can't believe this. Why do you always do this?"

"Because . . ." I felt a stirring of the emotions I'd been suppressing. ". . . Because I love you two . . . so much." Chloe gaped at me like I'd just told her I was actually a lesbian. Fortunately, the doorbell rang, signaling Mrs. Williams's arrival and my, somewhat relieved, departure.

Moments later, I was on Carly's doorstep. Even as I lifted the heavy brass knocker, I had no idea what I was going to say to her, but she had to be told. And if she already knew, she had to be comforted. When there was no response after several seconds, I tried again . . . and then again. Maybe she was downtown at a meeting? Or sharing a free Diet Coke with the vending-machine guy? I knocked one last time, and was just turning to go, when the door opened.

"Oh, hi, Paige," Carly said brightly. Obviously, she didn't know. She was wearing baggy navy blue sweatpants and a large white T-shirt that said "Molson Canadian Rocks." Around her neck were slung the headphones of the Discman she clutched in her hand. "Sorry, I didn't hear you. I was downstairs in my office, and I had my music on."

"Can I come in for a minute?"

"Sure." She stepped back to usher me inside. "Come on in." In Carly's three-bedroom abode, it would have been easy to forget that a male of the species existed. Her walls were faux-finished in shades of peach and cream, a border of stenciled miniature roses running around the periphery. Her couches were off-white leather, accented with peach and mauve throw pillows. I perched awkwardly on one, taking in the plethora of vanilla-scented candles in hand-painted ceramic holders on the coffee table before me.

"Can I get you anything?" Carly asked. "Cup of tea? Glass of wine? Diet Coke?"

"No . . . no thanks. Umm . . . why don't you sit down?"

"Okay." She plopped down beside me.

"I have to tell you something . . . something terrible."

"What?"

"Uh . . . It's . . . it's . . . Karen . . ."

"Karen? What is it?"

I reached out and took both her hands in mine. "I don't know how to say this, Carly . . . I just . . . I'm just going to come right out and say it. Karen . . . Karen has . . . passed on."

"What! Oh my God!" She pulled her hands from mine and covered the lower part of her face.

"I know, hon. It's just so . . . terrible, so . . . tragic."

"But she can't be dead. I just saw her this morning. What-what happened?"

I heaved a heavy sigh. "I don't know much, but it sounds like she fell and hit her head in the attached garage."

"Oh God," Carly said quietly, her soft voice muffled further by her fingers over her mouth. "Oh God. Oh God. Oh God."

"I know. I know. I know."

There was a long and mildly uncomfortable silence. I knew I wasn't doing a very good job of comforting Carly, but it wasn't like I'd had days to come to terms with the tragedy. In fact, I was in desperate need of some comforting myself. If Paul didn't get home soon, Karen wouldn't be the only one with a head injury. Still, I felt I should be hugging my friend or at least holding her hand. But

Carly stayed as she was, hands on her cheeks Macaulay Culkin–style, knees drawn up to her chest. Awkwardly, I patted her shin a couple of times. Finally, I cleared my throat and spoke. "Why don't you come to our house? It's not a good idea to be alone right now." Carly didn't respond. I wasn't even sure she'd heard me. "Carly, . . . come on. Let's go to my place."

She looked at me then, her hands finally slipping from their resting place on her cheeks. "Uh . . . no . . . No thanks, Paige. I'd rather be alone."

"Come on. We'll call Jane and Trudy. I think we should all be together at a time like this."

"No." Her voice was firm, resolute. She stood up, obviously my cue to leave. "I'll call you tomorrow."

And then I was alone in the cool evening air. I began to walk home but paused on the sidewalk in front of my neighbor's home. It had gotten dark, and I turned to stare at the warm lamplight illuminating Carly's sheer, frilly curtains. She was in shock, just like I had been—still was. I hoped I'd made the right decision, leaving her home alone to grieve. I didn't have a lot of mourning experience, thankfully. Aside from my grandparents and several hamsters, my life had been largely untouched by death. On TV, grief was best dealt with in large, sobbing groups. But maybe that was just in Mafia movies. This was Denver. This was Aberdeen Mists. This was real.

When I entered the warmth of my own home, Mrs. Williams was busy in the kitchen making tomato soup and grilled-cheese sandwiches for the children.

"Thanks so much, Mavis," I said, padding quietly into the kitchen in my stocking feet.

"Can I fix you something, dear?" She turned to face me. "You've suffered a terrible shock, and this must be so hard for you. I know you two girls were such good friends." As my chin began to quiver, Mrs. Williams put down the flipper and pulled me into her rose-scented bosom. And that did it. That gesture of sympathy released all the sorrow I'd been repressing. I felt a deep, painful sob shudder in my chest. I didn't want the kids to see me fall apart—at least, not until I'd had a chance to explain what had happened.

"Would you mind staying a little longer?" I asked, in a voice hoarse with emotion. "Just until Paul gets home?"

"Of course, dear. I'll stay as long as you need me."

And with that, I escaped to the quiet and seclusion of my bedroom, where I cried for all I was worth.

CHAPTER 9

Somehow, I managed to sleep that night. When Paul got home, he brought me a glass of brandy and some painkillers left over from when he'd had his root canal. That may have helped a little. "Take these," he'd said, handing me two small white tablets. "You need to rest. This has been such a huge shock to your system. You've just lost one of your best friends." This set me off weeping hysterically again, but I managed to choke down the pills and most of the brandy. While I knew mixing alcohol and narcotics was not normally a good idea, this was not a normal time. And I needed to numb myself, to turn off the pain, at least for a little while.

When I awoke, I enjoyed a brief moment of innocent contentment before the horrible reality of the situation descended upon me like a lead blanket. Paul had taken the kids to school and had offered to stay home if I needed him. I'd sent him off to work, confident that a little time alone would help me come to terms with Karen's death. But this morning, I suddenly felt so isolated, even uneasy in my empty house. Rolling over, I grabbed the phone off the side table and called Jane.

"How are you?" she asked, sounding much stronger than she had the previous night.

"I don't know. I'm as good as can be expected, I guess."

"Me, too. I'm devastated, of course, but I'm holding it together. Not like poor Trudy."

"Trudy?" I hadn't called Trudy yet, mostly because I wasn't worried about her. I just assumed that Trudy would be a pillar of strength, busily making casseroles for Doug and sweets for the eventual funeral.

"Trudy's fallen apart! She can't even get out of bed. Carly's gone to look after her. She even had to take Emily and Cameron to school. Ken's not back from his business trip until the weekend."

"Thank God for Carly," I said. "Did you talk to her?"

"She called early this morning."

"How's she holding up? When I left her last night, she was still reeling."

"She seems to have pulled herself together. And you know Carly . . . She's always there for everyone else. She's looking after Trudy and already baking muffins to take over to Doug."

"Good . . . that's good."

"I told her I'd stay with the kids this afternoon if she needs a break."

"Or they could come here to play with Chloe and Spencer." I was sure I could put up with the odious little creatures for one afternoon.

"I'll let her know."

"So . . . is it appropriate to go see Doug now?" I asked. "I've got some . . . banana bread that I wanted to take over."

"I think so. It will probably make him feel better to know that he has our support. Becca's whipping up some pecan bars right now. Daniel and I are going to take them over this afternoon and give him our condolences."

Of course, I had no banana bread. I didn't even have any bananas, but I had to see Doug. Maybe then, Karen's tragic death would feel real to me. Plus, I had to see for myself how Doug was handling the situation. I couldn't help but think that there was something fishy about Karen's sudden demise. No one else seemed to have a problem with the "fell-over-and-conked-head-in-garage" scenario, but then, no one else knew what I did.

I quickly showered, dressed, and headed downstairs. In the kitchen, I rummaged through the cupboards in search of a condolence offering for Doug. I really wasn't up for baking, not to mention the fact that I was short on a number of ingredients. At first, my search seemed futile: juice boxes, Fruit Roll-Ups, Goldfish crackers, cans of tomato soup . . . None of these seemed a particularly appropriate gift for a grieving widower. That's when I spotted the blue box at the back of the cupboard—individually wrapped Rice Krispies squares. Yes! Could there be any greater comfort food than the Rice Krispies square? And they were also low in fat and cholesterol. I'm sure Becca's pecan bars couldn't make that claim. Hurriedly, I retrieved the box and began ripping open the foil packets. When I had opened fourteen pouches, I placed the squares on a plate, squishing them with the palm of my hand for authenticity. I had just begun to cover the adequately misshapen squares with plastic wrap when I was interrupted by the phone.

"How are you doing, babe?" It was Paul.

"I'm okay—sad, but okay. How were the kids this morning?"

"They were good. I explained to them what happened, and that Mommy needs some time alone."

"What did you say about Karen?"

"I told them the truth. Karen had a very bad accident. She fell and hit her head, and now she's gone to heaven."

God, if only that was the truth. I don't mean the heaven part. Not being a religious person, I didn't believe in the traditional angels-and-pearly-gates kind of heaven. And even if it did exist, I wasn't sure they'd be letting the likes of Karen in; I've heard they frown on adultery there. But I wished her death were simply, as Paul said, a very bad accident. Deep in my gut, I knew it couldn't be that easy.

Paul continued, "So, do you have any plans today? Are you and the girls getting together?"

"Actually, I'm going to see Doug. I made him some Rice Krispies squares."

"Oh. Do you think he's ready to have visitors?"

"Well, I think it's important that he knows we're here for him. Jane agrees."

There was a brief pause before my husband spoke again. "You're right. He needs to know he's got friends who care about him. Give me forty-five minutes and I'll come with you."

"Uh . . . no, that's okay," I stammered. I didn't want Paul to accompany me. There were questions I had to ask Doug, questions that would undoubtedly sound strange to Paul. I didn't need him there to censor me. "You're busy, and you can see Doug later. We don't want to overwhelm him."

"I want to come, Paige. I want to be there for you." Oh sure, pick *now* to become caring and supportive. "Besides, Karen and Doug were just over at our house a few days ago. Christ. I still can't believe it."

"Okay, fine," I acquiesced. "But hurry up. If you're not here in forty-five, I'm going by myself."

Unfortunately, Paul arrived home thirty-eight minutes later. "There's no traffic at this time of day," he said, sounding very pleased with himself.

"Great," I mumbled, smoothing the plastic wrap around my "baking." "Let's go."

Paul held my arm supportively as we walked down the street toward Karen and Doug's house. Well, I guess it was just Doug's house now, but that was going to take some getting used to. I clutched the off-white ceramic plate with both hands, my fingers beginning to ache with the tension. My heart was beating loudly, and my throat was uncomfortably dry. I felt nervous and panicky. Was I really ready to face Doug? What if I somehow sensed that he'd had something to do with Karen's fall? What then? Did I call the police? Tell Paul? Would Paul be angry that I hadn't disclosed the information about Karen's affair sooner? God, I wished I had. But I couldn't bring it up now. It would be tasteless to slander the dead. And if it did turn out to be nothing more than a bizarre attached garage accident, I didn't want to sully Karen's good name.

"Here we are," Paul said, clearing his throat nervously as we stood on Doug's front steps.

"Yep," I agreed. "Here we are."

"Well . . . ring the bell."

"You ring it. I've got my hands full with these delicious Rice Krispies treats."

". . . Okay." Reaching forward, he pressed the mother-of-pearl button, then quickly stepped back to stand slightly behind me, the coward. We could hear the chimes sounding within the house. Moments later, the door swung open.

"Oh . . . Hi, Carly."

"Hi, Paige . . . Paul . . ." She kissed my cheek and then my husband's. "I just got here."

"I thought you were with Trudy?"

"She's asleep," Carly said, her voice hushed, as if Trudy were snoozing right behind her on the floor of the grand entryway. "She took a little something to calm her nerves. I'll go back when the kids get off school. I just realized that Doug was all alone. His sister is flying in from Vancouver on Friday."

"How's he doing?"

"Well . . . he seems to be holding up. I'm sure he'd love to see you. Come in." Carly ushered us into Karen's home. We stood awkwardly in the foyer, both of us unsure whether we should enter farther. "Take your coats off," Carly instructed. "I'll go tell Doug you're here."

"Hold these for a sec." I passed Paul the plate of squares and slipped out of my heavy fall coat, hanging it on the stainless steel coat tree. Karen's denim jacket hung on one of the pegs. I felt an involuntary shudder run through me.

Paul said, "I'll leave my coat on. I don't think we should stay too long."

Doug rounded the corner. He looked pale, drawn, every inch

the distraught husband. When he looked at me, his eyes welled with tears. "Paige . . ." His voice was hoarse. "Thank you for coming." I moved toward him and enveloped him in the tight embrace of mutual sorrow. As we held each other, I could feel his body shaking with sobs. Tears streamed down my cheeks, wetting the sides of my hair and Doug's collar. "I loved her so much," Doug whispered.

"Me, too," I replied. At that moment, I felt sure Doug's grief was real. He had lost the woman he loved, and he was devastated. There was no way he could have had anything to do with Karen's death. But when he pulled away from me, I couldn't help but notice that the tears that had pooled in his eyes had dissipated, and his cheeks were dry.

Doug turned to Paul then. "Thanks for coming."

"I'm so sorry for your loss," Paul said awkwardly. "Umm . . . Paige made you these Rice Krispies squares." He thrust the plate toward Doug.

"Let me take those to the kitchen," Carly intervened.

Paul continued in a strained voice. "We just wanted you to know that we're here for you. If you need anything, anything at all . . ."

"That's right," I squeezed Doug's forearm. "Anything . . . anytime . . . we're here for you."

"Would anyone like coffee? Tea?" Carly offered.

"Oh no," Paul said quickly. "We won't stay. We just wanted Doug to know that—"

"Actually, I'd love a cup of coffee," I interrupted. "If you've got some made?"

"I'll put a pot on. It's no trouble."

"You don't need to make coffee just for us," Paul protested. "Really, we should be going."

"We've got time for a quick cup," I said, slipping my shoes off. I turned to Doug. "You don't mind if we stay for a few minutes, do you?" I realized I was being pushy, but I wasn't about to leave without gaining some information.

"Oh . . . of course not."

"See?" I said to my husband, who was staring at me with angry eyes. "Doug doesn't mind. Why don't you give Carly a hand in the kitchen?" Then, linking my arm with Doug's, we moved farther into the house.

Doug and Karen's home was incredible . . . Really, it was almost what you'd call opulent. It had a floor plan similar to most of the new homes in Aberdeen Mists, but the difference was in the details. They had spared no expense: the floors were the highest-quality walnut, the millwork was detailed and exquisite, and the fixtures were stylish brushed nickel. As we passed the kitchen, I took in the glistening granite countertops and rich slate flooring. At the far end, was the door that led to the attached garage. In a flash, I saw an image of Karen, lying alone in her immaculate carport, the life slipping out of her. I shook my head to dislodge the disturbing picture. At the same time, I released Doug's arm.

I followed him into their formal living room . . . Actually, it may have been their casual family room. Both rooms were impeccably decorated with lavish furnishings, expensive art, and tasteful knick-knacks. Having no kids, it was easy for Karen to keep her home pristine. If she'd had the baby they had longed for, it would have been a different story. At least one of their living rooms would have been slated for demolition—spit-up on the couches, mountains of Cheerios crushed under the cushions, crackers ground into the carpet . . . This thought brought a lump of emotion to my throat: my friend would never have the frustrating, yet somehow fulfilling, experience of scrubbing her baby's vomit off her sofa. But I forced myself to focus on the task at hand. I had to get some details from Doug, and I had to get them before Paul and Carly joined us with the coffee.

"So . . . ," I said, sitting next to him on the plush divan. "Your sister is coming to stay with you?" I had to start with a *little* small talk.

"In a few days. She has to find someone to take care of her kids."

"It's nice that you have family to be with you during this difficult time."

"Yeah . . ." He looked and sounded exhausted, but still I pressed on.

"Umm . . . Jane mentioned that you had talked to Karen before . . ."—I trailed off, unsure of how to phrase it gently—". . . her accident."

"She called me in Chicago."

"What did she say?"

"That she wanted to talk to me about something when I got home."

"Did she say what it was? Do you have any idea?"

"Not really." He sighed heavily. "She just sounded a little down . . . a little blue. I thought it would be nice to surprise her by coming home early. But when I got home—" A painful sob broke free even as Doug tried to stifle it with his fist to his lips.

I leaned toward him and patted his knee sympathetically. "When you got home, what? What did you see?"

"Just . . . Karen . . . lying there."

"And she'd hit her head, is that right?" He nodded. "Was there anything on the floor?" I did not mean blood but quickly realized that's how it must have sounded. "Like, had anything spilled—oil, maybe? Could she have slipped?"

"I-I don't remember. I didn't notice."

"Could she have had a preexisting condition—something that could have caused her to black out and hit her head? Something you didn't know about?"

"Here's the coffee!" Carly entered the room, obviously making a conscious effort to sound upbeat. Paul trailed behind her holding a plate of delicious-looking apple muffins and my slightly squashed store-bought Rice Krispies squares. Idle chitchat ensued as we busied ourselves fixing our beverages and loading snacks onto side plates, but soon, the banter had been exhausted and we lapsed into an awkward silence.

"So . . . ," Paul finally said, "if you need any help around the house . . . you know, any yard work or anything . . ."

"Thanks," Doug murmured, staring into his coffee cup.

"And don't you worry about meals," Carly added. "I'll make sure you've got plenty of food in the freezer to get you through." Doug gave her an exhausted smile of gratitude.

I opened my mouth, intending to offer to clean his oven or scrub his toilets or make some other well-meaning gesture, but what came out was something quite different. "So . . . what did the police say about Karen's fall?" Paul's head snapped up, and he gaped at me like I'd just offered Doug a condolence blow job. Carly shoved a muffin in her mouth and busied herself tidying the coffee tray. "I mean . . . the police were here, right?"

"They were here," Doug replied. "They said Karen's injuries were consistent with a fall."

"But they'll do an autopsy?"

"Yes."

"And if it turns up anything suspicious, they'll do a full investigation?"

"I guess so. I-I don't know."

Carly spoke. "I'm sure they won't find anything strange, Doug. Soon, you'll be able to find closure and start the healing process."

"That's right," my husband agreed. "It was just a terrible accident."

"Yeah, but isn't it kind of weird to just, y'know, fall over—"

Paul cut me off. "We've got to be going," he said, shooting me a look. "Thanks for the coffee Carly. Doug, really, anything you need, anything at all . . ." And with that, he bustled me to the grand entryway.

Out in the brisk fall afternoon, we walked side by side in silence until we were an adequate distance from Doug's house. "What the hell was that?" Paul grumbled, not turning his head to look at me.

"What?" I kept my eyes forward as well. This way, none of the neighbors would suspect us of fighting—a useful and quickly learned trick when living in a small suburban community.

"All that stuff about the police and an autopsy! How could you be so insensitive?"

"Come on, Paul. Don't you think it's a little strange that Karen just fell over, hit her head, and died?"

"It was a freak accident. They happen all the time."

"Well . . . Did you notice how Doug seemed so upset, but he wasn't actually crying?"

"Christ, Paige! Some people just aren't criers. What is going on with you?"

"Nothing," I snapped. "It just . . ."

"It just what?"

"It just seems a little mysterious to me, that's all."

"Yeah, well, before you start playing detective, you might want to consider other people's feelings."

I started to respond but stopped myself short. He had a point.

CHAPTER 10

Paul was right: I'd been horribly insensitive. God, Doug probably hated me now. Every time he saw me, I was either drunk and obnoxious or rude and tactless. I vowed to handle the situation much more delicately from now on. Yes, I still had my suspicions about the nature of Karen's death, but I would keep them carefully hidden going forward. And if the police found nothing amiss after her autopsy, I'd let the whole thing go altogether. Although the police had been known to be wrong before . . .

My first sensitive and caring gesture was to spend some time with Trudy. Armed with a box of Safeway doughnuts, I rang her front bell. There was no answer. I rang it again. Surely she wasn't so incapacitated by grief that she couldn't shuffle over to the door? She had now had four days to deal with the shock. I bent over and yelled through the mail slot. "Trudy! It's Paige! Let me in!" I heard a faint rumbling of movement inside, and finally, the door swung open.

"Hi!" I said brightly, trying not to flinch at Trudy's appearance. She didn't look *that* bad, but she didn't look that good, either. Her face was drawn and tired, her eyes red and puffy. It was obvious that her hair hadn't been washed since she'd heard the news, and judging by the pizza, spaghetti, or some other tomato-based stain on her track pants, neither had her clothes. "I brought you some doughnuts."

"Come in," she said, ignoring my tasty offering and shambling back into the house. I trailed behind her until we reached the family room, where Trudy deposited herself prostrate on the couch and pulled a yellow floral comforter up to her neck. The piles of used tissues, dirty teacups, and empty cracker boxes made it evident that this was where Trudy had been spending the majority of her time. "So . . ." I took a seat in an overstuffed chair across from her. "How are you doing?"

"I can't . . . I can't cope with this," she said, tears instantly beginning to seep from her eyes. "It's too much."

"I know it's a terrible tragedy," I said gently, "but we have to go on. Karen would have wanted us to go on."

"Oh God," Trudy wailed. "Karen can't be gone. She c-can't be!"

"But she is . . . , and we have to deal with it."

"No!" she cried, reaching for a Kleenex. "This doesn't happen to people like Karen—so young, so sweet, so innocent . . . She was such a special person."

Trudy was talking about her like she was some sort of martyr. Maybe if I told her about the hot sex Karen had been having with a certain Spanish barista, it would help her deal with the situation. But I had already decided not to besmirch my friend's memory. "She was very, very special," I said. "But sometimes these awful accidents happen."

For some reason, this set Trudy off. She laid her head down and wept like—well, like one of her best friends had just been found dead in her attached garage. I moved over to her and stroked her hair as she cried. "Let it out," I murmured. "It's okay." Eventually, she managed to compose herself and reached around me for another tissue. "Listen," I said, "what time do your kids finish school?"

"Two thirty." Emily and Cameron went to a private school approximately twenty minutes' drive from Aberdeen Mists. Trudy didn't feel that the public system could adequately foster her children's innate creativity and cater to their unique learning styles. Theirs was an alternative school where they didn't get graded and they made their own notebooks out of bark.

"Chloe and Spencer aren't finished until 3:10. I can go pick up your kids and then bring them back to our place for pizza."

"Okay." She sniveled.

"That will give you some time to . . . you know, take a shower, put on some fresh clothes . . . try to get yourself together a bit."

"Mmm hmm," she mumbled noncommittally.

At 2:32, I pulled up across the street from the nondescript brick building that was home to the Foundation of Success, or "FOS," as it was commonly known. I instantly spotted Emily standing just outside the main entrance and, a few yards away, her little brother. "Yoo-hoo! Emily! Cameron! Hello!" I called, while scurrying across the road to meet them. As unlikable as I found Trudy's children, it was imperative that I remember that they were going through a difficult time. They had undoubtedly never seen their mother in such a state before, and it would obviously be traumatic. I would have to handle them with kid gloves. "Hi, guys," I panted, jogging up to them.

"What are you doing here?" Emily asked coldly.

"Where's my mom?" Cameron echoed.

"She's still not feeling very well, so I'm picking you up and bringing you back to our house to play with Chloe and Spencer. You can stay for dinner, too. We can order pizza. You like pizza, don't you?"

"Only plain cheese," Emily remarked, but they followed me to the car.

The drive to Rosedale was awkward. The kids sat sullenly in the backseat while I asked them a stream of inane questions about school, their favorite subjects, movies, singers, and ice cream flavors. Finally, I had collected my own offspring and made it home. As soon as I opened the front door, the children raced up the stairs and dispersed to their respective rooms. Instantly, I heard the sound of a bin of LEGOs being tipped onto the floor in Spencer's and the strains of a rather raunchy-sounding pop song behind Chloe's closed door. The girls were probably pretending to mud wrestle each other while wearing assless chaps, but at least it afforded me a little peace.

I went to the kitchen and began to putter—wiping invisible spills, organizing the salt and pepper shakers, and sorting through various school notices left on the countertops. It was imperative that I keep busy, no matter how mundane the task. I could not allow myself to slip back into grieving mode; it wasn't fair to the children. Nor could I let myself ponder the details of Karen's death. My misguided curiosity had caused enough problems. Maybe Paul was right. Freak accidents happened all the time. And some people just weren't criers; it didn't mean they were wife killers. No, I would bury these suspicious and doubtful feelings. Instead, I would be caring and sensitive . . . and also very busy and productive.

Digging in the junk drawer, I found my address book. There, nestled between the two pages allotted for "W" was my carefully folded Life Makeover list. This was the perfect time to focus on my self-improvement. It would distract me from my musings on Karen's demise and perk up my general outlook on life. I unfolded the piece of paper and laid it flat on the counter before me. But what I read seemed so incredibly . . . shallow. Was I really such a vapid creature that I thought pectoral exercises would improve my life? Or a stimulating hobby? And did I actually think giving my husband two blow jobs a month would improve our marriage? Well . . . it probably would, but that was the last thing on my mind at the moment. Karen was dead, for God's sake!

Of course, there were the kids . . . But in all honesty, Spencer's potty mouth had been much improved of late, and even Chloe seemed a little less disdainful toward me. Since Karen's murder, my daughter had actually been really sweet. She even poured her brother's cereal this morning and . . . My thought process trailed off. Did I just say Karen's *murder*? Oh God. I couldn't fight what my every instinct was telling me. Karen did not just fall over and whack her head. It was too bizarre . . . implausible. There had to be someone else involved.

At that moment, the front doorbell rang, sending a little chill up my spine. The timing was slightly unnerving. I'd just allowed my-self to acknowledge that Karen was actually murdered in her own home, and now an unidentified person was trying to gain access to mine. Bravely, I walked to the front door and stared through the peephole. On my front porch stood Janet Lawson, one of the neigh-borhood moms, holding a heavily Saran-wrapped package.

"Hi, Janet," I said, opening the door.

"Hi . . . I just heard about Karen Sutherland. I'm so sorry." We hugged briefly. "I made this orange poppy seed loaf for Doug." She thrust it toward me. "I don't know him very well, and I don't really feel comfortable . . . You know how it is. Would you mind?"

"Of course not." It was a sweet and thoughtful gesture, espe-cially since Janet and Karen would only have been passing acquain-tances. I knew Janet a little better since her son was in Chloe's grade at Rosedale. But she worked full-time as a receptionist for a gyne-colo-gist downtown, so we'd never spent a lot of time together.

"I realize I didn't know Karen well . . ." She seemed to pick up my train of thought. "But I was just so devastated when I heard. Es-pecially given her recent . . . *success.*"

"Yeah . . ." I nodded, only half following her conversation. "We've all been really rocked by this."

"Oh, I know you were so close to her. I can only imagine how you feel. It's just so sad . . ." Her eyes began to mist up. "She was in just over a week ago, and she was so happy, so full of joy . . . I mean, it was finally happening for her, after all this time."

". . . Right."

"In a way," Janet sniffed, "it's like two lives were lost."

Oh my God! Oh my God! I suddenly understood what the heck she was talking about! "Thanks for the loaf," I said hastily. "I'll make sure Doug gets it. I'd better get back to the kids."

"Right. Okay. I'm sorry. Please give him our condolences. And our loaf."

"Will do." I shut the door before she'd even had a chance to turn around.

Jesus Christ! Holy shit! Oh my fucking fuck! I paced the hall-way, the loaf squashed in my right hand. This changed everything—

made it more complex, more suspicious, more sinister! It had taken me a moment to catch on, but now it was crystal clear. Karen had been in to see Janet's gynecologist boss. She had been happy and full of joy! It was all finally happening for her! Karen was pregnant, and Janet obviously thought I knew!

I took a deep breath, intent on calming myself. I had to process this new information. I mustn't let it send me off the deep end. Okay . . . stay cool. *The number one cause of death in pregnant women is homicide by the father of the child.* I had heard that line on *CSI: Miami* only a few nights earlier. Oh God, oh God. What did this mean?

I knew Doug was desperate for a baby, so I felt pretty sure he couldn't have done it. Unless . . . the baby was actually Javier's! Doug did have that low-mobility sperm, after all. Perhaps, when Karen told Doug she was leaving him to live with Javier and raise their love child on canned ravioli and Ichiban, he freaked out and conked her on the head! Or . . . Karen invited Javier over to tell him the good news about their baby, but when he heard, he panicked at the thought of making such a huge commitment and bashed her one! Or maybe, somehow, one of Doug's sparse sperm had made it to the egg and it was his baby! Karen and Doug were finally going to have the child they'd always wanted. She broke it off with Javier, who, in a fit of jealousy, came to her house and shoved her. She hit her head on the concrete floor and—

"I want to go home now," Cameron said. I jumped a little at his sudden and silent appearance.

"Oh . . . hi, sweetie. It's not time to go yet. I'm going to order us some pizza."

"I want to go home. It's boring here."

Oh Christ. I didn't need this right now. "Why don't you go play with Spencer for a little while? The pizza will be here soon."

"Spencer's toys are boring. I want to go home. I want to see my mom."

"Listen . . ." I leaned down so we were at eye level. "Would you like to play a game with me? We've got Snakes and Ladders."

"No."

"We could do a puzzle?"

"I want to go." Cameron turned and started heading toward the front door.

"Spencer!" I shrieked, in need of reinforcements. "Get down here!" I trotted behind Cameron. "We could do some coloring?"

"No." He began to put his shoes on.

"Painting?"

Spencer appeared behind me. "What?"

"What could we do with Cameron that would be fun?" I asked, in a voice tinged with desperation. "Just for a little while . . . until the pizza comes."

"Umm . . . Play-Doh?"

"How about Play-Doh, Cameron? Do you like Play-Doh?"

"Yeah . . . ," he said hesitantly, dropping his shoe to the floor. "I guess."

"Great!" I said enthusiastically. "Let's go play with some Play-Doh!"

I set the boys up at the kitchen table with a large bucket of Play-Doh and various kitchen tools. Thankfully, they were giggling contentedly when I took the phone into the hall and dialed Domino's. When I returned, I sat down between the two youngsters. This couldn't be an easy time for either of them. They were too young to really understand what was going on with the whole Karen situation, but they must sense it. And in a way, the tragedy across the street was having an enormous impact on them. It was affecting the most important people in their universe: their mothers. I took a deep breath and vowed to be patient and kind. "Nice work, Cameron," I said encouragingly. "And yours is really cool, too, Spencer."

"What do you think this is?" my son asked, holding up his creation.

"Umm . . ." I took in the small creature with two legs, two tiny arms, and a long blue tail. "A kangaroo?"

"Nope. Guess again."

"A crocodile standing up?"

"Nope. Guess again."

"I give up."

"It's Dad."

"Ohhhh . . . ," I said, as if suddenly seeing the similarities. "Does Dad have a tail?"

"That's poo hanging out of his butt."

I was on the verge of a reprimand when Cameron burst out laughing. Well, at least Spencer was entertaining that sullen little monster. I decided to let it slide. "Right," I said. "Poo . . . yeah, of course."

"Guess what this is?" Cameron asked, with a gleeful grin.

"Uh . . . a boy sitting on a giant toadstool?"

"No!" He was practically breathless with excitement.

"Tell me."

"It's my dad, with a giant fart cloud coming out of his butt!"

Spencer squealed, and soon the two of them were clutching their sides and rolling on the floor with laughter. I would have to chastise them. Trudy took a hard line on inappropriate language, and I knew firsthand that she had an issue with the word *fart*. When their laughing seizure had subsided, I spoke sternly. "Okay . . . that's enough of that kind of language."

"Fart is not a swear," Cameron retorted.

"Well, it's still not a very nice or polite word."

"But *fart* is just a plain old word. What's so bad about saying *fart*?"

"You know your mom doesn't like you using that word, Cameron."

"So . . . that's just dumb. . . . Fart."

"Cameron . . . ," I began.

"Fart!" he screamed, much to Spencer's delight. "Fart! Fart! Fart!"

"Pass wind," I said helplessly. "Pass wind." The doorbell rang, and I scurried to meet the pizza deliveryman. If he was bothered by the chorus of *poo, fart,* and accompanying sound effects emanating from the kitchen, he didn't comment. Laden with two steaming pizza boxes, I made my way back to the kitchen, pausing at the bottom of the stairs to call up to Chloe's room. "Girls! Pizza's here!"

"Uh . . . uh . . . wanna make you sweat . . ."

"Chloe! Emily!"

"Uh . . . uh . . . wanna make you scream . . ."

"Girls! Pleeeeeeeeeeeeeeze!" I hollered, suddenly overwhelmed by the barrage of sexual innuendo coming from my daughter's CD player. Thankfully, it stopped. Now, if I could only turn off the sound of the boys discussing their fathers' toilet activities.

I was in a fog during dinner, nibbling on a piece of Hawaiian, consumed by my own thoughts. The children talked incessantly, and no doubt rudely, but I managed to tune them out. I couldn't get Janet's revelation about Karen's condition out of my head. It made her untimely death sadder still, and I fought to control my emotions in front of the kids. But it had also increased my conviction that there was something fishy about the way she died. I had to tell someone about her affair with Javier—it was the right thing to do. I could call the police, but did I really want to blow Karen's secret life wide open like that? I wasn't sure. When Paul got home, I would confess all to him. He was practical and level-headed. He'd know what to do.

Something brought my attention back to the table. It was the girls singing.

"Grinding . . . and moaning . . ."

"Okay," I said, standing abruptly. I'd had enough. "Time to go, kids."

"Already?" Cameron whined. "I don't want to go yet." He'd obviously had a change of heart since I'd let him say *fart* 240 times in the last hour.

"Yep. Get your coats on. Go! Go!"

Normally, we would have walked, but I was desperate to get rid of my extra charges. And at this point, I wasn't sure my legs would carry me a block and a half. Within two minutes, we had rounded the corner and pulled up in front of Trudy's house. It was dark, save for a faint light glowing from the family room. Trudy was probably still lying on the couch watching TV. "Emily and Cameron, out. Chloe and Spencer, stay here. I'll be right back."

At the front door, I rang the bell continuously. If I had to, I would annoy Trudy off the sofa. It worked. She opened the door within a matter of seconds. It was obvious she'd ignored my suggestions to shower and get herself together. "Hi, kids," she said weakly, kissing the tops of their heads as they filed past her. "Thanks, Paige."

"You're welcome."

"Listen, if it's not too much trouble, maybe you could have the kids over tomorrow, too? It's just hard for them to be here with me. I'm still so weak."

"Sorry, but no."

"Pardon me?" Trudy was surprised by my abruptness.

"I said no. You have to snap out of it, Trudy. We all miss Karen. We're all devastated by what happened. I am barely holding it together myself, but I am, somehow, holding it together. We have kids. We don't have the option of falling apart."

"W-well . . . ," she stammered. "You don't understand how hard this is for me. Karen was—"

"I do understand," I barged in. "I understand exactly how hard it is for you. And I'd like nothing better than to lie on my couch crying for the next six months, but I can't. And neither can you. You have a family to look after." And with that, I turned on my heel and marched back to my SUV.

In the darkness of the vehicle, the tears poured silently down my cheeks. This was just great. I'd already lost one friend to a horrible tragedy, and now I might have lost another. Maybe Paul was right. Maybe I wasn't being sensitive to other people's feelings, but I was having enough trouble coping with my own. I had never felt so alone, so completely isolated in my grief. The secret Karen had entrusted me with was overwhelming me. I felt confused, guilty, deceitful . . . And now, I knew about not only her secret romance but her secret pregnancy as well! I could no longer shoulder this burden alone; I just couldn't take the pressure. When Paul got home, I would spill the beans. He'd be annoyed that I had been duplicitous for so long, but he'd soon get over it. And he'd be able to provide the support system that I so badly needed.

But my husband got home late that night. By the time I had cleaned up the kitchen, helped Chloe with her homework, and read a bedtime story to Spencer, I was exhausted. I filled the bath with warm, lavender-scented water and submerged myself. When Paul finally popped his head in to say hello, I was nearly comatose. I barely had the energy to say a quick "How was your day?" let alone a quick "Sorry I didn't mention it before, but Karen was having a passionate love affair and was also secretly pregnant." My confession would have to wait. Soon, the perfect time would come, an evening when my mood was courageous and my husband's receptive. But the longer I put it off, the harder it became to reveal the truth.

CHAPTER 11

The funeral was on Friday afternoon. I took great pains with my appearance—I still don't know why. It was inevitable that I would become a sniveling, red-nosed basket case within moments of my arrival. Still, I blow-dried my hair, applied my makeup, and dressed in a black skirt, black panty hose, and a bright pink cowl-neck sweater. Perhaps not appropriate funeral attire, but it had been Karen's favorite.

Paul had taken the afternoon off and would soon be home to escort me to the service. I was grateful for his support. This day was not going to be easy for me, for a number of reasons:

1. One of my best friends was about to be cremated.
2. Her widowed husband thought I was insensitive, annoying, and an obnoxious drunk.
3. Another of my best friends probably hated me because I refused to pick up her children from school and told her she

was a bad mother if she continued to lie weeping on the couch.

But I steeled myself for the occasion. Taking in my reflection in the bathroom mirror boosted my confidence a little. Karen had always gushed over this sweater, commenting on how the bright color brought warmth to my skin and made my cheeks look fresh and rosy. It was a tribute to my friend, the fact that I was wearing this outfit to say our final good-bye. As I thought about Karen, a small, wistful smile found its way to my lips. At that moment, I felt glad that I hadn't divulged her secret to Paul. Karen was a kind, sweet, and special friend. She was a wonderful person who had made an error in judgment. If I could, I would keep the rest of Aberdeen Mists from remembering her as some out-of-control nympho.

The sound of Paul's key in the lock summoned me downstairs. "Hi," I greeted my husband. "We'd better get going."

"Okay. Why don't you go get changed? I just need to pee and brush my teeth."

"I am changed."

"Oh . . . That's what you're wearing to the funeral?" He stared at me like I was wearing nothing but a bra with the nipples cut out.

"Yeah," I replied uncertainly. "This was Karen's favorite sweater of mine. I thought I would wear it as a sort of . . . tribute to her."

"Oh."

"Do you think I should change?"

"No, no," Paul said, brushing past me. "I'm sure you know what you're doing."

"I can change!" I called after him, but he was already upstairs.

Twenty minutes later, we pulled into the parking lot of Saint Matthew's United Church, already burgeoning with well-wishers. Paul and I made our way silently up the walk, stopping only briefly to clasp hands or plant perfunctory kisses on cheeks. In my bright pink sweater amid a sea of black-clad mourners, I actually did feel like my nipples were poking out. But I managed to hold my head high as we filed into the church, taking a seat in a pew several rows back. The room was filling quickly, evidence of Karen's popularity, but the front of the church remained empty. Obviously, the first few rows were reserved for Karen's family. Jane blew me a kiss from her seat just across the aisle and one row ahead. She wore a demure but stunning black suit, her nipples safely tucked away from view. Her husband, Daniel, distinguished in his charcoal ensemble, nodded an acknowledgment, his hands busy clutching Jane's in support.

As we waited for Doug and the family to arrive, I scanned the room. There was no sign of Trudy . . . or Carly, for that matter. Oh no. I hoped my outburst the other night hadn't upset Trudy so much that she was unable to attend. Perhaps Carly was with her, comforting and consoling her. She was probably telling her how rude and unsympathetic I had been to Doug and "not to take it personally," because, obviously, I was the one with the problem, not Trudy. Maybe they were going to have their own private, "close friends only" service for Karen—a service that I, of course, would be excluded from.

"Who are you looking for?" Paul whispered.

"Oh . . . just Trudy and Carly," I replied. "It's getting late. I thought they'd be here . . ." Something caught my eye. It was a man, entering alone and awkwardly taking a seat in the second-to-last pew. Why he grabbed my attention, I'm not exactly sure, but he seemed so out of place, even uneasy in his plaid dress shirt and pressed black jeans. And it was odd, his being alone. Everyone else had come in couples or clusters. Oh my God! My body tensed as the sudden realization hit me.

Paul leaned over. "What's wrong?"

"Nothing!" I swung my head around to face him. "Nothing. Why?"

"You seemed startled or something."

"No. I'm fine." I smiled to appease him. "Just wondering where those two are . . . Carly and Trudy."

"They'll be here," he replied indifferently, staring ahead.

I forced myself to face forward, even as my mind raced with this startling revelation. The stranger at the back was Javier! Of course it was! If he really loved Karen as she said he did, he would want to come and pay his respects. The Spanish were a religious and ceremonious people, were they not? God, what did I know about the Spanish? But I did know that some people needed the closure of a funeral to say good-bye to a loved one. I had also watched enough detective programs to know that even murderers sometimes showed up at their victims' services.

I looked over my shoulder again. He wasn't exactly what I had expected, but it had to be him. He had thick, dark hair and tawny Mediterranean skin. His eyes were dark, but from this distance, it was hard to tell if they smoldered or not. Javier was a little . . . *beefier* than I had expected, but he had broad shoulders, and his face did have a lot of character. Yes, I could see how Karen would have been attracted to him. There was something so unique, mysterious, and . . . foreign about him. He would have been hard to resist.

There was a discernible shift in the crowd as Karen's significant others entered the church. Necks craned, then snapped forward, eyes darted, then returned to the front. No one wanted to be caught gawking as Doug walked slowly in, flanked by a woman who had to be his sister and Karen's diminutive mother. Following them was an assortment of siblings, aunts, and cousins, and then Trudy and Carly. Don't ask me why, but their inclusion in this "inner circle" irked me a bit. Jane and I had been just as close to Karen as they were. We were every bit as devastated by her sudden passing, and yet we were seated in pews five and six, respectively. And there were Carly and Trudy, easing into the second row, close enough to reach out and pat Doug's back consolingly, which they did periodically.

But when the minister appeared at the pulpit and began to speak about "a beautiful young life cut short," any feelings of jealousy or envy dissipated. My focus was on saying good-bye to my friend, my sweet and beautiful friend who was leaving us much, much too soon. Karen should have been sitting there beside me. We should have been paying our respects to some elderly lady who had lived a long, rich life, full of children and grandchildren. It was so wrong to be saying good-bye to a vital young woman on the brink of motherhood. That reminded me—somehow, I had to speak to Javier before he slipped away.

Finally, the minister's long-winded and rather generic sermon was over. I had endured it with great composure, having shed an ocean of tears in the privacy of my own bedroom. I was touched to see a silent tear trickle down my husband's cheek. I gave his hand a comforting squeeze. "Now," the minister said, "I'd like to introduce a dear, dear friend of the departed's . . . Carly Hillman."

Again, I felt an uncomfortable twinge of jealousy as I watched Carly make her way to the pulpit. Of course, she was a perfectly appropriate representative for our group of suburban friends, so why was I feeling that perturbed? It was juvenile, I knew, and somewhat disturbing, but I couldn't seem to help it. I was perplexed as to why this sudden tragedy was making me feel so . . . petty. Weren't these life-altering events supposed to make you more accepting, more patient, more "don't sweat the small stuff"? It seemed to be having the reverse effect on me. I felt almost . . . possessive of my friendship with Karen.

Carly addressed the congregation. "Hello everyone. Thank you for coming today to celebrate the life of our special friend . . . daughter . . . sister . . . *wife.*" She looked tenderly at Doug then. From my vantage point, I could just see his profile. He was staring straight ahead, a steely set to his jaw. Carly continued. "Not long after I met Karen, I suffered a tragedy of my own. My husband of just ten months left me for an older woman with two children. I was devastated. I wasn't sure I could go on, but Karen came to my rescue. She refused to let me fall apart, because . . . that's just the kind of friend Karen was . . ."

Of course, I completely understood why Doug hadn't asked me to speak at the funeral. He was probably afraid I'd show up drunk and spout inane gibberish about families and babies and who really needs them anyway . . . And it wasn't like I was really a *fan* of public speaking, but . . . I don't know. In a way, it would have been nice to at least have been asked. It would have been a gesture that validated the friendship I'd had with Karen. It might even have made the burden of secrecy I was carrying a little less heavy.

". . . Karen touched all of our lives, every one of us here today. In my case, she actually changed my life . . . maybe even *saved* it . . . and for that, I will always be thankful. I will always . . ." She stopped for a moment, as her emotions threatened her voice. "I will always love her."

Carly stood silently for a long moment, the tears she'd been holding in check now streaming down her face. The crowd shifted awkwardly, unsure of whether she was going to compose herself and continue or whether the eulogy was over. I was vaguely aware of a rustling in the second pew and watched as Trudy moved to the podium. Tenderly, maternally, she put her arm around our distraught friend and leaned in to the mike. "Thank you, everyone, for coming today. Your attendance is a tribute to Karen's memory. There will be tea, coffee, and cakes served in room nine. Just go down to the basement and follow the pink arrows with 'Remember Karen' written on them."

Somewhat thankfully, the congregation got to their feet. "Well . . . I'm dying for some cake," I said to my husband, by way of explanation as I launched myself into the aisle. There was no way Javier would stick around to make small talk with Karen's friends and relatives. What would he say? "Yes, I will miss Karen terribly. She gave the best head." I had to intercept him before he left. Unfortunately, the other mourners were not experiencing the same sense of urgency. The line inched forward, stopping every few feet to let another row of people into the aisle. I craned my neck to see if I could spot Javier. It looked like he was already gone.

"Hi, Paige," a voice behind me said.

I turned. "Trudy!" How had she gotten from the pulpit to row six so quickly? "Uh . . . how are you?"

"I'm fine. I'm better—thanks to you."

Was she being sarcastic? I couldn't tell. "Look, I'm sorry if I was hard on you. I'd had a difficult day, and I shouldn't have taken it out on you."

Trudy smiled. "I needed that kick in the pants. You did me a favor."

"Really?"

"I was wallowing in self-pity. All I could think about was how much I missed Karen. When you confronted me, it really shook me up. I was hurt and angry at first, but then I realized that falling apart wasn't going to help Doug. That's when I decided to get off the couch and get busy."

"Great."

"Carly and I have been working nonstop on the funeral preparations—baking, organizing dishes and flatware, making a photo collage of Karen . . ."

I suddenly felt completely left out again. ". . . I could have helped, too," I said in a small voice.

"It's okay." She squeezed my forearm. "We know you've been having a hard time with this. I'm just sorry that I was so self-absorbed that I couldn't see how much you were hurting."

"Umm . . . Thanks."

She reached out and hugged me then, even as we continued to inch up the aisle. "I love you, friend," Trudy said.

"I love you, too," I replied, a little awkwardly. We were in the midst of a throng of neighbors and acquaintances, after all.

Trudy released me. "If there's one thing this tragedy has taught me, it's to let the people you love know it."

"Good. That's good."

"Oh! There's Jane," she said, waving toward our friend, still working her way out of her pew. "Excuse me, Paige. I think that girl needs a big hug right about now."

For a few seconds, I watched Trudy struggle against the flow of well-wishers toward Jane. I also glanced at Paul, who appeared to be in deep conversation with Ed Winofsky from the country club. Seizing the opportunity, I forced my way through the crowd. Turning my body sideways, I bumped and jostled my way out of the church, mumbling a continuous stream of *excuse me's* as I went.

When I finally reached the vestibule, I scanned the room for Javier. Dammit, I was too late. I rushed toward the exit door and burst out into the silent parking lot. Hugging my arms against the autumn chill, I scurried toward the rows of parked cars, hoping to catch him just about to leave. My eyes roved back and forth, looking for an occupied vehicle. What would Javier drive? I envisioned a beat-up pickup truck or a rusted 1983 Honda Civic hatchback. But what met my eyes was a sea of large, pristine SUVs or family sedans, all of them unoccupied. Dejectedly, I turned back inside.

As soon as I entered, I was met by my husband. "Where were you? I was looking for you."

"I just needed some air," I lied. "Sorry. I should have told you."

"It's okay. Doug and everyone have gone downstairs for tea and cake. We should pay our respects."

"Of course."

We followed Carly and Trudy's pink construction-paper arrows until we arrived at room nine. Greeting us at the doorway was the photo collage Trudy had mentioned. I stopped to look at Karen as a toddler, an awkward girl of about twelve with braces and a bad perm, a pretty teenager looking tanned and lanky in cutoffs and a green T-shirt . . . There was her wedding picture . . . And a photo of Karen surrounded by Trudy, Carly, Jane, and me, taken at a New Year's Eve party two years ago. I felt the familiar lump of emotion forming in my throat. Tearing my eyes from the memories, I entered the room.

Amid the throng of familiar faces milling about, I sought out Doug. We hadn't spoken since the day after Karen's death. (I'd sent Paul over with Janet's slightly squished orange poppy seed loaf.) I didn't relish seeing him after my past behavior, but decorum demanded it. And I wanted to give my condolences to Karen's mom and brother, whom I had met one Christmas years before. With Paul's hand supportively at my back, we went to the grieving widower.

"... Doug," I said hesitantly. He appeared to be in deep conversation with Karen's brother's wife.

"Oh, hi, Paige," he said. Was it my imagination, or had a scrim of detached coolness descended over his eyes?

"We just wanted to give you our condolences ... again."

"Thank you."

I let Paul take over and moved on to kiss Karen's mother and immediate family. But I was not up to small talk. Emotionally, I was exhausted, and yet mentally, my mind was racing. If only I'd had a few minutes to talk to Javier, to get a feel for the kind of man he was. Was he capable of killing Karen? Or was he so distraught over her death that he would risk attending her funeral just for a chance to say good-bye? If that turned out to be the case, then I'd have to interrogate Doug further. Although he already thought I was a complete weirdo. I didn't see how I could gain any further information from him without his applying for a restraining order.

And then I saw him. I had to blink my eyes to make sure they weren't playing tricks on me, but there he was. Javier had not sneaked off. He was just across the room, pouring himself some coffee from the stainless steel upright urn. "I'm going to get a cup of coffee," I mumbled to Carly, who was standing closest to me. I made a beeline for Karen's lover.

Thanks to my swift movements, he was still stirring the sugar into his coffee with one of those tiny brown plastic straws when I approached. "Hi," I said, smiling pleasantly, as I reached for a Styrofoam cup.

He looked up briefly. "Hi." It was not an overly friendly greeting, but not dismissive either. I was going to have to approach my subject very carefully, play it cool ... If I was too aggressive, I might scare him off.

"So ..." I smiled at him as I reached for the minicreamers. His face really was full of character. "Did you know Karen well?"

"We had gotten close ... over the last few months."

"Oh." I had expected more of an accent. In fact, if he had one, it was undetectable to me. But maybe Karen had been exaggerating his Spanishness for effect? Besides, love was blind. One woman's smoldering, sensuous Latin lover was another woman's averagely pleasant guy. "It was such a shock," I continued, "her . . . *accident.*"

"Terrible," he replied, taking a drink of his coffee. "She was still pretty young."

Pretty young? Karen hadn't mentioned Javier's age, but it was now evident that he was only in his midtwenties. Wasn't that the most passionate and impulsive time of life? A young man of twenty-five would be much more likely to lash out violently at his lover than a more seasoned fortyish guy like Doug, right? I had to engage Javier further.

"Do you know many people here?" I asked innocently.

Javier picked up a date square and stuffed it in his mouth. "Not really," he mumbled.

"Well, I'll stay here and keep you company, if you like. I don't want you to feel uncomfortable."

". . . Sure." He gave me a bemused smile. He had nice eyes, but I wasn't really picking up any smolder in them.

"I was really close to Karen, too," I said leadingly. "She told me a lot of things . . ."

"Yeah?" He reached for a butter tart. Maybe the poor guy had stuck around because he was starving?

"Yeah . . . she told me things that no one else knew." I leaned in and whispered in his ear. *"Secrets . . ."*

He looked at me for a second and then nodded slowly.

"Look, I understand if you don't want to talk here. Maybe you could give me your number?" I began to dig in my purse for a pen.

"Well . . . ," Javier said, looking around nervously, "I don't know if that's such a good idea . . ."

"I can be very discreet."

". . . Okay."

"What's going on here?" The woman who spoke was about Javier's age, several inches shorter than me, and very curvaceous. She had long, wavy dark hair and wore bright red lipstick.

"Oh . . . hey, babe," Javier said, putting his arm around her quickly.

I was stunned! I could not believe that Javier had brought a date to Karen's funeral! Had he gotten over her so quickly? Had he been involved with someone else all along? Did that raise or lower the probability that he had killed my friend? "I was just talking to this lady—a close friend of Karen's."

"Yeah," she snapped, glaring at me. "So I see. Hands off, lady. He's taken."

"Oh, no, no, no!" I said. "I'm married." I pointed furiously at my wedding ring. "I'm not interested in Javier—that way. I just wanted to talk to him about—"

"Javier?" She gave a humorless laugh, then turned to her boyfriend. "First you turn up late, and now I catch you playing some kinky game with this . . . *woman*. God, you didn't even tell her your real name!"

"I didn't tell her any name," Javier said, his voice full of fear. "I don't know what she's talking about. She just came up and started making moves on me."

"Making moves on you?" I was outraged. "I wasn't making moves on you. I was . . ." I stopped midsentence. Oh shit. Oh shit, shit, shit. "Your name isn't Javier?"

"George."

His girlfriend spoke. "I'm Leslie, Karen's cousin from Montana. We just moved to Denver a few months ago. Karen and I were just reconnecting when . . . she had her accident."

"I-I'm sorry, Leslie . . . ," I stammered. "I wasn't making moves on George." I turned to him. "I wasn't, George. Honestly. I thought that you were a friend of Karen's who didn't know anyone else here. I was trying to be friendly."

"Whatever." Leslie held up her hand. "It's pretty pathetic trying to pick up a guy at a funeral."

"I wasn't," I cried. "It was a misunderstanding!" But they turned and walked away from me. My cheeks burned with humiliation.

"Everything okay?" Paul appeared at my side.

I turned to him. "Fine. Fine. I'm just a little . . . upset, that's all. Would it be rude if we left now?" I suddenly felt overwhelmingly weary, sad, and confused. It was more than I could cope with, this knowledge of Karen's affair. I wanted to be blissfully ignorant, oblivious to Karen's duplicity like everyone else was. I wanted to make butter tarts and photo collages and grieve for my friend properly. Instead, I was consumed by the mystery surrounding her death. Trudy was right. I was having a really hard time dealing with this.

Paul took my arm and kissed the side of my hair. "It's okay. Let's get you home."

CHAPTER 12

A s the days passed, I grew stronger. If there was one thing my humiliating encounter with George had provided, it was a new sense of determination. I had to meet the real Javier. I had to talk to him, to gain an understanding of his feelings for Karen. I'd let too much time pass to confess to Paul or Jane or Carly: I would have to handle the situation on my own. I would meet with Javier, and if he sparked even one iota of suspicion in me, I would go to the police. But if he seemed genuine in his grief, I would let the whole thing go, chalk Karen's death up to a tragic, freak accident. It was decided. Of course, I'd keep a close eye on the way Doug spent the life insurance money. Any new sports cars or hot tub installations would definitely signal cause for concern.

I turned my attention back to the deserted stretch of highway before me. A light snow was beginning to fall, tiny flakes whipping through the air and landing on the windshield with small, wet plops. I flicked on the wipers. They dragged against the largely dry surface of the glass with an unpleasant squeak. From the backseat, I heard the muffled sobs of my daughter. While my words of consolation had previously fallen on deaf ears, I decided to try again.

"Honey," I said sympathetically, "your new glasses look great. You look really beautiful and so grown-up."

"I look like a nerd!" she screeched.

Mr. Dennison had been right. Chloe was having a really difficult time accepting her new, bespectacled appearance. Unfortunately, I was too embarrassed by my previous flirtatious behavior to take him up on his offer of support. But it was okay. I was fairly sure I could handle this on my own.

"No, you don't," I said cheerfully. "You look smart."

"Mom, I don't want to look smart. I want to look cool."

"Well . . . glasses are cool."

"Oh, really?" she snapped. "If they're so cool, why don't any singers wear them?"

"What? Of course singers wear glasses," I said somewhat nervously. "Lots of singers . . . like . . . ."

"Who?"

"Well . . . Elvis Costello."

"I don't care about the guys."

"Okay . . . umm . . . Nana Mouskouri."

"Who?!"

"You don't know her?" I said. "Oh, she's very popular . . . a beautiful voice. A really great singer."

"What is she, like, eighty?"

"No . . ." I chuckled awkwardly. "Well . . . maybe. But there are others!"

"No there aren't," Chloe said sulkily. "Britney doesn't wear glasses. Neither does Christina or Jessica . . . or Beyoncé."

There was a long silence while my mind scrambled to think of some cool singers who wore glasses. "Lisa Loeb!" I said triumphantly. "Lisa Loeb wears glasses, and she is very hip and cool. And she's not eighty. She's probably around my age."

"I don't care about the old people!" my daughter shouted.

I sighed heavily. "You can get contacts in a year or two."

"I want the surgery."

"The surgery? You want laser eye surgery?"

"Yes."

"Kids can't get laser eye surgery."

"Why not?"

"Because," I said, frustration evident in my voice, "your eyes are still growing. If you had the surgery now, you'd need glasses again in a few years."

"Then I'd get the surgery again. I don't care!"

"Chloe, you'll have to be satisfied with contacts."

"You're so mean! Lynne would never make Britney walk around looking like a complete dork!"

"What? Who?"

"Lynne Spears—Britney's mom!" she shrieked. "They are best friends! Lynne supports her and believes in her and would never embarrass her like this!"

"You're probably right," I said resignedly. "I guess it's just your tough luck to have such a horrible mother who will only buy you a two hundred–dollar pair of designer glasses that look really cute and stylish and then offer to get you contact lenses in a year or two."

"I hate my life!" she wailed, sinking back into unintelligible sobbing.

"Yeah, well mine's not so hot either," I muttered, steering the SUV through the large wrought-iron gates marking the entrance to Aberdeen Mists. Some days, motherhood felt like a real chore. Between Chloe's hostility and Spencer's toilet talk, it wasn't really the most rewarding of career choices. And with the impact of Karen's sudden death gradually fading, Paul was once again immersing himself in work, leaving me to cope on my own. This was not easy— especially given the fact that I had a possible murder to investigate.

When I pulled into the driveway, Chloe barreled out of the car before I'd even had a chance to turn off the ignition. "That's dangerous, young lady!" I called after her, but she was already stalking toward the house. I suppose she didn't care if she was crushed under the wheels of a Ford Explorer. In fact, it would probably be a welcome relief from the pain of going through life looking like a hideous, bespectacled circus freak. When I unlocked the house, she stomped silently to her room. Spencer, at this point by far my favorite child, tugged at my hand.

"Could I watch a kids' show? Pleeeeeeeeeeeeze! I haven't watched any TV all day or yesterday either."

"Go on." I caved in. "Kiss first." With a peck, he scurried to the family room. I sighed heavily as I followed his path toward the back of the house. Once in the kitchen, I poured myself a glass of merlot and began dinner preparations. We were having Chloe's favorite, spaghetti, a meal I had planned before our trip to the optometrist. I had hoped it would cheer her up, but it was now apparent that a delicious bowl of pasta was not going to help my daughter deal with the trials of vision correction. If she didn't snap out of it soon, I would have to break down and call Mr. Dennison for some professional advice. Perhaps if I acted very businesslike, brusque even, he might think he'd imagined my previous suggestive behavior?

As I chopped the onion and celery into minute pieces (in hopes of rendering them undetectable to a certain six-year-old), my mind slipped back to Karen's case. Yes, I had begun to think of Karen's love triangle and untimely death as a "case." It was very Nancy Drew of me, but I couldn't help it. And just as I had been consumed by Karen's affair when she was alive, I now found myself completely obsessed with finding answers to her early demise. In some ways, I felt I owed it to her: she had trusted me and confided in me. But I had to admit, solving the mystery had started to feel crucial to my sanity.

I dropped the veggies into the pot, drizzled them with olive oil, and turned on the heat. Okay . . . I had to meet Javier—the real Javier. But how? I knew virtually nothing about him: no last name, no address, not even a neighborhood . . . All I knew was that he was Spanish, sexy, and worked as a barista. What—was I going to drive to every coffee shop in Denver looking for hot Latin men? Obviously, that wasn't logistically feasible—and I was jittery enough these days without going on a caffeine binge. With a discouraged sigh, I plunked a pound of ground beef into the saucepan and stepped back as it sizzled dramatically. No . . . there had to be another way to find him.

That's when my eyes traveled to the fridge, home of various alphabet magnets, school notices, and children's art projects. There, affixed with a green letter *M,* was Spencer's latest masterpiece. It was a pencil sketch, enhanced by watercolor paint in shades of gold and blue. Of course, I knew this was supposed to be a pee fountain, but if I disregarded that for a moment, it was really quite lovely. If I imagined that the yellow paint represented water, backlit by a setting sun, instead of actual *urine,* it was an impressive effort for a first grader. Then it struck me. Karen had met Javier at an art class! He was an artists' model! That was the answer! I would sign up for art classes.

Unfortunately, I couldn't remember the name of the studio where Karen had taken classes. Grabbing the cordless phone, I called Carly. She wasn't home. I tried Jane, who answered but couldn't remember the name either. Finally, I tried Trudy. "It was called Wild Rose Arts Center," she said helpfully. "I didn't know you had an interest in art."

"Well . . . I've been meaning to take up a hobby," I said, my cheeks turning pink despite myself. It's not like I was lying: I had even written "Find creative hobby" on my Life Makeover list. I was just omitting the fact that my newfound artistic bent was due in large part to a need to check out the model. "The kids are both at school now . . . and with Karen gone . . . I guess I need a distraction."

"I think it's a great idea."

"Thanks."

"I'm embarking on a new project of my own."

"Oh?"

"Carly and I are setting up a charitable trust in Karen's memory."

"Wow! That's wonderful."

"Well, you remember how much Karen wanted a baby. We've decided to make a donation in her name to the Alternative Infertility Clinic of South Denver. And we're setting up an ongoing trust so that her friends and family can pay tribute to her by donating to the cause." She paused for a moment. "I think it would make her happy to know that, thanks to her, fewer women will have to suffer a barren existence."

Ah yes . . . Karen's barren existence . . . The secret of her pregnancy weighed heavily on me, but I managed to muster the appropriate words. "I think it's really great, Trudy. Karen would be so pleased."

"Thanks, Paige." She sniffled.

"You can count on my support," I said. "Oh! Better run. My spaghetti sauce is bubbling over."

The sauce was actually simmering nicely, but I felt an urgent need to sign up for a class at the Wild Rose Arts Center. A glance at the digital oven clock indicated that it was 5:07, unlikely that a receptionist would still be there. But I quickly looked up the number in the phone book and dialed hopefully.

"Wild Rose Arts Center," a bland female voice answered.

"Oh! Great! You're still there."

"The office is open until eight on Wednesdays and Thursdays," she replied mundanely. "Can I help you?"

"Yes," I cleared my throat. "I'd like to sign up for a drawing class, please."

"Do you have the course number from our flyer?"

Dammit. "No—I don't actually have a flyer."

"We have a number of drawing classes," she explained in her bored voice. "I can have a flyer mailed out to you, or you can look it up online. Then you can call back when you know the class you want to take."

"I know the class I want," I said hurriedly. "A friend of mine took a great drawing class there. I can't remember what it was called, . . . but she was drawing people . . . uh, models . . . male models . . . I think it was."

"That would probably be Drawing the Human Figure," she said. "But the session started in September. The next one isn't until January."

"I want to start right away," I replied, my voice tinged with desperation. "Please, I don't mind if I've missed a few classes."

"You've already missed nearly half of them. And I don't know if

I'm allowed to prorate your enrollment fee. I guess I could ask my manager tomorrow."

"Don't worry about it," I said, already fishing my Visa card from my wallet. "I'll pay full price. When can I start?"

"Classes are Wednesday nights at 8:00."

"Wednesday? That's tonight!"

"Do you want to sign up or not?" The woman on the other end of the phone sounded needlessly exasperated.

"Sign me up. I'll be there."

By the time Paul arrived home at 7:35, the children had been fed, Chloe's homework had been done, and I was standing in the grand entryway, clutching a SpongeBob Squarepants notepad (with the cover torn off) and three HB pencils held together with an elastic band. "Hi," I said brightly. "I'm going to an art class tonight."

"An art class?" Paul responded, as if I'd just told him I was off to have my head shaved. "Since when do you like art?"

"*Like* art?" I retorted. "Of course I *like* art. Who doesn't *like* art?"

"I mean, since when are you interested in taking an art class?"

"I've been wanting to for ages," I replied defensively. "I need a creative hobby—something to feed my mind and nourish my soul."

"Okay," he said skeptically. "Have fun."

As I raced down the highway toward the lower downtown home of the Wild Rose Arts Center, I fumed at my husband's lack of support. Why couldn't he just get behind me and my newfound hobby? True, my sudden passion for drawing had come out of the blue, and I had never shown any proclivity for sketching before, but I wasn't entirely without creativity. This was typical of Paul. I took a deep breath and let my angry feelings dissipate. But once they were gone, I desperately tried to summon them back. My fury had been a good distraction from the acute anxiety I was feeling at the prospect of meeting Javier.

Twenty-two minutes later, I pulled into the darkened, potholed parking lot of the arts center. With my sketchbook and pencils tucked under my arm, I entered the aging two-story building and began searching for my class. Although it was eight o'clock sharp, the reception desk was vacant. Thankfully, I was greeted at the doorway by a small, round table holding a stack of flyers. Flicking frantically through the pages, I found my class.

DRAWING THE HUMAN FIGURE—ALLAN DRURY—ROOM 16
This class is suitable for all levels of artistic ability and will address
composition, line, and form, using pencil and charcoal.

Okay . . . I hurried down the fluorescent-lit hallway, looking for room sixteen. It was already two minutes past eight. I wasn't *late* late, but I wasn't making a very good first impression. Finally, I reached the doorway. Peering inside, I hesitated a few moments before entering. About ten of my fellow artists were surrounding a raised platform, straddling these bench thingies, with sketchbooks clipped to angled boards before them. Taking in their composed and relaxed manners, their obvious familiarity with these contraptions, I suddenly felt completely out of my element.

"Welcome!" the instructor, Allan, called, sensing my hovering presence. "Come on in."

"Uh . . ." All eyes turned to me. Was it my imagination, or did they all look very nourished of mind and soul? Besides, I was on a mission. "Sorry I'm late. I'm new." I stepped inside.

"Grab a drawing horse," Allan said. He had unkempt gray hair and was wearing dark brown corduroys, a soft, faded flannel shirt, and small wire-rimmed glasses. His deportment was calm and serene. "As I was saying . . ."

He continued to talk—something about line and form and negative space—as I found an available bench . . . I mean, drawing horse. Unfortunately, I was positioned very close to the central platform, giving all my classmates behind me an excellent view of my laughable lack of sketching ability. Glancing surreptitiously at my neighbor's setup, I clipped my SpongeBob pad of paper to the drawing board, chagrined to find it was about half the size of everyone else's pad. Okay. I was ready: ready to see the real Javier.

"In a moment," the instructor was saying, "I'll invite our model in to join us." He looked directly at me. "Some of you may be new to drawing from live models, but there is no need to feel uncomfortable or embarrassed. This is the human body in its most pure and honest form. Our model is a professional, who is entirely comfortable providing you with a form to sketch. Any questions?"

Someone asked something about depth of focus, which was way over my head, while I mentally prepared myself. I would have ample time to study Javier undetected—although, as a model, he would probably affect a vacant, expressionless stare, keeping his true feelings of guilt, remorse, or just plain loss well hidden. But after class, I could approach him ... maybe even invite him out for coffee. I hadn't yet decided if I would reveal my identity as Karen's friend or pretend to be a naïve stranger. I would play it by ear.

"Class, please welcome Javier," Allan was saying. My heart beat loudly as a dark-haired man in his late twenties wearing a baby blue bathrobe moved to the center of the room. Javier positioned himself on the raised platform, turning to face the class. He had hooded, sexy eyes, a chiseled jaw, and a slightly off-center nose that appeared to have been broken. It wasn't a classically handsome face, but it was compelling. Karen had been right, it had character ... lots and lots of character. In fact, I found I couldn't look away.

The instructor spoke again. "Javier would like to start tonight's class with a two-minute standing pose."

I tore my eyes from his face and stared at the paper before me, pencil poised to begin. Two minutes wasn't very long to draw the complete human figure. Javier dropped his robe. I dropped my pencil.

"Whoops! Uh ... Sorry." The pencil rolled across the floor, finally coming to rest at the foot of the platform where Javier stood ... stark naked. Jesus Christ. I hadn't been prepared for stark naked! In a crouched position, I scurried to retrieve my pencil. "Sorry about that," I muttered again, preparing to rush back to my station, but suddenly, I froze. It was probably only for a second or two, but to me, time had slowed perceptibly. Squatting at the base of the platform, I had just realized that I was mere inches away from the most attractive naked body I had seen in person since ... well, since Paul had an attractive naked body back in the early nineties. At that moment, I had completely forgotten that Javier was quite possibly Karen's murderer. I felt nervous and fluttery. I could almost feel the heat emanating from his golden skin, hear the blood pumping through his veins, his heart beating . . . Okay, don't look up, I instructed myself. Keep your head down and slink back to your drawing horse. But it was like some kind of compulsion. I raised my head.

I had a perfect view of two solid, muscular legs, reminiscent of a carved marble statue. And of course, dangling right above me was . . . his impressive, uh . . . well, to borrow a term from Spencer, his *wiener.* That snapped me back to reality. I turned quickly and duckwalked, in my squatted position, back to my spot.

Get it together, woman! I chided myself as I raised my pencil to the paper. You are here on a reconnaissance mission, not to ogle the prime suspect. What are you, fifteen? You've seen a hundred penises! What's so different about this one? Okay . . . maybe not a hundred, but probably ten or twelve—if you counted children. The rest of the class was focusing intently on drawing the human figure. They seemed oblivious to the fact that this was quite possibly the most perfect, muscular, sexy human figure on the planet.

I drew a light, sloping line, which could easily represent a shoulder . . . or possibly a tricep. I hadn't actually had the courage to look at Javier again, lest I collapse into childish, nervous giggles. God! What was wrong with me? When did I become such a perv?

"Two minutes are up," Allan announced. "Javier, please select another pose."

I followed the rest of the class in turning to a fresh sheet of paper, despite the fact that there was virtually nothing on my first. This time, it would be different. I was quite capable of looking at the human body as a pure and honest form. I was a wife and mother, after all, not some sick sex maniac. Besides, Javier was a wife stealer and a potential friend killer. It was sick to be feeling an attraction toward him. Sick! I looked toward the platform. Javier had moved into a modified kneeling position, his chin resting on his hand. At least now I couldn't really see his . . . you know . . . *private parts,* which made it a little easier to think of him in a nonsexual way.

But just as I was about to make my first mark on the page, all the hair on my body stood on end. A palpable tingling sensation, like an electric current, traveled through me, and my heart began to race. What was wrong with me? Was I having a stroke? An anxiety attack? My eyes shifted back to the platform, and that's when I realized the source of my irrepressible reaction: Javier was staring at me. I mean, he was really *looking* at me, and not in an "I just need somewhere to look while I crouch here naked" kind of way. Our eyes locked, like two magnets and— Oh my God! His were smoldering—really smoldering! I couldn't breathe. What was happening to me? Oh my God! Was I having a *moment* with Javier?

With an impressive force of will, I ripped my eyes from his and focused on the blank white page before me. Did that really just happen? Was I experiencing an intimate connection with that incredibly gorgeous, naked possible head bonker? It had been so long since I'd had a real *moment* of my own that I wasn't sure my instincts could be trusted. My mind traveled back to Carly's encounter with the Diet Coke man, and I mentally conjured her checklist:

- Our eyes met. (check)
- Time stood still. (check)
- It felt like we'd known each other forever. (check)

But this was all wrong. I was married! A mother of two! I was thirty-eight years old with two popped balloons hanging off my chest! I didn't have *moments* with gorgeous creatures like Javier. Besides, I was working a case. I had to regain my focus.

Sensing the instructor's presence behind me, I began to draw frantically—long, sweeping lines that in no way resembled a human body. For the rest of the hour, I sketched without really looking at my subject again. I imitated the movements of my neighbors: long, smooth pencil strokes, followed by short, quick bursts for shading. The results of this method were several Picasso/stick figure hybrids, but Allan didn't comment, other than a murmured "Interesting." Either he was not paying attention or he thought I was more of an impressionist.

Finally, the end of class was announced. As I gathered my pencils, I could see the baby blue robe being draped around Javier's nakedness. Now was my chance. I would stroll up casually and say, "Nice work." When he responded with a "Thank you," I would say, "Do I detect an accent? You're from Spain! I love Spain. How about I buy you a coffee so we can talk about Spain?" Or I could take a more direct approach. "Hello, Javier. I'm a close friend of Karen Sutherland's. I was wondering if we could talk privately—about Karen?" Yes, the direct approach would work better. No more of this insane eye contact and sexual chemistry. I would come right out with my reason for seeing him. Although . . . I didn't want to scare him off. Maybe we could have a friendly chat about Spain or art or something, just to break the ice? Then, when I'd put him at ease, I'd bring up the real reason for our meeting.

Allan's voice interrupted my internal dialogue. "Thanks, everyone! See you next week."

My head snapped up, and I looked around. Other than Allan, I was the only one left in the classroom. Everyone else, including Javier, had gone.

blew it! I completely blew it! For the next few days, I couldn't stop berating myself. My first serious attempt at getting to the bottom of Karen's death had been a huge failure. Well, I guess my initial conversation with Doug had been my *first* attempt—and that had bombed, too. I was no closer to finding out what had happened to my friend. And I was more than a little concerned that I had acted like some crazed nymphomaniac with Javier.

I blamed Paul for that—Paul and my hormones. If my husband had been more responsive to my resexualizing attempts, it would have been easy to keep my desires in check. If I were a sexually satisfied woman, I would have been able to look at Javier as nothing more than a model, an extremely muscular and sensual *object*. But no! Instead, I had sat there like some horny teenager, leering and salivating at the sight of his smooth, golden skin and rippling muscles; quivering from the intensity of his smoldering gaze. It was disgusting: *I* was disgusting. I should have been looking at Javier as

Karen's ex-lover, potentially the father of her unborn child, and quite possibly, her murderer.

But next Wednesday, I would be ready for him. I would not squander another chance to meet with Javier. My nerves would be steeled, my sexual instincts in check. Just to make sure, I planned to spend Tuesday night having wild, uninhibited sex with Paul. I would be completely satiated, entirely uninterested in Javier's chiseled pectorals and washboard abs. Those hooded, sexy eyes would have no effect on me whatsoever. Oh, I'd have eye contact with him, all right. I'd play along with his sick little game, but only to gain what I really needed: his trust. And then, when he felt completely at ease, close and connected to me, I'd bring out the big guns. "I know about your passionate affair with Karen Sutherland," I would say. "Would you like to tell me about it?" . . . Maybe I should also have sex with Paul Wednesday evening, right before I left for class?

My doorbell rang, startling me from my plotting. It was 2:30 in the afternoon, only twenty minutes before I had to leave to pick up the children, an odd time for visitors. Opening the door, I was slightly startled to find two unfamiliar men on my doorstep. The first appeared to be in his early forties, a little overweight but with an attractive face and full head of thick brown hair. He wore a dark blue suit with a crisp, white shirt and blue patterned tie. The other one was in his midfifties, with soft, nondescript features and sparse blond hair, wearing wire-rimmed glasses and a gray suit.

"Mrs. Atwell?" the younger one said.

"Yes?"

"I'm Detective Portman. This is my partner, Detective Conroy. We'd like to speak to you for a few moments about your neighbor Karen Sutherland."

"Uh . . . of-f course," I stammered. "Please come in." They wiped their feet meticulously before stepping into the grand entryway. I had known the police would come eventually, but I was ill prepared. What happened next? On *Law & Order*, the people who had nothing to hide were always friendly and cooperative, offering cool drinks or coffee. "Would you like some coffee?" I asked, because, really, I didn't have anything to hide—nothing tangible anyway. And when I did have something more concrete to tell the police, I certainly planned to. They should be thankful, actually. I was doing some of the legwork for them.

"No thanks," Conroy remarked. "Would it be all right if we came in and sat down?"

"Sure . . . yes, of course." I led them into the formal living room, where they each perched on opposite ends of Grandmother Maple's chintz sofa. Seating myself across from them on a slightly worn brocade chair, I said, "I have to go pick up my kids in about fifteen minutes." And then, in case that remark might be construed as uncooperative, I quickly added, "Could I get either of you a cool drink—or a snack? I have Rice Krispies squares."

"We're fine," the older one muttered.

Portman, with the cute face, spoke. "So, Mrs. Atwell—"

"Ms.," I interrupted.

"Sorry . . ." He smiled kindly. "*Ms.* Atwell."

"It's no big deal, really," I said, with a laugh and a wave of my hand. "I just prefer Ms. I always have. I don't know why. Not so *old-fashioned,* I guess. But please . . . call me Paige."

Detective Conroy, at the other end of the couch, did not find me charming. "We understand you were close friends with Karen Sutherland?"

"Yes. We were . . . very close friends."

"Her death must have come as a shock to you."

"A huge shock!" I said, eyes wide to reinforce my point. "It was so sudden . . . so unexpected." I leaned forward. "Have you found some clues as to what happened to her?"

"We can't discuss the particulars of the case with you, ma'am," Conroy continued. "This is just a routine interview. At this stage, we're still eliminating possible suspects."

Portman clarified his partner's cryptic explanation. "We found several sets of prints at the scene. We're trying to identify people who would have had a legitimate reason to be in your friend's garage before she died."

"Oh, okay. Well . . . my friend Carly Hillman spent a lot of time with Karen. I suppose she might have been there."

The cops' expressions remained blank. Portman jotted Carly's name in a small notebook. "Anyone else?"

"I borrowed a bicycle pump from her before . . . the accident, so my prints could be there. Maybe Jane McKinnon . . . or Trudy Young."

"We'll need to take your fingerprints," Conroy said.

". . . If you don't mind," Portman added. "It would eliminate you as a suspect."

"Sure, of course, but I have to pick up——"

Conroy interjected, "We've got a Live Scan in the car. It just takes a few seconds."

"Okay, then."

"Would the Sutherlands have had any male visitors?" Portman asked.

And there it was: the perfect opportunity to tell them about Karen's affair with Javier. Obviously, they knew she was pregnant by now. Once they were aware of *the other man,* they could interrogate him properly. I would no longer have to embarrass myself with my ridiculous lack of artistic ability at that sketching class. I wouldn't have to face Javier again after that silly "moment" we shared. It would be such a relief. The police could investigate Doug, too. I wouldn't have to poke and pry into my neighbor's business. I could go back to being a sweet and supportive friend, instead of Aberdeen Mists' own Jessica Fletcher—a much younger version, of course.

"Umm . . . ," I began, under the guise of contemplating which men might have been in their attached garage. But really, I was stalling. Did I want to blow Karen's affair wide open at this stage? If her death turned out to be nothing but an unfortunate accident, was it fair to tarnish Doug's memory of his wife? And what about her reputation in the community? Did I really want to turn my dear friend into "that slut who got what she deserved"? No, I couldn't tell them yet—not until I knew more. "I can't think of anyone. I don't really know Doug's friends."

"Well . . ." Portman stood up. "I think that's about it, Ms. Atwell—Paige. We'll let you go collect your children now."

"Right," I said, having momentarily forgotten I had any. "Yes, well, I hope I helped . . . at least a little."

"One more thing," said Conroy, still seated. "Can you think of anyone who may have wanted to hurt Karen Sutherland? For any reason?" His eyes bore into mine, and I felt the heat of panic rise into my cheeks. Was he on to me? Could he see that I knew more than I was telling?

"No," I said, eyes darting nervously from one detective to the other. "Everyone loved her." There was an awkward pause while Detective Conroy continued to sit motionless on my couch. This must have been some sort of "bad cop" tactic, like the pressure of his gaze would cause me to blurt out "Okay, okay . . . Her secret lover might have killed her or possibly her low-sperm-count husband."

But I held my tongue and soon was following the detectives to their unmarked car and placing my digits on a small scanner. Before departing, Portman turned to me. "If you think of anything else that we should know about . . ."—he proffered a business card between his index and middle fingers—"give me a call. My direct line is on the card."

"Okay." I took his number. "I will."

"Thanks for your cooperation."

"You're welcome." I smiled at him, grateful that he had been there to buffer his cold and somewhat abrasive partner. Detective Portman smiled back. He had such an attractive face, despite being a bit heavy. And I had to admit, cops were sort of sexy. I guess it was the power thing. I mean . . . he was carrying a gun and everything. I was still smiling. He was still smiling. What were we doing? Were we flirting . . . just a little bit? "Bye," I said, my voice sounding ridiculously seductive.

"Have a nice day," he said, eyes still connected to mine.

God, I really needed to have sex with my husband.

Half an hour later, I had gathered the children and taken them to their swimming lessons. I sat in the bleachers, giving the appropriate thumbs-up signals to their aquatic endeavors, but my mind was fixed on the case. The police interview was concerning me, and not just my slight flirtation with Detective Portman. I was almost getting used to my lack of self-control around attractive men. But their presence on my doorstep obviously meant there were suspicions surrounding Karen's death. I knew it couldn't have been as simple as an accidental fall. But now I was afraid I could be in trouble. I was withholding evidence—or withholding *motive* or something . . . Whatever the proper term was, if the cops found out that I knew about Karen's affair, they would be angry. They'd probably want to see me prosecuted for obstructing the course of justice—or something like that. What if they put me in jail? The kids would have to visit me at the state pen, where I'd be wearing one of those hideous orange jumpsuits. I didn't want to put them through that trauma.

When we arrived home, I sent Chloe to the guest bathroom to shower the chlorine off and drew a bath for Spencer. With the sounds of my son happily splashing in the background, I sat down in the hall holding the cordless phone. I had to talk to someone about my police interview today, but who? After a few moments' contemplation, I dialed Carly.

"Hello?"

I was relieved when she answered. Lately, both Carly and Trudy had been so busy catering to Doug's needs and working on Karen's charitable trust that they had been largely unavailable. "Hi," I said. "It's Paige."

"Oh, hi. How are you?" She sounded upbeat.

"Fine . . . fine . . . And you?"

"Busy." She launched into an explanation of the banking processes involved in setting up a memorial trust. I half listened to her, the other ear trained on the bathroom to make sure Spencer wasn't drowning. "So . . . ," she finally said, "what's new with you? How are the kids?"

"They're good." I paused briefly. "The police were here today, to talk about Karen's . . . death."

"They came to see me, too," she said casually.

"Really? What did they ask you?"

"Oh, it was just a routine visit—something about fingerprints in Karen's garage."

"They took my prints. They're eliminating possible suspects."

"Mine, too. That's right. They said they were eliminating suspects."

"Which means," I said, my voice escalating, "that they are looking for someone." I lowered my voice to a hiss. "A *suspect*."

"I wouldn't read too much into it," she said. "They have to do this whenever there's an unexplained death."

I continued, my voice hushed, "But if everything had checked out with the autopsy . . . If it had simply been an accident or the result of some preexisting condition that caused her to fall and hit her head, why would they care who was in her garage?"

"You've been watching too much *CSI*!" Carly laughed. "It was a routine procedure."

I felt defensive. Carly obviously thought I was on some kind of insane witch hunt. If only she knew Karen's secrets, too, then she would see the validity of my suspicions. If she knew, we could commiserate, hypothesize, and brainstorm together. Once again, I felt the overwhelming urge to spill my guts, but something stopped me. I wasn't sure how Carly would react to the information. She was still so hurt by her ex-husband's infidelity that she might feel betrayed by Karen. She might think that Doug deserved to know what kind of woman he had been married to. She might put a halt to the Alternative Infertility Clinic trust, thus prompting a number of questions from Trudy and others—not to mention all the barren women who needed her help! No, Carly was not an ideal confidante. And I had to admit, I did watch a lot of *CSI*.

"Yeah, I suppose you're right," I said. "I guess I'm still having a little trouble believing that Karen just fell over and died in her attached garage."

"Well, she did," Carly stated matter-of-factly. "There were no signs of forced entry, no signs of a struggle, Doug has an airtight alibi—"

"He does?"

"The coroner set the time of death at between 11:15 A.M. and 1:00 P.M. Doug was on a flight back from Chicago that didn't land until 1:45. There's no way he could have done it."

"How do you know all this?"

"I was there when the police called to tell him he wouldn't be considered a suspect." Why hadn't I thought to ask Carly all this stuff before? If Doug was out of the equation, that made it all the more imperative that I speak to Javier. He was definitely the prime suspect now. Carly interrupted my reverie. "It was an accident, Paige. That's all. Let it go."

I laughed awkwardly. "I know, I know. I'd better lay off the prime-time dramas."

"I've got to go," Carly said. "Trudy and I are getting together to discuss having a celebrity golf tournament with proceeds going to Karen's charity."

But of course, getting my mind off Karen's death wasn't as easy as forcing myself to watch *Everybody Loves Raymond* reruns. I had to admit that Carly made some sense, but I couldn't let go of my suspicions that easily. Until I spoke to Javier on Wednesday, I would be stuck living with a pervasive uncertainty. I was still obsessing when Paul got home from work at eight.

"How was your day?" he asked, kissing me quickly as he entered the kitchen.

"Fine," I said. "I made us some chicken curry. I hope you're hungry."

"Starving! I'll go kiss the kids and be right down."

When we were alone, seated at the kitchen nook, I spoke. "How's the curry?"

"Good," he replied, taking a large drink of milk. "Hot."

"So . . . ," I began casually, forking a piece of chicken. "The police were here today."

"The police? What for?"

"They had some questions about Karen's death."

Paul dropped his fork. "What kind of questions?"

"Routine." I shrugged, adopting Carly's casual manner. "Apparently, they have to ask certain things when there's an unexplained death."

"So what did they ask?"

"They asked who would have had a legitimate reason to be in Karen's garage. They found a lot of prints in there."

"What did you tell them?" Paul was staring at me intensely.

"Well . . . I said, me, Carly, Jane, Trudy . . ."

"I don't like this," Paul said, standing and moving to the fridge to refill his milk glass.

"Is it too spicy? I could add some more yogurt."

"Not the curry, Paige. I don't like the police nosing around asking questions when you're here alone."

"They weren't *nosing*. They were asking routine questions."

"There was a death across the road. You placed yourself at the scene."

"I *was* at the scene," I said, my voice rising in frustration. "I used to go to Karen's house all the time. My prints would be all over the place. They were eliminating me as a suspect."

He returned to the table. "Next time the cops come around, I want you to call me."

"Why? What's the big deal?"

"Just call me next time, okay?" he said forcefully.

"Okay!" I snapped.

"We have to be careful. Things get misconstrued. People can be falsely incriminated." Now who was watching too many prime-time dramas? "If they come around again, we should call a lawyer."

"They won't be coming around again," I fumed. "You're the one who said it was just a freak accident."

"And what do you think?" he growled. "That there's some murderer on the loose in Aberdeen Mists?"

"I never said that."

He put his fork down. "Do you think it was Doug?"

I hesitated. "Why, do you?"

"No! Christ, Paige, all you have to do is look at him to see that he couldn't possibly have done it. He's devastated."

I took a mouthful of food and chewed in silence for a few moments. Paul obviously hadn't noticed Doug's cool aloofness and detached air, but now wasn't the time to bring it up. "He has an airtight alibi, anyway," I said.

"How do you know that?"

"Carly told me. She was there when the police cleared him."

"Well . . . ," Paul said, scooping up some curry, "that settles it, then. There was nothing sinister about Karen's death. Can we please just drop the subject?"

"Fine."

"But if the police come around again, call me."

"Fine!"

We finished our meal in angry silence, until Paul excused himself and went to his study. I loaded the dishwasher noisily, banging dishes and slamming cupboards with frustration. It annoyed me that Paul wouldn't even entertain the possibility that Karen's death was anything more than an accident. And even more annoying was his attitude toward my police interview. "Next time the cops come around, I want you to call me." Did he think I was such a bumbling fool that I would somehow implicate myself in Karen's death? Ha! He obviously didn't realize what a savvy woman he was married to. I was fast becoming a master at keeping secrets and feigning innocence. And in a couple of days, I could very well be taking my wealth of knowledge to the police. After my meeting with Javier, I would decide whether he needed to be turned over to the law. Paul would be eating his words when the police thanked me for my contribution to the case. I might even get an award or citation of some sort.

With the kitchen clean, I decided a long, soothing soak in the tub was in order. As I headed for the stairs, I poked my head briefly into my husband's office. "I'm going to have a bath," I said shortly, then turned to go.

"Hey," he called, his voice conciliatory.

I stuck my head back inside. "What?" I was not ready to forgive him yet.

"I'm sorry. I just . . . I just worry about you, that's all."

"Worry about what?"

He sighed heavily and rubbed his eyebrows with his fingers. "This whole thing with Karen . . . I don't know . . . you've been acting strangely ever since it happened."

"Of course I have. She was one of my best friends!"

"But it's like you're obsessed with the way . . ." He trailed off.

". . . With the way she . . . passed away."

"I'm not obsessed. I'm not. I just think . . ." Suddenly, my words were blocked by a lump of emotion, and tears obscured my vision.

"Hey . . . ," Paul said gently, moving toward me and enveloping me in a warm embrace. "It's okay, babe . . . It's okay."

I cried for a little while, soothed by my husband's soft words and warm hands on my back. When I had spent some of the sadness in me, I nuzzled into his neck. "Thank you," I murmured. "I love you."

"I love you, too."

Our faces turned inward, and our mouths found each other. We kissed for a while—at first, small, comforting pecks, which eventually grew in intensity and passion. "Let's go upstairs," Paul whispered into my hair.

It was only Monday, a night before I had planned our session of wild, uninhibited sex. But hey—just like Jane said, sometimes you had to be spontaneous. "Let's go," I whispered back.

CHAPTER 14

The sex was great, really, really great. It had been ages since Paul and I had had an encounter like that. It had been ages since we'd had any sort of encounter at all. My earlier attempts at resexualizing had all failed miserably, and since the tragedy across the street, I hadn't been in the mood. Paul had tried once, shortly after Karen died, but I had called him an insensitive prick and he had been fearful to approach me again. I had been so absorbed in my loss and the mystery surrounding my friend's demise that sex had dropped dramatically on my list of priorities.

But now . . . well, now any sexual hunger I'd had had been sated. How could it not be? We had done it for an hour and a half—which, in case you have not been married for twelve years, is a very long time. We did it all: fellatio, cunnilingus, even 69! We tried all the positions: missionary, girl on top, doggy-style, spoons . . . It was incredible! Crazy, even! It was just what I had needed. There was only one problem. The entire time, I had been thinking about Javier.

It had sneaked up on me. When we first entered our bedroom, I had been completely into Paul. I had been so happy that we were fi-nally reconnecting, thrilled that I was having intense, passionate feel-ings about my husband again. But suddenly—during *spoons,* I think it was—Javier popped into my brain. It was no longer Paul taking me from behind; it was a sexy Spanish lothario, with smoldering eyes and a chiseled jaw. "Oh, Javier!" I wanted to cry out. "Harder! Harder!" But I managed to refrain—at least from the "Oh, Javier" part.

I was not a prude. I knew it was completely normal, even healthy, to fantasize during sex. It wasn't like I hadn't done it dozens of times before. But previously, my fantasies had been focused on the completely unattainable: George Clooney, Mikhail Baryshnikov, and for a while, Joe Sakic—when the Colorado Avalanche was having a particularly good year. But I had not made it a habit to visualize real, everyday people while screwing my husband. Certainly not people who were my friends' lovers! Okay . . . once, Trudy's husband, Ken, had popped into my head during the act, but it had been more of a quick flash of his face than a full-blown fantasy. Obviously, this was not going to make it any easier to face Javier at tonight's art class.

Staring into the bathroom mirror, I painstakingly outlined my eyes in kohl pencil. I didn't normally wear a lot of eye makeup, but I felt my upcoming encounter called for some. Adding a coat of mas-cara, I took in my reflection. Too much: I looked like Cleopatra . . . or else Alice Cooper. Grabbing a Q-tip from the bathroom drawer, I proceeded to remove some of the dark liner. There . . . that was bet-ter. I hoped Paul didn't notice that I was heading to the Wild Rose Arts Center wearing full evening makeup. Who was I kidding? I could have pranced out of the house wearing a tinfoil bikini and Paul wouldn't have noticed. Although . . . after our Monday-night session, he might have become a little more tuned in.

Hair and makeup done, I moved to my bedroom to dress. At my lingerie drawer, I hesitated, just for a moment, before extracting the red water bra and G-string. It wasn't that I expected anyone to *see* me in this sexy underwear. It was a confidence thing. I remember reading a quote from some supermodel who said all women should wear sexy underwear to feel sexier. Normally, I did not put a lot of stock in the opinions of supermodels, but this one seemed to make sense. And since my intention was to get Javier to notice me, the illusion of big breasts couldn't hurt either.

Over the red ensemble, I slipped a formfitting black sheath dress and put on a pair of black knee-high stiletto boots. The leather boots were a constant source of buyer's remorse: they had been ridiculously expensive, and I'd had ridiculously little opportunity to wear them. But tonight, they were the perfect complement to my femme fatale look.

"Whit woo!" Spencer fake-whistled when I walked into the kitchen, where my children were finishing a dessert of chocolate ice cream. "You look so beautiful!"

"Thanks, sweet boy." I kissed his head.

"Why are you so dressed up?" Chloe asked, almost snidely, taking in my outfit.

"I'm not *so* dressed up," I replied, silently thanking God that she couldn't see the red underwear. "I just wanted to look nice. I'm going to my drawing class . . . and then maybe out for a bite to eat with some of the other . . . artists."

Chloe shrugged. "You look like you think you're going to the Academy Awards or something."

"No, I don't!" I cried. "It's not like I'm wearing a sequined ball gown. Sheesh!" Paul's key in the lock distracted me from Chloe's criticisms. I hurried to greet him.

"Wow," he said, taking in my appearance. "Where are you off to?"

"I've got my drawing class tonight, and then after, there's a cocktail reception for all the artists." I hated lying to my husband and daughter, but I was working a case, and it wouldn't be prudent to involve them.

He helped me into my long winter coat. "Well, have fun."

"I will," I said. And with a quick kiss for the children, I was on my way to meet Javier.

Somehow, I found myself in the arts center's parking lot twenty-five minutes later. The drive had been a blur, a swirling collage of erotic fantasies starring a certain nude model, punctuated by pragmatic pep talks about getting to the bottom of Karen's death. When I turned off the ignition, I felt prepared, steeled for what lay ahead. Javier was a suspect in my best friend's murder, not my potential boyfriend . . . or one-night stand . . . or passionate, slightly rough encounter in the arts center's boiler room. He was not, as Karen had said, irresistible—at least not to someone as sexually satisfied and strong-willed as me. No, I had a job to do. I was to interrogate him, using all my feminine wiles and intuition. If I could get him to break down and confess—great. If not, I would watch his every move, each gesture and subtle tic. *CSI* had taught me that there were several physical manifestations of guilt: darting eyes, dry mouth, fidgeting hands. One dart! One fidget! One urgent sip of water and I would be on the phone to Detective Portman.

I strode confidently into the classroom and found a vacant drawing horse. I was obviously overdressed, but I planned to casually mention that I was off to a cocktail party after class. There was no need to feel insecure or conspicuous. Clipping my pad of paper to the drawing board, I prepared to straddle the bench. Unfortunately, swinging my leg over in the fitted skirt was proving impossible. Shit! What was I going to do now? I could sense my composure slipping and a nervous, jittery feeling taking hold. I took a deep, calming breath. Okay, this had to be achievable. I couldn't be the only art student to show up in a short, tight skirt and high heels, could I? I looked around the room at my largely bohemian classmates. Could I?

Finally, I managed to mount the drawing horse by standing behind it and shimmying myself forward with small hopping movements. Not a very elegant or sophisticated approach, but at least Javier wasn't in the room yet. Once in place, I clasped my bare knees tightly to the piece of wood between them, my high-heeled feet splayed out beside me for balance. It was tricky, but if I didn't make any sudden movements, I felt sure I could hold my precarious position for the full hour.

As we waited for the class to begin, I leaned over to my neighbor. "I've got a cocktail party after this," I announced loudly.

"Oh." The woman with long gray hair, a hand-knit sweater, Birkenstock sandals, and socks did not seem interested.

Soon, our instructor, Allan, walked to the front of the room. "Good evening, class. Tonight, we're going to focus on contouring and shading. Whether drawing still life, landscape, or portraiture, light and darkness play . . ."

I tuned out. This didn't apply to me: I was on a serious mission.

"And now," Allan said, drawing my attention back to the platform. "I'd like to bring in tonight's model."

Despite my serious mission, my heart began to pound like a frightened rabbit. Calm down . . . , I told myself. You can do this. Do it for Karen . . . your dear friend . . . your dear, dead friend . . .

"Class, this is Amanda." A dark-haired young woman clad in a white robe padded in her bare feet to the platform.

What?! Where was Javier?! Who the hell was this . . . tart?! Somehow, I refrained from jumping up and screaming it audibly. This was probably because my knees remained in a vice grip on the drawing horse, lest I provide Allan and the model with an excellent view of my transparent red G-string panties. But no matter how dejected I felt, I could not fall apart. Instead, I swallowed the lump of disappointment in my throat and breathed deeply to quell the slightly panicky feeling in my chest. Hopefully, no one had noticed the dismayed flush in my cheeks and the thin veil of perspiration covering my forehead. It was highly unlikely, as Amanda had now dropped the robe to reveal her annoyingly perfect human form. She had obviously not breast-fed anyone.

"All right, artists," Allan announced. "Amanda will begin with a one-minute seated pose."

There was nothing I could do. I couldn't flee—at least, not quickly, given my impractical outfit. I was forced to sit there, sketching the perfect curve of Amanda's stupid, perfect back. But by the end of the hour, I had several half decent sketches—maybe not very good compared to my classmates' but a huge improvement over last week's drawings of Javier. And more important, I had come up with a "plan B." When I left the house tonight, I had been intent on a meeting with Karen's former lover. The evening had definitely thrown me a curveball, but I was flexible, capable, working my case . . . I was not going to give up that easily. When Amanda had covered her flawlessness and most of the artists had packed away their paraphernalia, I approached our instructor.

"Hi, Allan." I smiled warmly and extended my hand. "I'm a new student, Paige Atwell."

He took my hand. "Hi, Paige. You started last week, didn't you?"

"Yes. I've been . . . out of town, so I started late."

"Great. Well, welcome. Do you have an artistic background of some sort?"

I took this as a compliment. "No, actually, this is my first art class ever. I didn't even take it in high school."

"It's good to develop new interests later in life."

I took this as an insult but decided it was time to get to the point. "So . . . I had been hoping to see Javier here tonight."

He gave me a knowing smile, as if he heard this from a lot of his "later in life" female students. "Javier and Amanda both pose regularly for the class. Javier was working tonight."

"Right . . . right . . . ," I said, as if Javier had told me he'd be at his other job. "What's the name of the coffee shop he works at again? It's slipped my mind."

"The Old Grind."

"Right. That's it, The Old Grind. Yeah . . . The Old Grind in uh . . . ?"

"Cherry Creek."

"Of course! The Old Grind in Cherry Creek . . . right, right, right. I might pop by there—before the cocktail party I'm going to," I added, indicating my outfit with a sheepish grin.

Allan continued to nod and smile. It was difficult to discern whether he was just a nice, friendly man or whether he found my pursuit of Javier amusing. I had to admit, it did not look good: a woman my age, dressed to the nines, ferreting out information on the whereabouts of a gorgeous nude model. I decided to do some damage control. "It's just that I have a message for Javier . . . from a mutual friend . . . from Spain. She just called me yesterday—from Spain—and she asked if I'd be seeing Javier. I told her I'd be seeing him at art class and that I'd be happy to pass on the message, . . . which is fairly urgent and . . . , y'know, all the way from Spain."

"Well . . . ," Allan said, "that's very nice of you to take the message to him." His smile was confusing. He was either impressed by my kindness or found my story comical.

"I'd better be off," I said. "See you next week." I already knew I'd probably be too embarrassed to show up.

I drove to Cherry Creek like a woman possessed. I had to get there quickly or I'd chicken out and head home. My mind raced, a multitude of thoughts playing in my head like a tape on fast-forward. . . . *Must find Javier . . . Must interrogate him . . . get to the bottom of this whole mess . . . He's not that good-looking . . . certainly not irresistible . . .* After much driving around the neighborhood in aimless circles, I finally found The Old Grind. Once I'd parked the SUV a block and a half away, I hopped out and tottered briskly toward the coffee shop. It wasn't until I was mere steps away from the building that I paused. Did I really want to do this? Was I getting in over my head? My cell phone was in my purse, as was Detective Portman's card. I could call him right now, apologize for not mentioning it before, but tell him there was someone he should speak to—a *person of interest,* I think they called it. I would tell him about Karen and Javier's affair and ask him, very sweetly, not to tell Doug unless it was absolutely necessary. He seemed like a nice guy. We'd had some sort of rapport. I'm sure he'd understand my efforts to protect my friend's reputation.

My hand dug inside my bag and searched fruitlessly for the phone. This moment of difficulty gave me pause to reflect. Would Portman even be at the office at this hour? A glance at my watch told me it was almost nine thirty. And what about that jerk Conroy? Portman might keep Karen's dalliance under wraps, but I doubted his partner would be as sensitive. My hand stopped its frantic search. No . . . I couldn't call for backup just yet. I would have to do this on my own.

CHAPTER 15

The coffee shop was on the corner, attached to a number of trendy shops and restaurants. I entered the long, narrow space and was immediately assaulted by a blast of warm air and the pungent aroma of coffee beans. The room was nearly deserted, save for two tables near the front window occupied by a well-dressed middle-aged couple and a college student with his laptop. I stayed near the door at first, unbuttoning my coat in the sudden heat. It had been stupid not to rehearse my next move, but I also knew it wasn't wise to overthink it. Even at this moment, I was seriously considering turning around and running back to my car.

But I didn't. I slowly entered the room, heading methodically toward the counter. I hadn't seen Javier yet, but I knew he was there. The sounds of cups rattling and an espresso filter being banged free of its contents signaled his presence. Even if he had been silent, I would have sensed it was him. It was like his being gave off some kind of electric current that found its way to me. I approached the counter and stopped. My heart was beating loudly in my throat.

Javier looked up, probably alerted by my audible pulse. A slow smile of familiarity spread across his sensual lips.

"Hi."

"Hi."

"Can I help you?" His accent was to die for! Not that he was irresistible or anything.

"Yes . . ." I cleared my throat. "I'll have a . . . hmm . . ." I decided to order something time-consuming to allow me to compose myself. "I'll have a decaf, soy milk, cappuccino . . . dry, please . . . and extrahot."

"No problem." His eyes twinkled at me.

Resist! I ordered myself. Don't succumb to his sexy accent and smoldering eyes! Think of Karen . . . Think of Karen lying in a pool of her own blood . . . likely put there by the very hands that are currently making your coffee!

"I know you, don't I?" Javier's voice over the coffee machine interrupted my internal ranting.

"Umm . . . ?" I leaned forward, as if looking at him closely for the first time. "You do look familiar . . ."

"You are an artist." It was a statement, not a question.

"Well . . . yes, I've been taking a class . . ." I paused, feigning sudden recognition. "Are you the model I was drawing the other week?"

"Yes. That is me." He put down the milk he had been steaming and extended his hand. "Javier."

I took it. It was warm and strong and calloused just enough. Dammit! Okay, okay . . . visualize Karen lying dead in a pool of blood . . . "Paige," I managed to croak out.

"You live near here, . . . Paige?" Oh, the way he said my name.

"No . . . I have a . . . umm cocktail party to attend in the area. I thought I'd pop in for a quick caffeine jolt to keep me awake. You know those boring formal cocktail parties."

"You ordered decaf, no?"

Shit! "Oh, I don't think so. Did I? I meant to order regular espresso. I'm sorry. Oh, you've already made it. I'll drink the decaf. No problem."

"No, I will make another."

"Really? I don't want to be any trouble."

"No trouble. I don't want you to fall asleep at your party."

"...Thanks."

Javier tipped the decaf down the sink and began tamping grounds into the filter for another cappuccino. I knew this replacement coffee would keep me up all night, but something told me I wouldn't be able to sleep anyway. At least, this had bought me a little time to converse with him. The Old Grind did not have stools at the coffee bar where you could sit and chat with your friendly barista. Once my drink was ready, I'd be relegated to one of the small wooden tables near the front, and my opportunity would be over. I had to act fast.

"So . . . I was just thinking . . . ," I said, over the whir of the steaming milk.

"Yes?" He looked at me, his eyes playful.

"I think we have a mutual friend." Even as I said it, I knew it sounded contrived.

"Really?" He turned off the steam. "Who?"

"Karen Sutherland."

There was no reaction. He turned his face away and focused on preparing my beverage. After a long silence, he slid the coffee toward me and looked me in the eyes. His were dark, unreadable. "I was very sad when I heard of her death."

"Me, too."

"She was a beautiful young woman. It is always sad when someone dies too soon."

"It is." I could feel myself softening under his gaze, and I knew I was no longer being a fair and impartial investigator. I had to snap out of it. "Did you know her well?" I asked, forcing a casual tone.

"Not too well. She was in the drawing class. We talked . . . We had coffee a few times."

"She talked about you . . . to me." I lowered my voice to a whisper. "Only to me . . ."

His face remained impassive.

"I was hoping we could talk . . . about Karen." With this statement, I was completely erasing the façade of just popping in for a caffeine jolt on my way to a nearby cocktail party—but he might have figured that out when I ordered the decaf anyway. Before Javier could answer, the college student approached the counter.

"Hey, man," the scruffy young guy said, "can I get a refill and one of those scone things?"

"Sure." He looked at me. "You will wait?"

"I will."

I found a table as close to the counter as possible but facing out toward the front entrance. I sipped my coffee, staring at the darkened streetscape, intensely aware of Javier's presence behind me—his every move as he poured the coffee, heated the scone thing, and loaded some cups into the dishwasher. My initial feeling was that he was innocent in Karen's demise. He was calm when questioned about her: no fidgeting, swallowing, or blinking. And his sadness at her loss seemed sincere. But was my intense physical attraction to him clouding my judgment? I mean, if Johnny Depp murdered someone, would I instantly believe his story, too?

It was imperative that I retain my focus. I took a deep, calming breath and did a visualization exercise: *Karen in a pool of blood . . . Paul's face on our wedding day . . . the children, laughing and eating Popsicles . . . Paul's love handles and back hair*—oops!

The sound of Javier pulling out the chair across from me brought my attention back to the room. When he was seated, facing me, I noticed that his features had turned cold and stony. God, maybe he *was* capable of murder?

"So . . . ," he said, "you came here to talk about Karen?"

I decided to take a direct approach. I cleared my throat. "Yes. Karen told me about . . . your relationship. I felt I needed to meet you . . . to talk to you . . ."

"Why?"

To figure out if you killed her. Obviously, I couldn't be that direct. "Karen loved you," I said.

"Well"—he leaned back in his chair—"Karen was a very nice woman, but she was confused."

"How?"

"She did not love me. She thought she loved me."

"Uh . . . what's the difference?"

"She was unhappy with her husband. She said he was boring and . . . —what is the word?—*predictable.*"

"Yeah . . ."

"I spent time with her. I listened to her . . ." He shrugged, as if drawing an incredibly obvious conclusion. "She thinks she love me."

I was confused, flustered . . . "So you're saying that you and Karen didn't have a . . . *physical* relationship?"

"No."

"You were not having wild, passionate sex with her?"

"No. We were friends. I think that the sex was, maybe, her fantasy."

Well, who could blame her? It was mine as well. But had Karen made up the whole affair? Could she really have been that delusional? She had been so convincing. I mean, she was considering leaving her husband for this guy, this . . . *friend.* I looked at Javier. The kindness had returned to his face as he sensed my inner turmoil. He reached out and took my hand in his rough, manly one.

"I am sorry," he said. "It hurts you to hear this."

"I just . . . She said . . ."

His fingers stroked the back of my hand in what was intended to be a soothing manner. Unfortunately, it was turning me on. "I know that women can sometimes be very lonely," he said. "My mother, in Spain, she was a very lonely woman. My father left us when I was a little boy. She was sad for a long, long time. She had only my sisters and me to love."

Oh God. He cared about his lonely mother. He *was* becoming irresistible. I could almost see myself concocting a rich fantasy in which Javier and I were carrying on a passionate affair and would soon run away together to live on love and canned spaghetti.

"When she died," Javier continued, "I came to America. But I always remember that look in her eyes. I saw that look in Karen's eyes. I wanted to help her, to make her feel happy. I did not want to . . ."— he paused for a moment, searching for the phrase—"to led her on?"

"*Lead* her on." I corrected his grammar out of maternal habit.

"Yes, lead her on. I did not want to do that."

"Well"—I managed to slip my hand from his grasp—"she told me you were in love. She told me she was thinking of leaving Doug for you."

He did not blink or twitch. "No. If she left her husband, it would not be for me."

I didn't know how to respond. He was basically telling me that one of my closest friends had lied to me, that Karen had concocted an elaborate, imaginary life to battle the suburban doldrums. When I had decided to meet with Javier, I wasn't sure what to expect: a vehement denial? a confession? But not this bizarre explanation! This virtual stranger was asking me to doubt the sanity of my close friend. And the most disturbing part was: I believed him. I stood up. "Well, thanks for taking the time to talk to me."

He stood, too. "You're welcome."

"I'll let you get back to work."

"There is no problem. I make you another coffee?"

"Oh, no, no." I waved my hand. "I've got to get going."

"To your party?" There was a twinkle of amusement in his eyes.

"I think I'll skip it."

"Well . . . It was nice to see you again, . . . Paige."

I wished he would stop saying my name like that. "Yes . . . you, too." I busied myself buttoning my coat.

"Will I see you next week, at drawing class?"

There was no need for me to go. My attendance had only confirmed the fact that I had very little artistic ability. I had met with Javier, and though I had yet to form a conclusion about his guilt or innocence, I had completed my mission. I also knew it was a very, *very* bad idea to see him naked again. "I don't know . . . ," I said. "I don't think so."

"I hope you will come. Or come have coffee with me again."

"Oh my goodness!" I started. "I didn't even pay you for the coffee. I'm sorry." With trembling hands, I dug in my purse for my wallet. A comb and a tampon spilled out onto the floor. Dammit! I bent to retrieve them. God, I had to get out of here. I righted myself and proffered Javier five dollars.

He shook his head and smiled sexily. "It is my treat . . . if you promise to come back?"

"Maybe."

"I was sad about my friend," he said. "It makes me feel better to talk to you."

"Okay . . . maybe." I turned on my heel and hurried out of the café.

I maneuvered the SUV through the darkened city streets and finally onto the highway. Alone in the darkness of the vehicle, I battled a heavy feeling of malaise. Meeting with Javier was supposed to bring clarity, but instead, I felt more confused than ever. I had also expected to feel some sense of accomplishment: I had met with Karen's lover and could now report my findings to the police. But what was there to report? Karen had coffee a few times with a sexy barista and then imagined a passionate affair with him. I couldn't let that get out. It was more embarrassing than having a *real* affair.

But as I gained more distance from The Old Grind and neared Aberdeen Mists, a new, niggling feeling surfaced in my mind: doubt. Had Javier just played me for a fool? Was he well aware of his power over women? Could he make us believe anything he wanted with stories of his lonely childhood in Spain and his sad-eyed mother? Maybe Karen and Javier really had been lovers? Maybe he had actually killed her? Maybe I had just been duped?

CHAPTER 16

I slept fitfully that night. When I did doze off, I had disturbing dreams starring Karen wearing a large blond wig and smeared red lipstick. But most of the time, I lay awake, listening to Paul's annoying, regular breathing and thinking about what Javier had told me. In the stillness of the night, my confusion seemed almost unbearable. I hoped things would look clearer in the morning.

They didn't, but thankfully, there was little time to dwell on the subject. I had slept late, which meant a frantic scramble to get my children dressed, fed, washed, and loaded into the car for the commute to Rosedale. As we sat in our driveway, the SUV idling, I did a quick mental checklist: lunches were packed, Spencer's field-trip form was signed, Chloe's homework was initialed and in her bag . . . We had done quite well considering the time constraints. And despite my foul, sleep-deprived mood, I hadn't even raised my voice. I put the vehicle into reverse and began to back out of the driveway.

"STOP!" Chloe shrieked from the backseat.

I slammed on the brakes in panic, thinking I was about to run over the neighbor's dog or small child. "What?" I screeched.

"I forgot the Jessica Simpson CD I was supposed to bring to lend to Alexandra!"

"Chloe!" I whirled on her. "Do you really think a friggin' Jessica Simpson CD warrants a scream like that?"

"God," she pouted, "you don't need to swear at me."

"What are you talking about? I didn't swear."

"You said *frigging*. Like, duh?"

"*Frigging* is not a swear word, young lady," I retorted. "It is a swear *replacement*. Now, if you want to get the friggin' CD, I suggest you hurry up."

She scurried into the house and was back within minutes, but we were already going to be late. I had just reached the wrought-iron gates exiting our community when Spencer said hesitantly, "Ummm . . . Mom?"

"Yes?"

"I forgot my friggin' reader."

Finally, after depositing my offspring at school, albeit twelve minutes late, I returned to the solace of my empty house. I felt exhausted, irritable, and still confused about last night's conversation. A cup of tea, some couch time, and a little mindless *Regis and Kelly* viewing seemed to be in order. I desperately needed a break from contemplating Karen's real or imagined affair and her accidental or homicidal death. As I filled the kettle, I checked the phone messages. There was one from Jane. Putting the kettle on the burner, I called her back.

"I want you to come over for coffee," she said. "I'm going to invite Trudy and Carly, too."

"Now?" The soft and welcoming couch seemed to beckon me.

"At around ten," she said. "It's about time we all got together like we used to. Karen wouldn't have wanted our friendship to fall apart because of her accident."

"Okay. I'll see you at ten."

I was the first to arrive at Jane's palatial home. Okay, *palatial* was probably too strong a word, but *grand* wasn't. They had built the six-thousand-square-foot home two years ago to Jane's exacting standards. While Karen's home was like an upscale version of all the others in our suburb, Jane's was in a different league. It perched, alone, on the top of a hill overlooking the rest of Aberdeen Mists. There was something regal about the McKinnon abode. It was like the *king* house, the rest of our homes its lowly subjects.

"Hi!" Jane opened the door and *mwa-mwa*'d both my cheeks. I stepped into her grand entryway, which, unlike mine, the name actually befitted. "Let me take your coat," she said, carrying it to a vast coat closet.

"The place looks great," I said, gazing around. It was a pointless comment. The place always looked great, thanks to Becca and the Wednesday team from Merry Maids. I turned to Jane. "You look great, too." Again, a completely unnecessary compliment, but she was looking particularly pretty in her white cashmere sweater and slim, dark denim jeans.

"Thanks. You look . . . really tired, actually." She took my hand. "Are you okay?"

"Oh, fine." I laughed away her concern. "I just had a terrible sleep. I made the mistake of having caffeine at about nine o'clock last night."

"You silly thing. Come, I've got coffee brewing, and Becca made a low-fat key lime pie this morning before she took Ainsley to preschool and Amelia to her swimming lesson."

I waited in the resplendent kitchen, nursing my coffee while Jane welcomed first Trudy and then Carly. We sat at the massive, hand-hewn oak table, set with sunny yellow place mats and blue and white Tiffany bone china. Our hostess cut us each a slice of low-fat pie and then joined us. "Okay," Jane said, when she had taken her seat, "there are a few rules for this morning."

"Rules for coffee?" Carly laughed, looking from Trudy to me.

"Yes," Jane continued. "This is to be a happy gathering. We can talk about Karen, of course, but there is to be no crying. We should honor her memory by reminiscing about the good parts of her life, not the sad ending."

"Agreed," we chorused, holding our coffee cups up in a sort of toast.

"So . . . ," Jane said, "what's new with everyone?"

There was not a lot new, or so it seemed to me. Carly and Trudy talked extensively about the Karen Sutherland Alternative Infertility Treatment charity. Trudy also mentioned Cameron's supporting role as boy number three in the Young People's Theater production of Oliver Twist and Emily's leap to grade-five piano.

"Good for them," Jane said exuberantly. "And what about you, Carly? Any luck tracking down the Diet Coke man?"

"No," Carly said, with a small shrug of her shoulders. "But I'm okay with it. If it was meant to be, I would have found him again. That's one thing Karen's death has taught me."

"What?" I asked, looking up from my pie. "What has it taught you?"

"Well . . . ," Carly said, "that we can't necessarily control our destiny. I think our lives are already mapped out for us. We don't know who we'll meet, who we'll fall in love with, or even when we'll die. Karen's short life inspired me to take each day as it comes and not put so much pressure on myself to find a man. I have a feeling that when the time is right, he'll look up and I'll be standing right there in front of him. "

"That's very accepting of you," Trudy said kindly.

"Or fatalistic," Jane chimed in. "I don't know, Carly. You make it sound like we have no control at all. We make choices, choices that define who we become, our happiness and success . . ."

"I agree that we have choice in our lives . . . ," Carly was saying, but I could feel myself losing interest in their existential debate. My mind slipped back to Javier's revelation about Karen's fantasy life as I waited for a break in the conversation. Then, mustering my courage, I addressed the group.

"How did Karen seem to you . . . before she died?"

There was a long pause. My friends were obviously taken aback by the abrupt change of subject.

"What do you mean?" Trudy asked.

"Well, you know . . . ," I said, "did she seem happy? Content? . . . *Sane?*"

"She seemed very happy," Carly said. "It gives me some peace to know that she was in a good place, mentally and emotionally, when she passed."

"I thought she seemed fine," Jane said. "I know she was some-times frustrated about not getting pregnant, but otherwise . . ." She trailed off with a shrug.

"So . . . she never said anything . . . *strange* to any of you?"

"Strange how?"

"I don't know, just . . . weird or out of character?"

"Why?" Carly asked. "Did she say something to you?"

"Not really," I said. "But I thought she seemed kind of . . . *discontent* with her life in Aberdeen Mists, just a little . . . out of sorts during the weeks before the accident."

"No," Jane said, "I can't think of anything."

Trudy, who had been silent up until now, finally spoke. "Well . . . ," she began hesitantly, "there was one thing I took as a lit-tle . . . odd."

"What?" I leaned toward her across the massive table.

"She asked me if I'd ever thought about living a simpler existence—like buying a small apartment, getting a cheap little car, spending less on clothes . . ."

"Oh my God!" Jane said, as if this were the craziest thing she'd ever heard. "Why would she say that?"

"I don't know," Trudy replied. "Of course, I told her that I felt blessed to have this life, but she was really on this *simplifying* kick. She was even talking about leaving Aberdeen Mists!"

"No!" Jane said. "And going where?"

"She didn't say, exactly . . . , but she mentioned Europe."

"Europe?" Carly asked.

"Europe." Trudy nodded.

"Did she say where in Europe?" I asked. "France? Spain, maybe?"

"Yes . . . I think it was one of those."

"Of course it was one of those," Jane said. "People don't dream of running off to Germany or Belgium do they?"

"I suppose not," Trudy said, "unless they really love beer . . . or waffles."

We all laughed, but my mind was preoccupied with Karen's admission to Trudy. She had obviously been thinking a lot about fleeing Doug and her suburban existence, but what did that mean? Was her relationship with Javier the real thing? Had he promised to whisk her away to Spain to save her the humiliation of facing all the perfect, happily married Aberdeen Misters? Or was she just bored and discontent, and running off to Spain with her dream boy was merely wishful thinking?

Jane's voice brought me back to the table. "Maybe Karen wasn't as happy as we all thought."

"Yes, she was," Carly said vehemently. "I spent the most time with her, and she was happy . . . very happy. She may have been a little frustrated, sitting around at home waiting to get pregnant, but she loved her life. She loved Doug." No one said anything for a long moment. Carly added, "He has an airtight alibi, you know."

"We know," I said.

"Of course." Trudy nodded vigorously.

Jane jumped in. "No one's saying Doug *killed* her, but maybe their marriage wasn't as picture-perfect as we'd all believed."

"Well, whose is?" This came, surprisingly, from Trudy. She instantly noticed our eyebrows raised in surprise. "I'm just saying that no matter how solid your marriage, everyone occasionally daydreams of running off to the south of France with some muscular young mailman."

I gasped. "You mean Leon!"

"No!" She blushed. "I was being hypothetical. I could just as easily have said muscular young . . . meter reader."

I pointed at her. "You *do* mean Leon!"

"Leon has great legs," Jane said.

"Particularly his calves," I added.

"He's twelve years old!" Carly cried.

"He's twenty-four," Trudy said. "Not that it matters because I wasn't talking about him specifically." She was beginning to sound a little flustered.

"Okay . . . I'm sorry," I said, patting her hand, "but you're right. Everyone has fantasies now and again."

"That's right," Jane seconded. "Even if you are happy, there's not a woman in the world who doesn't occasionally wonder about a different kind of life . . . a different kind of man."

"True." I nodded.

"So . . . Karen was probably perfectly happy," Carly said. "I mean, you three have it all, and you still have fantasies."

We all agreed that this was true. Fantasizing about living in a small apartment in Europe did not necessarily mean Karen had been seriously unhappy with her current existence. With that subject exhausted, we returned to more lighthearted banter: how Chloe was adjusting to being a bespectacled sideshow attraction, Becca's recipe for low-fat key lime pie (the secret was ricotta cheese), and the Foundation of Success's annual fund-raising craft sale . . . Before we knew it, Becca had arrived with Jane's two Ralph Lauren–clad daughters, signaling that it was time to go.

When I got home, I felt more lighthearted than I had since the tragedy. Jane had been right: it was important to keep up our coffee tradition in Karen's absence. She would have wanted us to go on. In fact, our coffee klatch was kind of an homage to her. Going to my pantry, I grabbed the two family-sized cans of soup and took them to the living room. Flicking on *The Young and the Restless,* I lay on my back and began working my pectoral muscles. It had been weeks since I'd felt motivated to tackle the Life Makeover list. Of course, lifting the soup cans was just a baby step, but still . . . It was a good sign that I was on the road to recovering my normal life.

As I lifted the cans and watched Malcolm (returned from the dead with really unfortunate cornrows) argue with his former lover/ sister-in-law, a realization crept over me. My carefree mood had to be attributed to more than just a good chat with girlfriends. In fact, I almost felt like I'd had an epiphany of sorts. Trudy's confession had been the trigger. If even perfect Trudy fantasized about running off with Leon—or, rather, some anonymous hottie—then perhaps Karen's make-believe affair with Javier wasn't so strange after all. I had feared my belief in his story was a result of my own gullibility, my weakness for attractive, sensual men, but now I realized he was probably telling the truth. We all had these momentary flashes of a passionate, exciting life outside the confines of suburbia. It was completely understandable. And the only difference between our fantasies and Karen's was that she had told me her amazing love affair was real. She'd told a little fib. So what? It probably made her feel happy to talk about it as if it were actually happening to her. I was glad to have brightened her final days by playing along.

Victor Newman walked out on Nikki for the three thousandth time, and I breathed a deep sigh of relief. I felt as though at last I could stop clinging to my doubts and suspicions and close the door on the mystery of Karen's death. It was just as Paul had said: a freak accident. It was just as everyone had said: everyone but silly, paranoid me. I could let it go. There was no need to ponder the circumstances of Karen's death, to question Doug's alibi, or to think about Javier . . . at all. I was finally free!

CHAPTER 17

This sense of lighthearted freedom lasted through the weekend and
on until Thursday. I was patient and fun-loving with the children,
kind and affectionate with Paul. On Saturday night, back on sched-
ule, my husband and I made love. It was very nice. Javier did make
an appearance in my mind's eye, but I no longer felt guilty about it.
Now fantasizing about Javier was no different than fantasizing about
George Clooney. Since I had decided to drop the art class, there was
no fear I'd be running into either one of them.

I would focus, with renewed vigor, on making over my life. Of
course, I had neglected this project ever since Karen's terrible accident, but now that I had put it behind me, I could take great strides.
There would continue to be moments of sadness, I knew that, but
her death no longer consumed me. I was at peace . . . , and it was
time to figure out what would make me happy.

A soul-nourishing hobby would be an excellent start. I flicked
through the Wild Rose Arts Center's flyer. Drawing was out, obviously. Unfortunately, my lack of artistic ability extended to most

other visual media as well. But the arts center also offered a number of dance classes: jazz, salsa, Highland dancing . . . Maybe that was the answer? As I recalled, I had shown a natural flair when I took ballet back in kindergarten. Yes, dance would be a good choice! I would be expressing myself creatively and getting in shape! Why hadn't I thought of it before? It was like killing two birds with one stone. And then, the phone rang.

"Ms. Atwell?"

"Yes?"

"It's Detective Portman calling from the Denver Police Department."

"Oh . . . hello." I was startled.

"I was wondering if I could come and talk to you?"

My husband's words flitted through my head—something about calling him and getting a lawyer if the police showed up again. "Sure," I said. "When?"

"I could be at your place within the hour."

"Fine. I'll see you then."

As I freshened up to meet with Detective Portman, my mind raced through the possible reasons for his visit. Had they found something fishy while investigating Karen's death? I didn't want to believe it. It felt so good to let go of my doubts and suspicions, to accept that Karen had simply fallen and hit her head. But as I put on a coat of mascara and some sheer berry lip gloss, I couldn't think of any other reason. Unless . . . unless our meeting was more personal in nature? I had sensed something between Portman and me that day—call it chemistry, mutual attraction, what have you . . . It hadn't been particularly intense on my part, certainly nothing I would have acted upon, but maybe it had been more pronounced for him? He hadn't mentioned bringing Detective Conroy along. I went into my bedroom and put on the water bra.

Dressed and made up, I took in my reflection in the full-length mirror. I didn't look too bad. The weeks of anxiety had taken something of a toll, but I was regaining my healthy glow. With this subtle, yet enhancing makeup, one would never know I'd just been through the wringer. And of course, my breasts looked fantastic. I felt a quick twinge of something uncomfortable—like guilt. I shook it off. I wasn't doing anything *wrong* wearing a water bra to meet with a cop. It just boosted my confidence . . . along with my tiny boobs. And it wasn't like he was going to find out the sad truth about them.

I skipped down the stairs and into the kitchen intent on finding something to do that would make me look busy and interesting. I could organize the cupboards? Busy but definitely not interesting. Or . . . I could bake something? Yes, baking would make me look busy, interesting, and charmingly domestic. Portman obviously liked to eat. Opening the fridge, I peered inside.

I would turn him down when he expressed his true feelings, of course. He was an attractive man but certainly not irresistible. "I'm flattered," I would say. "But my marriage is important to me. I'm sorry if you somehow got the impression that I might be available. What? I'm everything you ever dreamed of? Well, I'm sorry, but . . . Oh, please don't cry . . ."

The doorbell rang, startling me. I closed the fridge door and scurried to the front of the house. A quick glance in the hall mirror, a fluff of the hair, and I was ushering the detective into my grand entryway.

"Thanks for seeing me on such short notice," he said.

"Oh, it's no problem." He looked just as cute as he had at our previous meeting but was dressed a little more casually. Oh God. Was he visiting me on his day off? This could be serious. "Would you like some coffee, Detective Portman?"

"Coffee sounds great . . . And call me Troy." He followed me to the kitchen.

We made small talk while the coffee brewed. I tried to put him at ease; it couldn't be easy to admit these kinds of feelings to a married woman. Finally, when we were seated at the kitchen table facing each other, I decided it was time to cut to the chase. "So . . . ," I said, "what did you want to see me about, *Troy?*"

He cleared his throat nervously. "Well . . . I'm breaking department protocol by coming here today, but there's something I felt the need to share with you."

"Okay." I would be firm but gentle in my rejection.

"We received a letter."

"A letter?"

"An anonymous letter about Karen Sutherland's death."

Oh my God! I was so shocked that I barely felt the bruise to my ego. "Wh-what does it say?"

He reached into the inside pocket of his sports coat. "We're not supposed to show this kind of evidence to potential witnesses," he said, withdrawing a folded piece of paper inside a resealable plastic bag, "but I've got a feeling that you might be able to help. We've questioned a lot of Ms. Sutherland's friends, and you seem the most . . . *tuned in* to what was going on with her."

"Well . . . thanks." He shook the letter out of its bag and onto the table, gingerly opening it with the tip of his finger. Without using my hands, I leaned forward to read. It was written in pencil, using block, almost childlike letters. It said:

TO THE POLICE,

I WAS A FRIEND OF KAREN SUTHERLAND'S. I WAS WITH HER WHEN SHE DIED. WE HAD ARGUED, BUT I DID NOT HURT HER. I AM NOT A VIOLENT MAN. SHE TURNED AWAY FROM ME AND LOST HER BALANCE. SHE HIT HER HEAD ON A METAL TOOLBOX. IT WAS A TERRIBLE ACCIDENT, NOTHING MORE. I CANNOT GET INVOLVED, FOR CERTAIN REASONS, SO THAT IS WHY I AM WRITING TO YOU. DO NOT WASTE ANY MORE OF THE AMERICAN PEOPLE'S MONEY INVESTIGATING HER DEATH.

"What do you think?" Portman asked when I sat back in my chair, my face pale with shock.

"I-I don't know what to think."

"Any idea who might have written this?"

Oh, I had an idea, all right . . . So why wasn't I sharing it? "Not off the top of my head. I'll need some time to process it."

"Okay," Portman said, flipping the note closed with his pen and sliding it back into the bag. "We've analyzed the handwriting, but it's virtually impossible to trace a note written in pencil and block lettering. But there are a few obvious conclusions we can draw from this letter."

"Like . . . ?"

"It was written by a male, probably a foreigner."

"A foreigner?"

"His reference to 'wasting the American people's money.' A citizen would have said something like 'the taxpayers' money.' And he says he can't come forward for 'certain reasons.' It's likely an immigration issue."

I nodded my agreement. "But . . . could the note be true? Could Karen's death have been a simple accident?"

"The autopsy was inconclusive. We know her head wound was caused by a fall, but a wound that severe usually has some force behind it."

"Meaning?"

"Meaning she may have been pushed."

"Jesus . . ."

Troy Portman tucked the note back into his inside pocket and took a final sip of coffee. "Well . . . I'll let you get back to your baking."

"Yes, my baking . . ." I stood and escorted him to the front door.

"So . . ." He paused, his hand on the door handle. "You'll call me if you think of anything? You've still got my card?"

"Yep, I've got it. I'll give you a call if I have any ideas."

"Thanks again for your time, Paige." He smiled, and I caught the subtlest hint of flirtation. But suddenly, playing horny housewife-meets-hot-policeman was the furthest thing from my mind.

"You're welcome." He turned to go, but I stopped him. "Umm . . . have you tested the paternity of Karen's baby?"

"You knew she was pregnant?"

I explained about Janet Lawson's orange-poppy-seed-loaf delivery and the ensuing slipup.

"And you have reason to believe that the child was not Doug Sutherland's?"

"Well, I don't really know . . . Maybe it was, but wouldn't it be a good idea to check?"

"I'll look into it. We can perform a paternity test on a deceased fetus if it's older than six weeks."

I felt my stomach churn at his words. "I should go," I said shakily.

"I'm sorry if I've upset you." He reached out and squeezed my hand, a rather intimate gesture, but I took little notice.

"I'll be fine. I'll call you." And I shut the door.

But I was not fine, not at all. The last few days of solace and peace of mind had come to a gut-wrenching end. I didn't want to fall back into the abyss of doubt and suspicion, but I was already there. The note had obviously been written by Javier, so why hadn't I turned him over to the police? I couldn't put my finger on it, but I felt something for him, something strangely . . . protective. Until I knew more, I couldn't offer him to the cops on a silver platter. If I did, he'd be deported, at the very least.

My mind raced over the contents of the missive. It sounded entirely plausible to me. Javier must have gone to talk to Karen about her unhealthy obsession with him. They'd exchanged words, and in the heat of the argument, she'd turned and toppled over. Pregnant women were notoriously clumsy. And like Paul had said, freak accidents happen all the time. On the other hand, I couldn't discount the information I'd gleaned from the *CSI* team: the leading cause of death in pregnant women is murder by the baby's father. I'd call Detective Portman in a few days to check on the results of that paternity test.

I was going to have to see Javier again; there was no other option. God, I really didn't want to. It was much better when he was nothing more than a sexual figment of my imagination, the star of my own mental dirty movie. But I had to get the truth out of him somehow. And if I couldn't? Well, then I would have to turn him over to Detective Portman.

The phone rang, startling me. I almost let it ring, afraid it might be Paul. I wasn't sure I could hide my anguish from him, but I knew I'd have to. If he found out the police had been here again, I'd face another one of his boring lectures. But on the other hand, it could be the school calling to tell me one or more of my children had a broken arm or a fractured skull. I picked up.

"Hello?"

"Paige Atwell?"

"Yes?"

"This is Marion Chambers calling from Rosedale Elementary."

Spencer's teacher! Oh God! What's happened to my baby? When I spoke, I managed to sound relatively calm. "Is Spencer all right? Is everything okay?"

"Spencer's fine," she assured me, "but I would like to discuss some concerns I have about him."

"Okay," I said weakly.

"It's nothing to panic over at this stage, but I'd like to meet as soon as possible."

"When?"

"The children have their music class first thing in the morning. I'd have some time to speak to you then."

"Great," I croaked. "I'll be there."

When I hung up the phone, I immediately dissolved into tears. It was all too much for me to bear. I had been so absorbed in Karen's case that I had been shirking my duties as a mother. I had been distant, distracted . . . And when I *was* paying attention to the children, I had been snappish and irritable. Spencer had obviously developed some serious personality disorder due to maternal neglect and moodiness. Marion Chambers was undoubtedly going to tell me that he'd been throwing rocks at cats or torturing squirrels. Nothing to panic about yet but a sure sign that he was well on his way to becoming a serial killer.

I allowed myself to weep unabashedly for ten or twelve minutes before I dried my tears. Enough, I chastised myself. Pull yourself together. My first priority was my son and helping him cope with his problems. I would push all thoughts of Javier, Karen, and the police from my mind until I had ensured he would become a healthy, functioning member of society. If that took years, so be it. As much as I'd loved Karen, there was nothing I could do that would bring her back. I would focus on the living—specifically, my son, while there was still hope for him.

The next morning, I parked the car next to Rosedale's playing field and turned off the ignition.

"What are you doing?" Chloe's voice was shrill with panic.

"I thought I'd come into your class and give a presentation on the special love shared between a mother and daughter."

"WHAT?"

"Relax," I grumbled, undoing my seat belt. "I've got a meeting with Mrs. Chambers."

"Why?" Spencer's voice was shrill with panic.

"I don't know why, yet," I replied, fixing him with a steely gaze, "but you'll be the first to know."

I kissed Spencer good-bye outside the music room and waved at my daughter's hastily departing back. Then, taking deep, calming breaths, I walked purposefully to the first-grade classroom.

"Hi, Paige." Marion Chambers welcomed me into her classroom, closing the door behind us. "Why don't we take a seat in Creativity Corner?"

Creativity Corner was composed of four squat Formica tables pushed together, surrounded by a number of short plastic chairs. The tabletops were cluttered with plastic yogurt containers holding markers, pencil crayons, scissors, and glue sticks. I pulled out a yellow chair and lowered myself into it. Ms. Chambers sat facing me on a blue one.

"Thanks for coming in on such short notice," she began.

"Of course. If Spencer is having some kind of trouble, I want to help him."

"That's a wonderful attitude," she said, smiling at me like I was one of her particularly keen students. "And I'm sure that if we work together, we'll be able to get Spencer back on track in no time."

"He's off track? How do you mean, 'off track'?"

"Well . . ." She paused for a few seconds, just to torture me, I think. "I'm concerned about his use of inappropriate language."

I guess I knew this was coming. And at least he wasn't killing small animals.

"Spencer is very fond of using the word . . ."—she hesitated,

as though it were physically painful for her to utter the syllables—
"frigging." I tried to look confused. She continued, "The principal
and I feel that this is not a suitable word for a six-year-old, and he
has been reprimanded several times. However, your son maintains
that this word is perfectly appropriate. He calls it a *swear replacement."*

"A swear replacement?" I said, looking shocked, but slightly
amused in a "kids say the darnedest things" sort of way.

"Yes."

"Well . . . I don't know where he would have heard that." I
began to fidget uncomfortably in my small yellow chair. "I'll talk to
his father about it . . . We'll make sure to explain to Spencer which
words are appropriate for a boy his age and which are not."

"Thank you. I don't think there's any need to panic, but even the
use of such a benign expletive may be setting Spencer up for problems in the future."

"Definitely," I said, nodding vigorously. "And we don't want
that."

"No, we don't." She continued to smile at me.

"Well . . . I'll let you get back to it," I said, rising, with some effort, from my seat. "Off to bake some oatmeal carob-chip cookies."
For some reason, I felt the need to assert my caring and maternal nature.

Marion escorted me to the door. "Thanks again for coming in.
It's always wonderful to work with concerned and involved parents
like you."

"You're welcome." My voice was thin and shaky, yesterday's dormant emotions threatening to spill over. "My children are the most
important thing in the world to me."

CHAPTER 18

The swear-replacing lecture with Spencer went very well. Paul and I calmly explained that *frigging* was an inappropriate word for a six-year-old boy to use, and I apologized for setting a bad example. We even implemented a "swear-replacement box," like Trudy's naughty-word box, where anyone in the household caught swear-replacing had to deposit a favorite item. Spencer lost one Bionicle to it and hadn't said *frigging* since.

With that parenting crisis averted, I felt free to resume my search for the truth regarding Javier. The sooner I could put that baby to bed, the better it would be for everyone—especially me. I was eager to regain my former sense of peace, unburdened by this obsession with Karen's case. And I was eager to return to guilt-free fantasizing about Javier. Unless, of course, it turned out that he was a psychotic killer; then I would focus more on George Clooney . . . or maybe that sexy Croatian doctor on *ER*.

Unfortunately, a rendezvous with Javier necessitated a lie to my husband. I called him at the office.

"Oh, hi, hon," he said, tap, tap, tapping as usual. Normally, this would have annoyed me, but I felt I had no right to complain. It seemed rather petty, considering I was about to concoct a fabrication to allow me to see another man.

"How's your day?" It was best to start out with a little friendly chitchat.

"Good . . . good . . . What can I do you for?"

Normally, another enormous irritant, but I let it slide. "Remember Mary-Anne Campbell? We used to work together at Kellerman PR."

"Right . . . [tap, tap, tap] right . . ."

"Well, I haven't seen her since Chloe was a baby, but she just called me up out of the blue! We're going to meet for a late dinner tonight."

"Great . . . [tap, tap, tap] great . . . What time did you say you're going out?"

"What time will you be home?"

"I'll be here until at least eight. Is that too late for you?"

"No. We were thinking we'd meet around nineish, so that would work perfectly."

"Okay, babe. Gotta run. Love ya."

"Love you, too."

I had a light dinner with my children, cleaned up the dishes, and then hurried upstairs to find something appropriate to wear. Unfortunately, my closet offered little choice. Not that I was trying to impress Javier: it was more of a confidence thing. Obviously, I couldn't wear the boots again—and not because they were currently in the swear-replacement box (I could easily have sneaked them out after Spencer went to bed). But I didn't want Javier to think I was some sad suburban housewife with only one sexy and stylish outfit. Finally, I decided on a pair of snug blue jeans and a black V-neck sweater. First, I slipped into the red water bra. Not that I was trying to look sexy and desirable. Oh no! That was far from the purpose of tonight's meeting. But I had worn the bra at our last encounter, and if I suddenly showed up with noticeably smaller breasts, he might find that distracting and not be able to concentrate on answering my questions. When I was satisfied with my appearance, I went downstairs to wait for my husband.

"Whit-woo!" Spencer fake-whistled, his standard greeting anytime I had lipstick or earrings on.

"Thanks, sweetie."

Chloe looked up from her homework. "You're going out *again?*" she sniped, as if I routinely left my children home alone to go hang out at some singles' bar.

"Again? What do you mean *again?* I hardly ever go out!"

"You do so," she replied. "What about that drawing class?"

"I'm not even taking that class anymore—not that there's anything wrong with enriching yourself through a hobby. In fact, I'm thinking about taking a dance class."

"A dance class!" Chloe howled. "You're kidding?"

"No, I'm not."

"That's so funny!"

"Why? Why is it funny?"

"Well . . . it's just . . . just . . . you . . . dancing . . ." She was doubled over now, and Spencer was starting to join in.

Suddenly, Paul walked into the kitchen. His presence at the front door had been muffled by the sounds of my children's vicious laughter. "What's so funny?"

"M-m-mom . . . M-m-mom . . ." Chloe gestured at me frantically, trying to explain, but she had lost the power of speech.

"For some reason, they think it's hilarious that I might want to take a dance class."

The corners of Paul's mouth twitched, but the rest of his face remained grave. "Well, I think that's great, honey. You're a . . . *cute* dancer."

"Cute dancer?" I cried angrily. "I'm a cool dancer!" Chloe collapsed onto the floor. Paul lost his battle for earnestness and dissolved into giggles. I had to leave before my loved ones could do any more damage to my ego. "See you later, John Travolta and Jennifer Beals," I grumbled.

"Who?" Chloe managed, through her hysterics.

By the time I reached Cherry Creek, I had sufficiently recovered from my family's mocking. I parked just down the street and headed to The Old Grind. It had not occurred to me that Javier might not be working. He simply *had* to be there. I had steeled myself for this conversation, and my nerves could not handle a postponement. I also didn't want to have to lie to my family again—as cruel as they were about my dancing. Hopefully, I opened the heavy door and made my way inside. Again, there were only a few occupied tables: a young couple feeding each other muffins and giggling quietly; an older well-dressed couple (possibly the same one from my previous visit); and a lone man with a laptop, though this fellow was middle-aged, with wiry gray hair and small, round glasses—a poet or a writer of some sort. I didn't linger at the entrance this time but moved swiftly to the counter at the back. Tonight, there would be no silly pitter-pattering of my heart, no flip-flopping of my stomach, no enjoyable tingling in my genital region . . . This was serious. I was here for answers.

When I reached the counter, it appeared to be abandoned. I peered over the top, hoping Javier was crouched below, stocking the fridge or scrubbing the floor. He wasn't there. A sudden sense of irrational panic swept over me. Where the hell was he? He couldn't have just abandoned his post in the middle of his shift. The coffee shop didn't close for another twenty minutes. I mean, he couldn't just walk out while there were customers here. Unless he had fled? A door at the back slammed, and I knew it was him. That same strange electric energy crept through my body. All the hair on my arms stood on end before Javier had even entered the room.

"Paige," he said, a delighted smile spreading across those full lips. "You came back."

Pitter-patter. Flip-flop. Enjoyable tingle-tingle. Outwardly, at least, I was able to maintain my composure. "Hi," I said coolly. "I need to talk to you."

"Okay. I make you a coffee?"

"No thank you. . . . Well, okay."

"Decaf tonight? Or do you have a boring party to go to?"

"Decaf's fine."

"Dry cappuccino, extrahot?" His eyes twinkled at me.

"Yes." God, he even remembered my high-maintenance coffee order. But tonight I would not succumb to his charms. Tonight, I needed to get some answers. My sanity depended on it.

"So," he said, beginning to make my beverage, "you need to talk to me?"

I glanced around at the other occupants. "Could we speak in private?"

"I will close at nine. We could talk then?"

"Perfect."

When my coffee was ready, I insisted on paying. Then, I took my mug to a small table, where I flipped mindlessly through an outdated magazine. Mentally, I rehearsed what I was going to say, not the exact words but the gist of it. This time, I would not be distracted by his intense gaze. I wouldn't get flustered looking at those sexy lips, the outline of his pectoral muscles through his blue T-shirt. I would be mentally and emotionally prepared.

Those final ten minutes seemed to take forever, but eventually, the other patrons left, and Javier locked the door behind them. Once again, my heart began to beat frantically. It was a normal physiological response: I was locked inside an empty coffee shop with a potential murderer. But I was not afraid of being killed by Javier. I was more afraid of losing my focus or, worse, . . . losing control.

Javier took a seat across from me. "I am happy to see you again," he said, looking deeply into my eyes. "You look very beautiful."

"Well . . . thanks," I said brusquely. "I need to talk to you about something."

"What is it?" His voice was warm and full of understanding.

It was time. The question had to be asked. "Did you know . . ." I trailed off, suddenly frightened to bring this information into the open. "Did you know Karen was pregnant?"

I had expected some kind of start, a physical indication of shock or guilt. But if he was stunned or disturbed by this news, he kept it well hidden. "I did not know. A baby would have made her so happy."

A baby *would* have made her so happy. I suddenly felt very sad, but I had to compose myself. In an effort to stifle my emotions, I turned antagonistic. "Really? You had no idea? I thought you and Karen were close friends."

"I told you before, we were not that close."

"Well . . . she confessed to you that she was bored with her husband. Why wouldn't she tell you that she was going to have a baby?"

"I don't know." He was looking at me suspiciously. "Did she tell *you* she was going to have a baby?"

"Well . . . no . . ."

"Why not?"

He was turning the tables on me, and I didn't like it. "This isn't about me," I snapped. "It's about you."

"Okay," he said patiently. "What do you want to know?"

"Did you write a letter to the police telling them that Karen's death was an accident?"

This time, there was a reaction. He stood up, suddenly angry. "What! Why would I write a letter to the police? I know nothing about her death!"

I stood, too, matching his ire. "The police got an anonymous letter. The writer said that he was there when Karen died, that they argued, but she fell, accidentally, and hit her head."

"I did not write it."

"Are you sure?" I moved toward him, aggressively. "This letter was from a man . . . a foreign man."

"Well, it was not me."

"Really? I guess it must have been from one of Karen's many other foreign boyfriends."

"It must have been."

"Cut the crap, Javier," I said venomously. "It was you, wasn't it?"

He descended on me. "No!"

"I need to know!" I yelled at him. "It's driving me crazy!"

"Why?" he said, his voice controlled. We were only inches apart now, both of us breathing heavily from the outburst. "Why is it driving you crazy?"

"Because . . . ," I croaked, "Karen was my friend, . . . and . . . I need to know if you were involved in her death."

"And what about me?" he said, shifting his body almost imperceptibly toward me. "Am I your friend?"

"No," I said huskily. "I only came to see you because I wanted to know what happened to Karen."

"So, you are using me?" Again, he moved, ever so slightly, toward me. His proximity was like some kind of magnetic force, pulling me into him. I could smell his skin, clean and manly.

"Were you sleeping with her?" I asked, just barely holding my ground. "Please . . . tell me."

"I was not." He moved in. Our bodies were touching now, just barely brushing each other. I was frightened: afraid I might collapse, burst into tears, or jump on him and start humping his leg. I quickly tried to visualize dead Karen or my cute, Popsicle-eating kids, but I could summon neither image. Javier reached out and, with one finger, tilted my chin. Somehow, I managed to remain standing.

"Your eyes . . . ," he said, staring into them. "They are not sad, like my mother's."

"Oh . . . ," I said hoarsely. I cleared my throat. "Well, that's . . . good."

"They are beautiful."

"Thanks."

"So . . . so . . . beautiful," he said softly, moving in for the kiss.

Oh God! Oh no! I was married! A mother! I could not kiss my dead friend's lover—real or imagined. I tore myself away. "I have to go," I said shrilly, hurrying to the table to retrieve my coat and purse.

"Don't leave."

Without looking at him, I hastily buttoned my coat. "I have to, but thank you for seeing me," I said formally. "Good-bye." I rushed to the door, but of course, it was locked. I began to rattle the doorknob frantically, on the verge of some kind of panic attack. "I have to go!" I screamed. "Let me out!" Silently, Javier came and turned the lock, setting me free into the frigid night air.

I didn't look back as I scurried to the SUV, taking huge gulps of air as if I'd just surfaced from a deep pool of water. I pressed the remote locking device, and the car beeped, its lights blinking to signal that it was open, ready to receive me. Once inside, I locked the doors, then leaned my head against the leather seat, feeling hot tears pool beneath my closed lids. I didn't know why I wanted to cry exactly. There seemed to be a plethora of reasons: Karen was dead; Spencer was on a slippery slope with that whole swear-replacing business; Chloe thought I was a lame dancer, and Paul agreed. . . . And worst of all, I had come very close to cheating on my husband. Of course, I was fully clothed and had had virtually no physical contact with Javier, but I knew what was in my heart.

God, I was a horrible, horrible person. Not only had I come very close to cheating on my husband, but I had come very close to cheating on my husband with the man who may have witnessed my friend's death . . . possibly even *caused* it! I was sick! A sicko! I had a wonderful family at home, and here I was prancing around in a water bra and G-string playing Miss Marple.

There was a light tap on the window beside me. I jumped in my seat, a startled cry escaping from my lips. Turning, I saw Javier, standing in his T-shirt in the chill evening air. I could see his nipples through the thin blue fabric. Sick! I was a sicko! Turning the key in the ignition, I lowered the power window an inch and a half. "Yes?" I called through the tiny crack.

"Paige . . . ," he said, holding his lips to the small space, "please . . . I want to say . . ." He stopped. "Could you undo the window a bit more?" I pressed the Down button, lowering it another inch or so. Javier continued. "I want to see you again."

"I can't," I said. "I'm busy with my kids . . . and my husband."

"But there is something . . . ," he said, ". . . something between us. You feel it, too, no?"

Oh, I felt it, all right. I looked at the gorgeous, sensual man staring intensely at me through the window. His dark eyes locked with mine, and I felt their familiar, mesmerizing pull. His strong, manly hands were pressed to the glass as he leaned in close. At that moment, I wanted more than anything to believe in him. I wanted to open the window and kiss those sensual lips, to invite him into the SUV and have wild sex with him in the backseat. Of course, we'd end up covered in cracker crumbs and raisins, but I didn't care. I wanted him . . . maybe more than I had ever wanted anyone.

"No . . . ," I said, "I don't feel it. I came here for information about Karen. That's it."

He was silent for a long moment. "Okay," he finally said, stepping back from the window. His posture was dejected; his eyes, as he looked at me, were full of pain. "I guess . . . I was wrong. Good-bye, Paige." Then he put his fingers to his lips and blew me a kiss. I didn't know if it was a Spanish thing or Javier's own patented move, but it knocked me back in my seat. It felt like his lips had actually touched my face, just gently, just for a moment . . . I turned to say something, I don't know what—probably "Get in here and do me, you irresistible Spanish stud!"—but he was already jogging back toward The Old Grind.

CHAPTER 19

"Yes, hello," I said nervously into the receiver. "Is this Detective Portman?" Obviously, it was Detective Portman. He had answered his phone "Portman."

"That's me. Can I help you?"

"This is Paige Atwell calling."

"Hi, Paige. Thanks for checking in."

"Y-you're welcome. I, uh, have some information for you."

"Great . . . Would you like to discuss it in person?"

"Yes, please."

"I could come out to your place this afternoon?"

"No . . ." I didn't want Troy coming to my house again. The neighbors might start to get suspicious, and word could get back to Paul. "I'd rather meet you somewhere. I don't mind coming into town."

"Okay." He rattled off the address of a coffee shop near the precinct. "How soon can you get here?"

"I'll be there in an hour."

Within minutes, I was in the Explorer, hurtling down I-25. No lip gloss or water bra this time. There would be nothing flirtatious or even pleasant about this rendezvous. I had information to give to Detective Portman, nothing more. While a part of me was dreading revealing all to this virtual stranger, I knew it was time. I was in over my head. Last night had confirmed it.

I made it into the city in good time but spent several minutes driving around looking for a parking spot. Because I'd lived in the suburbs for so many years, my parallel-parking skills had suffered. And with a vehicle the size of mine, finding ample space in the business district was a challenge. Finally, I paid an exorbitant fee to stow my car in an underground garage and hurried to meet Detective Portman.

He was already seated at a vinyl booth in the small coffee shop—really, it was more of a diner. I walked toward him, feeling conspicuous despite the fact that none of the other patrons had taken any notice. They all appeared to be cops having coffee with informants—*stoolies,* I think they were called. I suddenly realized that I was no different: I, too, was a *stoolie.* Okay, I was a little different— I was far better dressed than the others, most of whom appeared to be homeless. But I was here for the same reason: to rat someone out. I felt like crap.

"Hi," Portman said, as I slid into the seat across from him. He looked cute again, back in a suit and tie. His jacket was off, and the sleeves of his tan shirt were rolled up.

"Hi," I mumbled.

"Let me get you a coffee." He called for the waitress: "Vera!" God, this felt so clichéd. I ordered a black coffee. Obviously, a dry decaf soy latte would have been out of the question.

"Thanks for coming down," Troy said.

"You're welcome."

"So . . . what have you got for me?"

Okay. It was time to lay it on the line, to release all the secrets that had been causing me so much pain and confusion. I took a deep breath and began. "Karen Sutherland told me she was having an affair."

"Really?" He leaned forward, interested.

"Well . . . maybe not really," I said. And then I let the words tumble forth. I told him everything: how Karen had confessed that she was in love with an artists' model / barista and thinking about leaving her husband; how I met Javier (by chance, I said, at my art class) and he denied that they were anything more than friends; how I had been trying to protect Karen's reputation so I hadn't shared her secret until now. I told Detective Portman all of it—except my own attraction to Javier. I refused to give it any sort of validation. And besides, Troy might have felt a tiny bit . . . *jealous,* if he knew I had been having adulterous feelings for another man.

"I know I should have come forward sooner," I said.

"You should have," he replied. "But I'm glad you did now."

"So, what happens next?"

"Well . . ." He dug in his jacket pocket, retrieving a notepad and pencil. "We'll need to speak to this Javier. Where does he work?" He jotted down the address of The Old Grind and the Wild Rose Arts Center.

"You won't tell him that it was me who . . . uh . . . *ratted him out,* will you?"

"No, that won't be necessary. Are you still taking that art class with him?"

"No."

"Good. It would be wise to stay away from him."

"Why?" I slid forward anxiously in my seat. "Do you think he's dangerous? Do you think he killed Karen?"

"I don't know at this point, but until we can rule him out, you'd better keep your distance."

"I will," I said. "Definitely."

"Well . . ." Portman pressed the button on the end of his pen before returning it to his pocket. "Thanks for coming down, Paige. I'll let you get on with your day."

"Umm . . . one more thing . . . , *Troy.*" I suddenly felt shy calling him by his first name. "The paternity test—have you got the results?"

"Not yet. It'll take a couple of weeks. Do you think the baby might be this Javier's?"

I honestly didn't know. For some reason, I still felt like Javier might have been telling me the truth about his relationship with Karen. But was it just wishful thinking on my part? After last night, I knew I could no longer trust my own judgment. "Maybe," I said.

I had expected to feel some sort of relief after finally revealing all the secrets I'd kept locked up inside. Instead, I felt mildly depressed and rather . . . guilty. Karen had confided in me because she trusted me, and I had let her down. And now it was very likely that the whole thing would be blown wide open. When Doug found out about Karen's affair, he would be devastated. Carly would be crushed that her best friend was no better than the hussy who had stolen Brian from her. Trudy would be disappointed. Jane, of course, would understand, but what of all the other perfect Aberdeen Mist wives? They'd all be looking down their noses, sneering at Karen's memory. And what would they think when they learned that I had known about the affair for months?

Unless, of course, Karen hadn't actually been having an affair and her death really was just a tragic accident. In that case, no one need ever know about her fictitious admission to me. I would have nothing to feel guilty about—except the fact that Javier was going to be interrogated and quite possibly deported. For all I knew, his immigration status could be totally legitimate, but based on the note he wrote to the police, I doubted it. I felt a strong wave of remorse wash over me at the thought of him being sent home. Not that I planned to see him again, *ever*, but I hated the idea of destroying an innocent immigrant's life. And I couldn't help but wonder if my motives were really pure or if I was just looking out for myself. Was I so weak-willed that the only way I could protect my marriage was to send the object of my desire across the Atlantic Ocean?

I needed a pick-me-up, a mood booster, something to get me out of this funk. As if on cue, the Aberdeen Mall rose up on my left, a sprawling mass of interconnected department stores, boutiques, and restaurants. Of course! Shopping was the answer! Shopping would numb me to these negative, self-defeating thoughts—at least temporarily. A new pair of shoes or even a new top would lift my spirits immensely. I would also buy the children each a gift and pick up a little something for Paul. As I took the mall exit off the freeway, I decided to look at this day as the end of an old cycle full of secrets and lies and the beginning of a new one. Really, it was a cause for celebration. And what better way to celebrate than an afternoon of shopping?

It worked. When I left the mall two hours later laden with a number of large shopping bags, I felt much more upbeat. I had purchased a striped purple sweater for Chloe, a hoodie emblazoned with a stylized snowboarder for Spencer, a blue zip-up pullover for Paul, and a hip shrunken blazer for myself. From now on, I was going to focus on the positive. I was not even going to allow myself to stress out over the money I'd just spent. This was a bright new day. Now if only I could find my car.

From my perspective on the sidewalk, I peered out into the sea of SUVs and family sedans. Okay . . . I had entered the mall through the Gap, so I had to be parked somewhere in the general vicinity. As my eyes scanned the area, I caught a glimpse of someone familiar in my peripheral vision. "Hey, Trudy!" I called.

Trudy turned toward me. She was burdened with several dry-cleaned garments and two overstuffed grocery bags. "Oh, hi, Paige."

I walked toward her. "Doing a little shopping?"

"Just a few errands."

I looked at her plastic-wrapped clothes. "Picking up Ken's suits? Is he back from his business trip?"

"Uh . . . he's still in Seattle. These are actually Doug's."

"Oh."

"He's been so busy at work that I offered to pick them up for him."

"That's nice of you."

"Well . . . you know how men are when they don't have a woman to look after them . . ." She trailed off with a laugh.

"True. Listen, have you got time for a quick coffee?"

"Ohhh," she said regretfully, "I can't. I was just picking up some groceries to take over to Carly's. We're going to whip up a few lasagnas for Doug to keep in the freezer. That way, he can just defrost them when he's hungry."

"Great idea." There it was again: that niggling feeling of . . . pettiness. Carly and Trudy had obviously appointed themselves Doug's caregivers. That was, of course, when they were not helping all of Denver's barren couples conceive, in the name of our deceased friend. And what was *I* doing? I was trying, with negligible results, to find out what really happened to her. But would anyone appreciate my efforts? Or were Karen's secrets best buried with her—or rather, burned and scattered across a picnic area at the foot of the Rocky Mountains with her?

Trudy gave my hand a squeeze. "I've gotta run. We'll see you soon."

"Right . . . Okay. Bye." I forced a warm smile. I had to stop being so full of doubt and negativity. This was a bright new day, the beginning of a happier, more positive cycle.

That evening, when I bestowed upon my family the gifts I'd bought, I felt incredibly upbeat, even jolly—like Santa must feel. Chloe adored her striped sweater, and Spencer, though slightly less enthusiastic about new clothes, thought his new snowboarder hoodie was really cool. Paul immediately tried on his pullover. It fit him perfectly and emphasized his broad shoulders. "Thanks, babe." He kissed my cheek. "What's the occasion?"

"Nothing special," I said. "I just realized how lucky I am to have such a great family." I could feel myself becoming emotional. "I wanted to buy you all a little present, that's all . . ."

"Well, thank you. Did you get yourself something, too?"

"A really cute blazer."

"Great. I thought you might have bought yourself a new dress to wear to the party."

"Party?" I asked, bemused. "What party?"

"The department's fiscal-year-end celebration for exceeding our sales quotas."

"You never told me about it."

"Yes, I did, Paige. Ages ago."

"No, you didn't! I would have remembered."

"Maybe you were just distracted. A lot has happened lately."

"You didn't," I muttered, but decided not to force the issue. I had been incredibly preoccupied. "When is it?"

"Friday."

"Friday? As in, tomorrow?"

"Yeah."

"Oh my God!" I went into panic mode, storming into the kitchen. Paul followed me. "I don't have a sitter! I don't have anything to wear!"

"Call Mrs. Williams. Or Katy Baldwin. One of them will babysit."

I rummaged violently through the junk drawer in search of my address book. "Why do I always have to take care of all this stuff? Why can't you ever book the babysitter?"

"I don't have their phone numbers at work, that's all. Here . . ." He stepped in and extracted my address book within seconds. "I'll phone them now. You go look through your closet for something to wear."

"I have nothing!" I cried.

"Wear that black dress . . . the tight one."

"I wore it to the last Christmas party!" I screeched. God, men could be so stupid.

"Okay. Sorry!" Paul was getting exasperated. "It's really nothing to freak out about."

"Easy for you to say! You've known about it for weeks. You've got tons of clothes. I've got one dress, one formal dress!"

"You can go shopping tonight."

"I volunteered to bake muffins tonight for Spencer to take to class tomorrow!"

"Okay . . . tomorrow morning, then."

"You really think it's that easy to find a new outfit? Well," I scoffed, "you obviously don't have to deal with a small bust and extra-long torso."

Paul looked at me in silence for a moment. "What's going on?" he asked slowly.

"What? . . . What?"

"Why are you getting so upset about this party?"

I busied myself putting away the dishes sitting in the drying rack while I tried to compose an answer. I could think of several reasons for my chagrin:

1. I really did have nothing to wear.
2. Paul's office parties were excruciatingly dull, especially for someone like me who had less than no interest in computer stuff.
3. They often culminated in an argument between my husband and me, since I found his colleagues painfully boring and he seemed to find them both entertaining and hilarious.
4. After my morning meeting with Detective Portman, my nerves were completely shot. I knew I was blowing the event out of proportion, but at the moment, it felt somewhat overwhelming.

I sighed deeply and turned around to face my husband. "I'm sorry. I'm overreacting."

"Yeah."

"I just wish I'd known about it sooner so I could have been prepared."

"Honestly, Paige, I really think I told you."

"Whatever . . ." I waved it away with my hand. "I think . . ." I sighed heavily again. "I think you and I need to reconnect."

"Oh," my husband said, seemingly surprised, "I thought we kind of had."

"Well . . . we kind of did, but I need more than that."

"Okay . . . ," he said thoughtfully. "Maybe when the kids have gone to bed, we could do it in the shower or something?"

"I'm not talking about sex this time."

"Oh. Sorry." This puzzled him. "So . . . reconnect how?"

"Emotionally. Spiritually." This appeared to puzzle him even more. Apparently, I would have to spell it out for him. "We used to be a team, Paul. Lately, I feel like we've been too wrapped up in our

own lives. You're completely immersed in your job, and I've been absorbed with . . ."—it took me only a millisecond to find the right word—"my grief. We need to come together again."

He moved toward me. "You're right." His arms reached out to embrace me. "That sounds good." We held each other in silence for a long moment, a contented smile playing on my lips. It was the new beginning I had hoped for; I could feel it. I would invest all of my energy in my relationship with my husband, in my family. It felt so right.

Paul pulled back and looked at me. "Maybe later we could still . . . you know, do it in the shower?"

"Maybe."

CHAPTER 20

We didn't end up doing it in the shower, but still, I felt positive about this next phase of our relationship. Paul and I needed to be more cohesive, less insular in our separate lives. I was glad I had finally spoken up about it. I was also glad that I managed to find a knee-length, champagne-colored dress that flattered my small bust and extralong torso. Plus, Katy Baldwin, a skinny blond teenager with a mouthful of braces, had agreed to babysit. Maybe this party wouldn't be as painful as I was expecting? I vowed to have a positive attitude.

I tried, I really did. The evening had started off quite well. When we first arrived at the upscale Italian eatery, Paul was attentive. He introduced me to his colleagues—or rather, reintroduced me. Over the last six years, I had spent approximately twelve evenings with these people, but I usually needed a quick refresher upon meeting them again. I smiled warmly as I shook their hands, asking about the ski chalet they had been building last time we met or their daughter who had just been heading off to college in Idaho.

But by the second cocktail, conversation was rapidly deteriorating. Paul seemed to have forgotten my existence as he immersed himself in animated discussions about difficult clients, crashing thingamabobs, and golf scores. I found another wife standing idly by and managed to strike up a conversation. Unfortunately, I soon found out that she was childless and extremely devoted to her career in banking. Since we had less than nothing in common, our idle chitchat quickly petered out. My husband, on the other hand, seemed to be having the time of his life. Thanks to a continuous stream of scotches, he was getting louder, more gregarious, and definitely more obnoxious. Surely someone would tell him to shut up soon? But to the contrary, the other guests seemed to find him incredibly amusing. I was grateful when we were summoned to the dining area for our meal.

The food was excellent. The conversation was not—at least not to someone who had no understanding of software protocols, had not been on that team-building retreat in Vegas, or dealt with the client Natalie Devon, a.k.a. Nastily Devil. I was used to this, from the past dozen or so events, so I smiled pleasantly and tried to concentrate on my veal and red wine. I couldn't help but feel some resentment toward my husband, though. After our heart-to-heart about reconnecting and presenting as a cohesive unit, he was basically ignoring me. He was so engrossed in relaying his many humorous anecdotes that it was like he'd forgotten I was there. When dessert had been served and it was apparent that the evening was going to proceed in this manner indefinitely, I knew I needed a break. I leaned over to my husband.

"Paul," I said quietly.

"No way, Damon! They *needed* that upgrade. Haven't you ever heard of *upselling*?"

"Paul . . . ," I tried again.

"Give me a break! You'd sell your grandmother the AP3000, and she doesn't even own a computer!"

Amid his cohorts' uproarious laughter, I snapped, "Paul!"

He turned toward me. He almost looked surprised to see me,

like he wasn't quite sure why I was there when I so obviously didn't fit in. "What?"

"I left my cell at home. Lend me yours so I can check on the kids."

"Okeydoke . . ." As he extracted his phone, he dove back into his previous conversation. "You're just in it for the free golf, man! I can see right through you!"

Dejectedly, I walked to the front of the restaurant and asked the pretty coat-check girl for my wrap. It was a chilly November evening, but I needed some fresh air. Hopefully, it would cool me off. By this time, I was positively seething at Paul's indifference to my presence. It was like our reconnection conversation had gone in one ear and out the other. This was going no better than my initial re-sexualizing efforts.

Standing on the sidewalk just outside the glass front doors, I dialed home. Katy Baldwin answered after a couple of rings.

"Hi, Katy. It's Paige calling."

"Oh, hi."

"How's everything going?"

"Good," she said, in her high-pitched, vaguely muddled voice. The plethora of metal in her mouth caused a slight speech impediment. "Really good."

"Did the kids get to bed?"

"Yep. Spencer went at about 8:30. Chloe went at 9:00, and then she read for a while."

"Great . . . great . . . Were they well behaved?"

"Yeah. They were really good."

"Good . . . good." There was a long pause as I scrambled for something else to ask. I wasn't ready to return to the party yet. "Spencer didn't say any, uh, *naughty* words, did he?"

"Not really."

"Not really?"

"No, he was fine."

"Okay . . . well, thanks, Katy. Hopefully, we won't be too much longer."

"Take your time."

I hung up and stuffed the phone into my tiny evening bag. Huddling into my wrap, I stared out at the darkened parking lot and the largely vacant highway beyond. At that moment, I really wished I smoked: it would have given me an excuse to stay outside, away from the party. I wondered how long I could stay away before Paul missed me—likely, until the restaurant closed at midnight.

Suddenly, I was assaulted by the stinging beam of headlights in my eyes. One of the dormant cars, parked across the lot and facing me, sprang to life. I squinted in its direction. It was a nice car, sleek and black. The hood ornament indicated that it was an Audi. As it sidled out of its spot, my first thought was one of envy: at least someone was getting to leave the party early. But the car didn't appear to be in any hurry to exit the lot. It eased forward, heading directly toward me. The driver, obscured by the glaring lights in my eyes, turned the wheel and pulled the car up beside me. I heard the electric whir of the passenger window being lowered.

"Paige. Get in."

I leaned down to peer inside. Holy shit! It was Javier! I felt a momentary flash of relief that he wasn't in prison or some immigration holding cell. But what was he doing here? How had he found me?

"What are you doing here? How did you find me?"

"I need to talk to you. Get in . . . please."

"I-I can't." I couldn't, could I? Paul might come looking for me—although that was highly doubtful. But Javier might want to harm me! Detective Portman's warning to stay away from him replayed in my mind.

"Please . . . ," he said again, looking at me with his dark, pleading eyes. Oh shit. He had some kind of Rasputin-like power! "I must speak to you." Before my rational mind could talk me out of it, I hopped in. With a piercing squeal of tires, we peeled out of the parking lot.

Javier was silent as we sped down the deserted highway. It was difficult to read his mood as I sat mutely beside him, frozen in my luxurious leather seat. There was definitely something titillating about being in this sexy car, so close to this sexy man. But I was also uneasy. I didn't know his intentions, and he was driving way too fast.

"Can you slow down please?" I said firmly. He ignored me. "Seriously, Javier! Slow down!" He did not decelerate. "Whose car is this anyway?"

"It is mine."

"Oh." I didn't want to be rude and ask how he could afford a car like this on his barista wages, but he must have read my thoughts.

"I saved for a long time. . . . And when my aunt died, she left some money to me."

"Really?" Skepticism had colored my voice. "Aren't you the lucky one? I wish I had a rich, dead aunt to buy me an Audi."

Suddenly, Javier flicked on the right-turn signal and began to slow the vehicle. When we reached the driveway of a darkened hardware store, he pulled in. He drove the car around to the back of the building and then slammed it into park. As he turned off the ignition, I felt my first real tremor of fear. Maybe Javier *was* violent? Unstable? Capable of stealing a fancy car and kidnapping an innocent mother of two? Maybe he was even capable of murdering that mother of two, like he had murdered Karen? But if he had murdered Karen, wouldn't the police have arrested him by now? It had been nearly twelve hours since I ratted him out to the cops.

He swiveled in his seat to face me. "Why did you do it, Paige?"

"Do what?" My voice was breathless with dread.

"Why did you tell the police I was sleeping with Karen? I told you that was not true."

"Yes, well, she told me it *was* true. The police asked, and I was honest. I told them that Karen said she was having an affair with you but that you denied it."

"I am so hurt by you," he said quietly.

"They're not going to deport you, are they?"

"No. I am legal to be here."

"How . . . ?" But I decided not to ask. "Well, that's good, then . . . for you." I looked into those dark eyes, and he really did look hurt. "Sorry," I said, "but what did you want me to do, lie to the police?"

He reached out and took my hands in his. They were warm, rough, perfect . . . "I want you to believe me. Karen was nothing more than my friend. I had nothing to do with her death."

Oh great. Here we go. Next thing I knew he'd be talking about his sad, fatherless childhood in Seville, and I'd be like putty in his hands. "I have to get back. My husband will be looking for me."

He said nothing for a long moment, just held my hands in his. Finally: "I did not write that note to the police."

"Okay." But it was obvious I doubted him.

"The day Karen died, I was working all day. I think that, maybe, someone is trying to . . . ummm"—he struggled for the word—"to make it look like I was there . . . like I wrote the note . . ."

"Someone is trying to *frame* you?" I encapsulated it for him.

"Yes. I think someone is trying to frame me."

"Who?"

"I don't know."

"But no one knew about your relationship with Karen except me, and I'm certainly not trying to frame you."

"Maybe she told someone else that we were lovers?" He squeezed my hand gently. "Even though we were not lovers."

I didn't respond. I was lost in thought. Who else could Karen have talked to? I had eliminated our close circle of friends when she initially confessed to me. Carly was too wounded by her ex's affair to be a good sounding board. Trudy was too prim and proper, and Jane, despite her adulterous past, had become this proactive, marriage-sustaining zealot. Besides, none of them would write a letter trying to *frame* Javier. There had to be someone else.

"You look beautiful in your new dress."

This statement jarred me from my speculation. I turned to face him, my eyes narrowed. "How did you know it was new?"

"It looks new," he said, releasing my hand and turning the key in the ignition. "I will take you back, before your husband misses you."

I continued to stare at him. "How did you know where I'd be tonight? Have you been following me?"

"No."

"Oh my God! You *have* been following me!" I suddenly felt the very real need to flee. I couldn't believe I had been stupid enough to get in a car with this . . . extremely good-looking stalker! I reached for the door handle, but he caught my arm.

"Let me explain," he said. "I did not follow you. I got your address from the art studio—from your registration. I had to talk to you, so I drove to your house. When I got there, you and your husband were just leaving."

"Jesus Christ! You came to my house? Why didn't you just phone?"

"I thought you would hang up!"

"Well, you were right!"

"And . . . I had to see you."

"Take me back to the restaurant, Javier," I said forcefully, staring straight ahead.

"You are angry."

"Damn right I'm angry!" I whirled on him. "I have children! I can't have some strange, possibly dangerous man lurking outside of my home!"

"I am not dangerous, Paige. Please, you must believe me."

"Just take me back to the restaurant! Paul's probably called the police by now."

There was no way Paul had called the police: We'd been gone less than half an hour. In fact, he probably thought I was still on the phone or in the bathroom. But Javier complied with my request, and soon we were back on the highway. We drove in silence, while I feigned continued fury. He had crossed a line, that much was certain, but I really didn't believe Javier was a danger to me. Maybe I was naïve or gullible, but he just didn't seem capable of violence. And if I was being totally honest with myself, I actually felt just a *teeny-tiny* bit . . . flattered. How many thirty-eight-year-old mothers of two could say they had a gorgeous guy like Javier lurking outside their homes, desperate to see them? God, I had serious problems.

As we neared the restaurant, I spoke authoritatively. "Pull up around the side." I pointed to a secluded area. When the car had stopped, I quickly jumped out. Before I slammed the door, I leaned in and hissed, "Stay away from my house."

I could feel Javier's eyes on me as I walked back to the restaurant. I could also feel myself, almost unconsciously, begin to swivel my hips sexily under his gaze. Yes, I would make an appointment with a therapist on Monday.

When I entered the dining room, the party had returned to the bar area. I slipped into the room, unnoticed, and stood by my husband's side. It took him a few seconds to become aware of my presence. He was deeply absorbed in a story he was telling about a rained-out golf tournament. "Hey," he said, smiling at me blearily. It was obvious his steady stream of scotches hadn't slowed during my absence. "Where you been?"

"I'm not feeling well," I said. It was true. At this point, my stomach was tied in knots.

"Oh . . . ," he said sympathetically. "Do you want to go?"

"Yeah, if you don't mind."

"You go on ahead," he said, kissing my cheek. "I'll grab a cab."

"Paul, a cab home will cost at least fifty dollars."

"I'll expense it. Go on." He gave me an affectionate, drunken headlock-type squeeze. "Feel better."

CHAPTER 21

In the morning, Paul was the one who wasn't feeling well. "Oh God . . . ," he moaned, when he heard me getting out of bed. "I feel like crap."

"I'm not surprised," I sniped, sounding like I'd never let a drop of evil alcohol touch my lips.

"I feel like a mouse crawled into my mouth and died."

Charming. "Go back to sleep," I muttered. "I'll make the kids breakfast."

I was somewhat annoyed at Paul's complete obliviousness to my disappearing act last night, but I had bigger things on my mind. It was actually a relief that he would be staying in bed. This way, I could relive my kidnapping and the ensuing conversation undisturbed. The children were enraptured by cartoons, so I set about making them French toast. As I beat the eggs and milk, my mind slipped back to the previous night's events.

It had been stupid to get in the car with Javier—stupid, wrong, scary—and exciting. Assuming I could trust my instincts at all, he wasn't a threat to my safety. Still, it was a bit *freaky* that he had driven all the way out to my house to talk to me—*freaky* in a thrilling and flattering sort of way. God, he could be out there right now, sitting in his car hoping to catch a glimpse of me. I hurried to the bathroom to fix my hair, just in case.

When I had served my children their breakfast, I puttered around the kitchen, making coffee, putting dishes in the dishwasher, and thinking about what Javier had said. If he really hadn't written the note to the police, then who had? As tight as our Aberdeen Mists social circle had been, Karen could have had any number of friends on the outside. Maybe I wasn't her sole confidante? Maybe she had confessed her affair—or fantasy affair—to someone else, someone who held a grudge against her and wanted her memory to be sullied? Say . . . a high school nemesis or one of Doug's ex-girlfriends? It was far-fetched, to be sure, but it was not impossible. If I was going to believe Javier's version of events, I would have to do some more digging.

But the digging would have to wait. Spencer had a soccer game, and Chloe had her hip-hop dance class. I managed to drag Paul from his bed to cheer on our son, while I raced to drop Chloe at the community center. I was not invited to watch her practice because ". . . only, like, *babies* have their moms watch them." I sincerely hoped her reluctance to have me observe wasn't really because they were learning the hip-thrusting, crotch-grabbing, nipple-tweaking moves so popular in today's music videos. With Chloe delivered, I raced back to the soccer field to catch the last half hour of my son's game. When he was finished, we all piled into the SUV and rushed back to retrieve Chloe.

"Who wants McDonald's for lunch?" Paul asked. It was like asking a drowning man if he was interested in a life preserver. The kids began screaming their agreement and shimmying around in their seats with excitement.

"Great idea," I grumbled. I tried to limit the children's fast-food intake.

"Come on," Paul said, "they love it."

"And it's so good for them!" I replied sarcastically. "I suppose this has nothing to do with your hangover?"

"Well . . . ," Paul said sheepishly, "it couldn't hurt." Laughing and shaking my head, I pulled into one of the approximately four thousand fast-food restaurants that lined our route home.

An hour and a half later, with grease oozing from our pores, we pulled through the gates marking Aberdeen Mists. As I brought the car to a halt in our driveway, Paul said, "Here comes Carly." Sure enough, my friend was walking across her front lawn toward us, carrying a large cardboard box. Exiting the vehicle, my husband called to her, "Do you need a hand with that?"

Though she was obviously struggling under the weight, she cheerfully called back, "No, I'm okay. Thanks, Paul."

Handing the house keys to my husband, I walked slowly to meet her at the edge of my drive. "What have you got there?"

"Well . . . ," she said breathlessly, dropping the box on the interlocking paving bricks, "I'm cleaning out my garage. Trudy and I are organizing a spring yard sale with all the proceeds going to Karen's infertility trust."

Oh, for Christ's sake! What was it with those two? It was like they had become compulsive do-gooders. But I managed to smile sweetly and say "Great."

"We're going to collect stuff from around the neighborhood and store it in my garage until the weather warms up. When I was going through my things, I found a lot of Brian's old stuff. I was wondering if Paul would want any of it."

I looked over my shoulder, but Paul had taken the children inside. "Uh . . . I don't know. What kind of stuff?"

"Hockey equipment, baseball glove, his camping gear . . . He obviously doesn't want it anymore, and there's no sense me keeping it."

"Well . . . I don't think he really needs anything like that."

"What size are Paul's feet? Brian's skates might fit him."

"He doesn't really skate."

"What about the camping gear? Your kids must love camping."

"We have all that stuff. Really . . ."

"Well, I'm also getting rid of some extra kitchen things. Do you need a lettuce spinner? An extra set of measuring cups?"

"I'm good . . . thanks. Keep that stuff for the yard sale."

"Okay . . ." She dug down the side of the box. "What about books? I went through all our old books." She retrieved a handful. "You like to read. How about these?"

Jeez . . . Carly had always been the generous type, but this seemed a little overboard. "Sure," I said, feigning appreciation, "I could use something to read." She thrust the small stack into my arms, and I briefly inspected my bounty: a couple of mysteries, a historical romance, and a bright pink chick lit. "Thanks. This is great. And it's really nice of you and Trudy to hold a yard sale for Karen's trust."

"Well . . . it's not completely selfless," my friend said, with a self-conscious laugh. "I've been meaning to clear some of the junk out of my life—particularly all the remnants of my life with Brian."

"Right . . ."

"I read in O magazine that you have to have room to let new things enter your world. If you keep adding and adding and never giving anything back, you end up with clutter—with your belongings, your emotions, your friends . . ."

"Makes sense . . ."

"It's about time, don't you think? I mean, it's no wonder I haven't been able to find a new man. My life has been too full of junk and baggage!"

I laughed agreeably.

"If you have anything to donate to the yard sale, we'd really appreciate it. There's no rush, obviously. We won't have the sale until probably the third Saturday in March."

"Okay. I'm sure I can get some things together by then."

Entering the house, I deposited the books in a corner of Paul's study and went in search of my family. Spencer was at the kitchen table drawing what appeared to be a giant toilet with lumpy, brown people falling into it—or more likely, turds with arms and legs. Chloe was locked in her room singing loudly into a deodorant-stick microphone, and Paul was lying on the family room couch watching football on TV. "How are you feeling?" I asked.

"Okay," he said, still staring at the box. "All that greasy food is soaking the booze out of my liver."

"Great. I've got a few things to do. I'll be upstairs."

Carly had inspired me. I would do a good deed by contributing to the fund-raising yard sale. Besides, my existence could do with a little decluttering as well. Not, in my case, to allow someone new to enter my life. *Au contraire!* But if I could simplify my environment, it might make my thoughts clearer. After last night, I was more confused than ever about Karen's accident.

I began in my closet, sorting through pilled sweaters, outdated blazers, and high-waisted pants. When in doubt, I tried things on, laughing at my reflection on several occasions. Why had I been hanging on to so much old crap? Yes, the eighties were now considered "retro," but I was fairly sure that jewel-toned sweaters with huge shoulder pads would never be back in style. Jeez . . . if your closets were a reflection of your psyche, it was no wonder I had been feeling so stale and uninspired.

As I pulled on a turquoise acrylic top complete with leather epaulets, I thought about Javier's suppositions. Could someone really be trying to frame him? He seemed so sincere in his belief. But if so, who was it? And why? Was that letter written by Karen's real murderer or just some nasty person who wanted to spill Karen's secrets? If that were the motivation, surely there were easier ways to besmirch her good name. Or was Javier lying to me—using his good looks and sexy accent to make me believe everything he told me? The uncertainty and speculation were driving me insane!

Suddenly, as I stared at my reflection in the hideous, military–meets–Sheena Easton sweater, I had a revelation. I needed to talk to Doug! True, our previous conversations had not gone smoothly—okay, they were disastrous—but now some time had passed. We had both endured a grieving period, allowing us to deal with our shock and loss. By now, he likely knew about Karen's pregnancy, the anonymous letter, and possibly even the affair—if it had actually occurred. I had to go and speak with him.

I barreled down the stairs and into the kitchen. Chloe was poking around in the fridge, and Spencer was sitting in the living room
playing with his sleeping father's pate. In my son's lap was a bottle of
hand lotion, which he was using to make impressive greasy sculp-
tures with Paul's thinning hair. Normally, I would have intervened,
but it seemed sort of an appropriate punishment for Paul's previous
neglect of me.

"I'm going for a short walk," I said to my daughter. "Wake Dad
up if you need anything."

"Okay," she said, emerging from the fridge. "Cool shirt."

"You like it? You can have it," I said.

"Really? Thanks, Mom."

"You're welcome, honey. Be back soon!" Throwing a coat over
Chloe's new shirt, I rushed out the door.

Okay . . . I told myself, as I stalked across the street in the crisp,
early-evening air, you can do this. Apologize to Doug for your earlier conversations. Tell him you were overwhelmed by your own
emotions and may not have been as sensitive to his feelings as you
should have been. Then . . . come right out with it. Tell him the police have been around to talk to you, that you know about the letter
and the baby. Don't say anything about Javier—unless he brings it up
first. If he does, you can admit that Karen mentioned him casually
but not that you knew anything about an affair. You want Doug as
an ally, not an enemy. Tell him that you met Javier briefly, just by
chance, at a drawing class. This time, you must be gentle and supportive with Doug. He's going through an incredibly difficult period: it was bad enough losing Karen, but now he has to deal with
all these doubts and suspicions.

As I walked up Karen's stone driveway, I felt prepared for the
conversation that lay ahead. There had been too many secrets and
too much speculation. I felt relieved to finally be sharing what I
knew with Doug. And I was sure he would appreciate having someone to discuss his feelings and concerns with. I was just about to take
the first step up to their front door when some movement from inside caught my eye. From this vantage point, I had a clear view of the
family room and part of the casual dining room. Seated at the table

were two figures: one, a man in a denim shirt—obviously Doug; and the other, a petite woman with blown-out, shoulder-length blond hair. They were each holding a glass of red wine and appeared to be in deep conversation. I watched silently as the woman threw her head back with laughter at something Doug said. I knew enough about body language to see that this was not a relative or a business associate. Their interaction appeared to be flirtatious, almost intimate. Then the woman stood, walking slowly around the table. There was something familiar about her fit, compact figure and confident gait. When she was standing behind Doug, she placed her hands on his shoulders and began to knead. He obviously enjoyed her ministrations, his head lolling forward. And then she looked up.

Holy shit! I dropped down on the bottom step, terrified she might have spotted me. Oh my God! It was Jackie Baldwin, my babysitter Katy's mom! I didn't know her well, but I knew enough. She had been divorced for years, and Katy was her only child. Jackie sold real estate or developed property or something similar that afforded her a Mercedes, a country-club membership, and a sexy, yet professional wardrobe. She was considered by most of the mom population to be the *cougar* of Aberdeen Mists.

Keeping my head low, I scurried back toward the street. God, I hoped none of the neighbors were watching me skulk around like some kind of Peeping Tom. But obviously, there was no way I could have a heart-to-heart with Doug while Jackie Baldwin was giving him a massage! In fact, I felt a little nauseated for having witnessed it. Karen had been gone for . . . what? Less than two months! And apparently, Doug felt sufficiently healed to be getting a rubdown by the neighborhood floozie!

This changed everything. In a matter of seconds, Doug had gone from a grieving, victimized widower to a promiscuous dirtbag! Perhaps my instincts were correct and Javier had been telling the truth all along? Doug had somehow fooled the police with his airplane alibi. How, I didn't know, but it had to be possible. Or he had hired someone to knock Karen on the head—a hit man . . . or a hit woman? Maybe he had been carrying on with Jackie Baldwin for months and he'd convinced her to murder Karen while he was on the plane. That bastard! Now I would be out a babysitter, too. I couldn't very well continue to hire the daughter of the woman who had bashed my best friend to death!

I scurried across the road and was soon on my own doorstep. I hesitated for a few seconds before entering and rejoining my family. My mind was reeling with this new possibility. Just when I thought I had figured out what happened to Karen, some new information cropped up. It was like I was forbidden any peace until the mystery was solved, like Karen was calling for help from the grave! Okay . . . maybe I was being a little melodramatic, but I knew what I had to do.

CHAPTER 22

My first instinct was to call Detective Portman and tell him what I had seen. Once he knew what a sex-crazed dog Doug really was, he would undoubtedly reopen the investigation into his alibi. But Paul talked me out of it. When I arrived home, my husband had just finished washing the hand lotion out of his hair. I joined him in the bathroom, where he was toweling off, and considered sharing the scene I had just witnessed. Part of me thought I should keep it to myself—just habit by this stage, I guess. But a larger part of me was bursting to disclose it. Besides, I didn't owe that pig Doug anything.

Unfortunately, Paul did not agree with my assessment of the situation. "What's the big deal?" he asked, rubbing his hair far harder than was necessary. It was no wonder it was thinning. "So he had a glass of wine with one of the neighbors. She was probably trying to sell him a condo."

"By rubbing his shoulders?"

"Hey . . . apparently she's one of Boca Development's top sales-people. Maybe that's 'the closer'?"

"Very funny," I grumbled. "I know what I saw, and it was not a business transaction."

"Well, even if there is something going on between them, it's none of your business."

I recoiled as if slapped. "None of my business? Karen was one of my best friends!"

"Everyone grieves differently, Paige. Everyone needs a different amount of time to move on. Maybe Doug's ready."

"Really?" I snapped. "So if I died, you'd be getting shoulder rubs from some realtor a month and half later, would you?"

"No . . ." He came toward me, a cheeky smile on his face. "I'd never let anyone rub my shoulders again. I'd stay in mourning until I finally died of a broken heart."

"Well . . . that's good," I said. "As long as you didn't let your grief interfere with raising the children."

"I'd try my best." He reached for me, but I pulled away.

"I've got to make some dinner."

We sat down to a wholesome feast of spaghetti and salad. (I was trying to compensate for a lunch the nutritional equivalent of card-board.) It was nice sharing a meal with my family. Despite his hang-over, or maybe because of it, Paul was in a buoyant, almost giddy mood. The lighthearted banter kept me from obsessing about what I had witnessed just hours earlier.

"So . . . ," Spencer said, pausing to noisily slurp a noodle into his mouth, "did you know that there is such a thing as worms that live in your intestines?"

"Not at the table," I admonished.

"But it's really true! And when they get bored in your intestines, they come out your butt!" My fork dropped to my plate with a noisy clatter.

"Oh my God!" Chloe screamed. "You are so disgusting!"

"I'm not disgusting," Spencer argued. "It's the truth. This one time, this kid had worms in his intestines, and then at night, his dad took a flashlight and he shone it on his butt—"

"SHUT UP!" his sister howled.

"Chloe!" I scolded, although I, too, was hoping that Spencer would shut up.

"But I'm gonna barf!" she protested.

Paul joined the fray. "Enough! Both of you! Now eat your dinner."

Sullenly, Chloe picked up her fork and silently twirled it in her spaghetti. Spencer took a drink of milk, then muttered, "Jeez . . . just 'cause I mentioned a true thing about butt worms . . ."

The fork was almost to my daughter's mouth when she retched. "Spencer!" I snapped. "One more word about butt worms and you will have all your LEGOs taken away for a month!" Chloe gagged again.

"Jesus Christ!" Paul growled. It was unlike him to lose his temper with the kids, but obviously, butt worms were not appropriate dinner conversation. "Just be quiet and eat your goddamn dinner!"

There was a long silence, broken only by the sound of Paul's and Spencer's forks on their plates. My husband looked up, his eyes meeting mine across the table. "What?"

"I can't eat this now."

"Me neither," Chloe agreed.

I stood up. "I'll make us a couple of grilled cheeses."

The next morning, I drove the kids to school and headed directly to the Willowbrook mini-mall, home of Boca Developments. Paul was probably right: it was too soon to go to the police with my suspicions about Doug and Jackie. But that didn't mean I couldn't do some investigating of my own. I had dressed professionally, in a pair of black slacks and my new blazer. I planned to meet with Jackie Baldwin on the pretext of business. Then, if she rubbed *my* shoulders, I'd know her encounter with Doug was entirely innocent.

"Do you have an appointment?" the receptionist asked when I requested Jackie.

"No, but I'm a friend of hers from the neighborhood. . . . Her daughter, Katy, babysits my children," I added. The receptionist showed no signs of recognition, and I realized that Jackie probably didn't advertise the fact that she had a teenage daughter. But she picked up the phone and called Jackie's office.

"Hi, Jackie. There's someone here to see you," she said into the receiver. Then, to me: "What did you say your name was?"

"Paige Atwell. I'm interested in buying a condo . . . for my mom."

Jackie had obviously heard my voice through the receiver, or possibly, through the thin, partitioned walls, because she appeared moments after the receptionist hung up.

"Hi, Paige," she said, walking toward me with a broad smile and her hand extended. "Nice to see you."

"You, too." I pasted on a false smile and took her hand. Jackie was an attractive woman in her early forties, but she had the look of someone trying too hard to hold on to—or, more accurately, recapture—her youth. Her hair was a little too big, her tan was a little too dark, and her business suit, while expensive, was a little too snug. Although, if I spent as much time working out as she did, I'd have been tempted to show off the results, too.

"Katy's always talking about how great your kids are," she said brightly.

I highly doubted that. "She's wonderful. They really love her."

"So . . . ," Jackie said, getting down to business, "your mother's interested in buying a condo in the area?"

"Yes, yes," I lied. "She'd like to be closer to me and the kids." Nothing could have been further from the truth. Not that my mother had anything *against* me or my children, but she was living the life she'd always dreamed of in Scottsdale. She and her second husband, Barry, a retired dentist, lived on the edge of a golf course and spent every day alternately on the links or in the pool. It was difficult to get her to visit us in frigid Denver, let alone move here.

"Let's go into my office." I followed her a short distance down the narrow hallway, until she stopped and ushered me into a tiny room. It was a typical, generic space with no personal touches—not even a framed photo of Katy. The desktop and credenza were immaculate and organized. I pulled out the fabric-covered chair and took a seat across from Jackie.

"We've got some great smaller units being built right now in the Cascade Development," she said, digging for a brochure in the filing cabinet at her side. "Is your mom alone?"

"No. She's with her husband." I paused a moment before proceeding. "I'd like to know more about the condos that Doug Sutherland is interested in."

There was only the slightest hesitation before she answered. Still fishing in her drawer, she said, "At this stage, Doug isn't looking at anything specific. He's considering downsizing at some point, so he just wants to know what's out there."

"Yes . . . well . . . I guess that makes sense," I said, "now that he's single."

"Yes," she agreed, righting herself. "Here's the brochure for the Cascade project." She slid it across the desk. "These units are being built with people just like your mother in mind. The complex has all the amenities that age group desires: whirlpool, gym, access to the new golf course being built at Sun Valley . . ."

"Great." I nodded and pretended to look at the brochure. "So . . . did Doug call you and tell you he was thinking of moving?"

"Uh . . . no." She was obviously taken aback by my bluntness. "I ran into him at the gym. He mentioned that he was interested in some of the new developments just south of us."

"So you two go to the same gym? Do you see him there often?"

"Once in a while," she said, nervously fishing in her drawerful of brochures again. "We're both very busy, so we sometimes work out early in the morning."

I noted the use of *we.* She was sounding very *couple-y,* all of a sudden. "I'm glad he's exercising. It must help him deal with the enormous grief he's experiencing after losing his wife so suddenly . . . and so *recently.*"

Jackie placed another brochure on the desk, but her eyes were slightly narrowed when she spoke. "I think Doug seems to be doing quite well, actually. He's healing nicely."

"It'll take years for him to really get over Karen."

"Of course. But that doesn't mean he has to stop living."

"No, but it doesn't mean he should be jumping into a relation-ship anytime soon, either."

"Well . . . I'm sure he'll do what's right for him."

"As long as he's not pressured into something before he's ready."

Jackie looked at her watch. "I've got another appointment," she said coldly. "Perhaps you'd like to pass these brochures on to your mother—if she is, in fact, interested in buying a condo."

"Of course she is!" I cried. She could not dismiss me until I'd gained more insight into Jackie and Doug's relationship! "Mom was just telling me on the phone how much she misses us and can't wait to move into her own place out here." Pausing, I began to rub my neck. "Man, my shoulders are so tight."

"Well," she said, smiling falsely, "when your mother gets to town, why don't you ask her to come see me?"

"I will. Ooooh . . . my neck is killing me."

"I've got to go, Paige. I'm meeting a client in ten minutes."

"Okay," I said dejectedly. "Thanks for your time."

As usual, my sleuthing had revealed nothing concrete. All I knew for certain was that Jackie was interested in Doug and that she defi-nitely did not rub the necks of all her potential clients. But I didn't know how intense their relationship was, how long they'd been see-ing each other, or any of the other important information I had hoped to ferret out. I certainly hadn't discovered that Doug had brainwashed her into killing his wife so they could be together. Maybe it was time I admitted to myself that my detective work sucked?

Twenty minutes later, I pulled into my driveway. Getting out of the vehicle, I stopped and stared down the street at Karen and Doug's empty home. I felt a bubble of emotion building in my chest. "Sorry, Karen," I whispered. "I guess I'm just not very good at this." Turning away before I dissolved into tears, I hurried toward the house.

After pausing to collect the mail from the brass box affixed to my house, I let myself inside. There were a number of missives—a good distraction from the despondency now setting in. As I walked to the kitchen, I sorted through the pile: bill, bill, low-interest credit-card offer, bank statement, pink scented envelope addressed to me . . . I flipped it over. There was no return address. Eagerly, I tore into it. At first, the envelope appeared to be empty, but as I tipped it on end, a single pressed red rose fell onto the counter. Confused, I stared for a moment at the delicate flower lying there before me. It had a white satin ribbon tied around the stem and a tiny card affixed to it. I opened it. It said only:

 Please?

J.

Damn him! I grabbed the torn envelope and looked at the top right corner: there was no stamp! He had been here again. Javier had hand-delivered this flower to my home. This was waaaaaaaaay too much! Why did he want to see me so badly? Why did he drive all the way out here to drop this note off? I had to admit, I'd been looking pretty darn good those nights I'd gone to see him at the coffee shop. And of course, Javier was under the illusion that I had perky, voluptuous breasts thanks to the water bra, but still . . . It was like he was in love with me or something. I mean, I didn't look *that* hot . . . , did I? Sheesh! It was enough to give a girl a big head.

But I was not going to go see him. If I ignored him, he would go away, eventually. Like a pimple . . . a very attractive pimple. I couldn't deny the fact that I still found Javier incredibly alluring, but I was committed to my marriage. Things were better between Paul and me lately. We had reconnected, at least a few times, and I was hopeful for more. Besides, I didn't know what, if any, role Javier had played in Karen's life . . . and death. It would be irresponsible, and just a bit twisted, to see him again.

The phone rang, startling me. For some reason, I scooped up the dried flower and tossed it in the trash before answering. It wasn't like the caller could *see* through the phone, but I felt better with it safely disposed of. If it turned out to be Paul on the line, I didn't want that stupid rose staring at me and making me feel all guilty and flustered.

"Hello?" I answered, forcing a light and airy tone. It was Jane.

"I've been thinking . . . ," she said. "We should get together for coffee again soon. I think we should make it a regular occasion, like we used to."

"Sounds good. We could do it at my house next."

"Okay. Do Wednesday mornings still work for you?"

"Uhhh . . . ," I said, checking the calendar for dentist appointments or volunteer field-trip supervision. "Yep. Wednesdays look good."

"Great. I'll call Trudy and Carly. And umm . . ." She hesitated. "I thought I'd invite Margot Bauman as well."

"Who?" My voice was a high-pitched squeak.

"Margot Bauman," Jane explained. "I'm sure you've seen her around. Tall . . . darkish wavy hair, quite attractive . . . Her daughter goes to preschool with Ainsley, and she has a son in third grade at Rosedale."

"I don't know her."

"She's really great. I've spent some time with her over the last few months, and I thought she'd be a good addition to our group."

Why was everyone so eager to replace Karen? First Doug and now Jane! "Well . . . ," I said, "I don't know that our group really needs an addition, does it?"

"It couldn't hurt," my friend replied. "It was great getting together last time, but it was a little . . . *maudlin*. If we get some fresh blood, it'll shift the focus. We can start living in the present again."

I couldn't believe she was talking this way! Did she think we could just plunk this Margot person into Karen's seat and move on as if she'd never been here? This coffee klatch was supposed to be a tribute to her memory! A special time dedicated to reminiscence! It was just wrong! Hopefully, Trudy and Carly would agree with me. "I don't know, Jane . . ."

"I'm not trying to *replace* Karen, for God's sake," she said, seemingly irritated by my reluctance. "But we have to go on with our lives. Do you really think it's healthy to spend every Wednesday morning reminiscing about our dead friend?"

"It's only been a month and a half!" I cried.

"It'll be two months on Monday."

"Oh . . . well, then, we should just forget all about her." My voice dripped with sarcasm.

"We will never forget her," Jane said emphatically. "But it doesn't mean we can't make new friends."

"How would you feel if Doug was making a new friend already?"

"That's different. Doug and Karen were married. They were exclusive. It's not like Karen told us we weren't allowed to have any other friends."

"Yeah. But how *would* you feel if Doug was making a new friend?"

"What do you mean by *new friend*?"

I told her what I had witnessed through the window last night as I was out for a casual evening stroll. She was quiet for a long moment. "You're sure it wasn't just a business meeting?"

"They were drinking wine! She was rubbing his shoulders!"

"It does sound a little . . . *friendly.*"

"I'll say. . . . Do you think . . ." I hesitated, unsure if I should ask Jane to ponder this possibility. "Do you think they could have been seeing each other before . . . ?"

"Before? Before when?"

My voice was hushed. "Before Karen died."

"Oh my God! What are you trying to say, Paige? That Doug was cheating on Karen with Jackie Baldwin? That they may have wanted her dead so that they could be together? Do you think they might have conspired to kill her?"

Laid out like that, it sounded incredibly far-fetched. "Ummm . . . I'm not saying that, exactly . . . I just wondered . . . Well, it's just so soon for him to be uh . . . getting his shoulders rubbed by someone else."

"Yeah, but that doesn't mean they're a pair of scheming murderers. God, you've been watching too much *CSI.*"

If one more person told me that . . . ! "Look, I've got to get going," I said shortly. "I've got some things to do before I pick up the kids."

"Okay. So, are we on for Wednesday at your place?"

"Sure," I said, with all the enthusiasm of scheduling a root canal.

"And what about Margot?"

I heaved a sigh of resignation. It wasn't really fair to exclude this poor Margot person because of my own hang-ups. "Bring her along," I said. "It's fine with me."

CHAPTER 23

The following afternoon, the phone rang.

"Paige?"

My heart skipped a beat at the sound of a male voice saying my name. All I needed was for Javier to start calling me and pestering me at home. But this voice had just said *Paige,* not *Paaaaaige,* with an incredibly sexy Spanish accent that made all the hair on my arms stand on end.

"Speaking," I replied.

"Troy Portman here."

"Oh . . . hello."

"Could we talk? Preferably in person?"

"Umm . . . okay. When?"

"The sooner, the better."

"All right. Same place? I can be there in an hour."

"See you then."

I arrived at the diner fifty-six minutes later. Detective Portman was already seated in the same booth, a cup of coffee before him.

This time, as I strode to meet him, I had no qualms about being a *stoolie*. If I could help the police get to the bottom of this mystery, I would. The uncertainty was destroying me. I was also just a little tired of Trudy and Carly getting all the accolades for their charity work and lasagna making.

"Thanks for coming," he said, half standing as I slid in across from him.

"Of course. So . . . is there any news on the case?"

"We got the paternity test results back."

I leaned forward anxiously. "And?"

"The baby was not Doug Sutherland's."

A queasy feeling came over me, and I flopped back in my seat. Oh God. So Karen had been sleeping with Javier. I had been such a fool to believe his lies—a sad, pathetic, later-in-life fool.

"The problem is . . . ," Portman said, pausing while Vera filled my coffee cup, "we don't know who the father is."

"Obviously it must be that Javier character," I said disdainfully. "Karen told me they were sleeping together."

"We have no way to prove it, though. He refused to give us a DNA sample."

"Well, that's like an admission of guilt, isn't it?"

"Unfortunately, it doesn't work that way."

"So . . . what happens now?"

Portman sighed and took a sip of his coffee. "With no evidence of a physical relationship between them, we have no reason to pursue our investigation of him any further. Mr. Rueda said he was working the day your friend died, and his coworkers confirm it."

Who? For a moment, I was confused. Then I realized that I didn't even know Javier's last name. Mentally, I had made love to him approximately thirty-seven times, and yet, I didn't even know his surname. I really was a pervert. "Well, his coworkers could be lying to protect him, couldn't they?"

"It's possible."

"What about fingerprints? His prints must have been at the scene."

"They weren't—which doesn't necessarily mean he wasn't there."

"It has to be Javier's baby. Who else could it be?"

Portman shrugged. "You never know . . . Karen Sutherland had a lot of secrets."

He was right: Karen had had a lot of secrets. Maybe she had been sleeping with someone else entirely, and Javier had been sort of a decoy? But that was ridiculous! I was just trying to protect my own ego by pretending that Javier had eyes only for me. He'd probably spent hours parked outside Karen's house, sent her numerous pressed flowers and cutesy notes requesting coffee dates . . . before, of course, he impregnated her and then possibly pushed her over.

"What if . . ."—I hesitated for only a second before plunging forward—"I could provide you with a DNA sample from Mr. Rueda?"

"Don't even think about contacting him, Paige. He could be dangerous."

"He wouldn't hurt me. I know it."

"I'm sure that's what Karen Sutherland thought, too."

"If you really think he hurt Karen, then how can you just let him go?" Desperation had made my voice shrill.

"I'm not convinced he did," Portman said. "This one's got me stumped. But I can't take the chance of you seeing him again. It's too risky."

He sounded very protective, almost like my big brother . . . or my *boyfriend*. It was sweet. "I won't see him again if you don't want me to," I replied, flirting just a tiny bit. "So . . . just out of curiosity, could you get DNA from a coffee cup or a spoon or something?" I was sure I'd seen them do that on TV.

"Yeah. DNA can be analyzed from any body tissues or fluids: hair, blood, bone, saliva, semen . . ."

"Oh jeez!" I said, blushing like a teenager at the mention of Javier's semen. I continued nervously, "Okay . . . so, hypothetically, if he drank out of a paper coffee cup, you could get his DNA from the cup?"

"Anything with trace saliva on it will have his DNA on it, so basically, anything he puts his mouth on."

This gave me another idea, but I was too embarrassed to ask if I could hand my lips in for analysis. Besides, Javier was becoming less attractive by the second. But still, I *needed* to know if he was the father of Karen's baby and what role he had played in her death.

"But there's a difference between obtaining DNA and obtaining *legally admissible* DNA," Portman was saying. "In order to use a DNA sample, we have to be able to prove that it wasn't contaminated by another party, and we also need to prove that the person had no further use for the object and . . ."

My mind drifted from his legalistic cop talk. I was sure that I could safely get some of Javier's DNA. It was as simple as taking him up on his coffee invitation—and taking the cup home with me. Then I'd turn it in to the police for testing. I felt confident that they'd find a way to make it legally admissible. I'd probably just have to sign an affidavit or something. I was pretty certain that was how it worked on *Law & Order.*

"So, you see, it's not as simple as just handing over an object with his trace saliva on it," Troy finished.

"Right," I said. "But there's something else I think you need to know." I leaned forward. "It's about Doug Sutherland."

He leaned in toward me. "Go on . . ."

"I think he might be involved with another woman . . . *already.*"

Portman did not look shocked. "Okay . . . well, thanks for passing that along."

"It's just so soon, don't you think? I mean, Karen's only been gone for a couple of months. It makes me wonder if maybe . . . they were seeing each other . . . *before.*"

This piqued his interest a little. He pulled out his small blue notepad. "Who is the woman he's seeing?"

"Her name is Jackie Baldwin. She works for Boca Developments selling condos. She says Doug's just interested in getting a smaller place, but I saw them together, and they looked rather . . . intimate."

"Can you be more specific?"

"They were drinking wine, which obviously isn't very professional. And then she began rubbing his shoulders."

Portman continued to jot notes. "And where did this take place?"

"In Karen's house! Well . . . I guess it's Doug's house, now. I saw it all through the window, as I was walking by."

"Had you seen them together when Karen was alive?"

"Uh . . . no, I don't think so."

"And did Karen mention to you that she suspected her husband was having an affair?"

"No." I could tell where this was going. "But Karen's only two months in the grave and Doug's getting shoulder rubs from another woman? That's just not right! Not to mention this Jackie character has a bit of a reputation in the neighborhood, if you know what I mean. A bit of a . . ."—I lowered my voice to a whisper—*"cougar."*

Portman suppressed a smile. "That's all very . . . interesting. But it's not evidence."

I felt a little insulted by his dismissive attitude. If he told me I'd been watching too much *CSI,* I would storm out and never come back. "I just thought you should know," I said sulkily.

"We'll definitely keep this in mind, going forward."

"Okay. Thanks."

When I got home, I was antsy. I was dying to head to The Old Grind, but the children would be out of school in less than an hour. Obviously, I couldn't take them with me. I would have to wait for Paul to get home before I could head into town again. It would be more than a little awkward to ask Katy Baldwin to babysit at this stage. Then an idea struck me. I could take the children to Trudy's! She still owed me one for looking after her little nightmares when she was paralyzed by grief. And I was sure she wouldn't mind. Spencer and Chloe were always well behaved for people who were not their parents. I picked up the phone and dialed.

Trudy was more than happy to have the kids over for a playdate while I went to my very important last-minute dentist appointment. Now I just had to give my husband the same excuse. As I called the office, I couldn't help but feel an uncomfortable swell of guilt rising in the pit of my stomach. I had been lecturing Paul on our need to reconnect, and yet, I continued to lie to him. Taking a deep breath, I pushed these feelings aside. Once I had solved Karen's murder, I would throw all of that energy into my marriage.

After several rings, Paul's voice mail answered. I have to admit I was relieved. I left a breezy message about a last-minute cancellation at the dentist's office and how I desperately wanted her to look at my receding gums on the lower left side. If the kids and I weren't home when he arrived, could he please pick them up at Trudy's? Of course, we'd probably be there, but just in case I got delayed or something . . . Hanging up, I changed into the water bra, applied a quick coat of mascara, and was on my way.

The Old Grind was busier in the late afternoon than it had been on my previous nighttime visits. Busy was good. It was much safer to meet with a potential killer in a crowded coffee shop than in some secluded alley or parking lot. I walked through the convivial din of coffee drinkers socializing and conducting business directly to the counter. It was so hectic in there that I hoped Javier would have time to take a break and have a cup of coffee with me. If he didn't, I wondered if there was any way I could get him to quickly lick a spoon or place his saliva on some other object for me? Patiently, I stood in line behind two other patrons, ordering a vanilla latte and a chai tea. The customers were being served by a cute young girl with a multitude of braids in her hair and an alarmingly large nose ring. But Javier had to be here somewhere, didn't he? Perhaps in the back, getting more soy milk or honey? This was peak time, after all.

When it was my turn, I got straight to the point. "Is Javier here?"

"No, not until tonight," she replied. "Can I get you something?"

"Uh . . . no, I was supposed to meet him . . ."

"Are you Paige?"

"Yes."

"He left this for you." I hadn't noticed the small white envelope propped against the tip jar, but as the braided girl handed it to me, I saw it was emblazoned with my name.

"Thanks." Snatching up the envelope, I hurried back to my car. I didn't want to open it in this crowded establishment and risk having a flower, a chocolate heart, or edible panties fall out on the floor. In the privacy of my vehicle, I tore it open with shaking hands. Inside was a tiny deep purple dried pansy. God, Javier must have garbage bags full of these things at home. There was also a small folded note. It read:

 Please?
303-555-4272
J.

The hand-drawn coffee cup had been kind of cute, but now, with this telephone, it was becoming kind of *cutesy*. I had to admit that Javier did have some artistic ability, but enough was enough! I was pleased that I was not swooning over Javier's little tokens like some lovesick teenager. Really, I was almost beginning to find him slightly . . . *annoying*. But still, I withdrew my cell phone and dialed the number on the paper.

"Hello?"

The sound of his voice sent an involuntary shiver through me. He's annoying, remember? I chastised myself. And a bit cheesy. Not to mention quite possibly lethal. "It's Paige," I said.

"Paige!" He sounded positively thrilled to hear from me. "You got my note?"

"Yeah, both of them. I was wondering if you wanted to get together for coffee?"

"I would love to," he said, and all the hair stood up on my arms, dammit. "Now?"

"Yes, now. I told Paul I was at the dentist."

"Of course, of course I can come now. Where are you?"

"I'm outside The Old Grind."

"We will go somewhere with more privacy, yes? On the same street, two blocks up, there is a place called Pear. I will meet you there."

I found the small, intimate bar easily and was seated at a table near the front within minutes. The place was nearly deserted, but I still felt relatively safe. Javier was unlikely to murder me in front of the bartender, the waitress, and the drunk salesman seated alone in the far back corner. I looked at my watch: 4:30. I should have ample time to collect the DNA sample and get home safely to my family . . . as long as Javier showed up soon.

He did. Less than five minutes after my arrival, he strolled into the dimly lit bistro. Obviously, he lived very close by. As he made his way toward me, a sexy smile spread across his lips, and I felt my breath catch in my chest. God, he was good-looking. But it was a physical reaction only. I couldn't forget that he had lied to me about his relationship with Karen, and I was here to prove it. Also, his habit of drawing little coffee cups and phones was really corny.

"I am so happy to see you," he said, as he sat down across from me. I let him take my hand and squeeze it, just for a moment. "You look beautiful."

"Thanks. Should we order a drink?" I wanted to expedite this process.

"I will get them from the bar. What will you have?"

"A glass of red wine, please." I hoped Javier would order a beer or, even better, a highball with a straw in it. I didn't want to have to steal a glass.

I watched him as he moved to the bar. He was wearing a dark brown leather jacket cut to accentuate his broad shoulders and a pair of perfectly faded Levi's. I was quite sure I'd seen Brad Pitt wearing a similar ensemble in a magazine. Javier obviously had style . . . and, somehow, money. But how did he afford a hip wardrobe and a luxury car on coffee-shop wages? There had to be another source of income, something that paid him extremely well. Oh God! Maybe he was a gigolo?

He returned a few moments later holding two glasses of red wine. Shit. "Thanks," I said.

"My pleasure," he replied. "I am just so happy you agreed to meet me."

"Well . . . yes. I wanted to ask you not to come to my house again."

He looked pained. "I should not have, but I was desperate to talk to you. Last time . . . it was not good. I am so sorry."

"Oh, for kidnapping me? Think nothing of it."

"I feel bad. Please . . . will you forgive me?"

"I suppose." I shrugged.

"I was so upset because of the police. They treated me like a guilty man. I am only guilty of being a friend to Karen. That is all."

"Right," I said. "That's a beautiful jacket you've got there."

"Thank you."

"I wouldn't mind getting one like that for Paul's birthday. Where did you get it?"

"It was a gift."

Of course it was . . . Probably a gift from one of his *sugar mamas,* or whatever the term was. "You're a lucky guy, Javier. Your aunt dies and leaves you money for a beautiful car, your *friend* buys you a beautiful jacket . . ."

"My sister," he said.

"Sorry?"

"My sister bought me this jacket when she came to visit from Spain. She is a wealthy lady . . . married to a politician."

"Oh. That's great . . . wealthy aunt, wealthy sister . . ."

He was beginning to eye me a little warily, and I realized I was being antagonistic. The anger I felt at having been lied to about his relationship with Karen was seeping into our discourse. I would have to tone it down. After all, I couldn't have him stalking off in a huff. He had to at least stay until his glass was empty.

"So . . . ," I said, smiling sweetly, "does your sister come to America often?"

"Not so often. But she comes once in a while. My other sisters do not come at all. They cannot afford the trip."

"That's too bad," I said sympathetically. "Do you go home much?"

"The last time I went home was two years ago, for my niece's wedding. It is hard to go home. I am busy. My life is here."

"Don't you ever get lonely?"

"Sometimes I feel very lonely." He gazed intently into my eyes. "But right now, I do not. I feel . . . like I am home." Oh brother. Was I supposed to fall for that line? Maybe it was because I'd recently discovered Javier was a liar and quite likely a killer, but it had no effect on me. Besides, I had bigger concerns. Javier's glass was still half full, and I was rapidly running out of idle chitchat. Fortunately, he picked up the conversation. "Tell me about your family."

"Well . . . ," I said, seizing the opportunity, "I'll need a stronger drink if I'm going to get into all that!"

Javier laughed. "What would you like?"

"I'll have a vodka and tonic. But please . . . let me get it. And can I get you another drink? Rum and Coke? Bloody Mary? Piña colada?" I rattled off all the straw drinks I could think of.

"No," he said, standing, "I invited you here tonight. I will buy."

Damn. As Javier went to the bar, I looked at his glass of red wine. It was almost like I could see his DNA crawling around on the rim. Not that I knew what DNA looked like, even if you could see it with the naked eye, but I had a mental image of little chain-link things with hundreds of legs. I had to get that glass to the police. (I would worry about its admissibility later.)

My mind scrambled for a plan. I could pour the wine into a nearby plant, stuff the glass in my purse, and tell Javier that a waitress had picked it up assuming he was done. My eyes were searching frantically for a potted fig when I felt Javier's gaze upon me. He was smiling in my direction and dropping a green plastic straw into my V&T. I noticed, with chagrin, that he had not ordered himself another beverage.

"Thanks," I said, trying to mask my dismay at his drinkless return. "You're not going to have another?"

"I will finish my wine first," he said, retaking his seat. "You were going to tell me about your family."

"Right. Yes, well . . . my mom's retired in Arizona, my dad's retired in Florida, and I have a younger brother who's a stock trader in New York."

Javier nodded, probably wondering why I would need a stronger drink to relay such a mundane story. "Do you see them much?"

"Once or twice a year . . ." I shrugged indifferently. Suddenly, like one of Oprah's lightbulb moments, I knew how I was going to get Javier's DNA. Picking up my highball, I took a small sip from the rim of the glass. "Ewww . . ." I made a face. "This doesn't taste right."

"Really?" Javier looked puzzled.

"Something's not right." I proffered the drink to him, the green straw pointed in his direction. "Taste it. Doesn't it taste strange?"

His lips descended upon the straw as if in slow motion. I just barely refrained from cheering *yessssssssssssss!* "It tastes fine . . . like a normal vodka and tonic."

"Vodka tonic?" I asked, taking the glass back. "I wanted a vodka *soda.*"

"I'm sorry. I must have heard wrong. I'll get you another."

"You know what? It's fine," I said breezily, surreptitiously re-moving the straw from the glass and holding it under the table. "I shouldn't have any more to drink, anyway. I've got a long drive ahead of me."

"Can I get you a coffee? A soft drink?"

"I should go." Hidden from view, my hands dropped the straw into my purse. "I didn't realize it was so late."

It was almost dusk as Javier walked me to my car. Surprisingly, I felt completely at ease with him, despite the darkening sky and rela-tively secluded surroundings. "I wish you could have stayed longer," he said, when we reached our destination.

"Sorry," I shrugged helplessly, "but I've got to get home to the kids."

"Could we . . ." He sounded almost shy. "Could we meet again sometime?"

"Honestly, Javier, I don't think it's a good idea."

"Paige, I understand that you are married and that you love your family. I would never ask you to forsake them. But since I met you, I can't stop thinking about you."

Oh great.

He reached for my hand. "I am not asking for a lot. I know you cannot give it to me. But please . . . tell me you won't cut me out of your life completely. You are such an amazing woman . . ." He smoothed a lock of hair from my forehead. "Beautiful . . . sensual . . . compassionate . . ."

Good God! I was half expecting to be billed for all this flattery. "Look, Javier, . . . if you promise not to come by my house again, I suppose I could meet you for coffee or a drink . . . sometime."

"Really? You would?" He looked like I'd just bought him another Audi. "I am so thankful. Our friendship . . . it means so much to me. *You* mean so much to me."

This was really weirding me out. We had only met briefly a few times. He didn't even know how old I was, the names of my children, or the true size of my breasts. He had lied to my face about his relationship with Karen, but now, suddenly, I meant so much to him? Whether he was a killer or not, the guy had serious problems. "Okay," I said, like he was a small child or mentally challenged, "I'll drop by the coffee shop again one day."

"Soon, I hope." He brought my hand to his lips. "Thank you."

No, thank *you,* I thought as I hopped into the driver's seat, for the nice little DNA sample.

CHAPTER 24

I was dying to take the straw in to Detective Portman for analysis, but first, I had to endure coffee with my friends and Margot Bauman. Admittedly, I was not starting out with a very positive attitude, but I still felt it was a little early to be filling Karen's seat at the table.

Before their 10:00 A.M. arrival, I scurried around the house, frantically tidying. I seemed to have so many other things occupying my mind lately that housework had fallen to the bottom of the list . . . or right off the list by the looks of my family room. I wouldn't have been so concerned if it was only Carly, Trudy, and Jane coming over, but I didn't want to give Margot a bad first impression. Not that I was particularly keen to make a new friend, but neither did I want her to judge me for my slovenliness.

By the time my guests arrived, I had knocked the dust off most of the furniture and thrown several armloads of toys, books, and games onto my children's bedroom floors. At least now the kitchen and family room were presentable. I welcomed first Trudy, then

Carly, then Jane accompanied by Becca and little Amelia, who quickly vanished into the playroom to enjoy some fun, yet educational activities. Margot had still not arrived as I poured coffees for my friends. Maybe she had decided that it was too soon to infiltrate our clique?

No sooner had I finished that thought than the doorbell rang. "That must be Margot," Jane said. "I'll let her in."

"Thanks," I called, joining Trudy and Carly at the kitchen table. Soon, Jane returned followed by a tall brunette with bright blue eyes and a friendly smile. She looked familiar; I had definitely seen her around Rosedale.

"Girls, this is Margot." Margot smiled and gave us a little wave. "Margot, this is Trudy, Carly, . . . and Paige, our hostess today." Trudy and Carly welcomed her, and even I greeted her warmly. It wasn't really Margot's fault that Jane had invited her to join us prematurely. It would be rude to be inhospitable.

"So, Margot . . . ," Trudy said, as I fetched our new addition a cup of coffee, "how many children do you have?"

"Two," she replied. "My daughter goes to preschool with Ainsley, and I have an eight-year-old son in the third grade at Rosedale."

"That's how we met," Jane explained. "Ainsley and Sophia have so much fun together that we've been having playdates every week."

"And where is little Sophia today?" Trudy asked.

"She's at her pottery class. I've got to pick her up in an hour."

"Oh, my Emily loved pottery class," Trudy said. "Actually, Cameron liked it, too. They both took classes a couple of years ago, but now they're involved in a number of other activities."

"And how old are they?" Margot asked.

"Emily's nine, and Cameron's six—almost the same age as Paige's kids."

"Yep," I said, sliding the cream and sugar toward Margot. "My daughter's ten, and my son is six."

"And what about you?" Margot turned to Carly. "How old are your little ones?"

I always felt pangs of sympathy for Carly whenever our conversations turned too *mommy*. It must have been hard for her to listen to us gush on about preschool and pottery classes and how fast they all were growing. I knew she was desperate to have a family of her own someday, but as far as I could see, she wasn't anywhere close . . . unless, of course, a man could impregnate you by handing you a free Diet Coke. When Karen was with us, we had had a nice balance in our group: three were mommies, two were not. It had ensured that our topics of conversation were wide and varied, not focusing too much attention on our various offspring. But with Margot in our circle, there was a perceptible shift, and Carly was definitely the odd one out.

But to my surprise, she smiled easily at the newcomer before answering. "I don't have any children *yet,* but, hopefully, one day . . ." She held up her crossed fingers.

God, she had become so Zen. Maybe she felt that decluttering her garage would make room in her womb for a couple of kids?

"I went through a difficult divorce a few years ago," Carly explained. "My husband ran off with another woman who had two young sons. I was angry and hurt for a long time, but given recent events, I've really been able to put things in perspective."

Jane leaned in to Margot. "I don't know if you heard about Karen Sutherland. She was a very close friend of ours."

"I did hear," Margot said sympathetically. "It's such a terrible tragedy. She was so young."

We all nodded silently. At the mere mention of her name, my eyes threatened to well up with tears. It just seemed so strange and sad to be sitting here drinking coffee without our treasured friend.

"It's been hard on all of us," Jane said.

Trudy added, "And her husband is devastated. They had been hoping to start a family."

"Although . . . ," Jane said—and by her tone, I could sense what was coming—"Paige thinks Doug might be moving on a little too quickly."

"What's this?" Carly asked.

Shut up, Jane, I silently willed her. Why do I tell you anything? You are such a blabbermouth.

"Paige saw Jackie Baldwin over at Doug's the other night. They were drinking wine and . . ." Jane paused for dramatic effect.

"What?" Trudy asked.

"She was rubbing his shoulders!" Her tone was exaggerated, as if I had witnessed something really incriminating, like *she was licking his testicles!*

"Well . . . ," Trudy said nervously, "she's probably trying to sell him a condo. He mentioned that he was thinking of downsizing."

"He did?" This came as a surprise to me, but then, I hadn't done more than wave to Doug since the funeral.

"It's normal to want to leave a house where such a terrible accident occurred," she continued. "He probably feels haunted by Karen's memory there."

"Yeah," Carly agreed. "But obviously, moving is a huge emotional step. He was probably tense, and Jackie was trying to get him to relax."

"True," Margot said, nodding. What did she know? She'd just joined us, and she was already making suppositions about Doug and Jackie's relationship.

"Although . . . ," Jane was saying, "Jackie does have a reputation for going to any lengths to make a sale." Her tone became suggestive. "She's rather famous for going *above and beyond* the call of duty to close a deal."

"Oh my gosh!" Carly said, looking at her watch. "I completely forgot I've got a conference call at 10:45." She hopped up. "I've got to go. Sorry girls."

"Oh no . . . ," we all murmured in dismay. "Could you come back afterward?"

"This will take a while," Carly said, pulling on her sweater. "Thanks for the coffee, Paige. Margot, so nice to meet you."

I couldn't help but wish that I had a conference call at 10:45 or some other reason to put an end to this gathering. Maybe I was overreacting, but their lighthearted banter about Doug having wine and massages with our sexually aggressive neighbor bothered me. It just wasn't right. It was too soon. And as warm and friendly as Margot was, maybe it was too soon for her to be sitting in on these conversations? It didn't feel right to have this virtual stranger listening to us discuss the length of Doug's grieving period.

With our only childless member gone, the conversation turned to our kids, their schools, and various extracurricular activities. I tried to keep my mind from wandering to the small green straw sealed in a sandwich bag nestled in my purse, but I was dying to get the evidence to Detective Portman. Once we knew for certain that Javier was the father of Karen's baby, then the police could begin their investigation of him in earnest—because if he could lie so convincingly about the nature of his relationship with my friend, then he could lie about his involvement in her death, too.

Finally, Margot excused herself to go pick up her daughter from pottery class. I made rumblings about having a number of errands to run, and my other guests got the hint. When I had seen my friends out, I hurried to the phone to call Portman.

"I need to see you," I said almost gleefully. "It's important."

"Sure . . . uh . . ." There was a pause, and when he spoke again, his voice was hushed. "Let's meet somewhere different this time. There's a Starbucks on the corner of Sixteenth and Lawrence."

"Okay. That's a bit of a walk for you, isn't it?"

"I could use the fresh air."

"See you soon!"

Portman was not there when I arrived. I decided to take the liberty of ordering us a couple of lattes. It was sure to be a treat for him after drinking Vera's weak and tepid diner coffee. I was still waiting at the counter when he walked in. He took off his sunglasses and scanned the room. When his eyes fell upon me, he smiled briefly and came over.

"I've ordered you a latte," I said.

"Great. Thanks. I'll go get us a table. There's one at the back over there." He pointed to a secluded corner near the restrooms.

I watched him take his seat. In this setting, there was something unmistakably authoritative about him, something that just seemed to scream *COP!!!* As usual, I couldn't ignore Detective Portman's almost macho attractiveness. But today, there was something differ-ent in his manner. Maybe it was the unfamiliar environment, but Troy seemed fidgety, uneasy, even . . . nervous. It was also odd that he had chosen for us an isolated table uncomfortably close to the men's toilet.

With a painfully warm paper cup in each hand, I hurried to join him. "Did you want sugar or anything?" I offered.

"This is fine, thanks. I can reimburse you the cost of the coffees if you give me a receipt."

"Don't be silly!" I waved away the offer. "It's my treat. I just ap-preciate you picking a meeting place where the coffee doesn't taste like dishwater."

"Ha-ha . . ." It was a forced laugh.

"Seriously . . . it's really nice of you. I know it's out of your way."

"Well . . ." He cleared his throat loudly. "I guess we should get down to business. What did you want to see me about?"

I felt a little flush of embarrassment at being cut off so abruptly. Apparently, Portman wasn't in the mood for niceties. "Okay . . . ," I said, fishing in my purse for the sandwich bag full of Javier's DNA. "I've got some . . . uh, *evidence.*" I whispered the word, sliding the plastic pouch across the table.

Portman looked at it. "What's this?"

"It's a straw with Javier Rueda's DNA on it."

"Paige . . ." He trailed off with an exasperated sigh.

"Now you can test the paternity of Karen's baby!" I was feeling quite proud of myself.

He took a long sip of coffee before answering; his eyes were fixed on the restroom's sign above my head. "There's no way I can get it into the lab."

"Why not?"

"I explained the other day about legally admissible evidence. This would never fly."

"Okay!" I suddenly felt flustered. "So maybe this wouldn't be admissible in court, but you can still use it to test the baby's paternity, can't you? Like, just for your personal knowledge? And once you know the answer, you'll be able to investigate Javier further."

"I don't think so."

"Why not?" God, he was so "by the book." Hadn't he ever watched *The Shield*?

"Look," he said, his voice tinged with frustration, "You don't understand police work, okay? Besides, my partner wants to close the case."

"Close it?" I shrieked. I lowered my voice before continuing. "How can you close it? We don't know what happened to Karen yet!"

"Well . . . we do know what happened," he said calmly. "She fell and hit her head. Conroy doesn't think there's anything more to it than that."

"Did you tell him about the affair? That the baby wasn't Doug's?"

"A lot of people have affairs." He shrugged. "And both the husband and the boyfriend have alibis."

"People fake alibis all the time!" I cried. "Once you prove Karen's baby was Javier's, he'll be your prime suspect. Did you know that the leading cause of death in pregnant women is murder by the baby's father?"

"Yeah, I know . . ."

"Well, does Conroy know?"

"Of course he does, but . . ." He fidgeted nervously in his seat. His face had suddenly gone alarmingly red. "He thinks that I might have a . . . *conflict of interest* in this case."

"What do you mean?"

Another heavy sigh. "He thinks that I may not be acting in an entirely professional manner with regard to the investigation."

"I don't get it? You've been very professional."

His face was getting redder and redder. "He thinks I may have personal feelings for you that are interfering with my objectivity."

"Oh my God . . ." To think that just a few months ago, I had felt completely invisible to the opposite sex. And now it appeared they couldn't get enough of me!

"It would be completely unethical for me to get involved with you," Troy was saying. "And I know you're married. I'm in a relationship, too . . . a good relationship that I don't want to ruin."

"So Conroy's wrong, then," I said, only a tiny bit disappointed. "So there's no problem pursuing the case."

"Well, to be totally honest here . . . I do enjoy your company. I'm afraid I may have given more credence to some of your theories than they deserved just so I could spend time with you."

This was both flattering *and* insulting. I didn't know how to react. I decided to go with insulted. "How can you say my *theories* don't have credence? A woman ends up dead in her own attached garage, and you think the fact that she told me she was having an affair isn't relevant?"

"Normally, it would be, but . . ."

"But because you enjoy my company, it's not? That's the stupidest thing I've ever heard." I flopped back in my seat and angrily took a drink of my latte.

My petulance seemed to fluster the detective. "Look, I probably shouldn't have told you all this . . . I mean, I definitely shouldn't have . . . I just wanted you to know what I'm up against if I try to process DNA that was obtained illegally."

"What about the note?" I snapped. "How can you ignore that note?"

"We're not ignoring it, but even the note maintains it was an accident. Usually, when we get an anonymous letter about a crime, it incriminates someone."

I suddenly felt incredibly frustrated, almost despondent. Tears were beginning to pool in my eyes as I leaned across the table and reached for Troy's hand. Maybe I was being manipulative, but if he did kind of "enjoy my company," I was going to use it. "Troy, *please* . . . ," I said. "I know Karen's death was more than an accident.

Don't ask me how, but deep inside, I know it. I won't be able to get any peace until her murder is solved."

"I'd like to help you, Paige, but Conroy . . ." He trailed off. "I don't know what I can do."

I gave his hand a squeeze. "Analyze Mr. Rueda's DNA for me, Troy. If we can prove he's the father, Conroy will come around."

CHAPTER 25

Now there was nothing left to do but hope that Troy would take Javier's DNA to the lab and then wait for the results to come back. Whatever they were, I had to pray that Conroy would see fit to keep the case open. I didn't know where this newfound conviction had come from, but I just knew someone was there when Karen died. I could feel it in the pit of my stomach. It could have been Javier, as the letter implied; or Doug, as I was beginning to suspect; or even Jackie Baldwin. Alibis-shmalibis! On the other hand, it could have been someone else entirely. Karen could have been involved with another man, using Javier as a decoy. God, she could have been sleeping with one of the neighborhood husbands! Yikes! Not that I feared it was Paul; there was just no way. For one, I trusted my spouse. And for two, Paul barely had the time and energy for me, let alone an extra girlfriend. Besides, he had always thought Karen was a little on the skinny side . . . or at least that's what he said.

Instead of torturing myself with endless speculation, I decided to focus on Christmas preparations. Thanksgiving had passed with an overcooked Grade C turkey, canned cranberry sauce, and Stove Top Stuffing. It wasn't like me to neglect a major holiday, but I had been so preoccupied with other matters that I'd practically forgotten about it until it was too late. But Christmas would be different. I would be ready.

Paul's parents were coming from Boulder to spend the holidays with us. His mother was what would kindly be called meticulous (or unkindly: fussy, nit-picking, and high-maintenance). This year, I would blow her away with my festive decorations, abundance of baking, and perfect, thoughtful gifts for everyone. Chloe, for one, was already full of fabulous ideas for her Christmas present.

"Mom!" She skipped into the kitchen where I was chopping carrots for dinner. In her hand, she clutched a glossy, full-color flyer from an electronics store. "I know what I want for Christmas!"

I smiled at my daughter. She looked so exuberantly childlike that it warmed my heart. "What do you want Santa to bring you, honey?"

She held out a page and pointed to a device in the top left corner. "This!"

"What is it?" I leaned in for a closer look.

"It's a karaoke machine! It comes with an ultimate starter pack and mike!"

"Chloe . . ." I hated to put an end to her gleeful excitement and prompt the return of her preteen angst, but . . . "It's two thousand dollars."

"I know it's a lot, Mom, but it'll be such great practice for becoming a singer. And if you get me this for Christmas, you don't have to get me anything for my birthday in February."

"Sweetie . . ."

"Please, Mom. It's my dream."

Oh God. This was going to hurt us both. "We can't afford a two-thousand-dollar karaoke machine. I'm sorry. Is there a cheaper one in the flyer?"

She snatched it away. "Thanks a lot!" she wailed. "I bet Tina bought Jessica a *fifty*-thousand-dollar karaoke machine when she was my age!"

"Umm . . . ?"

"Jessica Simpson! Her mom, Tina, always believed in her and supported her dream to be a star."

The difference being that Jessica Simpson could actually sing. Poor Chloe didn't realize it, but she was completely tone-deaf. I'd suffered through enough renditions of "Sk8ter Boi" to know she was not going to become a musical star.

I put down the knife I was holding and spoke calmly to my elder child. "Of course I want to be supportive of you, Chloe. That's why I asked if there was a cheaper model available."

"Just forget it," she said sulkily. "I don't want some junky one."

"Well, that's your choice, then," I said, resuming my chopping. "There's plenty of time before Christmas for you to think of another gift."

"Can I get my belly button pierced?"

The knife clattered noisily on the cutting board. "You're ten!"

"Eleven in February."

"Oh . . . okay, then."

"Really?"

"No, not really!" I growled. "I can't believe you'd even ask if you're allowed to mutilate yourself for Christmas."

"It's not mutilating! It's cool!"

"When you're paying your own rent, you can pierce a bone through your nose if you want to, but while you're living under my roof, I draw the line at earrings."

"Fine," she snapped, turning on her heel to huff out of the room. "When I become a famous singer in a couple of years, I'm going to become legally emaciated! Then I can do whatever I want!"

It was wrong to laugh at her slipup—possibly even emotionally scarring—but it was just so darned funny. "Really?" I said, my lips twitching with mirth. "Well, when you're legally *very thin,* I guess you can pierce whatever you want to."

"What?" She was confused for a second, and then, "You are the meanest mom in the world!" I heard her feet thudding loudly on the stairs and then the door to her bedroom slamming.

I highly doubted that I was the meanest mom in the world. While it was obviously not very nice to mock my daughter's improper word choice, I had heard of mothers who locked their kids in closets for days on end. Obviously, they were far meaner than I. Besides, I would show Chloe that I wasn't such an ogre. This would be the best Christmas ever. I would find her a gift that would make her forget she ever wanted a two-thousand-dollar karaoke machine or a pierced navel. It would be something original, thoughtful, and relatively inexpensive, like . . . hmm . . . tickets to a Christina Aguilera concert and a backstage pass! Or a day at the skateboard park with Avril Lavigne! She'd be so thrilled. Although . . . other than winning some radio contest, I wasn't exactly sure how to make it a reality.

The very next day, I embarked on my best-Christmas-ever mission. As I drove to Aberdeen Mall, I knew my motivation was not pure. I didn't particularly care how great this Christmas turned out to be; I just wanted to show up my mother-in-law. And if I was being really honest with myself, this whole operation was just an attempt to distract myself from Javier's paternity-test results. In the four days since my meeting with Detective Portman, I had been tempted to call him approximately eighteen times. Somehow, I had refrained. I was afraid that Troy might misinterpret my persistence as flirtation, and I didn't want to jeopardize his effectiveness on the case. I seemed to have an incredible power over the opposite sex lately: I had to wield it very carefully.

Parking the car as close as I could to the main entrance, I made my way through the massive automatic doors and into the shopping center. In the real world, it was late November; in Aberdeen Mall, it was Christmas Eve. The length of the hallway was festooned with gold and silver garlands, miniature Christmas trees, giant candy canes, and enormous wreaths adorned with colorful glass balls. Surprisingly, this did nothing to get me into the festive spirit. In fact, it just seemed to put more pressure on me to get ready for my in-laws' arrival. At least this newfound panicky feeling left less time to dwell on Karen's murder.

I wandered mindlessly through the largely vacant halls, unsure of where to begin. The males in my life would be easy to shop for. Spencer had been talking incessantly of a Bionicle called Krekka; Paul had been hinting about a new golf bag for months; and Ted, my father-in-law, had a standing Christmas order in for Godiva chocolates and a subscription to *The New Yorker*. The females, however, presented more of a challenge. Of course, there was the Chloe issue to overcome, but more challenging still was Pauline. (Yes, my mother-in-law's name was Pauline, and yes, she had named her son after herself. That says it all, really.) Just for once, I wanted to get her a gift that she couldn't find fault with, no matter how hard she tried. Although . . . if that failed, I could buy her any old crap and tell her Paul picked it out himself. Needless to say, anything selected by her loving son was absolutely perfect.

Pausing to get my bearings in the sprawling complex, I found myself standing in front of the Victoria's Secret store. There, on a rack near the front, hung my red water bra—well, its larger cousin. A feeling of guilt washed over me at the sight of it. It was silly—I had bought the ensemble to resexualize my marriage, but I couldn't deny that I had worn the sexy underwear to meet Javier on several occasions. Why? Why had it been so important to delude him into thinking I had perky, voluptuous breasts? What had I been playing at? Would I have crossed that line? Yes, I had been angry and disappointed with my husband then—I still was, sporadically—but would I really have done something so reckless? If I had learned one thing from this whole mess with Karen, it was that adultery was a bad idea.

And that's when I saw him. He was at the cashier's counter, just pocketing his wallet after paying for his purchases. Grabbing the small pink plastic bag full of lingerie, he turned toward me. Shit! It was too late to duck, and it would be too obvious if I turned and ran. On his face, I saw my own chagrin reflected, briefly, but he quickly replaced it with a friendly, if somewhat forced, smile.

"Hi, Paige."

"Doug . . . hi."

"Just getting a little early Christmas shopping done," he said, indicating the bag almost sheepishly.

"Yeah, me too, . . ."

There was a slight pause. "It's for my sister."

"Your sister?"

"Well, I'm actually shopping on behalf of my brother-in-law," he explained. "My sister loves this lingerie, and they don't have Victoria's Secret in Canada."

"Really?" I tried hard to keep the skepticism from my voice.

"Yeah . . . so I told him I'd uh . . . pick it up for him." He chuckled self-consciously. "I feel a bit weird buying a bra and panties for my own sister."

"It's a bit weird, all right." I made myself laugh along with him.

"How are the kids?" he asked, after a moment.

"They're good . . . How are *you* doing?"

"I'm all right," he said. "It's still hard . . . Some days are better than others. Christmas will be tough."

"It will," I agreed. In that moment, I felt really connected to Doug. Any suspicions I had about him were replaced by genuine, heartfelt sympathy. But since he was here, I might as well do a little digging. "I hear you're thinking of moving?"

He was caught off-guard. "Moving?"

"Jackie Baldwin mentioned you were interested in buying a condo." I felt the need to explain my encounter with his lady friend. "My mom is thinking about getting a place out here and asked me to check into the condo market."

Doug looked a little pale. "Oh, well . . . it's only a thought at this stage. Jackie and I go to the same gym, and she mentioned these new developments just south of here. The house feels kind of big and empty these days. I may want to downsize at some point."

"Well, I'm sure Jackie can help you out. She's really good to her clients, isn't she?" He was looking at me like he thought I was strange again. Or was that the look of someone who'd just been found out? I continued, "She really seems to go that extra mile, y'know?"

"Yeah, she's great." He looked at his watch. "I'd better get going. I've got to get back to the office."

"Well . . . nice seeing you. Have a great day."

I could no longer concentrate on shopping, that much was certain. Giving Doug a sufficient head start, I headed for the exit. Buying lingerie for his sister? Yeah, right! What kind of creepy brother bought lingerie for his sister? What kind of creepy brother-in-law would ask him to do it? What—did he just call Doug up and say "Would you mind popping into the mall and picking out a sexy bra and panties for your sister to wear? Something really skimpy and transparent would be great"? I doubted it. And even if there were no Victoria's Secret stores in Canada, they surely had the catalog. The brother-in-law could have ordered his wife's Christmas lingerie. They lived in Vancouver, for heaven's sake, not in some igloo on the arctic tundra!

The encounter with Doug plagued me the whole way home. He had to have been buying a gift for Jackie Baldwin. He had noticeably paled when I confronted him about moving. He'd been awkward and shaky when I mentioned her name. There were just too many signs. Sure, everyone had brushed it off when I told them about the wine and shoulder rubbing I'd witnessed, but this was different. This was something tangible! Tangibly sexual! Their relationship couldn't be discounted any longer.

When I pulled into the driveway, I was still feeling agitated. I needed to unload this burden to someone, but to whom? Paul would tell me to mind my own business. Jane would tell me I was watching too many cop shows. Trudy would get all uncomfortable and flustered at the mere mention of lingerie. My eyes traveled to Carly's silent house. We had been closest to Karen. Surely she would share my disapproval of Doug and Jackie's relationship?

Moments later, I was loudly banging the brass knocker on Carly's front door, in case she was in the basement wearing headphones again. She opened it a few seconds later, looking winded and disheveled.

"Sorry," I began, taking in her appearance, "am I interrupting something?"

"I was just doing a Pilates video," she explained, gesturing to her baggy track pants and too-large T-shirt. "I want to fit into that little black dress by Christmas," she added hopefully.

Good luck. Christmas was less than five weeks away. "Would you mind if I came in for a sec? I really need to talk."

"Sure. Are you okay?"

"Not really." I followed her inside and sat next to her on the ivory leather sofa. "I'm really upset, Carly. Maybe it's none of my business and maybe I'm just paranoid, but . . ."

"But what?" She sounded alarmed.

"I just ran into Doug at the mall."

"Okay . . . ?"

"At Victoria's Secret."

"Oh . . ."

I quickly detailed the ensuing conversation in which Doug pretended to be buying sexy underwear for his Canadian sister. "Am I wrong to be bothered by this?"

"No," she said, "it does sound a little far-fetched."

"A *little* far-fetched? He's obviously buying sexy underwear for Jackie Baldwin! It's way too soon! It's not healthy!"

"If it bothers you so much, maybe you should talk to him."

"*I* can't talk to him!" I said, shocked. "Doug doesn't like me."

"Of course he does."

"No, he doesn't. He thinks I'm aggressive and weird and a big boozer. Besides, what would I say?"

"Well . . . ," Carly said, shifting slightly in her seat, "just tell him that you think he needs to take more time to heal before he jumps into another relationship. Tell him that you don't mean to interfere but that you care about him and think he should wait for the *right* woman to replace Karen."

It sounded completely legitimate, but . . . "I can't." Then a marvelous idea struck me. "You're close to Doug! Why don't you talk to him?"

"I'm not going to talk to him! Paige, . . . this is *your* issue. I don't really have a problem with Doug seeing Jackie Baldwin. He's doing what he needs to do to heal."

"Fine," I said petulantly. "If everyone just wants to sit around and watch him throw the rest of his life away, then, well, whatever . . ."

"Don't be like that," Carly said, reaching over and taking my hand. She looked at me in silence for a moment, her eyes full of understanding . . . or was it pity? When she spoke again, her voice was slow and gentle, like she was speaking to someone mildly autistic. "Maybe you should just let it go, hon?"

"I-I don't think I can."

"It's over, Paige. Nothing we do or say will bring Karen back." I could feel a lump of emotion building in my throat as she continued. "You have a wonderful family to focus on. Don't let Karen's death take you away from them."

I was on the verge of collapsing into sobs when I stood up. "Yeah . . . you're right," I croaked. "I'd better let you get back to your workout."

"It's fine. I think I've done enough for today."

"I've got to go, anyway. Spencer has a dental appointment at two, so I need to pick him up from school."

She walked me to the door. I turned around and squeezed her hand. "Thanks for listening. I'm really going to try to move on."

"Please do," she said, with a sympathetic smile.

"Oh . . . one more thing," I added. "You haven't heard of any radio contests where you can win a backstage pass to a Jessica Simpson concert, have you?"

CHAPTER 26

On the ninth day after my meeting with Troy Portman, I broke down and called him. "Hello, detective," I said formally. "It's Paige Atwell calling."

"Oh . . . uh, hi." He sounded uncomfortable. I could just picture Detective Conroy sitting across from him, asking "Is that your girlfriend calling with more of her crazy ideas?"

I maintained my professional composure. "I'm just calling to check on the results of the paternity test we discussed a few weeks ago."

"Right . . ." I heard him shuffling through some papers. "Those results are not available at this time."

"Oh. Well, when will they be available?"

"It's hard to say."

"Troy," I said shrilly, "are you blowing me off?"

"Let me call you back." He hung up.

What was going on? Did he just hang up on me? Was he mad at me? Embarrassed by his earlier admission? Or was the case now closed so he didn't want to waste any more of his precious time talking to me? The phone rang again.

"Hello?"

"It's Troy." I could hear traffic noises in the background. He was obviously calling me back from his cell. "I couldn't really talk in the office."

"Is Conroy still insisting on closing the case?"

"Yeah . . . but I'm stalling him. I've got the DNA in the lab."

"Hooray! I mean, thank you so much. Once we prove Javier's the father of Karen's baby, then we can look at him more closely. Did you know that the leading cause of death in pregnant women is murder by the baby's father?"

"Yes, Paige."

"I mean . . . we already know Javier's a liar, and a pretty convincing one at that. I suppose it's quite a big jump—from lying to killing—but he would have had motive, right? Maybe he didn't want the responsibility of a baby? Or he could have been enraged if Karen chose to raise the baby with her husband. Of course, we can't discount Doug Sutherland either. He's got a new girlfriend, you know."

"You mentioned that."

"So . . . how long do you think it will take to get the results?"

"I really can't say. The lab's backed up, and this case is no longer a high priority."

"Well, the sooner we know, the sooner we can—"

"Paige." He cut me off.

"Yes?"

"There is no 'we.' We're not a team on this case. You are not a detective."

"I know," I said, slightly hurt, "but you said yourself that I was the most tuned in to what had been going on with Karen. I was the only one who knew about the affair."

"And I appreciate your input, but it's not safe for you to get involved in this. You need to leave it to the professionals."

"But most of the professionals think it was a simple accident!" I cried. "There was someone there, Troy. I know it!"

"I'm going to have to go, Paige. I'll call you when the results come in." He hung up.

Now, that was definitely a blow-off. I could sense that Detective Portman was beginning to think I was some bored housewife who dreamed of being a glamorous PI. Nothing could have been further from the truth. I couldn't wait until this was all over and I knew what had happened to my friend. But I had to admit, these test results meant more to me than just solving the mystery surrounding Karen's death. They were the key to getting Javier out of my life.

Placing the receiver back on the base, I returned to the kitchen, where I had been assembling a lasagna. It was a time-consuming project, and the surrounding area looked like a tomato-sauce bomb had exploded, but it was Spencer's favorite. Plus, Paul had called and said he'd be home in time for dinner tonight. I was looking forward to sitting down with my entire family and enjoying a delicious, high-carb meal.

As I was sprinkling the last layer of noodles with mozzarella, my mind drifted back to the paternity test. It had taken two weeks to rule out Doug as the father; how long would it take to incriminate Javier? I couldn't help feeling that I was living on borrowed time. When I'd last seen him, Javier had promised to stay away from my house if I agreed to come see him again. I had no intention of keeping my end of the bargain. Why would I? At best, he was a liar; at worst, a killer. There was no way I was going to pursue a friendship with someone like him—if friendship was really what he wanted. No, I needed to make sure he stayed away from me.

But when the police confronted Javier with the fact that he was the father of Karen's child, he would know that I knew. Portman would undoubtedly tell him I'd provided the straw for DNA testing. Even if he didn't end up in jail, Javier would never want to see me again. Until then, I lived in fear of finding another pressed rose or pansy in my mailbox.

I put the lasagna in the oven and began the arduous task of cleaning up. Paul had promised to be home by six, which gave me enough time to scrub the kitchen, toss a salad, and put a little makeup on. Since it was Friday night, I'd bought us a nice bottle of cabernet to share. We would enjoy some special family time and, when the kids were tucked into bed, maybe some romance.

But six o'clock came and went . . . then six thirty. At six forty-five, the children began moaning about dying of starvation, so I fed them. Finally, at seven twenty, I heard my husband's key in the front door.

"So much for our nice family dinner," I grumbled, loudly enough for him to hear. "I guess it was silly of me to have dinner ready at six o'clock just because you promised to be here. I hope you like crunchy, dry lasagna."

Paul walked silently into the kitchen. He was carrying a large basket of Scentual Woman bath products. "Oh, honey," I said, feeling instantly sheepish for complaining. "That's so sweet of you." I took the overflowing wicker basket from him. "You shouldn't have." I kissed him. "This must have cost a fortune."

"Uh . . . yeah."

Tearing off the crisp plastic wrapping, I dug in. "Oh! Sensual massage oil!" I winked at him. "Edible body powder!"

"Paige . . ."

"I got us a bottle of wine." I moved seductively toward him. "Why don't we have a bite to eat, a couple of glasses of wine, and when the kids are asleep, we can try out some of these products?"

"It's not from me."

"What?"

"I came home, and the basket was sitting on the doorstep."

Oh God. My heart began to beat erratically. He couldn't have, he just couldn't have!

"There's a card." Paul's face was a mask, his demeanor impassive.

"Right," I said, looking at the small white envelope nestled next to the chocolate-flavored body mousse.

"Aren't you going to open it?"

"Of course," I said, forcing a casual tone. "I wonder who it's from?" The shaking of my hands was barely perceptible as I slid my thumb under the seal of the envelope. I extracted the tiny card. It was made of high-quality ivory paper, embossed with an *S* for *Scentual.* I flipped it open. Paul stood close, reading over my shoulder. In familiar handwriting, it said:

> I C U ?
> J.

"Ohhhhhhhh," I said, feigning realization.

"What? What does it mean?"

"It's from Jane," I explained. "It's a . . . thank-you present."

My husband's posture relaxed instantaneously. "That's nice of her. What is she thanking you for?" He moved into the kitchen and fished in the cutlery drawer for the corkscrew. "You said you bought wine?"

"On the counter . . ." I gestured to a far corner. "I'll get the lasagna out before it's too dry. So . . . how was your day?"

"Good . . . good." He extracted the cork from the bottle. "So what did you do for Jane that warrants such an extravagant gift?"

Placing the lasagna on the counter, I reached for two wine-glasses. "Oh, I helped her with some PR stuff for a fund-raiser she's working on."

"That was nice of you." He took the glass I proffered and filled it. "What's the fund-raiser for?"

"Oh . . . uh . . ." I took a sip of wine, stalling for time. "It's for the uh . . . ICU!" I said it almost triumphantly. "Yeah, it's for the intensive care unit at Children's Hospital."

"Great." He moved toward me and kissed my forehead. "You're a good person, Paige. I'm going to go upstairs and see the kids."

Oh yeah. I was a good person, all right. What kind of *good person* received a gigantic basket of sensual bath products from another man? I was positively seething at Javier as I chucked the card in the garbage. I was tempted to throw the whole basket in the trash, but that would arouse Paul's suspicions. How dare Javier go back on his promise to stay away from my house! For all he knew, I was

still planning on coming to see him at The Old Grind. Was he trying to ruin my marriage? Or was there a more sinister message in
this gift?

The guilt and anger ate at me all night—especially when Paul
insisted he wanted chocolate body mousse for dessert. I tried to
let go of my fury as my husband licked the artificially flavored edible oil product from my stomach and breasts, but I really couldn't
get into it. It just felt . . . *icky.* Not physically: physically it felt kind
of greasy and a little bit sticky. But on an emotional plane, it
upset me to think that this chocolate-flavored body mousse was a
gift from Javier. I put on a sufficient show of enjoying it, at least
enough to fool Paul, but I couldn't quell the sick feeling in my
stomach.

The next day, I stuffed all the body products into the darkest re-
cesses of my linen closet and tried to forget about them. I really had
no other recourse. I wasn't going to see Javier: It would only en-
courage his stalkerish tendencies. And I couldn't bug Troy about the
paternity-test results again. It was evident from our last conversation
that he was beginning to think I was a bit stalkerish as well. I would
wait for the results to come in and Javier to be confronted by the
police. Until then, I'd just have to find multiple reasons to poke my
head out the front door checking for any unwanted gifts.

The rest of the weekend passed without incident. When Paul
went back to work on Monday, I continued my manic cycle of
checking the phone for messages from Detective Portman and the
front porch for romantic presents from Javier: neither arrived. But
on Tuesday, the phone rang.

"Hello?" I answered hopefully.

"Oh good. You're there."

"Oh, hi, Jane." Oops. I hadn't meant to let disappointment seep
into my voice.

It was evident in the tone of her reply that she'd picked up on it.
"I was calling to ask if you wanted to join me for a power walk, but
maybe you've got other plans?"

"No! Sorry! I've just been waiting for this, uh . . . *plumber* to call
me back."

"Everything okay?"

"Yeah, yeah . . . I just need an estimate for this thingie . . . It's no big deal." Lying was beginning to feel unnervingly comfortable.

"So are you up for a walk?"

I wasn't, really. I wanted to stay in the house, running between the phone and the front porch like some deranged hamster. But it was beginning to feel a little obsessive-compulsive, and I knew I'd been neglecting my friendships of late. Besides, my mother always said a watched pot never boils. Maybe if I left the house for a while, Troy Portman would finally call. "Sure," I said brightly. "Just give me a few minutes to change."

It had been months since I'd gone power walking with Jane. Our every-second-Friday routine had fallen by the wayside after Karen's tragedy. But judging by Jane's pace and enthusiastic arm pumping, her exercise routine had not suffered as mine had. In fact, I was struggling to keep up with her in the first five minutes. Thankfully, conversation was slow.

"How are the kids?" she asked, as we began the descent toward Rosedale Elementary. The slope allowed me something of a reprieve.

"They're good . . . Yours?"

"Good. Enjoying preschool . . . and swimming lessons."

"Great . . . You haven't heard of any radio contests where you can win backstage passes to a Christina Aguilera concert, have you?"

"No."

"I want to get Chloe a really amazing Christmas gift that doesn't cost a fortune."

"You'll think of something."

We rounded the bend past the school and enjoyed a long flat stretch. Despite the fact that I was breathing easily again, our discourse had not revived. Something was amiss with Jane. She seemed a little cool, distant, maybe even ticked off with me.

"Listen," she said, jarring me from my internal hypothesizing, "I don't want you to take this the wrong way . . . As harsh as this sounds, I'm coming from a place of caring and love . . ."

Well, this couldn't be good.

"We're all concerned about you."

"Concerned? About me?"

"Yes. You've been really . . . *different* lately."

"Different? How different?"

"When Margot came to coffee the other day . . . ?" Her tone implied that that one sentence fragment explained everything.

"I was very nice to her!" I replied defensively.

"It was obvious you didn't want her there."

"No it wasn't. I handled it very well, I think."

"So you admit you didn't want her there?"

"Well . . . I just think it's too soon to be replacing Karen."

Jane sighed with exasperation. "Why do you insist on looking at it that way? It's not healthy."

My back was up. "What way?"

"Inviting someone new to coffee doesn't mean we're *replacing* Karen. She was one of a kind! Irreplaceable! But we have to go on living, Paige. It's okay to make new friends. Trudy, Carly, and I all agree."

I was beginning to feel a little picked on. "I don't get this. Why does everyone think it's perfectly fine for Doug to have, like, a two-week grieving period, but when I want a few months, I'm *not healthy*?"

"Come on, now," Jane said chidingly, "Doug took more than two weeks to get over her."

"Well, I can't help the way I feel. I think it's too soon to be bringing someone else into our group when we're all still trying to heal."

There was a long silence before Jane said, "Okay . . . I suppose we should respect your feelings and give you a little more time."

"Besides," I said, skipping a little to keep up with Jane, who, despite our passionate exchange, was power walking faster than ever, "what about Trudy and Carly? I mean, they're acting like they're Doug's live-out nannies. They cook for him, clean for him, do his grocery shopping, pick up his dry cleaning . . ."

"That's different," Jane said. "Those two have got the disease to please."

It sounded quite accurate. Jane's preemptive marriage-counseling sessions had provided her incredible insight into the human psyche.

"They're classic people-pleasers," she continued. "They're reveling in their caregiver roles. Trudy has her own family to take care of, but Ken's gone so much that she doesn't get the appreciation she craves. And Carly . . . well, she just really loves being needed again. This tragedy has given her a real purpose in life."

"Yeah . . ."

"I'd like to see those two get together one day," Jane said, leaning into the incline for maximum gluteus toning.

"Who?"

"Carly and Doug. That probably would have made Karen happy, to see Doug with one of her dearest friends."

"Really? You think so?"

"Of course." She shrugged. "I mean, if I died, I think it would be nice if Daniel ended up with one of you."

Eww! Daniel was so . . . *old.*

"If you were single, of course. I mean, who better to love your family in your absence?"

"I guess so," I managed weakly. I felt especially thankful that Paul had promised to mourn me forever if I were to die.

"But unfortunately, Doug would never be interested in her in *that way.*"

"No?"

"Come on," she said, shooting me a look, "you know what I mean. Doug is a good-looking, successful guy, capable of attracting hot women. Karen was hot. Even Jackie Baldwin is hot in her own obvious way. Carly is lovely, but . . . I don't think she's his type."

"Yeah, I know what you mean," I admitted.

"But enough about that," she said, and her tone became gentle. "I'll talk to the girls, and we'll try to be more understanding of your feelings. But . . . do you think you might like to talk to a professional? To help you move beyond Karen's accident?"

"I-I think I'm fine with it . . . really."

"We don't want to stick our noses in where they don't belong, but we're worried about you. You seem almost . . . obsessed with it."

"I'm not. I just . . . Well, everyone grieves in their own way, Jane. I really need to *feel* the pain and the loss, to surrender to my emotions. I need to *own* the grief in order to move on."

Luckily, Jane had not watched the same *Dr. Phil* episode on dealing with grief that I had. As I had surmised, she was appeased. "I understand. But I want you to know that you're not alone. If you need any help . . . any comfort or support . . ."

We stopped at the edge of my driveway. "I'll call you," I said.

"We're always there for you—Trudy, Carly, and me."

"I know. Thanks for caring so much." I squeezed her hand. "See you later."

"Actually . . . could I use your restroom quickly? I think I'm going to run for a couple of miles now."

"Sure." I tried not to let on how winded I was as she followed me to my house. I bounded energetically up the stairs to the porch trying to give the impression that I, too, could run a couple of miles if only I weren't so busy. As I was about to put my key in the lock, Jane halted me.

"There's something in your mailbox." I could hear her lifting the brass lid and extracting it, but I was too frightened to turn around. Please just be the mail . . . all bills even . . . pleeeeeeeeeze.

"What is it?" I asked casually as I continued to open the door.

"Look." It was a small rectangular box, professionally gift-wrapped in gold paper with an enormous red bow. Damn that Javier! Damn him all to hell!!! I should never have left the house. "I saw the ribbon peeking out," Jane said excitedly. "Who's it from?"

"It's from Paul," I said, smiling beatifically. "I had a feeling he was going to surprise me like this."

"Well . . . open it!"

She followed me inside and, after we slipped our trainers off, on into the kitchen. "I think I'll wait until he gets home," I said, placing the box on the counter.

"Don't be silly. If he wanted you to wait until he got home, he'd have given it to you himself. It's got to be jewelry," she continued gleefully. "What's the occasion?"

"It's our anniversary," I lied.

"Your anniversary's in August."

"Not our *wedding* anniversary. Another date we celebrate . . . It's sort of . . . private."

"Oh! Aren't you two romantic! Open it. Open it!"

I feared she would never leave if she didn't get a glimpse of the contents. Removing the tiny card and tucking it into the pocket of my hoodie for later, private viewing, I began to tear off the paper.

"Hurry," Jane said, "I have to pee."

When the flat silver box was unwrapped, I began to remove the lid. Hopefully, Jane would attribute the trembling of my hands to anticipation. What was revealed was not jewelry. It was a small electronic device resembling a very thin cell phone.

"It's an iPod!" Jane cried. "Awesome!"

An iPod? Javier had bought me an iPod? It didn't seem to fit. He'd started out with pressed flowers and cutesy notes, and moved on to sensual body products. As cool as it was, an iPod just didn't conform to his romantic gifting pattern.

"This is even better than my model," my friend was saying as she removed the gadget from its box. "You'll love it, Paige. You can store ten thousand songs in here and multiple playlists. I don't know how I ever worked out before I got mine."

"Great."

"Let me see . . ." She pressed the wheel on the front. "He's put some songs on here for you." I made a frantic grab for it, but it was too late. "What?" She brought the tiny screen closer to her eyes. "These are all Spanish songs."

Now the gift made sense. If I could read Spanish, I would undoubtedly find that they were all highly romantic love songs.

"Oh! Paul's so sweet," I said, reclaiming the iPod. "It's the anniversary of our first trip to Mexico."

"Oh . . ." Jane sounded mildly puzzled.

"It was a really special vacation . . . the first time he . . . told me he loved me . . ." I smiled demurely.

"I had no idea Paul was so romantic," Jane said, impressed. "I'll just use your ladies room and be on my way."

While she was in the bathroom, I hurriedly removed the card from my pocket and tore it open.

 J.

Just when I thought he couldn't get any cheesier! I mean, did women really fall for this stuff? Had Karen fallen for it? Then I noticed, at the very bottom of the card, more tiny handwriting.

I must see you!

CHAPTER 27

When Jane had left, I sat down on the couch and stared at the tiny card. I felt sick, physically sick. My life was slipping out of my control, and it was only a matter of time before it all blew up. For the first time, I felt just the slightest hint of . . . fear. Was Javier becoming obsessed with me? Could I be in danger? I had always felt at ease in his presence, completely safe. But what did I know about hanging out with murderers? One thing was certain: Javier was more tenacious than I had realized. He was certainly not like a pimple that you could just ignore and it would go away. He was more like some nasty rash that refused to disappear without medication.

Adding to my angst was the fact that I hated lying. I didn't just hate it—I truly believed that it caused cancer. Now I found myself entangled in a web of deceit. How long could I keep up this charade? How long could I keep Paul and Jane apart? They were bound to run into each other, and the whole thing would unravel. Paul would say, "Hey, Jane. Thanks for the chocolate-flavored body mousse you bought for Paige. Yum, yum!" And Jane would say,

"Chocolate-flavored body mousse? What are you talking about?" Or Jane would say, "Hi, Paul, you romantic devil, you! I'm so impressed that you bought Paige an iPod loaded with Spanish songs to commemorate the first time you told her you loved her in Mexico." And Paul would say, "What? The first time I told her I loved her, I was drunk at the campus bar at DU. What are you talking about?"

And what was I supposed to do with this iPod? I couldn't just throw it away, could I? It was worth a lot of money. And it could store up to ten thousand songs! And it could finally be the catalyst to get me to start exercising! If Jane saw me out power walking, she would certainly wonder, where is her fabulous little iPod? I didn't want to arouse her suspicions. Oh, what was I thinking of? I couldn't keep it! It was a gift from a veritable stalker! It was loaded with romantic Spanish love songs intended to make me think fondly of the aforementioned stalker. Maybe if I deleted all the romantic Spanish love songs, I could keep it?

I knew what I wanted to do with the iPod. I wanted to drive down to The Old Grind, throw the door open wide, and march to the back counter. When Javier turned around, looking all gorgeous and delighted to see me, I would hurl the box at him. "Take your stupid gift!" I would scream. "You may have ruined Karen's life, but you're not going to ruin mine. Stay away from me, Rueda," I would growl threateningly. "You don't know who you're messing with." This, of course, would be foreshadowing for when the police told him I'd provided them with his DNA.

But I knew I couldn't do that. Portman had warned me to keep my distance from Javier, and I had to agree it was for the best. Perhaps I could donate the iPod to a women's shelter or a club for street kids? Someone should get some enjoyment out of it. A glance at my watch told me my decision would have to be put on hold. It was time to go pick up the children. Hurriedly placing the card on top of the device, I returned the lid to the box. I would hide it in the back of the linen closet until I could figure out the best way to dispose of it.

Life went on normally for several days, aside from the fact that I could almost feel myself developing a peptic ulcer. Portman did not call. I was beginning to fear that he never would. The green straw with Javier's trace saliva was likely languishing in some landfill by now. Troy probably told me it was in the lab to appease me and then planned to stall me indefinitely until I lost interest. Unlike Javier, this avoidance technique would probably work on me. I was already feeling incredibly defeated.

No one seemed to notice my general malaise, which only served to intensify it. That is, until Saturday evening. I was loading plates into the dishwasher after our supper when my daughter appeared in the kitchen. She had just emerged from the bath. Her hair was wet, pasted to the sides of her face, and she was wrapped in her yellow terry-cloth robe. "Hi," I said, as she rounded the corner. "Are you all clean?"

"Yep . . ." She was looking at me strangely, a wide grin splitting her features.

"What?" I felt a little paranoid. Was she laughing at me? Did I have something on my face?

But my elder child moved toward me and gathered me in a gigantic hug. "I love you, Mom."

"I love you, too, honey," I said, a little warily.

Her wet head was still pressed to my chest as she continued to speak. "I know I was acting like a spoiled brat about the karaoke machine. I'm sorry."

"It–it's all right."

"And I don't even want my belly button pierced anymore."

"I'm glad."

"And you're not the meanest mom in the world. You're the nicest mom in the world."

"And you're the nicest daughter . . ."

She released me. "I'm going to do some singing practice in my room for a while. Or do you need some help cleaning up?"

"Uh . . . I think I've got it under control. But thanks for asking." She skipped happily back upstairs.

I walked directly to Paul's office, where he was working on a proposal or a presentation or whatever for next week. "There's something wrong with Chloe," I said.

"What do you mean?" He swiveled around in his chair.

"She's acting really, really strange."

"What's she doing?"

"Hugging me, telling me I'm the nicest mom in the world, offering to clean the kitchen."

"Christ!" Paul stood up. "I'll go talk to her."

"She couldn't be into drugs already, could she?" I asked worriedly. "I've heard that ecstasy makes you act very sweet and loving."

"Don't worry," Paul said, bounding up the stairs, "I'll get to the bottom of this."

When the kitchen was clean, I put the kettle on and made a cup of Serenity herbal tea. Paul had still not returned, but I was sure he would summon me if he suspected our daughter was on "E." I flicked on the TV and put my feet up on the coffee table, immersing myself in the umpteenth season of *American Idol*. It wasn't until the episode was over that my husband appeared in the living room.

"I put the kids to bed," he said.

"Thanks, hon. What's up with Chloe?"

"Well . . . I think she found her Christmas present."

"What?"

"In the linen closet," he said, moving to sit beside me. "She found this . . ."

Holy shit! Oh my God! Fucking fuck, fuck, fuck!

Paul began to remove the lid from the flat silver box. "You didn't tell me you were getting her an iPod. It's a little extravagant for a ten-year-old, don't you think? She's thrilled, though."

Oh help! Please! I silently begged for an earthquake, a car to crash into the formal living room, a twister . . . anything to postpone or prevent what was about to happen.

"Wow," Paul said when Chloe's supposed Christmas present was revealed. "This is really nice. A guy at work has a—" He stopped, noticing the card. "What's this?"

I didn't know what to say. I was frightened, mute.

He opened it, taking in the little heart-shaped musical notes and the impassioned plea at the bottom. I had expected him to explode, to scream and yell at me for my obvious betrayal, but his voice stayed calm—which was actually worse in a way. "What the hell is this?"

"It's not what you think," I said, my voice quaking. "Please . . . let me explain."

"Yeah . . . ," he said coldly, "I think you'd better."

"Okay . . . ," I said, taking a deep, ragged breath. "I'm going to start at the beginning. It's kind of long, so please hear me out. But first let me tell you that I'm not having an affair."

"Good." There was no relief in his voice.

"Karen was."

"Karen was?"

"Yeah . . . well, at least she told me she was."

He was quietly angry. "Why didn't you tell me this before? Don't you think the police need to know this?"

"They do know."

"Oh. So you've been talking to the police and you haven't even bothered to inform me? You complain that we're not *connected,* and then you keep all these secrets from me. What the hell is going on with you, Paige?"

Tears had sprung to my eyes. "I'm sorry. I handled this badly, I know. But please . . . let me start at the beginning."

And I did. I began with Karen's confession and how she'd sworn me to secrecy. I explained how, after she died, I had wanted to protect her reputation and Doug's feelings, so I kept her affair hidden. I explained how I met Javier at drawing class, how I found out Karen was pregnant, how the police received an anonymous letter . . . I told him that Karen's baby wasn't Doug's and that I'd provided the police with a green straw with Javier's DNA on it. I told him everything—except of course, my own attraction to Javier. That was irrelevant now, anyway. At this point, the mere thought of Javier was sickening. And I had never appreciated what I had with Paul so much. In that moment, I knew how precious my marriage was: not perfect, not thrilling, but incredibly precious. If I had jeopardized it by playing Cagney or Lacey or whichever one was skinnier, I would never forgive myself.

"I don't blame you for being mad," I said tearfully. "I was stupid. It all got out of hand."

"You *were* stupid," he said. "And I *am* mad. You invited a possible murderer onto our doorstep."

"I didn't *invite* him . . . ," I began.

"You're the reason he's been here, to our home, at least three times. God, Paige, don't you care about your family? Your children?"

"I do!" I wailed.

"And what if he had hurt you? How do you think that would affect the kids and me? It would destroy us."

My sobs could no longer be held in check. "I screwed up. I know . . . I'm such an idiot. But please . . . Paul, I love you and the kids so much. Please forgive me."

Almost grudgingly, he took me into his arms, where I wept inconsolably for at least ten minutes. When my tears and snot had soaked through his shirt, Paul gently pulled away. "Listen to me," he said, gripping me firmly by the shoulders. "From now on, we're going to handle things my way."

"O-o-okay," I blubbered.

"I mean it, Paige. This amateur detective act is over. Do you understand me?"

"I-I do."

"Good. Now, why don't you go have a nice warm bath and then get to bed?"

"Will you be joining me?" I asked hopefully. His new take-charge attitude was a real turn-on!

"Later," he said gruffly. "I've got some phone calls to make."

I slept more soundly that night than I had for months. My deep slumber could probably be attributed to emotional exhaustion, but I also felt a tremendous sense of relief. With Paul's involvement, the burden of Karen's secret had finally been lifted. In the morning, my spouse still seemed disgusted with my behavior, but he was not overtly hostile. I pussyfooted around the house, making pancakes, ironing Paul's shirts, and playing with the children so that he could work in his study undisturbed. At this stage, he didn't seem open to a huge display of affection, but I hoped to subtly convey my appreciation.

But Monday morning brought an end to the cold war. At six thirty, when Paul would normally have been leaving for the office, he phoned in and said he'd be working from home. I wasn't sure what to think: Paul never worked from home. Did he feel I needed to be watched, in case I started playing detective again? Protected from my extravagant gift-giving stalker? Or did he really just want to work on his proposal or presentation in the relative quiet of his home office? I didn't ask. Instead, I focused on delivering my children to school in a timely manner.

When I returned, Paul was on the phone in his study. Quietly, I went into the kitchen and began to clean up the breakfast dishes. After a few moments, the audible murmur of his conversation ceased, and he called my name.

"Coming!" I called back, still contrite, scurrying to meet him. When I was in the doorway, I smiled sweetly. "Yes, honey?"

He swiveled in his chair to face me. "I just got off the phone with Ed Alahan."

"Okay . . . ?"

"He's a lawyer friend of mine."

"Oh . . ."

"We're going to take out a restraining order against this Javier guy," he stated. "Ed's bringing some forms by. You'll need to fill them out, and then he'll help you set a court date."

A restraining order? A court date? Was that really necessary? I mean, Javier had only left some bubble bath and an iPod on my doorstep, not a decapitated rabbit or something.

"Gee . . . I don't know if that's—"

Paul's formidable expression stopped me short. "I'm handling things now. Don't even think about arguing with me."

"Okay . . . ," I said meekly. "So, uh . . . do you feel like—I don't know—going upstairs and lying down for a while?" His forcefulness was making me so hot!

"Ed will be here in half an hour," he said coldly, turning his chair away from me.

Ed Alahan was a nice-looking Indian man about my age. He sat with me as I filled out a number of forms stating my name, age, address, and the nature of my relationship to the defendant (Javier). What *was* the nature of my relationship to him? Unrequited crush? Model and artist? Deceased friend's boyfriend? I decided the last one was the most accurate, and the most incriminating. Then I was asked to provide an incident checklist, indicating the approximate dates and details of my disturbing encounters with Javier. When the list was complete, it looked so . . . *benign*.

DATE (approx.)	INCIDENT
Dec. 6	*Defendant leaves iPod loaded with Spanish love songs in petitioner's mailbox.*
Dec. 2	*Defendant delivers basket of sensual body products and leaves it on petitioner's doorstep.*
Nov. 10	*Defendant leaves pressed rose in mailbox with card requesting petitioner meet him for coffee.*
Nov. 8	*Defendant shows up at restaurant where petitioner is dining and lures her into his car. Defendant drives petitioner to secluded parking lot to talk to her before returning her to restaurant.*

There was really nothing sinister about our interactions. In fact, except for the last one, all Javier had done was drop a couple of gifts off on my porch. That didn't make him a stalker, did it? It just made him . . . overly generous. What judge would grant a restraining order for that? Ed sensed my concern. "Don't worry . . . ," he said kindly. "The list will have more impact when it's placed in context. In court, we can explain that this man was the lover of your murdered friend."

"If Karen really was murdered," I added.

"Well, for the purposes of obtaining an order of protection, we'll be focusing on the fact that her death is still under investigation."

"Right. Of course."

"I'll be in touch with a court date."

I felt a sudden surge of panic. "Will I have to testify? Will Javier—*the defendant*—be there?"

"The first step is a temporary order of protection hearing. The judge will ask you some questions about the stalking, but Mr. Rueda won't be in attendance. If we progress to a permanent order, there will be a more formal hearing, and the defendant will be able to attend."

"I hope we won't need to go that far," I said.

"Me, too." His smile was reassuring.

"Thanks for all your help." I shook Ed's hand.

Paul appeared from his study. "You all finished here?"

"It's taken care of," Ed said, gathering the papers.

"I'll walk you out," Paul offered.

When he returned, he joined me at the kitchen table. "You okay?" His voice was still cool, but I was touched by his concern nonetheless.

"Yeah . . . I just wish I didn't have to go to court and everything . . ."

"Yeah? Well, I wish you hadn't been seeing a strange, potentially dangerous man behind my back, but you were."

Obviously, he was still pissed off. I took a deep breath. "I don't know, Paul," I said frankly. "I'm not 100 percent sure Javier's the killer. He certainly seems obsessive and a bit . . . *misguided,* but . . ."

He stood up. "We'll see what the police have to say. They'll be here in an hour." Jeez . . . when Paul said he was taking control of things, he wasn't kidding. I went upstairs to freshen up a bit and then put on a pot of coffee.

Detectives Portman and Conroy showed up punctually at 11:00. Paul ushered them inside, shaking hands and exchanging introductions. I hung back, standing awkwardly at the edge of the grand entryway. "And of course, you know my wife, Paige," Paul said, with a hint of derision.

"*Ms.* Atwell," Detective Conroy said, nodding in my direction.

Portman cleared his throat nervously. "Yes . . . hello." His greeting was overly formal. The poor guy seemed really uncomfortable being around my husband and me. When we were seated at the kitchen table with mugs of coffee before us, Conroy began. "So, Paul, . . . you said on the phone that you have some additional information on the Sutherland case that might be of interest?"

"Yes. My wife hasn't been entirely forthcoming with you. . . . Have you, Paige?"

"Well . . . no. I mean, I wasn't purposely being deceitful. I just didn't think it was relevant before, but Paul says—"

Paul cut me off. "Karen Sutherland was having an affair with Javier Rueda. My wife struck up some kind of friendship with him . . ." His eyes darted quickly, accusingly to my face. So did Troy Portman's. "He's been coming by the house . . . leaving her notes, dropping off gifts . . . He's obviously got an obsessive personality."

"What kind of gifts?" Conroy asked.

"Oh . . ." I shrugged. "Just a pressed flower, . . . some bath products, and . . . an iPod."

"Loaded with Spanish love songs," Paul added.

Troy was back in professional-cop mode. "Do you still have any of these gifts?"

"Yes."

"Go get them," Paul ordered. His take-charge attitude was rapidly moving from sexy to just plain bossy, but I complied. When I returned, I laid the overflowing wicker basket and the iPod on the table before them. Both detectives inspected the bounty.

"Did you use any of these products?" Conroy asked, noticing

that the Scentual Woman basket was in disarray and the plastic wrapping removed. His tone wasn't particularly accusing, but it set my nerves on edge. I didn't like Detective Conroy, and I *really* didn't like him asking if Paul had licked edible body mousse off my breasts.

"Uh . . ." I blushed and looked to my husband for help.

"Before I knew they were a gift from Rueda, I suggested she use one of them, yeah," he said.

Portman was inspecting the iPod. "This is an expensive model. And these songs . . . You say they're Spanish love songs?"

"Well, I'm not fluent, but . . . they appear to be."

"We'll get them translated. There could be some message in them."

"Yep," Conroy said. "We'll need to take all this stuff in with us for closer inspection."

Paul said, "We're taking out a restraining order against him. We might need the gifts as evidence at the permanent hearing."

"They can be made available to you, if need be," Conroy explained. He stood up. "Thanks for bringing this to our attention." He was addressing Paul, of course, his body angled purposefully away from me.

When Troy spoke, he excluded me as well. "Rueda's behavior toward your wife is definitely cause to take a closer look at him." Oh sure . . . now that Paul had taken charge, they were willing to investigate. Suddenly, it was no longer just a *simple accident*.

"Don't forget about Doug Sutherland," I added. "I saw him at the mall buying sexy lingerie for his sister."

All three men looked at me like I was speaking in tongues. "Right," Conroy said dismissively. "We've got it under control."

When they were gone, my husband silently helped me pick up the coffee cups. "Are you going in to the office now?" I asked, a little hesitantly. He was obviously still mad about the whole stalker business; I hoped he hadn't picked up on the fact that Detective Portman "enjoyed my company."

"I'm going to work at home for a while," he said, tipping the remains of Conroy's coffee into the sink. "At least until we get the re-straining order sorted out."

I stopped and looked at my husband. His shoulders were tense and his jaw was set in a tight line of anger, but he was still the man I loved. He felt my eyes upon him. "What?"

"Nothing. I just love you, that's all," I said. "I just . . . really love you."

CHAPTER 28

So it was over. Paul and Ed Alahan escorted me to court, where I managed to convince a judge that Javier constituted a threat to me and my family. With Javier not allowed within ten feet of me, Paul felt comfortable returning to work, the kids continued to go to school, and life went back to the way it was before . . . waaaaay before, when Karen was alive and I had nothing to be suspicious or concerned about. I had promised my husband that I would let the police handle the investigation from here on out, and I meant it. I would not call Troy Portman to check on their progress. I would not contact Javier (obviously). I would not spy on Doug or visit Jackie Baldwin under the guise of buying my mom a new condo. I would focus on Christmas, which was now less than two weeks away.

Paul and I agreed that we basically had to get Chloe an iPod. It would have been too cruel to tease her like that. I purchased one very similar to my gift from Javier and loaded it with songs by her favorite singers—avoiding all lyrics pertaining to *getting dirty, getting sweaty,* or *getting your freak on,* of course. Spencer would receive his coveted Bionicle set; Paul, his new golf bag; and I'd even found a beautiful brooch for Pauline. At least *I* thought it was beautiful. If she didn't agree, I'd just tell her that her beloved son picked it out.

I threw myself into the Christmas preparations with a fervor bordering on mania. Three consecutive days were spent at Aberdeen Mall purchasing gifts, a new red tablecloth and matching Christmas napkins, Christmas crackers, and various twinkle lights and ornaments. I cleaned. I decorated. I baked. The house was spotless, festive, and gingerbread-scented. It was a veritable winter wonderland, . . . and there were still five days to go until my in-laws arrived.

Intent on keeping my word to my husband and not obsessing about the case, I had to find something else to occupy my mind. It needn't be a huge project: the children would soon be out of school for the holidays. But it had to be engaging enough to keep me from calling Troy Portman, peeking through the front curtains to observe Doug's comings and goings, or driving by The Old Grind hoping to catch a glimpse of Javier. I was far from cured, but I was taking it one day at a time.

I was in Paul's study, placing some cheerful sprigs of holly on top of his computer, when I noticed the pile of books. I had completely forgotten about the stack of paperbacks Carly had virtually forced upon me. Reading was the perfect solution! Sifting through them, I selected a mystery. The blurb on the back said it was the story of Patty Hanover, a beautiful, blond divorcée whose ex-husband was found floating in her pool. Did Patty kill him, as the police suspected? Or was it the beautiful young nanny she'd brought over from Britain, Annabelle Swinton, who was in line to become the third Mrs. Hanover? Of course, a butler with a mysterious past, a disgruntled business associate, and Patty's intensely passionate new lover served to complicate the case. Could Patty solve the murder before she ended up in jail?

God, it was right up my alley!

I immersed myself in the mystery, relieved to be focusing on a fictitious murder for a change. The writing was fast-paced and lively; the author, a former detective, was masterful at building suspense.

When the phone rang, partway through chapter eight, I jumped off the couch, startled.

"Hello?" I answered breathlessly, my heart still beating audibly in my chest.

"It's Carly. What are you up to?"

"Nothing much . . . just reading. You?"

"I'd like to have you girls over for coffee if you're free. Just a little pre-Christmas get-together before everyone gets too wrapped up in the holidays."

"That sounds great. When?"

"Now . . . Whenever you're ready."

"Okay. I'll be there in a few minutes."

"Great!" She sounded excited. "Trudy's on her way, and I'm just going to call Jane."

I hurried to the kitchen, where I loaded shortbread cookies, gingerbread men, and rum balls into festive cookie tins purchased for this occasion. Every Christmas, we exchanged tokens of our friendship, just a little something heartfelt and homemade. I had only bought three tins this year, one each for Carly, Trudy, and Jane. Oh damn, what if Margot had been invited? Surely, even Jane would agree that it was a little early to be exchanging heartfelt friendship tokens with her? Since Carly hadn't mentioned Margot's name, I surmised that three cookie tins were enough.

When I arrived, Trudy was already there, and Jane was just pulling up in her Lexus. Everyone had come bearing gifts. We knew that, within days, the Christmas chaos would descend and it would be impossible to get together. Carly welcomed us all warmly and led us to her kitchen table. Atop the red tablecloth overlaid with a delicate lace pattern, she had placed a warm apple-cinnamon coffee cake, a knife, and four serving plates. It looked and smelled scrumptious, but before we could dig in, Carly spoke.

"Thanks for coming on such short notice, guys," she said, smiling at us each in turn. "I know things are about to get hectic. Paige, you have your in-laws coming; Jane, you're off to Cancún soon; and I know Trudy, you'll be busy with Cameron's seasonal play and Emily's nondenominational holiday piano recital . . ." We all nodded our agreement. "So I thought we should do our gift exchange now . . . since we won't have another chance to get together."

"Great idea," I said, handing out my cookie tins. "Just a little Christmas baking . . ."

My friends peeked inside the tins and made the appropriate gushing remarks. "Looks delicious!"

"Oh, the girls will adore these gingerbread men!"

"Your rum balls are to die for!"

Jane went next. She had given us each a nice bottle of red wine in a festive bag made of red velvet and white rabbit fur. In Jane's case, heartfelt and homemade meant that she picked an idea from a craft magazine and Becca turned it into a thoughtful token of her friendship. But it was a lovely gift, and we were all equally demonstrative with our appreciation.

Trudy, had of course, outdone us all in thoughtfulness and craftsmanship. "I hope you'll like these," she said, placing a plain brown bag on the table in front of her. From it, she extracted a matching hat and scarf in the finest angora wool. "The charcoal set is for you, Paige." She passed it to me. "Jane, . . . yours is winter white . . . And Carly, . . ." She removed the final garments from the bottom of the bag. "I thought you'd like lilac."

"They're gorgeous," I said, trying them on. "When did you have the time?"

"Oh, I love to knit," Trudy said dismissively. "Really . . . I find it so relaxing."

"Well, this is absolutely beautiful," Jane said, tying the scarf around her neck.

Carly rubbed the soft wool against her cheek. "I love them, Trudy. Thank you so much."

When Trudy was becoming uncomfortable with our heaps of praise, Carly stood up. "Now it's my turn. I'll be right back." She hurried off to the spare bedroom, which I knew was dedicated solely to her craft projects. Moments later, she returned holding three stacked shoeboxes against her chest. "Take one," she instructed, walking around the table.

Simultaneously, we removed the lids and rustled through the wads of pale pink tissue paper inside. I heard Trudy's gasp before I'd found my gift, but when I did, I understood her reaction. Nestled in the soft pink bed was a tiny, cloud-shaped pillow. Transferred onto the soft white fabric was a photograph of Karen. I recognized it from the New Year's Eve picture of the four of us displayed at her funeral. Beneath her smiling face, Carly had embroidered:

KAREN SUTHERLAND
OUR ANGEL
1968–2005

I heard a ragged sob catch in Jane's throat, and it brought one to mine as well. Normally, I would have found such a creation a little . . . tacky, too reminiscent of wearing a photo of your dog or your kids on your T-shirt. But under these circumstances, it was incredibly meaningful and touching.

"It's for the Christmas tree," Carly explained, holding Trudy's cloud up by the loop of ribbon affixed to the top. "I thought it would be a nice way to keep her memory alive."

"Of course," Trudy said hoarsely. "Every Christmas, we'll put our angel on the tree and take a moment to really remember her."

"Oh, Carly," Jane said, moving over to hug her. "It's so special."

"It is," I added tearfully, reaching over to squeeze Carly's hand.

"Could we . . . ," Trudy began, before her voice broke. She took a few seconds to compose herself and then continued. "Could we take a moment right now to remember our friend? I feel like we've all been so focused on healing that we maybe haven't spent enough time . . . remembering."

"That's a great idea," Carly said.

"Let's join hands and say a prayer," Trudy suggested. She turned to me. "Paige, I know you're not one to really *pray,* but if you'd like to join our circle and just . . . think positive, loving thoughts . . . ?"

"Sure," I said, feeling like a practicing Satanist at a Billy Graham crusade.

We all joined hands around Carly's frilly Christmas table and closed our eyes. Trudy spoke. "Let's thank the good Lord for bringing Karen to us for as long as he did . . . and let us pray for the soul of whoever was involved in her mysterious death."

My eyes popped open and met Trudy's. Wordlessly, we shared a moment of complete understanding. It was the first time any of my friends had vocalized the fact that they had suspicions about Karen's death, too! In a flash, it was over. Trudy closed her eyes and began moving her lips in silent tribute. I looked quickly from Carly to Jane, but they were each immersed in prayer—or in Jane's case, as in mine, probably positive, loving thoughts. But I knew what I had heard. Trudy suspected that Karen's death was more than a simple fall.

The rest of our visit was more upbeat. When we had adequately recovered from our prayer circle, we dug into the coffee cake and shifted the conversation to Christmas plans. Trudy regaled us with details of the upcoming seasonal play and piano concert; Jane talked of her five-star holiday in Mexico; and Carly filled us in on her plans to spend Christmas Eve volunteering at a soup kitchen and then spend Christmas morning with her parents and sister in Highlands Ranch.

"What about you, Paige? Are you ready for Pauline?" Carly asked teasingly.

"I'm ready," I said. "At least I think I'm ready. I'm sure when she shows up, she'll find a million things that I've forgotten to do."

"Don't let her stress you out," Jane said. "Don't let her ruin your Christmas."

"I'll try not to."

"You're a great hostess," Trudy said, patting my hand. "She's lucky Paul married you."

"I'm going to take the next couple of days to rest and rejuvenate before she arrives. If I can get myself into a state of complete relaxation and acceptance, then maybe she won't bother me so much."

"Like a trance," Jane joked.

"Basically," I agreed.

After we spent another half an hour of lighthearted banter, Jane had to go home and pack. "I'd better get going, too," Trudy added. "I'm putting the finishing touches on Cameron's singing-snowman costume."

"I should go and meditate," I joked.

At the front door, we all hugged and wished one another happy holidays. "I'll probably see you before the big day," I said to Carly. Since we lived so close, our paths were bound to cross.

"If you need a break from Pauline, you can always hide out here."

When I got home, I didn't meditate. I cleaned and puttered until it was time to pick up the kids. With my children home, I made their after-school snacks, did homework with Chloe, and played Snakes and Ladders with Spencer until I had to fix dinner. We were having tacos: another family favorite that would definitely not pass muster with Pauline. When my mother-in-law was visiting, we had to have a roast of meat and three vegetables for every meal.

My husband got home shortly after the kids were tucked into bed. While his anger at me had dissipated, there was still an underlying tension between us. He resolutely refused to discuss Karen's case with me. For all I knew, Detective Portman could have called him with Javier's paternity-test result ages ago. In fact, Javier might have already been charged with my friend's murder. Paul was not about to tell me—and I was too afraid to ask.

"How was your day?" he asked, joining me in the kitchen.

"Good." I kissed him. "Yours?"

"Busy."

"Do you want tacos? Or I could make you something else?"

"No, tacos are good. I'm going to kiss the kids and change clothes. I'll be right back."

I fixed him a plate and sat at the table across from his seat. When he joined me, he immediately tucked into his food. "Thanks, hon. I was starving."

"You're welcome. So . . . the girls and I exchanged Christmas gifts today."

"Great," he mumbled, through a mouthful of taco.

"Check these out." I lifted the plastic Safeway bag filled with my afternoon's haul and extracted the bottle of wine. "This is from Jane."

"Great."

"And from Trudy . . . ," I modeled the hat and scarf for him.

"You look cute."

"This one . . ." I said, gingerly removing the angel pillow, "is from Carly." Paul looked at it silently for a long moment. "It's for the Christmas tree," I elaborated. "So we can remember Karen every Christmas."

"That's really nice," he said softly.

"So . . . ," I began, my voice catching in my throat. Paul might be angry with me for what I was about to ask, but there was no better segue. "Have you heard anything from the detectives . . . about Karen's case?"

He sighed heavily. "Conroy called yesterday."

"And?"

"They interviewed Rueda, but they got nothing."

"Got nothing? But what about the paternity test? Did it prove he was the father?"

"The DNA sample was inadmissible. They couldn't process it."

Damn that Troy Portman! I knew he was blowing me off!

Paul continued, "Without proof that he was the father of Karen's baby, they don't have much of a case against him."

"Oh." I didn't know what to say. I didn't know how I felt.

"If the police can't touch him, we might want to consider a permanent restraining order . . . just in case."

After a moment, I replied weakly, "Okay. . . . I think I'm going to take a bath now." Grabbing my detective novel off the coffee table, I headed upstairs.

When I was immersed to my popped balloons in warm water, I let myself feel the impact of my husband's words. The paternity of Karen's fetus would never be known. I would never find out if Karen had been telling the truth about her relationship with Javier. I would never find out if he had been there when she died. Karen would fade to a distant memory, eventually thought of only at Christmastime, when we hung our slightly tacky, yellowing angel pillows on the tree, and we would never know what really happened to her. Javier would go on to live a happy, carefree life. He would move on, get married, possibly even have children . . . I thought about Trudy's prayer for the soul of whoever was involved in Karen's demise, and I didn't know if I could be so forgiving. But I would have to be, wouldn't I? If not forgiving, at least accepting of the fact that I would never know. The case was closed. There was nothing I could do.

I slid down deeper into the water so only my head bobbed above the surface. With my right hand, I fumbled for the mystery novel on the bath mat. Finding it, I flipped it open and began to read. There was no point in thinking about Karen any further. It was over . . . really over this time.

I stayed in the tub until the water began to cool and my fingertips became pruney. The novel held me transfixed, the mystery slowly, deftly unraveling. I was afraid to stop reading. I knew that the minute I put the book down, my mind would return to the ambiguity of Karen's demise. It was too hard, too much to deal with a few days before Christmas and my mother-in-law's arrival. I preferred to throw all my attention into the story in my hand, unfolding itself methodically toward a tidy conclusion.

Suddenly, I sat up with a start. A mini–tidal wave of water sloshed over the edge of the tub, soaking the tan bath mat and turning it a dark brown. My body was shivering now, but I was barely aware of my physical response. Standing in the tub, I reached for a fluffy beige towel and wrapped it around me. I stepped onto the sodden bath mat, then hurried to perch on the seat of the toilet. With shaking hands, I opened the book again, finding the page that had caused such a violent reaction in me. I reread it, my heart beating loudly in my throat and blood rushing audibly through my veins. "Holy shit," I said to the empty room when the passage was complete. "I don't believe it."

CHAPTER 29

"Patty Hanover?" the man at the door asked. He was new to the case, razor-sharp and rough-hewn. It was the drink that had given his features that hard edge . . . although Patty had no way of knowing that. To her, he was just another cop, looking to cause her trouble.

"Who wants to know?" she asked, in her gravelly, scotch-soaked voice.

"Detective Meyers," the man said, flashing his LAPD badge. "Mind if I come in?"

"Suit yourself." She let the door fall, but he caught it with a deft arm. Stepping across the threshold, he followed her to the kitchen, where her tumbler of scotch sat waiting. He tried hard not to notice she was wearing only a short silk robe. But God, the woman had an amazing pair of legs. "Drink?" she asked.

Christ, how he wanted one, but it had been eight years

since a drop of liquor had touched his lips. He wasn't about to blow his sobriety over some dame with great gams. Besides . . . she was now the prime suspect in her ex-husband's murder. "No thanks," he replied. "This isn't a social call."

"Why don't you get to the point, then?" she snapped, taking a seat on a kitchen chair and crossing those magnificent pins. "I've got some drinking to do."

"We received a letter, ma'am," he said, pulling out a chair and sitting down next to her.

"A letter? What does that have to do with me?"

"This letter states that you killed your husband."

"*Ex*-husband."

"We're going to have to take you in for questioning."

"Let me read this letter," Patty said calmly, holding out a perfectly manicured hand. Myers passed it to her and watched as she delicately unfolded it. Then, she began to read aloud, her words slightly slurred from the drink.

TO THE POLICE,

I WAS A FRIEND OF NIGEL HANOVER'S. I DON'T WANT TO GET INVOLVED, BUT I KNOW WHO KILLED HIM. HIS EX-WIFE, PATTY, WAS CONSUMED WITH JEALOUSY WHEN HE LEFT HER. HE WAS FINALLY MOVING ON WITH HIS LIFE, AND SHE COULDN'T BEAR IT. WHEN HE CAME TO COLLECT SOME OF HIS BELONGINGS, SHE LOST HER TEMPER AND BASHED HIM OVER THE HEAD WITH A LEAD CRYSTAL VASE. UNCONSCIOUS, HE FELL INTO THE POOL AND DROWNED. THE MURDER WEAPON CAN BE FOUND IN PATTY'S CHINA CABINET AND WILL HAVE HER PRINTS ON IT. DO NOT WASTE ANY MORE OF THE AMERICAN PEOPLE'S MONEY INVESTIGATING OTHER SUSPECTS. PATTY HANOVER IS THE KILLER.

"Annabelle . . . ," Patty murmured, almost to herself. "I know it was her."

"The letter is anonymous, ma'am."

"I brought that ungrateful tramp over from Britain to be our nanny. I invited her into our home, to be a part of our family. And look how she repays me: steals my husband, kills him, and then tries to frame me for it!"

"Why would Annabelle Swinton want Mr. Hanover dead?" Meyers asked. "They were in love."

"I don't know, but . . ." Suddenly, Patty reached for the detective, clutching his hand desperately. "Analyze the handwriting! Please! You'll see for yourself!"

"Unfortunately, Ms. Hanover, the letter was written in pencil, using block lettering. Those two elements make it virtually impossible to trace."

"Damn her!" Patty wailed. "She's going to get away with it!"

I closed the book and threw on my husband's navy blue bathrobe, which was hanging on its hook on the back of the door. Clutching the detective novel under my arm, I rushed down the stairs. "I'll be right back!" I called to Paul, ensconced in his office. Whether he heard me or not was difficult to say, but it didn't matter. I had to go, I had to do this. He was not going to talk me out of it. In the grand entryway, I slipped into a pair of Paul's running shoes and burst out into the night. Clutching the baggy robe around me and hobbling in the too-large shoes, I hurried to Carly's house. I was aware that I probably looked like Igor lurching up her walk, but luckily, she answered my insistent knock.

"Paige!" She took in my outfit and alarmed expression. "What's wrong?"

"I need to talk to you," I said urgently.

"Okay . . . come on in."

Stepping out of my husband's shoes, I padded in my bare feet into her living room. A fire crackled in the fireplace, giving the room a homey glow. Carly followed me in and stood opposite me. I took a deep, calming breath. At least, I had intended it to be calming. "Remember when you were getting rid of Brian's things?"

"Yeah . . ."

"You gave me one of his books." I held up the novel.

"Uh-huh . . . ?"

"Well, what you don't know is that the police received a letter a while ago implicating someone in Karen's death. His name is Javier Rueda, and he's from Spain. He was a *friend* of Karen's . . . maybe more."

"Really?"

"Yeah, and in Brian's book, there's also an anonymous letter to the police. Listen to this . . ." I frantically searched for the incriminating passage and then read it aloud to her. "Did you notice how it said 'Do not waste any more of the American people's money . . .'?" She nodded vaguely. "That's the tip-off that the letter was written by the British nanny. An American would have said something like 'the taxpayers' money.' "

"Okay . . . ?"

"The letter the police received incriminating Javier used the exact same wording! The police even said that the note must have been written by a foreigner." She looked at me blankly. "Don't you see, Carly? Whoever wrote the letter to the police must have read this book. That's how they knew that saying 'the American people's money' would make the cops think the letter was written by someone other than a citizen."

"It's probably just a coincidence."

"There's more!" I said excitedly. "The letter the police received about Karen was written in pencil and block lettering! It says right here in the book that that makes handwriting impossible to identify. Whoever wrote that letter had to have read this book!"

"So . . . what are you saying?"

I had never considered Carly *thick* before, but come on! "This is Brian's book, right? He must have written the note trying to frame Javier! He must have, somehow, been involved in Karen's death."

"Oh, I don't think so," she said with a dismissive laugh. "He barely knew her. Why would he want to hurt her?"

"I don't know," I said desperately. "Maybe to hurt you? Or maybe they were closer than you realized?"

"No. Brian's a cheating scumbag, but he's no murderer."

"But he had to at least have written the note. This is his book!"
I shook it in her direction.

"Paige, I'm sure it's just a fluke that the letter to the police used
the same line that's in the book. And plenty of people know that
using pencil and block lettering make a note untraceable. It's probably been on lots of detective shows. It's really not that incriminating."

"It is!" I cried. "No one watches more detective shows than I do,
and I didn't know it!"

"Listen, hon . . . ," she said soothingly, coming toward me, "didn't
you promise Paul that you'd let the police handle the investigation
from now on?"

"Yeah, but they're not doing anything. They've closed the case."

"Then obviously they believe her death was an accident. Just
let it go . . ." Reaching out, she gently removed the book from my
grip. "Maybe you shouldn't be reading detective novels in your current . . . *state*? I'll go put this back on my bookshelf."

Oh God. Carly was right. I had done it again—flown off the
handle, jumped to conclusions, stuck my nose in where it didn't belong . . . Maybe I did need some professional help to get over this.
But I had been so sure! No . . . it was stupid of me. Brian had only
known Karen a matter of months before he ran off with the busty
insurance adjuster. What possible reason could he have had to kill
Karen? Or frame Javier, for that matter. I was just relieved I hadn't
expressed my suspicions to Paul. I wasn't sure our marriage could
survive another of my insane theories. Slipping into my enormous
shoes, I waited at the door for my friend to return. I owed her an
apology, and I wanted to ask her not to tell Paul the reason for my
late-night visit.

"Oh, you're still here?" Carly said, returning to the living room.

"I wanted to apologize," I said sheepishly. "You're right. I've got
to let it go."

"You do, Paige."

"I will." I noticed that Carly still had the novel clutched behind
her back. "Why do you still have the book?" I asked.

"Oh." She shrugged and laughed a little nervously. "I was going to put it back on my bookshelf, but I decided to get rid of it." Her eyes moved involuntarily to the blazing fireplace. "I'm not in the mood to read this kind of stuff anymore . . . too morbid."

"It was *your* book . . . ," I said softly, suddenly remembering that day in my driveway. Carly had been clearing out her own belongings as well.

"No, it was Brian's," she replied flippantly.

"Carly . . ." I looked at her, and I could feel my heart breaking. "It was *your* book. You wrote that note to the police."

"What are you talking about?" she asked defensively. "You're going off the deep end again. Just stop, okay? Seriously, that's enough."

But it had all come into focus: Carly's insistence that Karen's death was just an accident and that I needed to let it go; the way she had insinuated herself into Doug's life, revelling in the feeling of being needed by someone again. Karen's demise had given Carly purpose—preparing for the funeral, setting up the charitable trust, taking care of the grieving widower, making memorial Christmas ornaments . . . "Oh God," I said, as the horror of realization dawned on me. "It was you!"

In movies, when the main character discovers that her best friend or boyfriend or whoever is the killer, I had always felt incredibly frustrated. "Don't just stand there waiting for her to kill you, too!" I would scream at the screen. "Get out of there! Call 9-1-1!" But either I was as dumb as those characters or I was numb, too stunned to feel any fear. This was Carly, after all. Until about three seconds ago, I would have trusted her with my life.

"Paige," she said, her voice tinged with desperation, "this fixation of yours . . . It's not healthy."

"You knew about Karen and Javier, didn't you?" I continued, standing stock-still in my clown shoes.

"No . . ." But her voice was weak. "I-I didn't know."

"Tell me, Carly. Tell me what happened."

Her cool façade crumbled, and tears instantaneously began to pour from her eyes. "It was an accident, okay? I didn't mean for her to die."

"Of course you didn't," I said gently. "What went wrong?"

She began to pace, stalking around her living room like a caged animal . . . a roly-poly black bear or something. "I caught her with that Javier guy," she said, not looking at me. "It made me sick, Paige. It really did. I saw them making out in her car outside the Dairy Queen. It was disgusting. They were like a couple of horny teenagers. They were like Brian and that slut of his."

I felt a slight twinge at the mental image of Karen and Javier getting jiggy with it behind the DQ. So there was no need for the paternity-test result. This confirmed that Javier and Karen were lovers. If I was surprised, it was only at my own gullibility.

"They were making a fool of Doug," Carly continued, wiping at her eyes. "He didn't deserve that. He deserved someone who appreciated him, who treasured him . . ."

"He's a good man," I said, encouraging her to continue.

"And then she told me she was pregnant."

"She told you?" I thought *I* had been Karen's confidante.

"We were like sisters. I loved her . . . I really did." Carly moved to perch on the leather arm of her ivory couch. Her eyes stared blindly into the fire. "She was so happy," she continued, in a soft voice. "She had everything she ever wanted . . . everything any woman could want . . . a good, faithful husband . . . a baby on the way . . ."

"So . . . what happened?" I gently prodded.

She looked at me briefly before returning her eyes to the fire. "I asked her who the baby's father was, and she said she wasn't sure. To Karen, it didn't really matter. She was going to decide which man she wanted and raise the baby with him. 'You can't,' I told her. 'That's deceitful . . . and wrong.' " Carly stood and began pacing again. "I wouldn't let her do it. I *couldn't* let her do it to Doug."

I waited on tenterhooks for her to continue, but it appeared she'd said enough. There was so much more I needed to know. My voice was quiet but commanding. "What happened next?"

"Karen . . . Karen got so angry at me. I'd never seen her like that before. She said it was none of my business how she lived her life. She accused me of being jealous and . . . and pathetic. She said I could never be happy for her because I wanted everything she had.

I wanted to *be her*." She turned to me. "I *was* happy for her, Paige. But it wasn't fair. She was lying and cheating, and yet . . . all her dreams were coming true."

"Uh-huh," I said breathlessly.

"She said if I told Doug, she'd call me a liar. She'd tell him that I was psychotic, that I was secretly in love with him. She'd tell everyone in the neighborhood that I was a bitter old maid who couldn't get a man of her own so I made up horrible stories to try to ruin Karen's happiness."

Carly looked at me then, tears streaming down her cheeks. "She was walking to her car—probably going to meet her *lover*." She spat out the word. "I needed her to stay and talk to me, but she wouldn't. She was so angry. I . . . I grabbed her arm but she pulled away and . . . and she fell and hit her head on the toolbox."

My voice was barely audible. *"Oh God."*

"It was an accident, Paige. I didn't want—" Her sentence was cut short by a painful sob.

I gave her a moment to compose herself before I pressed on. "And the letter?" I asked, when she had blown her nose loudly. "Why did you write the letter to the police?"

"Because . . ."—her voice had suddenly turned angry—"Javier was getting away scot-free. I mean, if anyone should be punished, it's him. He was using her and abusing Doug."

"That's true . . . Then why didn't you write a letter naming him as the killer? Why pretend that he wrote the letter and claimed it was an accident?"

She held up the novel, still clasped in her hand. "A letter accusing someone of murder is too obvious. You knew right away that Annabelle was trying to frame Patty. It didn't take much for the cops to figure it out. I thought if I cast just a little suspicion on Javier, made it seem like the letter was written by an immigrant, the cops would find out about the affair and assume he was responsible for her death."

"Oh . . ."

"He's the villain here, not me. What happened was just an accident."

"But . . . why didn't you call 9-1-1 when Karen fell? Why didn't you try to save her?"

"I panicked," she said, coming toward me. I involuntarily jumped back a little. "I heard her head hit the toolbox. I saw the blood. I knew there was nothing I could do. I just . . . I just ran home. Please, Paige." She was close to me now, and her hands reached out to grasp mine. "You don't need to tell the police all this. They won't understand, and it won't bring Karen back. She's our angel now, our precious angel. Please . . ." She squeezed my fingers, uncomfortably hard. "Let's just keep this between us. We're friends. I love you."

Tears were now pouring down my cheeks as well. "I love you, too," I managed to mumble. "I have to go."

"Paige," she said again, as I opened the door. Her voice was cold and devoid of emotion. "If you love me, don't destroy my life."

I stepped out into the chill night air and stopped on her doorstep. "I won't," I said, turning to face her. "You've already done that."

Paul met me in the grand entryway upon my return. "Where the hell did you go?" He took in my ensemble. "What the hell are you wearing?"

"I need the phone," I said wearily, brushing past him.

"Why? What's happened?"

But I was too overwhelmed to explain. With the cordless in hand, I turned to my husband. "Do you have a cell-phone number for Detective Portman or Conroy?"

"Yes . . . but can't this wait until morning?"

"It can't," I said, tears spilling from my eyes. "I have to talk to the police . . . now."

"Oh God," Paul said softly, and somehow, he knew. "I'll get the number."

CHAPTER 30

Carly was charged with first-degree manslaughter. There would be a trial and I would have to testify against her, but that was months away. For the moment, I would focus on my grief: there were now two lost friends to mourn. Trudy and Jane and I pulled together. In the days following Carly's arrest, we clung to one another, talking endlessly of Karen, of Carly, of what went wrong . . . It was all out in the open now: the affair, the baby, and Carly's unhealthy obsession with a life she so desperately wanted but couldn't achieve.

To be honest, I had briefly considered Carly's request to keep her role in Karen's death a secret. She hadn't intended for our friend to die; that much I believed. But that night as she confessed, I saw in her a rage and desperation that frightened me. Who knew what could provoke her to another act of violence? Catching Doug and Jackie Baldwin on a date? (They had recently brought their relationship out in the open.) Witnessing the Diet Coke man handing out a free beverage to some other single office worker? She was a loose cannon! Besides, I was done keeping secrets.

The fact that my mother-in-law arrived a few days later turned out to be a blessing in disguise. Given my current turmoil, Pauline was more than happy to step in and take over the Christmas festivities. "There's no need for Paige's melancholy mood to ruin this occasion for the rest of us," I heard her tell her husband. "I'll do my best to salvage the holidays—for the sake of Paul and the children." Normally, this would have irked me, but under the circumstances, I just felt grateful. I wanted my family to have a wonderful Christmas, and I knew Pauline would do a better job than I could this year.

I rested. I took long walks where I cried until my eyes hurt. I played with my children and had deep conversations with my husband. When Christmas was over and Paul's parents had left, I felt renewed. Yes, Carly's role in Karen's death had been another staggering blow to suffer, but for the first time, I had closure. There was no more doubt, no more suspicion . . . Karen's ghost no longer hovered above me pleading *Solve my murder! Solve my murder!* Not that Karen's ghost ever actually did that, but I had kind of imagined it to justify my obsession with the case. In a few months, I would have to go to court and send one of my closest friends to prison, but I found solace in the fact that I was doing the right thing. Finally, after so many lies and deceptions, I was being truthful.

There was only one loose end left. I don't know why it bothered me so much—God knows I tried to dismiss it—but it lingered. No matter how satisfied I was with the current state of my life, I couldn't let it go. Despite his creepy, stalking gifts; his corny, illustrated love notes; and his out-and-out lie regarding the nature of his relationship with Karen, I couldn't stop thinking about Javier. I felt bad for him, even a little guilty. He was an innocent man, and yet, he had been treated like a murderer. He'd been interrogated by the police, rejected by me, and slapped with a restraining order by a process server. All he had done was love my friend—my *married* friend, mind you, so it wasn't like he was an angel or anything, but that didn't make him a killer. I finally knew that my instincts regarding him had been correct. Javier wasn't dangerous. He was never a threat to me. In fact, he had lost someone he loved, just as I had. It was normal for him to seek comfort from me, to reach out to a friend who could understand what he was going through. He was alone, so far from home . . . And I had turned the cops on to him.

The restraining order was still in effect, but I had to contact him. I decided a letter was the most prudent way. I didn't want to show up at The Old Grind hoping for a conversation and have him run screaming from me. I also didn't want my husband to know I had unresolved feelings about my stalker. So when Paul was at work and the children were occupied with their recent Christmas presents, I sat at the kitchen table and drafted a note.

Dear Javier,

I felt the need to contact you. I'm not really sure why. I guess I feel I owe you an apology. You lost someone you loved—at least, I hope you loved her. Karen was a really special person, and we were both lucky to have her in our lives for even a short time. It must have been hard for you to mourn her all alone, trying to keep your secret. I suppose my slapping you with a restraining order didn't make it any easier.

I'm sure you have heard by now that my neighbor Carly Hillman has been charged with Karen's murder. She maintains it was an accident. At the very least, it was a crime of passion. Carly was jealous of Karen and obsessed with everything she had. Her rage just got out of control on that terrible afternoon.

I also wanted you to know that I forgive you for lying to me. For whatever reason, you felt you had to deny your true relationship with Karen. I'm sure you had your reasons. Maybe you thought I was interested in you in *that way*, which I certainly was not. Maybe you thought that if I knew the truth, I would cut you out of my life completely. I wouldn't have. I would have supported you in your grief . . . because, like I said, I was not interested in you in *that way* . . . Though I do think you're a very attractive man.

It is not a good idea for us to see each other. My husband was very angry about my subterfuge, and rightfully so.

272 ○ Robyn Harding

My marriage and my family are my number one priority, so please don't leave any more gifts on my doorstep—though the ones you left were really lovely. Thank you. Just know that I feel for you, in my heart, and hope you will go on to have a happy life.

Sincerely,
Paige Atwell

I reread it. It seemed to get the point across. I scratched out *subterfuge* and replaced it with *sneaking around*. Yes, if I could get this note to Javier, it would be the final page in this painful chapter—not counting the trial, of course, which I had resolutely decided not to dwell on. When my sympathies had been conveyed to the poor, misguided foreigner trying, fruitlessly, to find love in his new land, I could close the book on this experience for good.

But the letter sat in my purse until the new year. I didn't know where to send it: The Old Grind? The Wild Rose Arts Center? With all Javier had suffered, who knew if he still worked at either place? Thanks to my siccing the cops on him, he had probably been fired from one or both. And was popping the letter in the mail really going to give me sufficient closure? Mail got lost or misdirected all the time. If I posted it, I would never know for sure that he had received it.

There was no way around it: a little surveillance work was going to be necessary. Don't get me wrong, I was more than happy to hang up my private investigator's license, but this mission was vital to my peace of mind. I would find out whether Javier still held either of his previous jobs and deliver the letter to him there . . . Not to him in person, of course. That was too risky. I didn't want Paul to find out, and I certainly didn't want Javier to fall head over heels at the sight of me and begin bombarding me with gifts again. I would leave the letter in the hands of one of his coworkers at The Old Grind or at the front desk of the arts center. That would ensure he received it safely.

On Tuesday morning, I drove to the coffee shop, but that proved futile. From my parking spot across the street, I couldn't see in through the window well enough to tell if Javier was working or not. And I didn't have hours to sit in my car watching for his entrance or exit. Besides, this was just a bit creepy. I mean, it was like Javier needed the restraining order against me. After twenty minutes, I pulled the SUV back onto the road and headed home. I would stake out the Wild Rose Arts Center on Wednesday evening. If he hadn't been fired, there was at least a fifty-fifty chance that he would be there to pose for Allan Drury's drawing class.

Not surprisingly, Paul had become a little more suspicious of my extracurricular activities. Telling him that I had plans to meet an old coworker or that I was taking a night class was not going to fly anymore. He would definitely nail me on the specifics: Who? Where? When will you be back? Undoubtedly, he'd call me, possibly even drive by to check up on me. I couldn't blame him. It was going to take some time to regain his trust. But Paul couldn't deny his children milk and cheese slices, both of which we conveniently ran out of at 8:30 that evening.

"Damn," I said, poking my head into the refrigerator. "We're out of milk."

"Do you want me to go get some?" Paul offered distractedly, staring at the TV.

"Oh, we can make do," I said casually. "Oh, great! We're out of cheese slices, too."

"I'll go," my husband said, eyes still transfixed by the hockey game being played out on the screen before him.

"No, you stay and watch the game," I said sweetly. "I'll go."

"I don't mind." Paul started to stand.

"I need to get some tampons and stuff, anyway," I added.

"Oh . . ." Paul sat back down. I kissed him quickly before hurrying out the door.

If my estimate proved correct, I should arrive at the arts center approximately seven minutes before the Drawing the Human Figure class was let out. If Javier was the model tonight, and not that annoyingly perfect Amanda person, he should emerge from the building at roughly 9:06. I would confirm his continued employment, watch him drive away in his Audi, then hurry inside and leave the envelope, addressed to Javier Rueda, propped prominently on the reception desk. That would be it. I would be free.

I pulled the SUV into the lot and parked in a remote back corner. From this vantage point, I had a perfect view of the main doors, from which I felt sure Javier would exit. The digital clock on my dash glowed in the darkness: 8:52. Close enough. Slouching down in my seat, I waited.

At 9:05, the first students began to leave. I spotted my former neighboring artist, instantly recognizable in her maroon sweatpants, Birkenstock sandals, and socks. A few more artists straggled through the doors, some in small clusters, others alone. I had not seen Javier yet, but neither had I seen Amanda. It was possible that they had hired a new nude model, but I doubted it was one of the motley crew I'd just seen exiting. At least I hoped it wasn't. The doors remained quiet for several minutes, until the instructor, Allan Drury, walked through them at 9:12.

Something was wrong. Where was Javier? Where was Amanda? Had Drawing the Human Figure been changed to something else— like Drawing the Bowl of Fruit? Perhaps Javier had been posing for the class when he was hauled in for questioning by the police or served with the restraining order? Allan might have decided that live models were too much of a liability. How was I ever going to find Javier? How was I ever going to express my remorse for the way he'd been treated? How long could I sit out here before Paul began to wonder if I really was just buying milk, cheese slices, and tampons? Dejectedly, I reached for the key in the ignition.

Suddenly, the movement of the exit doors caught my eye. I looked up, and there he was, emerging into the night. My stomach did a little dance. Javier had become quite attractive again, now that he was no longer stalking me and I'd confirmed he was not a murderer. He paused there in the doorway, as if holding the door open for someone to follow. I could see the steam of his breath in the cold air, his hands burrowed deep into the pockets of his expensive leather jacket for protection against the chill. His hair looked a little longer, stylishly disheveled. I slid down farther in my seat as his eyes

seemed to scan the parking lot. Poor Javier. He was probably paranoid that the police or a process server would pop out at any moment.

Then a woman appeared behind him. She was clutching a
sketchbook to the front of her white rabbit fur coat, and she wore
snug jeans tucked into stiletto boots. Talk about overdressing for an
art class! Her hair was shoulder-length and pale blond, but as she
turned in my direction, I caught a glimpse of her face in the halo
of light emanating from the single outside bulb. Despite her impec-
cable makeup, it was clear she was another later-in-life artist . . .
quite a bit *later,* in fact. The woman was at least in her early fifties.
Okay . . . maybe that was a bit of an exaggeration, but she had at least
eight to ten years on me. It was sweet of Javier to escort this elderly
woman to her car.

The pair began to move down the steps, and I watched Javier's
arm slide around the older lady's waist. She stopped, obviously delighted by his attentions, and turned to face him. Her arms slid
under his leather coat and wrapped around his taut young body. She
said something then—obviously something hilarious, as they both
threw their heads back in laughter. When they had composed themselves, they stood, talking quietly, for a long moment on the steps.
There was something so intimate in their pose, so . . . *carnal.* But it
couldn't be, could it? She was twice his age. And then, casting his
eyes quickly around the silent parking lot, Javier leaned in to kiss
her. Ewwwww! She could have been his grandma! I covered my
eyes, peeking, horrified, through my fingers.

The old lady reached in the pocket of her fur coat and handed
Javier a set of keys. I watched them, through my splayed digits, walk
briskly to a steely Mercedes. Javier opened the passenger door for
her before hurrying around to the driver's seat. Moments later, he
peeled out of the parking lot.

When they were gone, I reached into my purse and extracted
the note. So, Javier had moved on; that didn't change anything, did
it? It was obvious he had a proclivity for mature women, preferably
with a lot of money to buy him cars and leather jackets and immigration lawyers, but still . . . He wasn't a dangerous stalker or a killer.

And it wasn't fair that he had been treated like one. Really, his only crime was falling for Karen . . . and falling for me. Exiting the car, I walked purposefully toward the building, my heartfelt condolences clutched in my hand. This was it. This was closure, finality, the end of a strange and disturbing episode in my life. When I reached the main entrance, I stopped. There, on my left, stood a large plastic garbage can. After tearing the missive into tiny pieces, I dropped them into the bin. That was all the closure I needed.

CHAPTER 31

Carly was sentenced to eight years in jail. With time off for good behavior, she'd be out in four. Testifying against my friend was the hardest thing I had ever done. I tried my best to give an accurate account of events while still demonstrating Carly's kind and generous side. But every time I tried to bring up the frozen lasagnas she made for Doug, or Karen's memorial Christmas decoration, the prosecutor shut me down. As she was led from the courtroom, Carly looked over at me, just briefly. Tears streamed down my face, but hers was dry, emotionless, her expression unreadable. Carly was obviously in shock, but I hoped she could see how much this had hurt me.

Back in Aberdeen Mists, life began to regain a sense of normalcy. Carly's house went up for sale and was quickly bought by a family from Portland. They seemed like nice people and were friendly enough, but both parents had careers, leaving little time for mingling with the neighbors. I was secretly thankful. Call me superstitious, but I didn't want to get too close to the next residents.

Jane, Trudy, and I continued to socialize. Margot Bauman was often included, and I grew to really like her. Of course, Jane frequently invited preschool or ballet-class moms, trying to fill that fifth seat vacated by Carly, but we had yet to find someone with whom we clicked.

Our incarcerated friend still weighed heavily on my mind. I couldn't help but feel responsible for sending her to the "big house," no matter how many people reassured me that it wasn't my fault. Logically, I knew that was true, but what did Carly think? Obviously, given her psychotic behavior, logic wasn't her strong point. For my own peace of mind, I knew I had to contact her. It wasn't like with Javier, where seeing him necking with some old granny had allowed me to close the door on our relationship forever. Carly and I had shared a much deeper bond! I decided to send a letter to the Colorado Women's Correctional Facility. But what could I say?

Dear Carly,

How are you? I hope you are enjoying jail.

I wanted the letter to be somewhat upbeat but not patronizing. After much forethought, I sat at my sunny breakfast nook and put pen to paper.

Dear Carly,

I hope you are keeping well. This must be a difficult time for you, but I have noticed that many women who are released from prison have really amazing complexions. Martha Stewart looked several years younger after her short incarceration, so I'm sure you will look incredible after eight years.

Oh God, that was no good. I crumpled the page into a ball. No, there was no room for niceties in this missive. It would have to come straight from the heart.

Dear Carly,

I'm writing to try to explain, if I can, why I had to be honest and testify against you in court. It was truly the hardest thing I've ever done, and the pain of that day will stay with me *forever.* But I had no choice. You see, I couldn't live a lie any longer. Karen had confessed her affair to me as well, and keeping her secret was eating me alive. That day, when I discovered you had been involved in her fall, I knew the truth had to come out . . . all of it.

Of course, I would like to ask for your forgiveness, but I understand if you can't give it to me. I want you to know that I hope you have a good life when you are released. I'm sure, with some therapy, you can learn to be happy again. You will still be a young woman, Carly (and if other released prisoners, e.g., Martha Stewart and Mary Kay Letourneau, are any indication, you will probably look far younger than your years). You can still have the life you dreamed of: husband, children, good friends. . . . I want that for you, Carly, I really do.

Sincerely,
Paige

Without rereading or overanalyzing, I stuck it in an envelope and handed it directly to Leon.

Whether Carly believed the sentiment in that letter, I don't know. She never responded. I was left to ponder whether the missive actually reached her through all the bureaucracy and security now surrounding her. Perhaps her silence meant she'd never received it? Or maybe she had and she was too emotional, too ashamed to make contact? Other times, I felt certain she'd read it and it had only fueled her anger. I could almost feel her hating me from her jail cell. But the gesture of reaching out to my former friend provided me some solace. Besides, I had expended enough energy on Carly, Karen, and Javier. It was time to focus on me.

I needed to find a hobby—although *hobby* seemed a rather lackluster term to define what I was looking for. What I craved was a *passion*—something to expand my mind, broaden my horizons, and nourish my soul! It had to be something that made me feel like I was living again, a part of the great big world outside of my kitchen and SUV. Despite the chaos and turmoil of the last few months, I had somehow managed to learn several hitherto undiscovered truths about myself:

- I treasured my husband and children, but there was an emptiness inside me that needed to be filled (and not by some studly barista or the like).
- While my drawing undeniably sucked, I was not completely without artistic talent. My heart yearned for some type of creative outlet!
- Dancing was not the answer. Was my dancing a complete joke, as my daughter and husband seemed to think? No, I was not *that* bad—but one afternoon spent trying to keep up with the *Shall We Dance?* DVD had confirmed that this was not the right avenue for me.

But I needed something, something that was mine alone, completely separate from my role as wife and mother. And then, one ordinary evening, I was making Spencer a pea butter sandwich for his school lunch. (Yes, *pea* butter: a peanut butter substitute derived from a moderately tasty form of peas. A child in Spencer's class had a severe allergy that would cause her to go into anaphylactic shock if she so much as smelled a peanut on a classmate's breath.) As I smeared the brownish green paste onto the bread, my eyes drifted to a vase of candy pink tulips on the kitchen table. Outside the window, the summer sun was just setting. Its final, deep orange light streamed into the room, illuminating the vibrant blooms and their delicate crystal vase. It was so simple and yet so beautiful. It stirred me somehow, and I dropped the knife. I felt an intense desire to capture that image, to preserve it. It was really too bad that I couldn't paint or draw.

And in that moment, it struck me: photography! Oh my God! Why hadn't I thought of it before? I could do photography! I'd need a camera, of course. All we had was a digital and an outdated Instamatic. And I'd have to take classes. No more pointing and clicking for me! I would learn about real film photography! I'd take photos of the children, of the mountains, of the setting sun shining through the window on a bouquet of tulips! I was going to do it!

And I did. I bought a secondhand Pentax and signed up for classes at a nearby college (the Wild Rose Arts Center was too risky). As my knowledge of lighting, depth of field, and aperture grew, I began to take some pretty impressive photos. My specialty was extreme close-ups: a leaf or a flower petal cropped to show the intricate and delicate detail of the plant. The children were another favored subject—or more accurately, their *parts* were: Chloe's cherry red lips, Spencer's boyish hand clutching a daisy, the downy back of my daughter's neck . . . I loved taking photos, I really did. In fact, it was a love that bordered on a *passion*. God! I had finally found it!

Paul supported my new hobby wholeheartedly. (I think he realized how much trouble I could get myself into when I was bored.) He made it home from work in a timely manner when I had a class. For my birthday, he gave me a newer, more expensive, and complicated Pentax. But it was the gift he bought me for our thirteenth wedding anniversary that really blew me away.

It came in the form of a generic, rather syrupy greeting card. "For the Woman I Love" the flowery script read, above the hazy image of a yellow, dew-kissed rose.

"Thanks, hon." I leaned over to kiss him before I'd even opened it. It was a little cheesy, a tad predictable, but it was still sweet of him to remember. Besides, I wasn't expecting anything significant. It was only our thirteenth, after all.

"Look inside," Paul said, and for the first time, I noticed his barely contained excitement.

Embossed on the pink parchment paper within was a schmaltzy

poem—something about me making his life complete and how he'd marry me all over again. Beneath it, my husband had written:

Happy anniversary, Paige!

How would you like to photograph the kids splashing in the Caribbean? A tropical sunset? Or maybe some Mayan ruins?
     We leave in three weeks.

I love you,
Paul

Mercifully, there were no little illustrations of tropical drinks or sombreros. I looked up at my husband, and he was positively bursting. "I've booked us ten days in Mexico, on the Mayan Riviera," he gushed. "It's a five-star resort, with a great kids' club so we can have some time alone. There are daily tours to Chichén Itzá and other historic sites—you know . . . if you want to do some photography . . ."

"Oh my God!" I squealed, and jumped into his arms. It was beyond fantastic! We hadn't gone on a beach vacation since before Spencer was born, and after the year we'd endured, we really needed it! Paul and I could decompress and spend some quality time together! The kids would have a grand adventure and learn about another culture! We would reconnect as a couple, as a family! It was going to be great!

And it was . . . pretty great. Except that we experienced some turbulence on the flight down, and Chloe puked all over Paul's left forearm and leg. Spencer, usually such a fan of throw-up, diarrhea, and the like, turned alarmingly pale. "Are you okay?" I asked him.

"I don't feel so good," he responded weakly.

"Let's go to the bathroom and wash your face." While Paul tended to Chloe and himself, I led my ghostly son down the aisle to the lavatory. "I'll come in with you," I offered.

"No," Spencer insisted. "I want to be by myself."

"Let me help you, honey."

"No, it's too small in there. I'll be fine."

"Are you sure?"

"I'm not a baby!"

"I know, honey," I said apologetically, as he stepped inside. I heard the click of the sliding lock, and the little green Vacant sign turned to red, Occupied. I coached Spencer through the folding door. "Just splash some water on your face, sweetie, . . . and go to the bathroom if you need to. You'll be okay, big guy." Several minutes later, I heard the loud gush of the toilet flushing. "Wash your hands, love!" I called.

"I'm coming out now!" Spencer called back. I heard the jiggling of the lock, but the rectangle beside it remained red.

"Spencer, come on out."

"I can't!"

"Why not?"

"When I move the lock, it goes dark in here."

"I know. The lock's connected to the light. Just slide the lock over and then quickly push on the door."

"I can't," he wailed. "I don't want to be trapped in a dark bathroom!"

"You won't be! It'll be unlocked. I'll come in and get you."

"No! You won't see me, and you might trample me!"

Trample him? What was I, a herd of rhinoceroses? "Spencer, calm down. I'll just reach in and grab your arm, okay?"

"No! No! I don't want to be alone in the dark."

Paul approached, his left side completely soaked from sponging off Chloe's vomit with airplane water. "What's going on?"

"He won't unlock the door," I cried. "He doesn't want the light to go off."

"It's okay, son," Paul said commandingly. "Daddy's here. Just slide the lock over, and I'll come in and get you."

"You're too big! I'll be crushed!"

I left to check on our daughter while Paul tried, for another twenty minutes, to cajole Spencer into unlocking the door. Finally, as we were preparing for our descent, the crew stepped in. They lifted up a small metal plate beneath the "locked" sign, then slid the latch underneath to the side. The door opened and, pale and tearstained, our son was released. When we finally exited the plane, I was flooded with relief. I was so happy that I was only mildly bothered by the disdainful looks the flight attendants gave their most troublesome passengers as we filed past.

Despite its inauspicious beginnings, the rest of the trip was wonderful. Of course, we each got hit with a case of Montezuma's revenge—to a greater or lesser degree. "Don't eat your ice cubes," Spencer would wisely counsel the guests lounging by the pool. "That's how you get Montezuma's revenge. I had it a couple of days ago. I got it so bad it was like I was peeing out of my butt."

We visited the nearby ruins, me with my new camera in hand, and reveled in the ancient history of the area. I also took a solo trip to a local market, where I shot the array of brilliantly colored fruits and vegetables, the deep red chilies drying on racks, and the stacks of terra-cotta pots and handwoven baskets. But most of the time, we just hung out . . . together. Sometimes, the children went to the kids' club for the day, leaving Paul and me to swim, lounge, eat massive quantities, and sip frothy beverages. Other days, the four of us spent the day in the pool or at the beach, splashing and frolicking, leaving only to lunch on hot dogs and French fries.

In the evenings, we put the kids to bed and sat out on the balcony, enjoying a slushy margarita or an ice-cold cerveza with lime. Paul and I talked about everything and nothing; the only untouchable subject was that of Karen's death and the ensuing madness. And it felt really good to spend time with my husband again—as a friend *and* as a lover. Since we'd been in Mexico, our sex life had picked up dramatically. Oh, it wasn't wild and crazy (the children were just in the other room, after all), but it was regular and loving and special.

On one such balmy evening, Paul and I stayed up late, having imbibed a few more margaritas than was our norm. We were laughing hysterically about something inane, falling toward each other in our frenzy, when suddenly, Paul kissed me. It was a hard, passionate, tongue-thrusting kiss, and it took me by surprise.

"Whoa . . . ," I said, when he finally pulled away.

"I'm so hot for you," my husband growled drunkenly. "You look so beautiful . . . your tan . . . your hair . . . Let's do it right here, right now."

"On the balcony?" I tittered. "Are you crazy?"

"Everyone's asleep," Paul cajoled. "Come on. Crawl on over here and sit on my lap. Even if someone's awake, they won't notice."

"Oh . . . I don't know!" It was risky, potentially embarrassing . . . and so exciting! I looked at my spouse, who was very handsome and tanned himself, and I suddenly realized how lucky I was. I had two sweet, healthy kids, a passion for photography, and a wonderful, caring husband with whom I was about to have daring and hot balcony sex. God, I had it all, I really did! Why had it taken so much drama for me to realize it?

"Come here, gorgeous," Paul said, pulling me by the hand. I had no sooner plunked into his lap when:

"Mom! I peed the bed!"

"Oh no!" I whispered.

"Aw, Spencer," Paul groaned, "you're killing me here."

I stood up. "I'll go change the sheets."

"Naw, I'll do it," Paul offered, moving to the sliding glass door. "You stay here and finish your drink." He gave me a naughty wink. "I'll be right back."

Leaning back in my lounge chair, I took a sip of my tart, half-melted beverage and stared out at the darkened palms surrounding the balcony. A small, self-satisfied smile curled my lips: airsickness, Montezuma's revenge, wet sheets . . . Yeah, I had it all, all right—and I couldn't have been happier.

ROBYN HARDING was born in Vancouver, British Columbia. In her indecisive youth she studied English literature, journalism, and marketing before embarking on a seven-year career in the advertising industry. She is married and has two young children. She is also the author of *The Journal of Mortifying Moments.*

ABOUT THE TYPE

This book was set in Bembo, a typeface based on an old-style Roman face that was used for Cardinal Bembo's tract *De Aetna* in 1495. Bembo was cut by Francisco Griffo in the early sixteenth century. The Lanston Monotype Company of Philadelphia brought the well-proportioned letterforms of Bembo to the United States in the 1930s.